R

"Super
with a
line. Ma
of Den
fan."

"*A Murder of Mages* was another hit for me, a fantastic read from a new talent whose star continues to be on the rise." —Bibliosanctum

"Books like this are just fun to read."
—The Tenacious Reader

"*[A Murder of Mages]* is the perfect combination of urban fantasy, magic, and mystery."
—Kings River Life Magazine

"Marshall Ryan Maresca has done it again. After introducing readers to Maradaine through the eyes of criminals in *The Thorn of Dentonhill*, he focuses now on the constabulary, the ones catching the criminals, in *A Murder of Mages*. . . . Another rollicking adventure of magic and mayhem." —The Qwillery

"Maresca's debut is smart, fast, and engaging fantasy crime in the mold of Brent Weeks and Harry Harrison. Just perfect."
—Kat Richardson, national bestselling author of *Revenant*

"Fantasy adventure readers, especially fans of spell-wielding students, will enjoy these lively characters and their high-energy story." —Publishers Weekly

DAW Books presents the
novels of Marshall Ryan Maresca:

*Coming soon from DAW

MARSHALL RYAN
MARESCA

The Imposters of Aventil

A Novel of Maradaine

DAW BOOKS, INC.
DONALD A. WOLLHEIM, FOUNDER
375 Hudson Street, New York, NY 10014

ELIZABETH R. WOLLHEIM
SHEILA E. GILBERT
PUBLISHERS
www.dawbooks.com

First Printing, October 2017
1 2 3 4 5 6 7 8 9

Acknowledgments

So here we are at *The Imposters of Aventil*, which is an incredible place to have reached. This book is definitely a milestone in the overarching saga of Maradaine, and I'm blessed to have come this far with it. That is in no small part due to the people who helped make these books happen.

My wife, Deidre, is the foundation that has helped me achieve this. Of course, every married writer praises their spouse in these, but she has truly gone above and beyond to enable me to do this work. Her faith and belief in me is humbling. Further thanks are owed to my parents, Nancy and Louis, my mother-in-law, Kateri, and my son, Nicholas. Additional familial thanks go out this time to my cousins Eddie, Tommy, and David Tini, for inspiring the Crownball game in Chapter Twenty.

I've been extremely fortunate to have two incredible beta readers in Kevin Jewell and Miriam Robinson Gould. On top of the two of them, I have a network of other writers who form a strong base of support and advice and camaraderie, including (but far from limited to) Rebecca Schwarz, Melissa Tyler, Amanda Downum, and Stina Leicht.

There's also my agent, Mike Kabongo, my editor, Sheila Gilbert, and the whole team at DAW and Penguin Random House: Betsy, Josh, Katie, Kayleigh, Alexis, and several more who do work that I don't even see.

And of course, there is Daniel J. Fawcett—my friend, my sounding board, and the person who understands this world as well as I do. Maradaine lives, Maradaine *sings*, because of his advice.

But enough of this. I'm sure you're anxious to see what sort of trouble the Thorn falls into this time. Enjoy.

The
Imposters
of Aventil

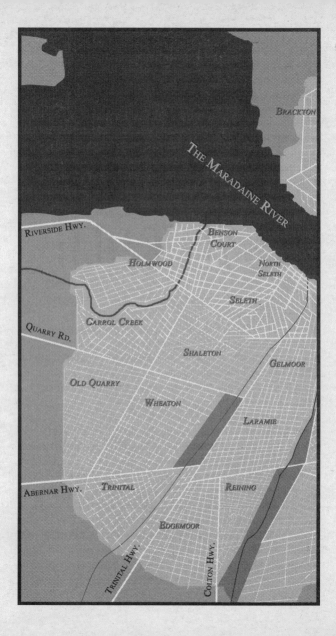

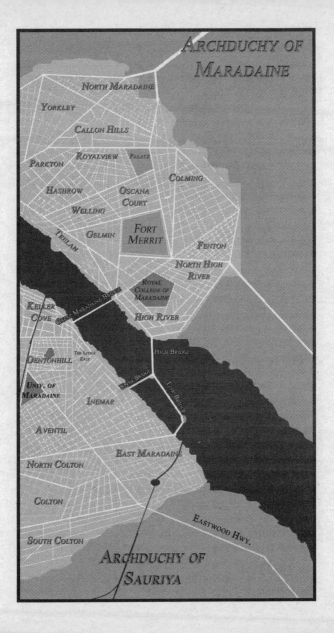

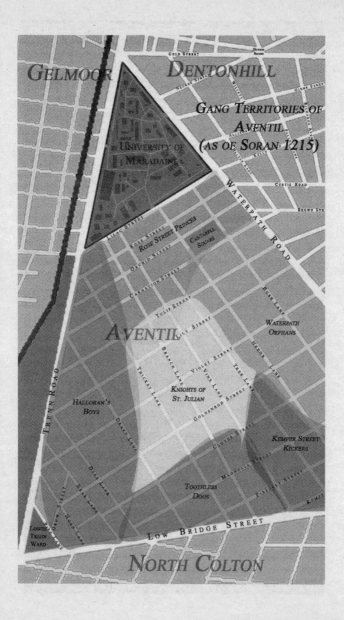

GELMOOR

DENTONHILL

GOLD STREET

GANG TERRITORIES OF
AVENTIL
(AS OF SORAN 1215)

CURTIS ROAD

BROWN STR

UNIVERSITY OF
MARADAINE

WATERPATH ROAD

LILAC STREET

ROSE STREET
ROSE STREET PRINCES

ORCHID STREET

CANTABELL
SQUARE

CARNATION STREET

TULIP STREET

LILY STREET

AVENTIL

WATERPATH
ORPHANS

BRANCH LANE

TRICKET LANE

DRAKE LANE

VIOLET STREET

VINE LANE

TREE LANE

HEDON LANE

BUSH LANE

TREN ROAD

HALLORAN'S
BOYS

KNIGHTS OF
ST. JULIAN

GOLDENROD STREET

DELL LANE

REAP LANE

CLOVER STREET

KEMPER STREET
KICKERS

WHEAT STREET

BRAMBLE STREET

MAGNOLIA STREET

TOOTHLESS
DOGS

TISSLEY STREET

KEMP

LOWER
TREEN
WARD

LOW BRIDGE STREET

NORTH COLTON

Chapter 1

THE AVENTIL STREETS teemed with Uni kids, and Lieutenant Benvin had to be a damned prefect to the lot of them. The captain had made it clear that he didn't give a barrel of sewage what Benvin was working on. The Grand Tournament of the High Colleges was starting, so every able body in Green and Red needed to show the color on foot, horse, and wagon throughout Aventil.

Benvin knew it made sense. With the Tournament, the population of the Uni campus, and therefore Aventil, increased tenfold. Athletes came from every major college in Druthal, as well as friends, families, and other supporters. Every bed was filled, every pub was packed, and folks were pressed against each other so tightly in the street that even the city's worst pickpocket could make a year's pay.

Add in the sweltering summer heat that hadn't broken all month, and the neighborhood was a stinkhole of trouble just waiting to burst.

"How many nights of this, Left?" Pollit muttered. "Because if it's more than three, I can't promise folks won't be eating their teeth."

"It's eight," Benvin said. "And I wouldn't believe that promise anyway."

Pollit flashed a smile. Pollit was part of Benvin's Loyals, the squad he had put together of those he trusted weren't in anyone's pocket. Just four footpatrol regulars—Tripper, Pollit, Wheth, and Mal, and two cadets, Jace and Saitle. The rest of the Aventil Stationhouse, they were fine enough folk, but Benvin didn't have faith that they would really have his back in a pinch. Only his Loyals, and he knew they gave their best because he believed in them. All of them had been outcasts amongst the Aventil regulars. Benvin had made them his.

"You don't totally hate this, Left," Pollit said.

"What makes you say that?"

"You usually don't wear that pin on your uniform."

Benvin glanced down at the pin on the lapel of his coat, marking his first-place win in oars for Riverview University at the Grand Tournament of 1202. "Man has a little pride in his school . . ."

"Wouldn't have pegged you for a Uni type, Left. Certainly not one of the Elevens."

"Drop it," Benvin said. He wasn't in the mood to talk about the things that led him from prominent law student at a prestigious university to street stick busting up cider rings and dice games. "Something over there."

A handful of Uni boys—Royal College of Maradaine lads by their purple and yellow colors—were getting heated in front of the Rose & Bush. Looked like the server was telling them they couldn't come in, and they weren't pleased with that at all. Also, they clearly had had their fill of any pub for the night.

Saints, it wasn't even seven bells yet. The sun was still casting long shadows down Rose Street.

"Gentlemen," Benvin said, Pollit right at his arm. "What seems to be the dispute?"

"She won't let us in!" one of the RCM boys said, wagging an accusing finger in the server's face. "We gotta eat something before the opening ceremonies!"

"We're full up!" the server snapped. "Ain't barely room for me to walk from bar to tables. Can't put another soul in the place!"

"Find another place," Benvin said. "Or perhaps your beds for the night."

"Pfff," the lead RCM boy said. He didn't seem to have registered who he was talking to. "We ain't about to head in yet. We got—"

"Oy," Pollit said. "Maybe you should note who's telling you. Unless you want us to find you some special bunks for the night."

The RCM boy looked at the two of them, his friends now all growing quiet as they recognized the Constabulary coats in front of them. This boy had definitely had too much cider, though, as his eyes didn't focus on them for a moment. When they did, they settled on Pollit.

"Saints," he snarled. "You a bird or a bloke?"

That was the wrong thing to say.

In a flash, Pollit had knocked the boy in the teeth. Before he could even blink, the boy was facedown on the cobblestone, irons going around his wrists. "Someone found a new bunk for the night!" Pollit shouted.

"Pollit—" Benvin tried to give a gentle rebuke, if Pollit would pick up on it.

Pollit looked up at the rest. "Any of you?"

"Going somewhere else," the other RCM boys all said, hands up defensively. They quickly dispersed.

"Good." Pollit had the boy up on his feet, arms bound behind him. "You see a lockwagon nearby, Left?"

Benvin leaned in. "We can't arrest the boy just for firing your hairs, Pol."

Pollit whispered back, "Can we have him sit in a wagon with irons on for an hour or so to cool off?"

"Twenty minutes," Benvin said. "There's one over there."

Pollit gave a salute to Benvin, and then one more to the Rose & Bush server with a wink, and took the RCM boy over to the wagon.

Folks in the stationhouse talked about Pollit in not-so-hushed whispers, but Benvin paid them no damn mind. Pollit was a damn good stick, that was all that mattered.

Whistle calls pierced the air—and not just a general call. Three sharp trills: long, short, long. Corpse call.

"Pol!" Benvin didn't need to look to know that Pollit

would soon be on his heels as he ran in the direction of the whistles. He hoped Pollit at least left the Uni with a wagon driver.

"Aside, aside," he shouted as he approached the source. A crowd had inevitably formed at the mouth of a narrow alley—not that every damn inch of this neighborhood wasn't a crowd right now—and Benvin nearly had to beat his way through. "Constabulary, people, stand aside!"

The crowd parted just enough to let him pass, to see a young man blocking the alley entrance, whistle in his mouth. He stopped blowing as soon as Benvin approached.

"Hey, Left," he said, dropping the whistle out of his mouth and catching it. "We've got some nasty business here."

"Jace," Benvin said, looking the cadet in the eye. "You're supposed to be off-duty." The boy was in civvie clothes, at least. But this kid, he never stopped working. Benvin admired him, to be sure, because he had a heart that was pure Green and Red as he had seen. Came from a family eight or nine generations deep in the Constabulary. When that crazy stampede went through the neighborhood two months ago, Jace had nearly got himself killed jumping onto the lead horse to blow out warnings. That was why Jace was part of the Loyals, but Benvin had to fight the boy to get him to go home sometimes.

"I was, Left, honest. On my way home when a couple folks spotted this. Had to put in the call, and then keep these folks off the scene."

"Fair enough," Benvin said. "Body?"

Jace nodded into the alley, while popping the whistle back in his mouth to make a new call, signaling that an officer was on the scene and they would need inspectors and the bodywagon to come.

Not that Benvin really wanted any of the Aventil Stationhouse inspectors to come. None of those chairwarmers were worth their rank, none of them could be counted on. Odds were they would come, glance at the body, and leave the work to him.

Pollit was now at the scene, giving a slight nod of regard to Jace. "Sorry about that, Left. Just getting that tosser comfy in the wagon."

"Anything good?" Jace asked.

"Ain't you supposed to be home?"

"In this crowd?"

Benvin ignored them, instead looking at the body. Definitely a murder. Four arrows were buried into his chest. Young man, about twenty or so. Scruffy, dirty, and unkempt. Face beat bloody, head cracked. Shirtless, but wearing a fur-lined coat. "A Red Rabbit."

"Ain't seen many of them since the last big street row," Pollit said.

"No," Benvin said pointedly. He pointed to the chevrons on the coat, and tattooed to the boy's neck. "And a captain at that. Is this Keckin?"

"Could be," Pollit said. "Saints, this is brutal."

Benvin had to agree. The four arrows were all from head-on. Keckin—if this was Keckin—wasn't running or even fighting back very well when this happened. Looked like he was shot, beaten, and then shot again. Someone wanted to make him suffer.

"Didn't happen here," Benvin added. He looked up to the top of the building. "Maybe on the roof, and he was dropped down after shooting him?"

Pollit gave his own glance up and down. "Makes sense. This couldn't have gone down around this crowd."

Benvin pulled one arrow out of the body. "And not too many people would use a bow in this neighborhood."

"You think it's him, boss?" Pollit asked.

"Nah, couldn't be," Jace said. He seemed almost spooked. "I mean, he's never left a body like this before."

"Then he's stepped up his game. Let's add it to the list of charges we'll lay on the Thorn when we catch him."

"I don't like it, boss," Jace said. "It ain't that simple."

Benvin didn't like it at all, either. With everything else going on in the neighborhood, the last thing they needed was for the Thorn to move on from being a vigilante menace to a vengeful murderer. This might have been a Red Rabbit scum that Benvin would have ironed and locked up given the chance, but he didn't deserve a death like this. Nobody did.

But it did mean one thing. Now Benvin had the cause he needed to act.

"Spread the word, boys," Benvin said. "As of right now, I'm calling an All-Eyes out on the Thorn."

On a night like this, Colin Tyson didn't care that he had been effectively exiled to Orchid Street.

Sure, he was still a captain in the Rose Street Princes, in charge of holding their territory against the Red Rabbits, but that didn't mean a thing to him. Ain't no one seen much of the Red Rabbits since Vee—since the Thorn—demolished the Trusted Friend, as well as the brewery where they were cooking their version of *effitte*. Old Man Jensett was dead—everyone presumed by the Thorn's hand, though Colin knew better—and most of the Rabbits ended up in Quarrygate. Whoever was still left out there was staying out of sight. The Waterpath Orphans moved in on their blocks without even a scuffle, from what Colin heard.

Orchid Street—at least his block between Bush and Waterpath—had nothing worth his time. Sure, the cheese shop was nice, and The Old Canal was a decent enough place to sit with a cider and plate of sausages, but it wasn't right. There wasn't any business worth hustling here, nothing to draw Uni kids over to drop some coin.

The only thing this block really had that was worth taking from the Rabbits was the sew-up and his offices, but he was so damn annoying that Colin wanted to crack him across the skull. He gave them no trouble, so long as there was some bird servicing his pisswhistle, but Colin didn't have any interest in feeding that vice. He certainly wasn't going to turn out any of the birds in the Princes to that end.

And, of course, there was his new crew, the dullest bunch of bonecrushers he had ever met. Ment, Kiggy, Vandy, and

Sella. The first three were the kind you wanted around if you had to crack some skulls, but good for nothing else. Not an ounce of thought or charm in the lot of them. Sella, she could scrap well enough and muster up some charm if she wanted, but most of the time she laid about the flop, dosed on the sew-up's *doph* supply.

None of that mattered on a night like tonight. The streets were filled with folks from every part of Druthal, all looking to have a good time and drop plenty of coin. Every inch of wall and lamppost was plastered with paper jobs, promising food, drink, and companionship at affordable prices. The Old Canal was bustling. People stood around gawking. They were eager to experience "the real Maradaine," whatever the blazes that meant to them.

What that meant to Colin was full pockets all around. He dropped a crate on the walkway right between the cheese shop and the sew-up and started running a five-card switch game with anyone and everyone who would dare to get close to him. He hadn't done that in ages—wasn't a soul living in Aventil who would fall for a five-card switch—but tonight it seemed like just the sort of classic swindle that these wander-throughs *wanted*.

Saints, it was like being fleeced was part of some show, and they loved it.

The two Uni girls from some southern school were eating it up.

"Come on, ladies, come on. You find the Duchess, you walk with five crowns."

"It's that one!" the fair-haired girl told her tall friend, pointing to the card that was torn and bent in the corner—just like the Duchess card they had seen earlier.

That one was not the Duchess.

"No, no!" the tall girl said. "You said it was that one last time and we lost!"

"I'm telling you—"

"I don't know!"

"Ladies, tell you what," Colin said. "I'll take these two cards off the table." He flipped over the two—Two Moons and The Soldier. "Now you've only got three cards to choose from. Surely you can find the Duchess with only three cards."

"It's got to be a trick," the tall girl said.

"No trick, no trick," Colin said. He held up his hands, flipping them back and forth. "Ain't got nothing palmed, and nothing up my sleeves. Blazes, ladies, my sleeves are rolled up!"

They both laughed as he showed them his arms.

This was the most fun he had had in months.

"Wait," the fair-haired girl said, her accent getting even thicker. She pointed to his tattoo. "So you're a Rose Street Lad, right?"

"Rose Street Prince, ma'am."

"Aren't we on Orchid?"

"That we are. If you're lost, though, I can see what I can do about getting you a guide through the neighborhood."

The tall girl flipped the card with the torn corner. Man of the People.

"Not the Duchess!" Colin said. "'Fraid I keep your coin, ladies."

The tall one was reaching into her pocket for another half-crown. She was ready for another round.

The fair-haired one grabbed her arm. "Ketara, we need to stop. Opening ceremonies are starting any moment now."

"One more," Ketara said. "I think I figured—saints, look at that!"

She pointed up to the top of the building behind them. The fair-haired girl gasped, and Colin glanced up—making sure to sweep up all the cards before he did. He wasn't about to take his eyes off them, if she was trying that old shift.

"Is that the whoever we heard about?" the fair-haired girl asked. "The Thorn?"

Colin couldn't believe it. There he was, just crouched on the roof of the sew-up's building with a bow and a crimson cloak. Just up there, in plain view.

Colin wondered what the blazes Veranix was thinking,

because it was the stupidest thing he had ever seen the boy do.

Ketara and her friend both cupped their mouths and shouted. "Woo! Thorn! Woo!"

That got his attention. He dashed out of sight. Maybe he realized how dumb it was.

"Is it true what they say about him?" Ketara asked.

"I don't know," Colin said. "They say a lot of crazy stuff, though."

The girls went on for a bit, but Colin was only half listening. He was still in shock. Since the Trusted Friend, Veranix had been cautious, even prudent. The Thorn was still hitting the *effitte* dealers in Dentonhill, but he wasn't making a point of being noticed. Colin had thought he had learned to lay low.

If he was getting careless again, Colin wasn't sure what to do. He had already risked everything he had keeping his cousin safe, and now he was out here on Orchid. More than that, he was indebted in more than one way to the reverend over at Saint Julian's.

Colin found himself saying a silent prayer that this was just a slip, and not a sign of terrible things in store for Veranix.

Delmin Sarren didn't even have to look in Almers Hall to know that Veranix wasn't there. Not that he had expected him to be there, but he needed to at least give the appearance that he was looking.

More to the point, Delmin realized that he didn't, in fact, need to look. His magical senses had always been his strongest asset as a student—Professor Alimen had even said that Delmin was one of the most gifted he had ever taught in that regard—but over the course of the summer he had grown even more adept with understanding what those senses were telling him.

Specifically, he had learned Veranix's unique flavor— that seemed the best word to Delmin—to the point where

Delmin could sense whenever Veranix was nearby. That might have been due to the incident at the end of the semester with Cuse Jensett's *numinic* batteries, fueled with Veranix's magic. Delmin had been so inundated with Veranix's *numinic* flavor he couldn't help but notice even a hint of it.

Not unlike how a scent would trigger a memory of nausea.

Now Delmin was thinking of Veranix as Aunt Iasta's mushroom soup, instead of doing the thing he actually needed to do, which was find Veranix before the Grand Tournament opening ceremony began.

A glance around Almers and the other dorms—just looking at the buildings themselves—told Delmin all he needed to know.

Delmin ran down the walkway toward Bolingwood Tower, and more importantly, the carriage house. If Veranix was anywhere on campus—besides where he was actually supposed to be, which was the opening ceremonies—he would be at the carriage house. But there was no sign that he was currently there.

Delmin felt the faintest whispers that he had been there recently, and the tendrils from those whispers—delicate smoke of *numinic* traces—left the carriage house and went off to the campus wall. Delmin could barely sense them, but if he really needed to, he could probably follow them along whatever route Veranix took once he left the carriage house.

If nothing else, this had convinced Delmin that his *numinic* senses were, in fact, more sensitive and finely honed than any other mage on campus—student or otherwise—including Professor Alimen. If the professor could sense Veranix with this much detail, he would have long ago figured out about Vee's secret life as the Thorn and put a stop to it.

Delmin ran back to the Haveldale Center. Veranix knew where he needed to be, and when he needed to be there. Even though "when" was ten minutes ago, there was nothing more Delmin could reasonably do.

He was capable of tracing Vee through the streets of Aventil and Dentonhill, following him to whatever danger-holes Vee decided to jump into in his quest to stop every *effitte* dealer in town. But actually doing that, going there—that was not something Delmin was emotionally prepared to do. Twice he had put himself in danger that way, and that was two times too many.

What he could do was report back to the opening cere-monies and honestly say that he couldn't find him, and hope that Veranix wasn't bleeding in a ditch somewhere.

Crowds were still filing into Haveldale Center, but they were all using the main entrances, not heading to the load-ing entrance that led underneath. That was where Delmin needed to get to. Just as he was approaching the wagon-wide tunnel, he felt the sharp, distinctive taste of Veranix sud-denly come up on him, strong and hard.

A moment later Veranix Calbert was standing in front of him, as if he had flown in with the wind.

"Saints almighty!" Delmin shouted. "How— what— why in the blazes—"

"Sorry," Veranix said. "Didn't realize how late it was, had to cheat a bit to make it."

"Cheat?" Delmin asked. He noted that Veranix was, if nothing else, dressed appropriately for the ceremonies, in his University of Maradaine uniform, with gray-and-red striped scarf and hat, fourth-year pips on his collar. All just like Delmin was himself. But something seemed off about Veranix's appearance.

"I've got to be honest, I don't fully understand what I'm *doing* when I do it. Am I making myself fast, or everything else slow, or am I changing how time works around me? I don't know."

Delmin didn't even have the words. Changing time? Could magic do that? Could Vee do that? And so casually to not even realize? It sickened Delmin to think, yes, if any-one could be so skilled yet so careless, it would be Vee.

"The point is, I ran here, *really* fast. I don't recommend doing it often."

Delmin grabbed Veranix's arm and pulled him into the entrance. "Vee, do I have to remind you that we actually have to *perform magically* in about five minutes? I'm kind of counting on you not to make me look like an idiot up there."

"I'll be fine," Veranix said. "This is showmanship, not real magic."

Something was off in Veranix's *numina* flow. Delmin was surprised he didn't notice it at first. "Vee," he said quietly. "Are you wearing it?"

"Do you mean—"

"Yes." Delmin's annoyance was surely coming through in his clipped tones.

"I did say I had to rush to get here on time."

"You said you had to cheat."

"And I'm not going to take it off while doing delicate and powerful time-changing magic," Veranix said. "That would be crazy."

Sometimes Delmin wondered if anything worked properly in that addled skull of Veranix's. That Veranix even owned a smuggled, Poasian-made cloak woven with napranium, the incredibly rare *numina*-drawing metal that fueled him with incredibly powerful levels of magic when he was being "the Thorn"—that alone made Delmin deeply uncomfortable. Delmin didn't even want to think about its intended owners and the original intent behind making it. The idea that Vee was about to wear it—this thing that in no way he should be in possession of in the first place—in front of a crowd of thousands was enough to make Delmin want to scream.

"Fine," Delmin said. "I mean it's not like if something goes wrong, you're dressed as the Thorn under all that."

"Umm—"

"Of course you are. You probably even have your weapons."

"I'm not losing another bow—"

"What am I—"

"There you two are!"

Madam Irianne Castilane was an official from either the College of Protocol or the Office of Intercollegiate Relations—or possibly both—but she missed her true life's calling as a parade sergeant. The opening ceremonies were her orchestration, planned in meticulous detail. And part of that detail involved a display of spectacle and wonder performed by the two fourth-year magic students she was informed were Professor Alimen's best students.

And she utterly refused to listen to any argument regarding how Delmin and Veranix were Alimen's "best students" in completely different, perhaps even contradictory, ways. She did not care for one moment that Delmin was not her man to perform a display of spectacle and wonder.

Delmin had pleaded to Professor Alimen to clear this up, but the professor merely suggested this was an excellent opportunity for him to test his practical skills.

"I managed to find him," Delmin said meekly.

"Madam Castilane, I deeply apologize—"

"Spare me, Mister Calbert," she snarled. "You missed nearly every rehearsal, so I'm not interested in hearing your apologies. What I want is you up on that platform ten minutes ago."

"Yes, of course," Veranix said. "Delmin, do you think I could do that?"

"What?" Delmin asked.

"Get there ten minutes ago."

Delmin bit his lip to keep from screaming in horror. "Sweet saints above, don't even joke about things like that."

They hustled through the tunnels to the backstage area, where a myriad of random performers from the University of Maradaine were all gathered—athletes of some sort, some army cadets with drums, and the Girls' School Ovation Squad. Delmin had a hard time believing that the last thing was something that actually existed.

"You're late," Vellia Sansar, captain of the Ovation Squad said with a sneer.

"Impossible," Veranix said, matching her sneer with a smile. "We can't start without us."

Vellia Sansar was definitely not a mage, because her gaze would have set Veranix on fire.

Veranix clapped his hands and looked around the gathered group. "All right, let's do this! University of Maradaine! U of M! U of M!"

Vellia's sneer melted away, and, turning to the rest of the Ovation Squad, she called out, "U of M! U of M!"

The squad, athletes, and cadets all joined in. Delmin started doing the same, despite himself.

Veranix was still going strong, and there wasn't any sign on his face that he was doing this as a facade or joke. Right now, in this moment, he was giving his full energy to the performance, the ceremony.

He kept clapping as the athletes ran up the steps to the stage, followed by the Ovation Squad.

Veranix pulled Delmin closer to him. "All right, Del. Like we practiced. Track me and follow the energy, use that to guide you."

"I know that," Delmin said.

"Good." He looked out at the stage as the athletes did a series of acrobatic maneuvers across it. There was something in his expression that was almost wistful. Then he turned back to Delmin. "One of us is supposed to be on the other side of the stage, right?"

"Yes," Delmin said. "It's you."

"Right. And it's blue, blue, white, fire, blue, white, blue, lightning, and then the big finish?"

"Switch the lightning and the fire," Delmin said. "Like every single other time you asked."

"I'm telling you, it's dramatically better—"

"Vee! The drums are starting! Other side!"

"Right."

A buzz of *numina* wrapped around him, and then he was gone. For half a moment, that signature flavor of Veranix's magic was a solid wall of energy stretching to the other side of the stage.

"All right," Delmin said to no one in particular. "Blue,

blue, white, lightning. You can do this." He almost believed it as he stepped up to the stage.

>◇◇◇◇◇◇<

Even from her place high up in the topmost level of Haveldale Center's seats, Kaiana Nell found the opening ceremony performances awe-inspiring. She had never seen its like, and from the sounds of the packed audience, many of them felt the same way. Bodies flipped and bounded in unison, as the Ovation Squad leaped from one part of the stage to the other, clapping and chanting. The drumbeats punctuated each moment, each stop of a foot, and each one hit Kaiana deep in the center of her body.

And then there was the real show.

Veranix and Delmin had refused to talk about what they were assigned to do. Veranix had refused out of his love for drama, milking the surprise out of it. Delmin, on the other hand, had kept quiet out of sheer terror.

The two of them took their places at opposite sides of the stage—from her vantage, two tiny figures in school uniforms—and then the stage lit up.

Of course, a series of oil lamps, lenses, and mirrors were already lighting the stage, but it changed completely when Vee and Del took their places.

An arc of blue light stretched between the two of them, which then pulsed and burst into a bright blast of blue that shot out over the crowd. Shouts and shrieks pierced the air as the blue light flew over their heads.

Then again with a white light, and then blue again, and then a blast of lightning that danced over the performers and the crowd.

A tap came on her shoulder. "Miss Nell?"

She turned to see Ebbily, one of the new young men on the campus grounds crew. A good forty more people were hired just for the games, and they were going to need every one of them to keep the playing fields and the rest of the campus in shape.

And once the games were over, most of them would be out of work.

"What is it, Ebbily?"

"We, uh, found something that requires your attention. At least, I was told it did."

Kaiana sighed. "Requires your attention" was the game the old hands on the staff were playing on her. Most of them resented her promotion to grounds supervisor, second to Master Bretten. Bretten, of course, had been grounds supervisor when Master Jolen was killed, but Kaiana had almost never interacted with him. Jolen had made a point of keeping her isolated from the rest of the staff. Now she was dealing with all of them.

The staff all hated and resented Kaiana's promotion—the Napa girl living in the carriage house, the new supervisor? But the school administration wasn't hearing any of that. Kaiana, as far as they were concerned, had saved the whole university from Cuse Jensett, and the promotion was her due.

So the game: she was the supervisor, so any and every annoyance or problem "required her attention." They were all going to make sure she never got a moment's peace again. Pulling her away from the opening ceremonies was more of that.

"All right," she said, getting up from her seat. She slipped her way down the back stairs of the grand auditorium to one of the service exits, and then followed Ebbily to the problem.

Down on the lawn outside the Haveldale Center two of the old hands—Lash and Rennie—were standing around, leaning on their tools, smug expressions on their faces.

"Sorry to disturb you, Miss Nell," Lash said. "It's just, we're cleaning up the mess these kids made—"

"Yes, of course," Kaiana said, striding over and glaring at him with everything she had. Her eyes were the one weapon she knew she had—she was going to lock on to the gaze of every damn one of these men and hold it until they broke and stared at the ground. They wanted to intimidate her, but she'd fought Red Rabbits and Jensett. These guys weren't going to scare her one bit. "What's the situation?"

"Well," Rennie said, "we're used to the regular junk and mess they all make. But we found something different, and thought maybe you should take a look at it."

This had to be a joke, she thought. Someone threw up in the bushes, or a student passed out, or some other absurdity.

"All right," she said. "What is it?"

"Right here," Lash said, pointing to the ground at his feet. "These."

Kaiana crouched down, keeping her eye on him. She wouldn't put it past him to do something crude. As soon as she got down all the way, she looked at where he had pointed.

Even in the moonlit night, it was clear what she was looking at. Three glass vials.

She grabbed one and stood up, holding it up to the light of the moon to get a better look at it. A thin film of fluid lined the inside of it.

Effitte. Here on the campus.

She crouched down and grabbed the other two vials. "Thank you, this is very important, indeed. I appreciate you bringing it to my attention."

"You do?" Rennie asked. He wasn't sure what to make of it.

"Yes. In fact, if any more of these are found, I want to know about it immediately. Am I clear?"

"Yes, Miss Nell," Ebbily said.

"Well, sure," Lash said. "We'll let you know. You going to stop it, Miss Nell?"

"Maybe she's the Thorn," Rennie said, laughing.

"That true, Miss Nell?" Lash added. "You been out there, killing gang boys?"

"Pardon?" Kaiana asked. That was unexpected.

"You didn't hear about that?" Lash asked. "Yeah, everyone was talking about it. The Thorn killed some gang boy, and the sticks are going All-Eyes on him."

"When?" Kaiana asked, not bothering to hide her interest. "This was tonight?"

"Why do you care?" Rennie asked.

"Because I like to pay attention to what's going on, Rennie," she said. "That's how you stop trouble before it happens. Now you must excuse me."

Holding back her anger, she walked as quickly as she could until she was confident she was out of their sight, and then broke into a run around the Haveldale Center to the service entrance. Veranix should be done with the performance by now. He needed to know about the *effitte*, and she needed to know who he killed and why.

The performance had ended by the time Kaiana reached the backstage area. Veranix was engaged in animated conversation with no fewer than four members of the Ovation Squad, who all fawned over every word he said. Delmin hung about a few feet away, clearly intimidated by everything around him. He spotted Kaiana and came straight over.

"Did you see it?" he asked.

"A bit," Kaiana said. Seeing his face drop, she added, "What I saw, you did wonderfully. I got pulled away. The usual game."

He nodded. "Sorry about that."

"This time it actually was important." She glanced back over to Veranix. She was not catching his eye, which she could understand, him being engulfed by Ovation like that. All four of them, traditional Druth beauties, with fair skin and light brown or honey blonde hair. Kaiana would have stuck out standing with them, with her tawny complexion and dark black hair.

Not that Veranix really cared about things like that. He just loved an audience, no matter who it was.

She gave a sharp whistle, and he immediately took notice. With a polite word, he extracted himself from the quartet and came over.

"Did you see it?"

"You were fine," Kaiana said. "We have a situation."

He nodded and kept walking, until the three of them were out of eavesdropping distance from the rest of folk backstage.

"What's up?"

"Two things," she said. She opened her hand to show him the vials. "These were found on campus."

His eyes hardened, and for a moment his entire appearance seemed to ripple. "When?"

"Just now," she said. "There's more, though. You're going to have to be careful—"

"I'm always careful, Kai . . ."

She declined to remind him of the incident two months ago where she had to rescue him from Cuse's device.

"Apparently the Aventil Constabulary has called an All-Eyes out for you tonight."

"They have?" A look crossed his face that seemed both perplexed and proud. "I wonder what that's about."

"I hear it's about the person they think you killed."

Now his face was just confusion. After a moment of stammering, he finally said, "Tonight?"

Delmin looked uncomfortable. "You were just out there, Vee. I mean, maybe someone—"

"No, that's not right," Veranix said. "I didn't kill—I didn't even *fight*—anyone out there tonight. Blazes, I wasn't even in Aventil."

He looked back and forth at Kai and Delmin, as if he needed to find reassurance from the both of them.

"I swear, whatever it is that happened . . . it wasn't me."

Chapter 2

V ERANIX RAN THROUGH the events of the evening in his head as he stalked through the campus walkways, Delmin and Kaiana right on his heels. The whole thing didn't make any damn sense.

"But if—" Delmin started to say for the fifth time.

"Not here," Veranix hissed. The campus was far too crowded—as crowded as he had ever seen it. All year long everyone had been talking about the Grand Tournament of the High Colleges, but he had never really conceived of how big and encompassing the whole thing would be. He could barely walk from Haveldale Center to Almers or the carriage house without bumping into a few dozen other people.

It occurred to him, with the cloak on, if he bumped into another mage or magic student, it could be very problematic. He was still focused on the illusion of his school uniform, but that wouldn't withstand the scrutiny of direct contact.

As they crossed out to the south lawn, it became clear that the crowds would make things more difficult. It was filled with people, wearing the uniforms of twenty-four different schools, all standing about, shouting, dancing to the music from the band that had spontaneously formed on the lawn.

"Blazes," Kaiana muttered from behind him.

"Right," Veranix said. "We go into the carriage house, it's going to get noticed."

"I was thinking about the lawn," Kaiana said. "It's going to take all autumn to recover, and only then if we get some decent rain."

"Come on," Veranix said, leading them into Holtman Hall.

"Am I allowed to go in there?" Kaiana asked.

"Probably," Veranix said. Holtman was the services center for this cluster of boys' dorms—kitchens and dining halls, laundry, custodial, maintenance. As it was part of the boys' dorms, female students were forbidden from entering—Jiarna Kay caused a stir when she followed them in last semester—but since female staff ran most of the things in Holtman, Kaiana surely could enter without trouble. Surely. Especially given her new position.

"So why are we going in here?"

"Did you never follow the Spinner Run to the end?" Veranix asked.

"Oh, right," she said, glancing around the hallway. Holtman was quiet and relatively deserted right now. Probably was only unlocked because the housing staff was just now having supper. A bit of conversation and activity could be heard over in the dining hall.

"This way," Veranix said, leading them to the storage room where the Spinner Run started. It was little more than a large closet, where the housing staff stored mops, buckets, barrels of vinegar, and whatever else they used to clean. It was almost always locked, but Veranix had long since mastered flipping the latch with a wisp of magic. The trapdoor down to the run was in the back corner, virtually unnoticeable if you didn't know it was there. Veranix only knew it was there because the other end was in the carriage house, and he had first come through from there. There wasn't even a way to open it on this end—it was clear the original use was to get from the carriage house to here without being seen.

He had always wondered about its history—why was a tunnel built from Holtman to the carriage house, why was it forgotten about, and why was it called the Spinner Run? He only knew that because of the brass plaque at the bottom of the ladder, which just added to its mystery.

Delmin stopped in the storage room. "Is this private enough?"

"It could be," Veranix said. "But if someone happens to come in, there's going to be questions about what the blazes we're doing here."

Delmin glanced back at the door. "True. Did Professor Alimen ever do any masking work with you?"

"Masking?"

"Yeah, you create something like a wall between us and the door, so someone looks in, they see an empty room, don't hear anything."

"No, never," Veranix said. That did sound like a practical thing to learn how to do, though he wasn't sure how to do it. It wouldn't be too different from the shrouding and appearance changes he did with the cloak's help.

"The professor probably presumed he didn't need to encourage Veranix to be more secretive," Kaiana said. "Let's move on. We'll definitely have the carriage house to ourselves."

Veranix magicked open the trapdoor and went down the ladder, conjuring up a floating ball of light for them to see by. Kaiana and Delmin came down behind him.

"You really come down here?" Delmin asked.

"It's been useful," Veranix said. He sometimes thought that he—or Kaiana—should make some effort to clean up the tunnel. At least clear out the cobwebs. But there was something to its mystique as a true secret passage that he loved. "It certainly has been a good place to hide my gear."

"This is true," Kaiana said. "Though having a special tunnel that leads right to where I would sleep never gave me much comfort."

As they reached the other end of the tunnel, Veranix wondered who, if anyone, might have lived in the carriage house decades ago, and if "spinner" meant something in those days that was long forgotten.

Best not to think about it.

He climbed up the ladder into the carriage house, and immediately found that they weren't going to be alone in there. Two voices cried out, followed by the sound of scrambling bodies. By the time Veranix was out of the trapdoor, he could clearly see who was in the carriage house, as Phadre Golmin was brushing dirt off his coat and slacks, while Jiarna Kay had her back to them both, fastening up her blouse.

"Evening," he said dryly. "I take it you two didn't come to the opening ceremonies."

"Veranix," Phadre said, flushed and out of breath. "Capital to see you here, old sport. Wasn't expecting . . ."

"Anyone?"

"No," Jiarna said, turning around to face them.

"Oh, Saint Hespin," Kaiana said, coming up the ladder. "You two do know I still live here, don't you?"

"I thought you had moved into the staff apartments," Jiarna said. "Aren't you entitled to that?"

"Mine aren't going to be ready until the fall," Kaiana said. "That's what I'm told." Many of the detail perks of Kai's promotion had been delayed. Though Veranix did wonder what he was going to do when the carriage house was no longer Kaiana's space.

"Sorry," Jiarna said.

"Where are you staying right now?" Delmin had come out of the trapdoor. "I know you were using the extension provision after getting your letters, but didn't the Tournament kick you out of the dorms?"

"Yes," they both said in unison.

"We had to be out of our rooms by today," Phadre said. "But our residencies at Trenn College don't start until the first of Oscan."

"And the caravan we're taking to Yin Mara isn't until the twenty-second of Soran," Jiarna added. "Meaning we have over two weeks with no place to live."

"One week, really," Phadre said. "We can rent rooms in Aventil, but not during the Tournament. Nothing around."

"Obviously," Veranix said. "Sorry about that."

"So what's up, chaps?" Phadre asked. "You all here on some Thorn business, then?"

Veranix felt his throat tighten for a moment. When he could find his voice, he glared at Jiarna. "You told him?"

"I told him," she said shamelessly. "You can trust him."

"Yes," Phadre said excitedly. "I mean, I was a bit skeptical with it all at first, but Jiarna reminded me of the business with that Jensett fellow, and what you were doing to stop him, and I remembered the incident at the dinner. And the dining hall. And . . ."

"Thank you, Phadre," Veranix said.

"I will say, it certainly made the events around my defense make much more sense."

"All right," Veranix said. No need to be coy or circumspect. "So, Kai. You found vials?"

She reached into her pouch and pulled them out, handing them over. "Three of them, right by Haveldale Center."

Veranix held one of them up to the lamplight. Thin residue. Had to be *effitte*.

"What's this, then?" Phadre asked.

"Drugs on campus," Kaiana said. "*Effitte,* specifically. Which is coming in over from Dentonhill."

"Presumably," Delmin said. "We *presume* it's coming in from Dentonhill."

That got Veranix's blood boiling. "Oh, come on, Del, where else would it come from?"

"It probably is from there," Delmin said. He then looked at Jiarna and Phadre, "You know he mainly had a thing with stopping the drugs and the drug lord out of Dentonhill. Fenley."

"Fenmere," Veranix growled.

"Right, yes," Phadre said. He reached out for the vial and took a look at it in the light. "Well, I certainly can't say I approve of filth like this on campus. Right?" He looked to Jiarna.

"So, with the tournament on, you've got hordes of new

bodies on campus, and with that, their bad habits," Jiarna said. "Through that, you're going to get a few users. What can you do about it?"

"Find the source, shut it down," Veranix said. "And then find the source's source, and so on."

"Problem is, Calbert," Jiarna said, "all you've got to go on is the fact that it's here. You've got nothing else to work with yet."

"She's right," Kaiana said. "And you can't just go out there and smack around students like you do the scrubs in shady pubs."

"Especially with an All-Eyes out for you," Delmin said.

"What's this?" Phadre asked.

Veranix sighed. Might as well say it all. "Apparently the Constabulary in Aventil are hunting for me. At least, that's what we've heard."

"Why?" Phadre asked. Constant questions. He seemed genuinely curious, but there was a tone of pointed accusation in there. Maybe Veranix was just imagining it. Phadre was a true academic, and perhaps he was employing the Method of Questions.

"What was it?" Veranix asked Kaiana.

"Dead body somewhere in Aventil," she said. "I don't know more than that."

"I should verify that," Veranix said.

"Colin?" Kaiana asked.

"Or Reverend Pemmick."

"There are more people on the team, here?" Phadre asked.

"Not now," Jiarna said quietly.

"All right," Phadre said. "Forgive me, Veranix, it's just . . . I mean, you were here on campus, performing in the opening ceremonies, so we know you weren't out there killing anyone."

"Do we?" Delmin asked. Veranix turned hotly on him. "You were out there, Vee. Blazes, you're still wearing your Thorn clothes and weapons under an illusion of the uniform."

"He can do that?"

Veranix relaxed the illusion, showing Phadre the full effect. "I was out there, but not in Aventil. I wasn't even . . ."

Everyone was looking at him expectantly.

"There are other situations I'm dealing with. Finding the dens in Dentonhill. Fenmere's people trying to expand into western neighborhoods. Missing kids . . ."

"Missing children?" Phadre asked.

"Tonight I was . . . see, a few months ago some boys from a doxy camp told me kids are going missing. Kids—especially children of doxies and other street folk—are vanishing in Dentonhill, and elsewhere in the city. Since then, I've kept in contact, tried to find out what I could, but . . ."

But he hadn't done a damn thing. He wanted to help them, find out what was going on, save the kids if he could. Problem was, he didn't have the first clue what to do about it. Scouting around Oscana Park wasn't working. He wasn't an inspector.

"You're trying to tackle all of that?" Phadre asked. "Saints, you're . . . I don't know how you do it."

"With help," Kaiana said.

"Right, right," Phadre said. "So you first need to figure out who is selling the drug on campus, and stop them. How do you normally do that?"

Veranix took off the bandolier holding his bow and quiver and sat down on a bench. "Normally? Find some low-level user or dealer, and scare them into telling me their source. But in Dentonhill, it's not that hard to find someone who's connected to *effitte*. On campus, with hundreds upon hundreds of visitors and guests? Kaiana's right, I can't do that."

"Then something top down?" Kaiana offered.

"As in, find one of the upper-level folk, and squeeze them? The only one I really know of is Bell. Problem is, he's gone completely to ground. Haven't seen a bit of him. He might have ended up in the river for all I know."

"So," Delmin said, "different kind of plan needed."

"I'm open to suggestions," Veranix said.

Delmin furrowed his brow. "All right, if it's on campus, then we need to find who is buying. Buyer leads to seller. To find who's buying, we need to find who is using."

Jiarna's eyes went wide. "A social strategy!"

"Pardon?" Veranix asked.

"It's very simple," she said. "Whoever is buying the *effitte* is doing so to use it, probably in some sort of social atmosphere. People are here for sport and revels. So we must all engage in sport and revels—as much as we can—to interact with as many people as possible to find the *effitte* users."

"Your plan is we go to events and parties of the Tournament?" Veranix asked.

"Isn't that what you wanted to do already?" Phadre asked.

"Yes, but now we're doing it for science. And justice." She glanced around the room. "It is justice, yes?"

"Yes," Veranix said hotly.

"And saving lives," Kaiana said quietly. "Most of these kids probably don't even know what *effitte* does. I mean, do they even have it in other cities?"

Veranix didn't know. He knew it was brought in from the Napolic Islands—the Poasian-controlled ones. It was made there, and smuggled here by Fenmere. Surely there were other smuggling rings all along the west coast. Maybe Fenmere was just one part of a grander network.

"Social strategy," Jiarna said sternly. "Aren't you supposed to be helping with the tetchball squad?"

"Yes, and I have been," Veranix said. "Batting coach, primarily. Professor Alimen says it's a good activity for me." The professor had been trying to occupy Veranix with tasks all summer—the opening ceremonies, the tetch squad, special tutoring. "Come the autumn," Alimen had said more than once, "there will be several first- and second-year magic students in need of mentoring, Mister Calbert. I am counting on you being available to them."

Jiarna nodded, now pacing around the carriage house. "Good, excellent. The tetch matches are the centerpiece of the Tournament, so that positions you perfectly for one aspect. Tie yourself to that squad. Engage with them on and off the field, and you might be privy to something useful."

Veranix was skeptical. "That's not going to be—"

Jiarna cut him off. "Yes, it is. Kaiana?"

"I've got enough work with my new position."

"Exactly," Jiarna said. "But you can use that. You've been given scruff, right? Folks below you challenging your authority?"

"Every little thing 'requires my attention'."

"Oh, that is perfect. Use that. Make it clear that you want to know every irregular thing they find. Embrace every time they pull that on you."

"Right," Kaiana said, nodding. "Maybe I can figure out where on campus it's concentrating."

Jiarna went into one of the empty stables. "I've got a map of campus that I drew up a couple years ago which should help." She started rummaging through the pile of crates, cases, and trunks that occupied it.

"Are all your belongings in here?" Kaiana asked, going to the stable.

"Both of ours," Phadre said. "Sorry, Kai, but we . . ."

"Vee," Kaiana said sharply. "The apartment."

"What?" Veranix asked.

"The apartment over the laundry press."

Veranix hesitated. That was one of his few safe refuges in Aventil, a place where he could hide his Thorn gear and rest.

"Vee!" she said sharply.

"Right, yes," he said. "Sorry, but . . . I've got a place you two could stay at, keep your belongings. It's just for a few weeks, right?"

"Yes," Phadre said. "You don't mind?"

"Not at all," Veranix lied on Kai's harsh stare.

"Thank you," Jiarna said coolly. She unrolled the hand-drawn map and laid it on a table. "We've got one location, by Haveldale Center? Delmin, what can you do?"

Delmin hesitated. "I've been chummy with several of the

other interim prefects in the dorm cluster." That was another job Alimen had tried to nudge Veranix into for the Tournament. He managed to squirm away from it, but Delmin had embraced the idea. "We've been meeting casually."

"All saints and sinners, that is perfect," Jiarna said. "You stick to them like flies in a butcher shop."

"And us?" Phadre asked.

"Simple," Jiarna said. "I still have quite a few friends in the social clubs, and they are hosting events with all the schools over the course of the Tournament. I will need a proper escort at those events."

"Your plan is you go to social club parties?" Veranix asked.

"It is a burden I am taking on to help you," Jiarna said, with the slightest hint of a smirk. "Believe me, I've been to quite a few of these things, and if there is *effitte* coming onto campus, it will filter there."

Veranix sighed. "All right. This is as good a plan as any. But if one student ends up in *'fitte*-trance, then I'm going to go into full skull-cracking mode."

"As you wish," Jiarna said. "And I have something to help you with that."

She went back to her belongings and came out with something wrapped in cloth. She put it on the table next to the map.

"Is that?" he asked trepidatiously. He unwrapped it to find his napranium-laced rope bundled in there. "You repaired it?"

Jiarna hesitated. Pointing to the leather strap wrapped around the rope where it had been cut in his fight with Bluejay two months ago, she said, "More accurate would be to say that I patched it. I don't have the materials or know-how to truly repair it, but I used a few different techniques to stem the *numina* bleed and blockage."

"Del?"

Delmin was already staring at the rope as closely as he could without making contact. The rope required strong command of magic to even handle, and in Delmin's hands it would be out of control. "She's right, in that there aren't the same snarls in the flow around the damage. But the flow is weaker overall."

"True," Jiarna admitted. "My method was essentially one of introducing impurities."

Veranix picked it up, feeling a surge of *numina* from it— but Delmin was right, it wasn't anywhere near the same degree of power he used to feel from it. He willed it, magically, to coil up at his belt like he always did. The rope responded to the magic, but it felt almost like a numb limb, and it took more effort than it used to. Not as much effort as trying to magically control a normal rope would, but effort nonetheless.

"Thank you," Veranix said. "This means a lot."

"All right," Jiarna said. "Now, where is this apartment you can lend us?"

Normally, Corman relished the summers. Much of Mister Fenmere's household staff had gone with him to the summer house on the Yinaran coast, as had Gerrick. They had all expressed their regrets. "Poor Corman, having to stay behind to keep an eye on things."

Mister Fenmere knew it wasn't a burden, though. Mostly because he knew that Corman loathed the beach, the ocean, and everything else involving the summer house.

Keeping an eye on Mister Fenmere's business and household for the summer months? That was usually bliss for Corman.

Usually.

This summer had been sweltering, and even opening up all the doors and windows did little to create a breeze in the house. Corman would be in shirtsleeves, drinking Scallic lime ricks, and he'd still be coated in a layer of sweat. It was vile.

Plus there was the fact that managing the business was

going nowhere near as well as it should have. He knew Mister Fenmere would not blame him for that, but he was ashamed nonetheless. The summer had been filled with minor disasters.

One disaster was the expansion into the western neighborhoods. The recent death of Mendel Tyne and the crumbling of his empire was a plum opportunity for them to take control over Keller Cove, and, from there, cement their hold on all of West Maradaine. Bell had been sent out to lay the foundation there, but he had gone silent. Bell had suffered humiliation from the Red Rabbits and the Thorn, and Corman wondered if it had been a wise move putting that man in charge of anything. Corman's presumption was that he had failed, bad enough that he was now rotting in a creek bed somewhere.

The larger disaster was still looming on the horizon. Dejri Adfezh was coming to Maradaine for a meeting with Mister Fenmere. Nothing good could come from that ghost setting foot on Druth soil. Adfezh sent word he was coming on the nineteenth, which was the same day Mister Fenmere was due to return from the coast. Corman had sent a letter, but at this point little could be done to change Mister Fenmere's return plans.

Corman felt it was important to let disappointment rain on those below him. He had gathered several of the corner bosses together, and made them stand in sweltering silence in Mister Fenmere's game room while he casually played billiards.

"Sales continue to plummet, friends," he said after sinking another ball. "At least, the sales that are being reported."

To their credit, none of the five bosses assembled looked uncomfortable or ashamed. Heads high, eyes hard. Benny, the shaven-head bruiser who ran a tight operation of captains and sellers in Dentonhill's north point, nearly snarled. "What's that supposed to mean?"

Nyri, the Waishen-haired and Tsouljan-skinned woman who ran a handful of upscale dens in secretive locations, answered him. "He means he thinks you're claiming losses to the Thorn and pocketing the difference." She sucked on her *hassper* pipe, adding, "My numbers have been stable, Corman. I don't appreciate being called out with no call."

"Stable isn't entirely true," Corman said. "They've been creeping downward, though at a slower pace than everyone else."

"That's because I don't rest my entire business on *effitte*."

"This isn't fair," Smiley said. He was the oldest one of the bunch, a former soldier who handled the western point of the neighborhood. "I'm the one who's getting hammered every time the Thorn comes around."

Jullick, the young buck, shot back, "You're not the only one." Corman did not care for Jullick. Far too ambitious. Mister Fenmere felt it was worth channeling that ambition to his own ends, but Corman thought that some form of rebellion was inevitable. It was just a question of when.

"And what are you all doing about that?" Corman asked. "Are you stopping the Thorn? Tracking him, chasing him, setting up a trap for him?"

"No, they aren't."

This did not come from Jads—the distribution and warehousing mistress that Corman had more than a little personal affection for—but from the door behind Corman. He was not expecting anyone else.

"No one is doing anything about the Thorn," the speaker continued as Corman turned around. Corman had to admit, he was genuinely surprised to see who it was.

"Mister Bell," he said, keeping his voice level. "I had presumed you were dead."

"No, just staying out of the wind," Bell said. The man barely looked like himself. Thinner, leaner, more hair. "Not that anyone here cared much."

"Don't say that," Smiley said. "Many of us would have helped."

"That doesn't surprise me." Bell stepped into the room, and before Corman knew what was happening, Bell had picked up one of the billiard balls and pitched it right into

Smiley's face. Blood spurted out of Smiley's nose as he shouted.

"Very uncivilized," Nyri said.

"Terribly sorry, ma'am," Bell said. "Best watch that nose, Smiley. Mister Fenmere would hate blood on the carpet in his game room."

"Very true," Corman said. "Mister Bell, your presence and your behavior are quite unwelcome."

"Quite unwelcome?" Bell echoed. "How genteel, Corman." In a flash, Bell snatched the billiard cue out of Corman's hand. "Let's do nothing foolish, then."

"Just because Mister Fenmere isn't here doesn't mean there aren't guards in the house."

"I know there are. I also know where they are." He held up his hands peacefully. "Don't you worry, I didn't do anything permanent to any of them. Unlike Smiley's nose."

"I'm going to make you eat your pisswhistle!" Smiley shouted, blood gargling in his mouth.

"Not today," Bell said. "Your guards are fine. Now, if the Thorn knew which house this was, if he got in here . . . that wouldn't be the case, Mister Corman. None of you would be fine."

"You aren't going to bring him here, are you?" Jullick asked.

"No, of course not, you simpering toad," Bell said. He pointed the cue at the man. "You know, I never liked you, Jullick."

"Why should he care?" Jads asked. "What were you, other than a glorified errand boy?"

Bell chuckled, and leaned over the table. "None of you should be upset with me, you know. Because unlike the rest of you, I actually understand our problem." He took a shot, failing to sink anything.

"What problem is that?" Jads asked coolly. She was watching Bell with wry amusement. "Are you saying you understand the Thorn?"

"I do, actually, but that's hardly the point," Bell said.

Corman had to admit, he was more than a little intrigued

by the moxie Bell was showing. It took having nothing left to lose to make him interesting. "What is the point, Mister Bell?"

"You haven't been able to stop him, because no one knows who the Thorn actually is. But that's just it . . . no one knows, so anyone could be the Thorn."

"I don't understand," Jullick said. "We already know that anyone might be the Thorn."

"That isn't what he said, imbecile," Nyri said. "Anyone *could* be the Thorn." Whatever nuance she had picked up from that distinction wasn't clear to Corman.

"I've taken a bit of initiative, Mister Corman," Bell said, laying the cue on the billiard table. "Some business that was, of course, personally satisfying. But I'm also going to handle your Thorn problem."

Corman was genuinely confused. Bell had done little but get repeatedly beaten by the Thorn. "And how will you do that?"

"By setting everyone after him," Bell said with a smirk. "And taking care of other business in the process."

"You're an idiot, Mister Bell," Corman said. He was more than tired of this absurdity, both with Bell and the Thorn. Even though Mister Fenmere had instructed him to not bother with the Thorn at all, he decided to take his own initiative. "All of you, spread the word. Two thousand crowns for the Thorn, dead or alive."

"Really, Corman?" Benny asked.

"Yes, really," Corman said. The two thousand could be spared, he knew that, especially if the Thorn was taken out of the equation. And if no one claimed the bounty, then it didn't matter.

"That won't work, Corman," Bell said. "But that should be interesting."

"Someone get rid of him," Corman said, indicating Bell with a nod of his head. Benny was the one to oblige, jumping over the table while drawing a knife out.

Bell didn't even blink, merely taking a step back. From nowhere, there was a twang and Benny screamed. He hit the floor where Bell had been standing, an arrow through his knife hand. A man stepped out of the shadows. He was wearing a burgundy cloak, hood hiding his face, and held up a bow with another arrow drawn. He gave a cocky smile. "How's that, Bell?"

"Perfect."

"You brought the Thorn here?" Corman shouted.

"Of course not, don't be stupid. Like I said, Mister Corman, if the Thorn had been here, you would all be in a lot of trouble." He gave a mock salute and stepped out the way he came. His bowman walked with him, keeping an arrow trained on Corman. Bell glanced back and added, "But you helped prove my point. Anyone *could* be the Thorn."

Then there was a burst of colored smoke. When it cleared, he and his friend were gone.

Corman looked at the five bosses, now feeling nauseous. "Clean this all up and get out of here."

"You're serious about the crowns, though?" Smiley asked.

"Two thousand for the Thorn? Dead serious. Tell everyone who might care to know. And if they get Bell's friend by mistake, all the better."

Chapter 3

ALMERS HALL WAS filled with athletes: archers, runners, riders, rowers, throwers, and, of course, tetchball players. On the third floor, the only actual University of Maradaine students were Delmin and Veranix, who had been given special dispensation to keep their room for the summer by Professor Alimen. This was the first summer where Veranix hadn't spent it largely on his own, the whole floor to himself. Even Delmin usually went home to his North Maradaine family. The crowded, raucous dorm in the middle of the summer was rather disconcerting.

A lot of these athletes were disciplined young men who got up with the dawn to begin their morning routines. Veranix found this incredibly unnatural. Also he was unable to sleep further once they all started going.

He reminded himself this was only going to be seven more days.

"So what's your plan for today?" Delmin asked from his bed when Veranix got up and went into his set of morning stretches.

"We all have a plan, remember?" Veranix shot back. "I'm tying myself to the tetch squad."

"Right, so where are they?" Delmin was clearly seeking solid details to ease his anxiety.

"Most of those boys live in the social houses. Tosler is

one of the Seated Men in Whisper Fox House, and the ones who aren't in that house or another, he's put up there for the summer."

"Whisper Fox is a good house," Delmin said. "My uncle and my cousin were both Foxes back in their day." Veranix nodded, remembering back to second year, when Delmin was more than a little frustrated to learn that magic students were barred from joining the social houses.

"So I'll be meeting up with them. Today they have a match against Trenn College, and I'll be there until I see trouble."

"Good show," Delmin said. "And . . . what do you do when you see trouble? Are you going with all your gear, masking it?"

Veranix dropped down to do his lower back stretches. "Thought about it, but I can't see how do to it without it being unwieldy. Bow and staff don't hide well."

"I've noticed."

"I'm going to bring the cloak and the rope in a rucksack and keep that on me, just in case."

Delmin gave him a disapproving look.

"Something happens, I want to be on it."

The look didn't change.

"I'll be careful."

"What's the plan after the match?"

"No clue," Veranix said. "Whatever the squad does, I'll do." He wasn't too keen on that. Tosler was a decent enough sort, but the idea of spending the evening in the company of the whole squad filled him with dread.

Someone pounded on their door. "Hey, Maries! Your boys are going to swallow dust on the field tonight!"

Veranix popped onto his feet and threw the door open, to find four boys—tall, muscular boys—gathered outside the door. They were just in shirtsleeves and slacks, so he couldn't determine what school they were from.

"What field?" he asked. "I mean, saints, if you're going to spin the sewage, I need to know for what."

"In the quint, you clod," the one in front said. "Just you watch, Maries."

"The quint?" Veranix asked. "The blazes you all leering about for that? Quint's a one-man event."

"That it is, Mary," the boy in front said, flexing his arms. "And Pirrell University is going to sweep that up, just like everything else."

"Fine," Veranix said, refusing to let this tosser bait him. "In the meantime, I'm going to go to the water closet."

He pushed his way past the group, only to have a hand grapple his shoulder. "Don't you walk off on us."

Veranix twisted out of the clod's grip easily, stepping back and turning to face them. "Are you trying to start a fight?"

"Vee," Delmin warned from the doorway.

"It's fine, Del," Veranix said. "I'm not going to fight these guys."

"Oh, the Mary thinks he's too good for us?" the Pirrell leader asked.

"You know I'm not one of the athletes, don't you? I'm not doing the quint or anything else."

"Then what the depths are you doing here?" The big guy moved to shove Veranix, which he easily dodged just by shifting his body. The big guy stumbled and bumped into the far wall.

"I live here," Veranix said, taking another step back. "And I'm going on with my day now."

He took two steps toward the water closet when the brute did exactly what he had expected.

"Vee!" Delmin shouted.

Veranix was already lunging to the side and dropping his head, so the bruiser's punch sailed through empty air. With a quick pivot he was behind the boy, who seemed genuinely confused that Veranix hadn't been clobbered.

"What are you, a rabbit?" he asked.

"Certainly not."

As Veranix suspected, the three still behind him made their move. They were as loud and slow as a broken wagon, so when they came to grab him, he had dropped down in a split and rolled back between their legs. He popped back up as they cracked into each other's skulls.

"Gents, I do really need to get to the water closet," he said.

"You're going to get such a creaming!" the leader shouted, and he charged down the hallway, arms in a wide tackle.

Dodging that was too easy.

"Delmin," Veranix said calmly as he slipped past the guy. "You are the interim prefect, yes?"

"Yes," Delmin said cautiously, as two fists came flying at Veranix's head from opposite sides. Veranix flattened himself against the wall, and the two boys managed to punch each other.

"When you report on this, which I'm sure you will—"

Veranix dodged another wild punch, and then another, and then a third—guiding the group's leader to punching his own friend in the face. Three of the four down, only the leader still standing.

"Make sure you note that I didn't lay a finger on them."

With that, he blew on the leader's face, sweetening his breath with enough magic to turn that blow into a gale force. The guy bowled over onto his friends, the four of them now in a pile on the floor.

Delmin laughed out loud. "I suppose that's technically true."

Veranix winked back at Delmin. "I wasn't kidding about the water closet. Gentlemen, it's been invigorating."

Lieutenant Benvin had taken to sleeping in the apartment over the Broken Spindle, a taproom on Violet Street that was favored by some of the Waterpath Orphans. It wasn't their "official" pub where their captains and bosses would congregate, but it was close to where their "territory" met the Knights' and they kept a close eye on it.

Benvin had acquired this apartment a month before,

paid out of his own pocket, even though it was for Constabulary operations. He had tried to explain why he needed it to Captain Holcomb, but the captain didn't care. He wasn't about to hand over an extra pence to clean up this neighborhood.

So Benvin got the apartment on his own, and made it the special operations center for his squad, away from the stationhouse. They were the only ones who knew about it, and they kept copies of all their files and work here. There had been enough mistakes with crucial documents back at the stationhouse: "filing errors" and "cleaning accidents." Corruption or incompetence, it didn't matter. Benvin wasn't going to take any more chances trusting the fools he was surrounded with.

Of course, the apartment was a shabby hole. No water closet—just a backhouse in the alley below and weak pump spigot in the room. There was no proper stove, just a countertop with a metal plate drawing heat from the Spindle's oven. With enough time, it could get a teapot to something resembling hot enough for tea. Benvin even had a teapot, tea, and honey, but only because someone in the team had brought them over from their own place. Benvin didn't remember who it was, but he was grateful for them as he waited for the water to heat up.

Someone knocked on the door. There were only a handful of people who would: his crew, the landlady, and one other. Benvin grabbed the crossbow off the bed—he had slept with it loaded next to him, a stupid thing to do—and went to the door.

"Who's there?"

"Blazes, stick, just open."

It was the one other. Benvin lowered the crossbow and opened the door. Yessa—one of the Waterpath Orphan captains—slipped in and slammed the door behind her. She glanced nervously around the room, as if expecting some sort of ambush. Then she took a good look at him—in shirtsleeves and skivvies, crossbow in hand—and chuckled.

"You're having an interesting morning, Left."

Benvin scowled at her, putting the crossbow on the rickety table. "You here for tea, Orphan?"

"If you're offering."

Benvin grabbed his trousers off the end of the bed and pulled them on. "Once the water gets close to hot."

"Didn't know I was staying all day."

Benvin took a good look at her while he grabbed his shirt and put it on. There was a smart young woman under the dingy hair and Orphan scars on her face. A better neighborhood would have had a school for her as a child, and she might have ended up one of these Uni kids instead of an Aventil ganger.

"Doubt you could. Your 'crew' would notice you gone, huh?"

"Crew, bosses, everyone else," Yessa said, sitting on the bed. "But I could always make excuses." She leaned back on her elbows, giving him a look that he could only categorize as lascivious.

Yessa had gone from spitting at him to making advances rather quickly, as soon as she had begun feeding information to him about gang activity. Benvin could not pretend that he wasn't tempted by the idea, but the potential problems it would cause outweighed any carnal benefits. Even still, the sticky heat of the unyielding summer had led her to wearing a sleeveless blouse with the bottom tied off to expose her stomach, sweat dripping down her chest . . .

Benvin straightened up and turned to the teapot plate. "No need for that."

"All business," she said with a sigh. "At least pour me a tea."

Benvin found two cups—all the cups were clean, probably thanks to Jace or Tripper—and poured out the weak, lukewarm tea. "You staying safe?"

"I'm fine, Left, but thanks for pretending you care." She sipped at the tea. "You signaled for me, so what do you want?"

"Body was found last night, a Red Rabbit named Keckin."

"Keckin?" She shook her head. "Thought him and Sotch left town."

"Aren't any Red Rabbits around anymore," Benvin said.

"Just the ones you've got locked up," she said. "Which is a good chunk of them. The rest, though, they all went to ground. You know that."

"So why is Keckin dead now?"

"Blazes if I know, Left. I guess somebody found where he was hiding."

"That's right," Benvin said. "Pretty sure it was the Thorn."

"Really?" She sounded very skeptical.

"Four arrows in the man, thrown from a rooftop. Seems pretty much like the Thorn."

"He was beefing with the Rabbits, that's what cracked them. You think he's hunting the last of them?"

"You tell me. What are they saying about the Thorn?"

She sighed. "Nothing new. We've been over this. He ain't tight with the Orphans, and we ain't giving him cause to tussle. Let him fight it out with Fenmere, or hunt down Rabbits."

"So you think he is the one hunting them?"

"Do I think so? Sure." She took a slug of her tea. "But that's just my gut telling me that, same thing you have going on."

"Right," Benvin said, drinking his weak tea. It really was awful, just a hair above the room temperature, which was sweltering hot. "He isn't just hunting them. Like I said, Keckin had four arrows in him. The bodyman in the stationhouse said they were hours apart. Marks on his wrist show that Keckin was tied up. The Thorn didn't just hunt and kill him. He tortured him."

"Blazes," Yessa said quietly. After a moment, she finished the tea and tossed the cup over to him as she hopped off the bed. Benvin caught the cup ably. "I need to get out of here."

"Anything comes up with the Thorn . . ."

"I will let you know," she said. "Especially if he's in

league with the Princes." They had had this conversation several times, and she was clearly tired of it. Though this time there was a hint that she was spooked.

"Good."

"You might want to steer any of the Uni crowds away from Vine south of Clover. I hear Dogs and Kickers are pressing on each other again, so that could be a spill."

"That ain't news," Benvin said.

"I hear it's a bit more heat than usual, but who knows." She sighed heavily. "I'll tell you if I hear anything about the Rabbits. I can tell you one thing, if Keckin was just killed—especially killed like you said—Sotch is probably running, and running hard."

"If she's still alive," Benvin said. "Stay safe out there."

She winked as she went to the door. "Always do. Except when you ironed me."

Whisper Fox House was far to the north and west of the campus, amongst a row of other Gentlemen's Social Houses, right at the border between the Ladies' College and the rest of the University. On the other side of the walkway, of course, were the Ladies' Social Houses. This whole area was the part of the University for the privileged, from noble families to scions of newer money.

Rich kids who weren't accepted into the Royal College of Maradaine, mostly.

Social house events were a fairly good way to spend an evening, especially when it was a joint event with a Ladies' House and Gentlemen's House.

An older man in a dark gray suit stood at the front stoop of Whisper Fox House, apparently not letting the morning heat perturb him at all.

"Are you calling upon anyone?" the man asked when Veranix came up the stairs.

"I am," Veranix said, used to the formality in approaching the houses when there wasn't an event. There was a list of who would be allowed in, but Veranix was on the list.

"Veranix Calbert, here for Mister Tosler and the tetchball squad."

"Absolutely, Mister Calbert," the suited man said. "Mister Tosler will be pleased to see you." He opened the door and let Veranix in.

Veranix had been through here enough times over the summer to find his way to the dining room, which is exactly where Tosler and the rest of the squad would be at this time. And they all were there, gathered around the long table, eating an absurdly bountiful breakfast, with three gray-skirted women serving them.

"Calbert!" Tosler shouted, standing up from his place at the head of the table. Tosler had always been friendly, staying in touch with his friends in Almers after he left the dorms to join Whisper Fox. He had been the one who had asked Veranix to coach the team. "Glad to see you here!" He crossed over and clasped both of Veranix's shoulders warmly.

"Calbert!" many of the boys called out, all while stuffing their faces with eggs, sausages, biscuits, butter, jam, and all sorts of other delights. All eleven of the squad—including Tosler—were already dressed for the match. Uniform for tetchball was a pullover jersey—in University of Maradaine blue and white—with matching short trousers and high stockings, along with fingerless gloves and page caps. If Veranix didn't already know the whole squad, he wouldn't be able to tell them apart.

"Have you eaten?" Tosler asked, gesturing to an empty chair.

"I can always eat," Veranix said. "Thank you." He had already had a Holtman breakfast, but that was shabby fare in comparison.

"Issie! Plate for Calbert!"

Veranix sat down while one of the servant women brought him a steaming plate of eggs and sausages. "So are we ready for the match?" he asked them all.

"Are we ready, boys?" Tosler asked.

"Woo-ha!" was the unanimous response.

"You're going to be there, right, Calbert?" This came from Ottie, a lean fourth-year who was eighth or ninth in line for a Barony, who played the Rail on the tetch field.

"Damn right I'm going to be there," Veranix said. "You think I would miss your matches after all the work I've done with you?" Taking a bite, he raised his voice so everyone could hear him. If he wanted to attach himself to whatever exploits these boys would get into over the course of the games, they had to all love him. And they all liked him fine, but it was time to add a bit more to the show.

"I mean," Veranix went on, "it's not like today's match is going to be all that exciting, because you boys are up against Trenn College. I mean, come on, Trenn? Weak-legged cabbage eaters, that's what they are."

There was a general cheer.

"Really, boys, if there's someone I feel bad for, it's Deeds."

"Why me?" Deeds asked. Good kid, second-year, built like a horse. Played Triple Warder.

"Because not one of those goose-armed chipmunks is going to even hit past the Jack Line, so you'll just be standing bored by the Triple all damn game!"

More laughter and cheers.

He pointed to a group of four others: Hoovie, Chippit, Needle, and Marmot, whose positions were in the Double zone. "I don't want you guys getting too restless, though. Just because nothing is coming to you doesn't mean you can start playing cards out there, hear? Got to keep up appearances."

Those four all laughed.

"Stay sharp, so when we're on the batting line, we crank it every blasted time. I want to see some Triple Jacks. I want to see some six-pointers. You hear?"

They all cheered.

Veranix tucked in more to the breakfast. "So you boys already have the victory party planned?"

Tosler chuckled. "Blute has a blazes of an idea." He pointed to the bull of a boy at his left, who played the Wall.

"Let's hear it."

Blute swallowed the mass of food he had just shoveled into his maw. "I call it the Aventil Amble. Though by the end it would be the Aventil Stumble."

Veranix wasn't sure he liked the sound of this. "How so?"

"Ten pubs, all through Aventil. We go to each one, do a pint, and move on to the next one. I got the path all worked out: the Old Canal, the Rose & Bush, the Shady Lady, the Broken Spindle, the Myrmidon—"

"Blazes, that's where I'll be down for the count," Veranix said.

"You need meat on your bones, Calbert," Ottie said. "Then you can keep up."

Blute had continued his list without stopping. "And then finally the Turnabout."

"Did I hear you right?" Veranix asked. "You all want to go into the Turnabout?"

"It's a pub, ain't it? Public house."

"Students do not go into the Turnabout," Veranix said. They had to know it was a Rose Street Prince hangout. A group of Uni athletes going in would probably start trouble. A group of thoroughly sauced Uni boys would surely cause a small riot.

"They will tonight!" Tosler shouted. "All right, gents, finish up! We've got a match to get to."

Veranix continued to eat, but his stomach was already churning. Staying close to this group might get him in a whole different mess of trouble. Colin had made it very clear that Veranix should never go into the Turnabout. If that old Red Rabbit could tell he was Cal Tyson's son, surely there were some old salts among the Princes who could spot it. Especially if they saw him near Colin.

Veranix shook it off. The Turnabout was the end of the Amble, and it was unlikely these boys would actually make it all the way there. Worst case, he would beg off before they reached the Turnabout. The other pubs were no problem, as far as he knew. Almost no Princes, and certainly no Colin.

Colin had mixed feelings about spending his time in the Old Canal. It was a fine pub, no doubt, and he didn't have any complaints about the quality of the beer or the sausage sandwiches. They were actually quite good.

But it wasn't the Turnabout, and he was the only Prince in the place. The rest of his crew stayed out, hiding up in the flop most of the time. They only came in when they needed something. This was noticed by the staff of the Old Canal, and the way they reacted approached frightened reverence. Colin would sit at a table in the back corner and be treated like a boss. They stopped even asking him to pay, often coming over to check if he needed anything else. Colin had always imagined that would feel great, but instead it was hollow and troubling.

Someone sat down at his table with him before he even noticed they had approached. "I don't need any—" he started.

"Yeah, but I do." A woman, hood half pulled over her face, but it didn't hide the fact that her hair had been badly dyed. It looked like she had tried to make it black and landed on something more purple.

"I know you?" he asked.

"Yeah, Tyson, you know me," she said. The voice wasn't familiar, nor was what he saw of the face.

"Not hitting the chimes," he said. "Did we roll back in the day or something?"

"Saints, no," she said. She pulled back her hood a bit. She looked familiar, but he couldn't place her. "Ain't you got eyes, Prince?"

"Sorry, I—" He tried to imagine what her proper hair color might be, how she'd look. Then it hit him. "Sotch?"

"Say it louder, why don't you?"

"Why shouldn't I?" he asked. "Didn't know I owed you

the courtesy." He should shout her name, if not pull out his knife and shove it in her heart.

"You don't, fine," she said. "Was never any love between the Princes and the Rabbits, 'cept the pact, and we broke that."

"And look what happened to the Rabbits."

"Blazes, I know that, Tyson. You don't think I know that?"

"So why is this my problem?"

She glanced around the room. "Because you know the Thorn."

Colin's heart jumped in his chest. "Who told you that?"

"Everyone knows that you threw in with the Thorn a couple of times. And the morning he wrecked the Trusted Friend, you took his cloak and ran off pretending to be him so the preacher could get him out."

"That's some sewage."

"Don't tell me it's sewage; Keckin and I saw that with our own eyes."

"So, yeah, I helped the Thorn. Didn't want him to get pinched by the sticks, especially since he was cracking on your skulls for breaking the pact."

"I don't care why you did it. You can reach out to him."

"Maybe I can, what of it?"

She leaned in. "I need to make some kind of deal. A truce or something."

"Truce for what?"

"For me and the few Rabbits I've got left. We just want to be left alone. Blazes, we ain't even in Aventil anymore!"

Colin didn't understand what she was talking about. Last he knew, the Rabbits were gone, and Veranix was back to knocking dealers around in Dentonhill. Was he hunting the Rabbits? He signaled to the barman for two beers.

"So you're saying you're gone? Out of Aventil?"

"We were, holed up way out in Benson Court," she said. That was extreme. Benson Court made Aventil look like the estate houses in Callon Hills. "But the Thorn found us. He got Keckin and dragged him back here to make a show of killing him." Anger cracked through her voice as her eyes welled up.

Colin didn't trust this story one damn bit. Nothing she was saying sounded like something Veranix would do. He'd certainly go after Fenmere and his folk, and *effitte* itself with that kind of tenacity, but he wouldn't make a macabre display of it. And he never indicated that he was interested in finishing off the Rabbits, certainly not hunting them.

It didn't add up, but listening to Sotch was the best way to find out the truth. But not here. "You hungry, huh? They do good sausages."

"Yeah, course," she said.

He made like he was signaling for sausages, but actually he was telling the barman to get his boys.

The barman nodded and bolted off.

There might be something to this frightened reverence. "So you saw the Thorn, then? When he came after Keckin?"

"Came after *us*," Sotch said. "I saw a piece of him, you know? Like, we were holed up in our flop, and out of nowhere there was smoke and flashes of light, and then all of a sudden he swoops in. I just saw a figure in a cloak, swinging his staff. But that was how it was in the brewery, too. Before I knew it, Keckin pushed me into the chute—"

"The what?"

She growled and rolled her eyes. "Our flop, we had this chute that dropped down to the sewer. You know, to escape real quick? He threw me down and slammed it shut."

"Thorn's a dangerous bloke," Colin said. "Wanted to keep you safe." He needed to keep her talking until his boys showed up.

"By the time I got back up, the place was a wreck, they were gone. Plenty of blood, though."

"And you tracked it back here?"

"My boys did, once we heard about the spectacle the Thorn had made. Did you hear?"

"I heard Keckin was killed, that's all," Colin said. "The rest was just rumors."

Except Colin had seen Veranix, up on the rooftop, right around that time. He certainly could have done it. Why, Colin had no idea. It was stupid.

Of course, doing something stupid tended to be Veranix's usual method.

"All right, so, let's say I can reach the Thorn. What's the offer?"

"Offer is he leaves us alone, and we stay the blazes away."

Colin shrugged. "Might not work for him. You were the blazes away, and he came for you."

"I don't know!" she said. "I have nothing, you hear? A few boys who were in my crew or Keckin's, and that's it."

"Hmm," Colin said. "And how do I know this isn't a trap?"

"A trap for what?"

"For the Princes. For the Thorn. I don't know. You were working for Fenmere. Maybe that's where your loyalties are."

"My loyalties are to my own lungs, and keeping them filled with air, Prince."

"All right, let's say I get in touch with him, and he's willing to talk it out with you. Let's just say that. How do I set up a meet? And what do I offer that makes it worth his while?"

"Church meet," she said. "I'll check in with you here tomorrow."

"No, no you won't," he said, as Kiggy and Vandy had come up towering behind her. "Boys, take her up and make her comfortable. Have Sella check her for weapons and then sit on her."

"Really, Cap?" Kiggy asked, as his hand came firmly on Sotch's shoulder. "Keep her comfy?"

"Gentlemen," Colin said. "Treat her with the utmost of care."

"I'm going to slice your belly open for this, Prince," Sotch growled.

"It's good to dream, Sotch, old girl," Colin said. "Bring her up."

She made to bolt, but Kiggy and Vandy grabbed her arms and lifted her up. She couldn't get any leverage to twist away, and her legs weren't long enough to effectively kick either of them. Not that she didn't try. Kiggy and Vandy carried her off while she screamed a series of creative invectives.

The barman came over to Colin, bringing a fresh beer. "I appreciate that we could help you remove her with minimal disruption. We didn't want a fight or an accident here."

"Of course," Colin said. "A plate of sausages and mustard when you get the chance."

"Yes, sir," the barman said.

Colin sipped at his new beer. Somehow, it tasted better than usual. Perhaps because he now had something to bring Old Casey and the other bosses that could get him back in their good graces, and hopefully back to Rose Street proper.

Chapter 4

THE STANDS AROUND the tetchball pitch were wild with fans from the University of Maradaine and Trenn College. Of course, the U of M folks greatly outnumbered the Trenn fans, but Veranix was still surprised to see scores of them hooting and hollering before the match even began. He couldn't imagine that they would all trek up from Yin Mara just to watch a match. Maybe the Grand was a big deal to them.

There was no ceremony approaching the pitch. Both teams just strolled in, waving and smiling, and then they set up camp on opposite sides, in the yellow out of bounds zone. As a coach, Veranix was forbidden, during the game, to step off the yellow onto the green.

"All right, boys, warm it up!" Veranix shouted to the team. "Drop it down, work the legs!"

The team got down on the ground and began their best attempt at the stretching exercises Veranix had been doing since before he could even walk. Some did it fine, others—like Blute or Hoovie—were just pathetic. Still, it was good to see all eleven drop down in unison and make a good effort.

He glanced across the pitch to the Trenn team over on their yellow. Many of them were gawking, confused over just what the Mary team was up to.

Good.

"Hey, Vee!"

Veranix glanced over to the stands, where Jiarna and Phadre were in the front row. They both wore full University of Maradaine uniform regalia. Jiarna even carried blue-and-white flags.

"I thought you were going to work the social events," Veranix said as he came over, trying not to shout despite the roar of the crowd.

"We will," Jiarna said. "This is part of it."

"You just want to watch the match, don't you?" Veranix said with a grin.

Jiarna raised a finger, as if to highlight her point. "I will have you know, we were both very torn with this match."

"How so?" Veranix asked. He turned to the squad. "Lower backs! Push it, Catfish, you can go further than that!"

Phadre answered, "Trenn is to be our new home, so there was a real moral dilemma who we should root for."

"A real moral dilemma?" Veranix repeated dryly. "Are you kidding me?"

"A brief moral dilemma," Phadre said. "Then Jiarna pointed out we've yet to step foot on Trenn College grounds."

"Nor did we have anything in their colors," she said, noting their team in orange and yellow. Some of the Trenn boys were trying to imitate the stretches, as if they were afraid the Maradaine team had hit on some secret. "I want to thank you, Veranix, by the way. We're very grateful for use of the apartment."

"Right, well, be discreet," Veranix said. "The woman I rent from is vigilant against any untoward activity in her building."

"Untoward?" Jiarna asked in mock outrage. "What do you take us for?"

"Strangers who will set her off, that's what," Veranix said, noting that the Watcher for the match was taking a position near the Arm's Circle. "Talk to you later."

The Watcher blew his whistle, and Tosler and the captain of the Trenn team ran out to the Arm's Circle to talk to him. After a coin flip and handshake, they both came away. "We're fielding first," Tosler said as he returned.

"Good match, all," Veranix said as the team got to their feet, heading out to their places.

"And the boys of the University of Maradaine are taking the field for the top of the first interval, strapping lads all," a voice boomed through the area, clear and crisp. It took Veranix a moment to figure out where it was coming from, as it seemed to be everywhere and right next to him at the same time. A young woman—a magic student, Veranix realized—was standing up on a perched lectern right behind the Squad Line at the back end of the field. She was the one speaking, magicking her voice so everyone could hear her.

As the team got in place out in the field, the Trenn team filled up the space between the Hold Line and the Squad Line, save their first batter, who took a place at the Tetch Rail. Tosler, in the Arm's Circle, received the ball from the Watcher.

"And Tosler's getting ready for the first throw, while the first batter for Trenn College is Uston. Uston is at the Rail in good form, let's see if Ottie can knock him from his game."

Ottie's position was Rail, standing just a few feet from the batter. The Rail's official job was to restore the Tetch Rail before the batter could score, but the unofficial role was to harangue the batter as he was trying to hit.

Ottie gave some patter while Tosler stretched out his arm a bit. He then took his place in the Arm's Circle, wound back and fired the ball past the Tetch Rail. The batter swung with everything he had, but missed the ball entirely. Blute, in position as the Wall behind the batter and in front of the Hold Line, caught the ball in both hands. He gave out a signature grunt.

"No crank from Uston! He goes back to the Batter Squad while the next up comes along . . ."

The second and third batters both swung no crank, but then the fourth knocked a solid hit.

"Arpig's hit sails high over the Arm's Circle and— it does not clear the Jack Line! It's far to the left, not quite in the yellow, so Pinter, U of M Jack Warder, is charging to it. Arpig is running to score, but Bool at Close Bumper is on his heels! Bool knocks Arpig down, but the boy from Trenn is not letting that stop him. Pinter has the ball and throws to Ottie, and Far Bumper Catfish has now jumped on Arpig as well. Despite having Bool and Catfish hanging on to him, Arpig is still moving to the Jack Line."

The Watcher blew his whistle. "The Rail is restored. No point!"

"Tough break for Trenn. Still seven batters to go this interval, so they might still have a chance to score, but the U of M boys will not be making it easy for them."

Veranix strolled over to the stands, where Jiarna and Phadre were. "And you were doubting who to root for."

"Still early in the match, Vee," Jiarna said. "Don't get too cocky."

Delmin was trailing along with two other interim prefects, though they had made the most boring decision possible for their plans. The Endurance Run was going to be underway for most of the day, and the boys he had attached himself to decided that the best use of their time was to plant themselves at the finish line—right by the south gate of campus— and make camp so they would be there for the end of the race. Which meant sitting on the walkway of Lilac and Hedge for a good five hours.

Delmin regretted being a part of this plan.

He sat down on the empty crate one of the others had scrounged up. "So, anyone have any real trouble so far? I had a few boys from Pirrell try to start a fight."

"Really?" This came from Dannick, who was prefecting down on the first floor, and probably would be the one keeping the job come the autumn. "That's more excitement than I've had."

"You're telling me you've had no excitement?" Garibel asked Dannick. "Brother, I would trade you. Over in Gonners Hall, I have most of the team from Glennford. They've got no morals whatsoever."

"I'm sure—"

"None whatsoever," Garibel said.

"Really?" Delmin asked. "What are they doing?"

"I had to kick out no less than a dozen Glennford girls—adoring fans—out of the rooms. Most of them in their skivs or less."

"Blazes, I should have asked for Gonners," Dannick said.

"It's a wastepit. And the whole campus is going to get that way, let me tell you."

"No, I'm sure . . ."

"We have hundreds of athletes from twenty-four schools, men and ladies. All in their physical prime, and supervision is near nonexistent. What do you think is going to happen, Dannick?"

"Doesn't sound that terrible," Dannick said quietly.

"Depravity is what it is, am I right, Delmin?"

"Right," Delmin said half-heartedly. "But at least we haven't had any drug problems, am I right?"

"Drugs?" Garibel asked. "I wouldn't put it past them. They won't slip by me, though. I know what *hassper* smells like."

Delmin slouched down and sighed. This was going to be a very long day.

"Fourteen-Aught!"

Many mugs of beer went high in the air, and then down the throats of the tetchball squad, a horde of other University of Maradaine students—boys and girls both—as well as Veranix. The beer of the Old Canal was passable enough, nothing to complain about. The place was packed to the rafters, and the barman and the rest of his staff didn't seem to know if they should be thrilled or angry. At least, until Tosler threw down a fifty-crown goldsmith note. Then they seemed thrilled.

"Where's Pinter, where's Pinter, that rutting bastard?" Tosler shouted. "Another pint for Pinter! This bastard hit a Triple Jack and scored six rutting points!"

The crowd whooped.

Veranix did the same, raising up his mug, but made a point to sip at it instead of slamming it down like everyone else.

"Damn right!" Pinter shouted from his seat, wedged against the wall. "Thanks to Vee! He knows how to knock the stuffing out of the ball!"

"Vee!" they all shouted, holding up the beers.

"Saints, Vee," Blute said. "Sit down and drink. And why do you have that rucksack on?"

"It's magic stuff," Veranix said, winking. "Not to scare you or nothing, Blute, but you wouldn't understand."

"Oh, saints, saints, Vee," said Pinter. "Do a thing, pal. Like you did in the ceremonies."

"Do it, do it!" Veranix realized that several members of the Ovation Squad were part of the crowd here.

"Vee, Vee, Vee!" they chanted.

"Hey now, hey now," Veranix said, tweaking his voice just enough with magic to drown them out. "I won't do that in this fine establishment. The proprietors would not appreciate it. And we should appreciate them. To our hosts!"

"Hosts!" they all shouted, and mugs went up and slammed down again. Tosler added, "More all around!" while pulling another fifty-crown note out of his pocket.

The barman made a hissing noise at Veranix and beckoned him over. Veranix leaned in, and the barman passed over the plate of sausage sandwiches that Veranix had ordered earlier.

"Thanks," Veranix said.

"Oy," the barman said. "You're gonna let your brother know we were good to you and yours, yeah?"

"My brother?" Veranix asked. That was jarring. He

hadn't seen one hair of Soranix in five years. The idea that he was in Maradaine, in Aventil, was more than a little disturbing. "What do you know of my brother?"

"The Prince captain who's always here," the barman said. "We treat him good and you as well, and there's no trouble."

Veranix sighed. They were on Orchid. He didn't even think of that. Of course Colin had been spending time in this pub.

"I'll . . . I appreciate it," he said to the barman. He picked up the first sandwich and was about to bite into it when he felt someone move up close next to him.

"That looks good," a soft female voice said. "Care to give me a bite?"

Veranix stopped short, surprise freezing him. This woman—long dark hair, sultry eyes, and creamy olive skin—made his heart skip just at a glance. Gorgeous, in a strangely familiar way.

"A what of huh?" he said, all composure leaking out his brain. "I'm sorry, I mean. . . . You are?"

She leaned in, grabbing one sandwich, and whispered, "Help a girl out, hezzah? There's a Pirrell boy in the corner whose been gawking at me."

"Sure," he said, brain still reeling, not catching up with other parts of his body. He turned around casually, noting there was a lone boy in Pirrell maroon and gray leaning against the far wall, nursing a beer, staring intently at this young woman. Then he looked back at her, really seeing her. She was wearing a Royal College of Maradaine uniform. "You're on the wrong side of the river."

"I'm where the action is," she said. "That's where my feet took me, all the way here." She bit deeply into the sandwich, and then wiped the juice off her chin with the back of her hand.

"You cross over the bridge for the games?"

"No, for the sausages," she said dryly.

"Right, of course," he said, taking the sandwich back from her. "I meant, you competing, or you just here to watch?"

He took a bite, doing his damned best to not look like a fool with sausage grease on his face or onion in his teeth.

"Compete," she said. "Floor and Beam, over the next five days."

"An acrobat?" he asked. She had the figure for it, and her arms were muscled like any he had seen in the circus days.

"Gymnast," she said. "At least that's what the Unis call it. They're not tenters like you."

"You calling me a tenter?" he asked. And she said "hez-zah" before?

"You have that look about you," she said. "I mean, you look like one of these Maradaine kids, but you've got Racq in your blood."

That's why she looked familiar. She was also Racquin, or at least was raised it. Like him, she looked enough like the regular Druth that she passed it off.

"Veranix Calbert," he said, extending a hand.

"*Sescha*, Veranix," she said. "You don't even hide it, do you?"

"My name's my name," he said, hand still held out. "You are?"

"Emilia Quope," she said, taking his hand in return. "At least, that's the name I use at school."

"What's your real name?" he asked quietly.

She leaned in, almost close enough for her lips to brush his ear. "I don't give that easily."

Veranix pulled back slowly, and let his eyes stay locked on hers. "I can be patient."

"Pirrell boy still staring?" she asked.

Veranix let his gaze dart away for a moment. "Raven-ously."

"Creepy," she said.

"To the Rose & Bush!" Blute shouted from the main table. The rest of the squad slammed down the last of their drinks and got to their feet.

"Your party is leaving," she said.

"Apparently so," Veranix said. Though the last thing he wanted to do at this very moment was step away.

"Well then," she said, taking his sandwich from his hands. "I guess it's to the Rose & Bush. Shall we?"

Lilac Street was a new kind of crowded mess, the likes of which Benvin had never seen before. Frankly, he hadn't been warned about what this was going to be, and it made him incredibly angry.

The University had arranged to block off streets for the Endurance Run—seventeen and a half miles' worth, ranging through Gelmoor, down south through Laramie, Reining, and the Colton neighborhoods, and then turning back up Waterpath to finish on Lilac right in front of the gates.

So in addition to keeping the general madness of the Tournament under wraps, Constabulary had to block off streets, guide traffic, and keep the crowd on the sidelines from being a menace. All while coordinating that effort with four other houses. Holcomb didn't bother to mention any of this to Benvin and the other lieutenants until this morning, so they all had to scramble to get the work done. The fact that U of M won its match in tetchball didn't help.

Captain Holcomb assigned Benvin and his people—including the cadets, because it was all-boots-out time—at the heart of the madness, the finish line of the Endurance. Barricades kept the fans and onlookers on the walkways, the crowd pressed tight against each other in near frenzy. And this was before the runners even arrived.

"At least we've got a good view of the finish line," Mal said.

"That hardly matters," Benvin said. "We got word on when the runners will come?"

"Not yet, Left," Mal said. "Jace hadn't come back."

"Right," Benvin said, grumbling. He glanced through the crowd. A whole mix of students, professors, Aventil locals, and who even knew what. Then he spotted a bunch of rose tattoos over near the gates.

"Mess of Princes," he said to Mal. "Where's the rest of our squad?"

"Lost sight of them," Mal said. "Except Saitle. He's near the gates."

"Stay here, and call Saitle over. I'm going to talk to those Princes."

"Don't do nothing stupid, Left."

Benvin frowned at Mal while he wormed his way through the crowd to the Princes. There were about six of them, and they seemed to be focused in purpose, leading a group of out-of-towners through the crowd.

"Oy," Benvin said, tapping the one with the captain stars on her shoulder. "What do you think you're up to?"

"Helping you out, stick," she said like a whip. She gestured for him to join her under the awning of one of the shops.

"What makes you think you're helping me out?" he snarled at her.

"Listen, you have a mess of a crowd here for the Endurance, and that's boss, but you also got folks who just want to get around town to the pubs."

"Well, they're going to have a tough time with that."

"See, that's where me and my crew come in. Safe walks for Uni kids is what we do, Left. We're getting them through the crowd to where they want to go."

"And find their purse missing when they get there."

"No jot, Left. Nothing of the sort," she said. "We're helping out the neighborhood, just like you."

"Don't you dare say you're like me, Prince," Benvin said. "What's your name?"

"Deena," she said. "You think I done something wrong, Left, then throw on the irons. But all we're doing is helping folks get around. Making your life easier."

"I don't need you to—"

"Hey, look sharp," she said. "First racers are coming in."

"How do you—"

"Got ears, Left," she said. She pointed down Lilac. With a wink she slipped into the crowd, and Benvin lost sight of her. He couldn't pursue her, not with the first runners about to approach.

He pushed back to his position. "We got them coming in?" he asked Mal, who now stood with Saitle.

"Haven't heard yet," Mal said. "No sign of Jace or the rest."

"Something's coming," Saitle said, peering down the street. "Crowd's agitated."

"Why are—" Benvin asked when it became apparent. Clouds of colored smoke filled the street, bursting forth in quick succession, approaching the finishing line. "Sharpen up."

He pulled out his handstick, hearing the thunder of hooves from inside the smoke. A horse burst forth out of the closest cloud, with a rider in a maroon cloak on top. As soon as the horse was clear, the rider leaped off, flipping in the air and landing gracefully on his feet, a fighting staff drawn.

The Thorn.

"Constabulary!" he said joyfully. "Just what I was hoping to find!"

Benvin didn't look to see if Mal or Saitle were with him—of course they would be. "Take him down, irons on!" he shouted, and charged in.

The Thorn had suddenly ridden into the middle of the square, and was fighting Constabulary. It was impossible. Delmin knew it was impossible.

This was not Veranix in the middle of the street, goading the Constabulary to fight him. The smoke was not magic, either. There was nothing magic at all here, no *numinic* flow around the person purporting to be the Thorn. Knowing these things didn't make watching it any easier for Delmin.

"Saints, is this really happening?" Garibel asked.

"I don't know," Delmin said, transfixed. He really couldn't believe what he was seeing.

"Ha ha!" the ersatz Thorn shouted, spinning his staff around and cracking it across the skull of the Constabulary cadet who had charged in on him. "Come on, sticks, I don't have all night!"

The two other constables—one a patrolman, the other a lieutenant—were on this imposter with their handsticks. The false Thorn parried both of their attacks, spinning his staff faster than Delmin could see. Whoever this fraud was, he could move like Veranix. He knocked the patrolman off his feet, letting him concentrate his attention on the lieutenant.

"Shouldn't we do something?" Dannick asked.

The fake Thorn was now striking at the lieutenant brutally. The lieutenant had held his own defense briefly, but soon the barrage of attacks was too much for him. The imposter cracked the lieutenant across the arm, knocking the handstick to the ground. With the constable disarmed, the fake Thorn smashed the lieutenant across the skull, and then whipped the staff around to do the same to the other side.

The constable dropped to his knees, clearly dazed out of his senses. The staff came up high, and was about to brain the man.

Despite himself, Delmin jumped out into the street and fired a blast of white and blue sparks and flame at the imposter. Doing even that made his knees buckle, and he almost dropped right next to the fallen lieutenant. The fraud dropped the staff to cover his eyes, backing off from his attack. Delmin knew he didn't have much power behind what he just did, and the fake Thorn was more surprised than injured. Nothing Delmin could have done would have really hurt him; he simply wasn't that magically strong. He was already winded, heart thundering in his chest.

But this fake Thorn had no way of knowing that.

"Not another step," Delmin said, holding up his hands in something that might seem menacing. "That was a warning."

The patrolman jumped up on the fake Thorn, trying to grapple him to the ground. The imposter was having none of that, twisting his body in such a complicated way that the patrolman was flipped over and thrown off. The patrolman rolled with it and was back on his feet, ready to give this fake another round.

But the fake Thorn had his bow out, and put an arrow in the patrolman's chest.

And then another.

And then a third.

It all happened too fast for Delmin to even react or understand what was happening before it was too late. If he were a better mage, a stronger one, maybe he could have knocked those arrows out of the air before they—

They killed the patrolman.

This was the vase exercise all over again, and like every damn time in practicals, Delmin had failed.

Except the vase was a man.

The imposter turned to the lieutenant, arrow nocked.

Delmin made his hands glow, which was all he had strength left to do. Even that made him feel like a gust of wind would knock him down, but he kept up a stern face. "Don't even try." He was angry enough to make it sound like something resembling a threat.

The fake Thorn—whose face was obscured by hood and a mask over his mouth and nose, nothing at all like Vee's magical shadow—winked at Delmin. "I suppose it's good enough."

Suddenly more bursts of colored smoke appeared around him—nothing magical, Delmin would feel that— and when they cleared away, he was gone.

Delmin dropped the glow and let himself fall to his knees. Glancing around, the crowd was still in a stunned stupor. The constable cadet was laid out on the ground, blood trickling from his head. The patrolman was clearly dead. Delmin looked to the lieutenant, with great purple welts on either side of his head. One eye was open, spinning wildly in its socket, while the other was shut.

Delmin turned to Garibel and Dannick. "Yellowshields! Hurry!"

The two of them ran off, while the rest of the crowd stood in stunned silence.

Delmin glanced at them all—hundreds of people—and realized that each and every one of them would swear blind to every saint that the Thorn just assaulted two Constabulary officers and murdered a third.

Delmin was the only one who knew that wasn't the truth, but there was no way he could possibly make anyone else believe that. Not without telling the whole truth.

And the whole truth wouldn't be any better for Veranix. No matter what, he was doomed.

Chapter 5

DAWN CREPT INTO Veranix's awareness like a thief, bringing him out of a deep, restful slumber, the likes of which he hadn't had in as long as he could remember.

He had no idea where he was.

There was a blur of events in his memory, which involved various pubs in Aventil, several beers, and a stunning young woman.

A stunning Racquin young woman.

Emilia. That he remembered. That was why he had ended up drinking more beers than he had ever intended. Because she was.

It looked like he was in a dormitory room, but it certainly wasn't his. It wasn't even Almers—the paint of the plaster walls was a warmer shade of beige, the woodwork was a little more refined. The differences were subtle but noticeable.

"Morning," a soft voice said near him. *"Vek se voa?"* *How are your feet?* She spoke in Sechiall, the Kellirac tongue Veranix associated with his grandfather and the old Racquin at the circus.

"Khe nias ra," he replied. *They'll keep moving.* That exhausted most of his Sechiall, but there was also something familiar about the exchange that he couldn't put his foot on.

"Glad to hear it," she said, pulling herself up to sit. They were definitely in the bed together. His clothing was definitely in a pile over across the floor. As was his rucksack with the cloak and the rope. At least he had managed to hold on to that.

"Where are we and when did we end up here?"

"We're in my room," she said. "Or rather, the room they put me in on your campus for the Tournament. My room is across the river, and you were in no state to stumble that far. Nor was I."

"So how did we get past the prefects and floor matrons?" he asked. "I mean, even in the summer, there's rules about boys in the ladies' dorms."

"You were ranting for a while about having a flop in Aventil that we couldn't use," she said.

"I loaned it to some friends," he said.

"Yes, Phadre and Jiarna. I remember that. You mentioned them quite a few times."

"Your memory is remarkably clearer than mine," Veranix said.

She leaned down and kissed him, slowly and softly. "Do you remember that?" she whispered.

"It has a vague familiarity that I'm willing to keep exploring," he said with a smile.

"Good," she said. "But I imagine those prefects and floor matrons are already up and about, with watchful ears." She paused and laughed. "Or whatever phrase would work for ears."

"Attentive," Veranix offered.

"Attentive," she said, grabbing a shift off the end of the bed and pulling it on. She dropped down off the bed with a preternatural grace.

"How did we avoid them before?" he asked.

"We're on the second floor," she said, "Which you declared as 'child's play,' and scrambled up the wall to the window."

That memory found its way back to Veranix's mind. As did several others.

She began a series of floor stretches, not unlike the ones

Veranix usually did, the ones his grandfather had taught him since he was a child.

"When's your match?" he asked.

"Over the next three days, first round is this afternoon at two bells," she said absently. "And I should probably go to training for a while." She stood up and began working balances.

"I should—get on a few things as well," he said casually. She seemed to have shifted her focus to her exercises, and he was probably overstaying his welcome.

She turned her head to him, without wavering from the one-footed bird pose she was in. "You don't need to run off, not if you don't want to."

"I don't *want* to," he said with a grin. "But if I have to go out the window, I should probably do it before there are too many people wandering about outside."

She nodded. "Of course. But I will be seeing you around?"

He got out of the bed and started to pick up his clothes. "Well, I know where to find you, with only a bit of a climb."

"I certainly won't complain if you climbed in sometime after midnight," she said. She switched legs in her pose. This time she winced and wobbled a bit.

Veranix pulled on his trousers. "Problem with your right foot?"

"A bit," she said. "Twisted it on a bad landing from a sloppy Pantix Throw a couple months ago."

That triggered another memory—doing a sloppy Pantix Throw in the midst of a crisis. A couple of months ago. In which the woman he had thrown up landed badly. But that would mean she was—

"I'm just glad it's healed enough—what?"

Veranix's face must have shown what he was thinking.

"Nothing," he said, regaining his composure. He pulled on his shirt and vest and grabbed the rucksack. "I just was—nothing. It was stupid."

Recognition crossed her face. "And that's been your theme for the night?" she asked tentatively.

Her eyes narrowed ever so slightly, and her stance changed from one of graceful balance to poised for a fight.

Veranix snatched up the rucksack, his fists balled up and ready.

"Well," she said coolly, "I guess you've figured out one of my other names, Thorn."

Veranix didn't even stay to retort. With a burst of magic he blew the window open and dove through it before she could say anything else. As he dropped to the ground, he pulled the cloak out of the rucksack and magicked it around him. He shrouded into near-invisibility while landing softly, and ran off as fast as he could until he reached Almers.

Leaning against the wall of his home dorm, he took a moment to glance back where he came from. He wasn't being pursued, at least not that he could tell. But it didn't matter. She knew who he was, where he lived, everything about him. Saints only knew what he had babbled about during the night.

He felt like kicking himself. The whole night he kept thinking there was something familiar about her but couldn't figure out what it was. Now he knew. Just a few months ago she was trying to kill him.

Blackbird.

He had spent the night with Blackbird.

This had to rank among the stupidest things he had ever done. And that was an already impressive collection of idiocy.

Veranix was ready to head to the bathhouses and scrub himself within an inch of his life when he noticed a ribbon tied around the tree branch next to the entrance of Almers Hall. Signal from Kaiana. Maybe she found something out, which was more than he had managed to do for the past day.

Grumbling to himself, Veranix stalked down the lawn, early rising athletes already working their exercises in preparation for their Tournament events. There were more than a few runners, probably training for the Quint. There were also a couple of archers setting up some practice targets. Veranix sighed a bit as he made his way to the carriage house. Archery was a tournament game he would want to participate in, and he probably could have represented U of M quite well, save the restriction on mages as athletes.

That was a stupid rule made by close-minded people.

Alternatively, the Tournament should have a flat-out magic competition. That would be something he'd also earn the University some merit for.

And was there anyone here who could win at Floor better than him? Not that Veranix knew. That meant it would surely go to RCM because Emilia—Blackbird—she was. . . .

Veranix pushed that out of his head. He didn't know what rutting game Blackbird was doing, but he'd be damned if he'd let her get the best of him. He was just glad to get out of there alive, with the cloak and the rope. Next time he saw her, he'd deal with her like an assassin deserved.

Approaching the carriage house, he spotted the tree outside the south wall, where Colin used to leave signals for him. For the first time in ages, there was one—white and red. Emergency.

What happened last night?

Veranix went into the carriage house, where Kaiana, Phadre, and Jiarna were all pacing about in quiet concern.

"Something going on?"

"Vee!" Phadre exclaimed. "You're finally here."

"Yes, I noticed," he said. Their faces were all somber. "What's happening?"

Kaiana actually brought him over to a chair and sat him down. "Were you out there as the Thorn last night? At all?"

"No, not a bit," he said. "I . . . I stuck to the tetch squad, like we talked about, but . . ." He hesitated. No need to tell Kai or the others about Blackbird and everything involved with that. "It didn't lead anywhere but too many mugs of beer."

"I told you," Phadre said. "I knew it wasn't him."

"I just said we needed to ask," Jiarna said.

"What wasn't? Ask what?"

Kaiana sighed. "Last night, while you were with the squad, the Thorn attacked a few Constabulary at the end of the Endurance. Killed one."

"No," Veranix said. "I wasn't out there. I couldn't have—"

"Exactly," Kaiana said. "Someone is pretending to be you out there. The Red Rabbit who was killed, and now the constables. Except hundreds of people saw this."

"Where'd you hear this?"

"That's what's being said out there," Phadre said. He dropped a copy of the *South Maradaine Gazette* on the table, with the headline, "Thorn Turned Stick Killer."

"Well, that's not good," Veranix said.

"Well, we don't know exactly what happened," Jiarna said. "But there's something else."

"What?"

"Delmin," Kaiana said. "He's at the stationhouse for questioning."

"What? Why is he there?"

Kaiana handed over a smeared sheet of newsprint paper. "Constabulary sent copies of this to campus this morning. List of students who were arrested, detained, or otherwise brought to the stationhouse." She pointed to Delmin's name, where it said "Witness Statement" next to it. Veranix recognized the names of the other prefects Delmin was going to be spending the day with.

"Well, that's good," Veranix said. "I mean, if Delmin was a witness, he would know—" Veranix stopped himself. "Of course, he couldn't explain how he would know that the person who attacked the constables was an imposter."

"This is who killed the Red Rabbit the other night as well, right?" Kaiana asked.

Veranix nodded. "I would imagine."

"So someone is pretending to be you, but killing gang members and constables?"

"Must be Fenmere's people," Veranix said. On Kaiana's

harsh look, he added, "Think about it! They've been unable to get at me directly, so with this, they attack my reputation."

Jiarna shook her head. "Or possibly you've inspired someone who isn't quite as noble as you are."

"I don't . . . it doesn't matter why. Someone is trying . . . saints!"

"What?" Kaiana asked.

He almost blurted out the revelation he just had: everything Blackbird did the night before—cozying up to him, engaging him as a Racquin, keeping him drinking, and seducing him—all that must have been a ploy to keep him distracted so the imposter could do his job. They must be working together.

"I realized how much time I wasted last night is all," he said. He pulled the cloak and rope out of the rucksack. "This whole social strategy is a losing plan."

"But it's not!" Phadre said. "Jiarna and I were at the Grand Sable House party last night."

"And how were the ladies of Grand Sable?" Veranix didn't imagine Vellia Sansar had any insights into the *effitte* trade.

"Grand, of course," Jiarna said. "But there were quite a few ladies from Grand Sable at other schools, and they had their gentlemen escorts. We overheard quite a few people talking about wanting to get drugs and determining where to buy them."

"And what did you find out?"

"Well, none of them wanted to tell me where when I inquired," Jiarna said.

"You did sound like a constable when you asked," Phadre remarked.

"I was being factual."

"All right, not a constable. A professor."

"Really?" Jiarna sounded pleased by that.

"A professor more interested in using the drugs for scientific experiment than recreation."

Jiarna smirked a little. "I can accept that assessment. And that might actually be a study of merit . . ."

"Also," Kaiana interrupted, "we found more vials discarded by the tetch field, as well as all around the boys' dormitory area."

"Any dorm in particular?" Veranix asked.

"Any. All."

"How many vials are we talking about?"

Kaiana's expression darkened. "At least thirty."

"Saints, this—it can't stand."

"I know," Kaiana said. "But I can tell you the tetch field was the only section of the Tournament sites where we've found them. Sticking to the squad, keeping an eye out is the best bet."

"I don't like it," Veranix said. "Where are my weapons?"

"Why?"

"Because I'm going to go talk to Colin, and with imposters, assassins, and constables all looking for me, I'm not going to be unprepared."

"Assassins? Which—"

"There's always assassins," Veranix quickly said. He did not want to explain about Blackbird, certainly not to Kaiana.

"Fine, Spinner Run."

Seeing the concern on all their faces, he said, "I'll stay shrouded, I won't engage first."

"Fine," Kaiana said. "I don't think it's safe for you. I could go meet Colin."

"You can't."

"I can't?" she asked sharply.

He hadn't told her this yet—it hadn't come up before, and Veranix had been hoping to avoid the subject. "The Princes—the bosses in the Princes—they know who you are, that you're in contact with the Thorn."

Several emotions danced over Kaiana's face, mostly anger and fear. "How . . . Colin told you this?"

Veranix nodded. "They know there's a Napolic girl who knows the Thorn, who gave Colin information, and after you made the newssheets . . ."

"Right," she said, then whispered, "Rutting saints and

sinners." She went down to the Spinner Run silently and returned with Veranix's weapons.

"Thanks," he said quietly.

"Do they know about my dad?" she whispered as she handed them to him.

That surprised him. "Not that I'm aware of."

"I should try to see him," she said, her voice still low. "After the Tournament is done. I should do that."

"If you want to," Veranix said. "I could—" He let it hang as he slung his quiver over his back. Going to Lower Trenn Ward would be dangerous and heartbreaking. His mother was on the same floor as Kai's father, both in a state of near catatonia. The one time Veranix had been in there—ostensibly to see Parsons, the former classmate in a similar state from *effitte* overdose—his mother had reacted to him. Fenmere supposedly had eyes on her, eyes everywhere. Going up there could risk her life and his.

And going there would mean seeing her in that state. That might be more than he could bear.

"We'll talk about it later," she said. Stepping back, she raised her voice a bit more, though it was clear that Jiarna and Phadre had heard everything. "You've got work to do out there."

"Best get to it, mate," Phadre said. "While the streets are still quiet."

Veranix gave Phadre a mock salute while shrouding himself. But he was right; things were probably going to get noisy very soon.

Sergeant Tripper hadn't slept a bit. He had been storming all over the stationhouse in futility. He'd been down to the examinarium, where Mal was laid out with three arrows in his dead body. He'd been in the task force office trying to pry answers out of Saitle, who had nothing useful to say. And he'd been up in the stationhouse ward, where Lieutenant Benvin was being cared for. The ward doctors said he might or might not wake up today. Maybe tomorrow. Maybe never.

There were a whole score of witnesses down in the sheephold, just ready to talk about what they saw, but he wasn't going to be allowed to go talk to them. No statements, no questions. At least, not from Tripper or anyone else on the squad.

At this point, all of the squad proper was him, Pollit, and Wheth. Saitle was on his feet, but his senses were addled. That boy should go home and sleep it off. Jace hadn't even checked in yet, which was the strangest of all. That boy was never late.

"So why can't I talk to them?" he asked the desk clerk in front of the sheephold. "They're just sitting right there waiting."

"You ain't allowed, captain said," the clerk responded.

"Then who is going to blasted well do it, and why ain't they already?"

"I ain't been told that," the clerk said. "But I was told definitely not you, or the chomie, or the freak."

That set Tripper's blood on fire. "Those your words or the cap's?"

"I was told what I was told."

Tripper wanted to make the clerk eat his blasted teeth, but that wouldn't have helped. But it would have felt good. Enough people in this stationhouse gave Wheth and Pollit a hard time, or worse, and Tripper was fixing to see it stop. Even if it got him busted back to cadet. Didn't matter— Wheth and Pollit were two of the best damn sticks he had had the privilege of serving with, full stop. Benvin had showed him that, and he wasn't going to let his lieutenant down. Especially not now.

He stomped up the stairs, pounding through the inspectors' floor, where the handful of specs just sat around chatting, none of them looking like they had anything urgent going on. He strode past them all and went to Captain Holcomb's office.

The captain sat corpulently at his desk, looking over the newssheet while gnawing on a pastry of some sort.

"Am I disturbing you, Captain?" Tripper barked as he went in.

"The blazes is your problem, Sergeant?" The captain didn't even look up from his newssheet.

"You want a list?"

"No, I want you out of my damned office."

"We have a man dead, a lieutenant laid up, and what the blazes are we doing about it, Cap?"

"Nothing," the captain said.

"The rutting—"

The captain slammed the paper down. "Nothing, Sergeant, and you know why? Because those are the regs. Something like this happens, it doesn't get handled by our house. None of us. Not you or your two little friends that Benvin likes to put up on the plinth. None of my specs, or even the cadets here. Out of house."

"Someone is going to come in here, and—"

"That's the rules," the captain said with a shrug. He picked up his paper and took another bite from his pastry. "You can take that up with the commissioner if you want."

"Don't think I wouldn't!" Tripper snapped, but that was an empty threat.

"Cool yourself, Tripper. Word has already been sent, and we'll get some inspectors in here to look after things."

"Who? When?"

"I ain't got any idea," Holcomb said. "Now get the blazes out of here."

The hard stare from the captain told Tripper not to push any further. He stalked out, still fuming. He glared at the inspectors, as if to dare them to make a comment.

Jace came running over from who knows where. "Sarge! Found you!"

"Where the blazes you been, Jace?" Tripper snapped. "We're hip deep in misfortune, and we can't do a damn thing about it . . . ."

"I did something about it," Jace said quietly. Tripper

must have looked shocked or confused, as Jace leaned in and whispered. "Soon as I heard, I knew the rules meant inspection from out of house."

"Ain't right," Tripper said. "Ain't no way someone'll come in here and care what goes on in this part of town. If they ain't already in someone's pocket, even."

"I know, but I called in a favor, trust me—"

"A favor?" Tripper thought his skull was going to explode. "Saint Marguerine, Jace, you're a blasted cadet. What kind of favor can you call in?"

Two strangers in inspector's vests walked up onto the floor, glancing about and taking the room in. One was a woman—Tripper had no idea there even was a skirt inspector in Maradaine—with red hair like a Waishen. The other was a skinny young man with wide, penetrating eyes. He took a few more steps onto the floor, and looked about as if expecting someone to greet them.

"Pardon me," he said to the room at large. "I'm Inspector Minox Welling, and this is Inspector Satrine Rainey. We've come from the Grand Inspectors' Unit to investigate the assault on one of your lieutenants."

Tripper turned back to Jace, who was grinning a bit too much, given the circumstances. "Grand Inspectors' Unit? How did you—"

"Simple," Jace said, pointing to Inspector Welling. "That's my brother."

Chapter 6

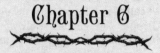

DELMIN DIDN'T KNOW where he was or why someone was shaking him awake, not at first. He had dozed off while sitting on a bench, and his neck was in a terrible position.

"What, what?" he mumbled.

"Mister Sarren, is it?"

Delmin's eyes focused on the woman waking him up. Older woman, red hair, Constabulary inspector's vest. Constabulary. He was at the stationhouse. Now he remembered what was going on.

"Yes, that's right," he said. "Am I—I've been waiting a while . . ."

"Quite all right," she said gently. "I apologize for the delay—rules and bureaucracy—but we've kept you waiting far too long."

"It's fine," Delmin said, getting to his feet. Glancing around, he noticed that there was no longer the throng of witnesses present. Even Garibel and Dannick were gone. "I see you've gone through many of the witnesses already."

"We've dismissed several of them, satisfied that their statements would not bring additional revelations." This came from another inspector—a younger, thinner man. Something about him immediately raised the hair on Delmin's neck. "We are interested in what you have to say, however."

He gestured for Delmin to enter a private room. "You must be hungry," the woman said.

"Yes, rather," Delmin said.

"Have something brought for Mister Sarren and Inspector Welling," she said to a desk clerk. "Quickly."

Delmin took a seat at the table, head still full of sleep and confusion. The inspectors shut the door and sat opposite him.

"So, Mister Sarren," the man said. "I'm Inspector Welling, and this is Inspector Rainey. We're with the Grand Inspectors' Unit."

"Grand Inspectors?" Delmin asked. That sounded impressive, whatever that was. "You're who they call in when other constables get attacked?"

"It's more complicated than that, but that's essentially right," Inspector Rainey said.

"Is the lieutenant all right?" Delmin asked.

"His condition is stable," Inspector Welling said. "Though Patrolman Malored was killed."

"I know, I saw," Delmin said. The image of that man, three arrows in his chest, that was still burned in his memory. Delmin had seen some disturbing things since getting mixed up in Veranix's business, but that was the first time he had seen someone killed right in front of him.

"Tell us what you saw."

"We were waiting for the end of the Endurance, when suddenly there were bursts of smoke in the road. A man came riding up through the smoke, and he started fighting the constables there—"

Delmin paused, noticing that the two inspectors were giving each other a look.

"Something wrong?"

"Not at all," Inspector Rainey said. "Tell me, Mister Sarren, if you were to speculate, where do you think the smoke came from?"

"Some form of smoke powder, I suppose, or some other chemical reaction. I really don't know, exactly."

"And the man?" Inspector Welling asked. He leaned in

across the table, and for a moment Delmin felt another chill pass through him. "How would you describe him?"

"Maroon cloak, face covered in a hood, fighting staff."

"I was correct, Inspector Rainey," he said. "This witness has proved invaluable."

"How is that?" Delmin asked, when a clerk came in with a plate of pastries.

"Thank you," Inspector Welling said, taking the plate from the clerk, and then giving him the sign to scurry off. He took one of the pastries for himself, and held out the tray to Delmin with his left hand.

His left hand was gloved for some reason.

And it made Delmin's magical senses fire madly, like a loud pop in his ear.

"What is—your hand—" Delmin started to say, and on the shift in Inspector Welling's expression, everything became clear. "Are you a mage, Inspector?"

"I'm not sure how that's—"

"What Circles allow their members to be in the Constabulary?"

"That's enough, Mister Sarren," Inspector Rainey said sharply.

Delmin was shocked into a stammer. "I—I'm sorry, I was just confused, and—" Now that he was seeing what it really was, understanding it, the inspector's gloved hand was fascinating. It seemed to be swirling and sinking with *numina*—like a tiny maelstrom confined to the inspector himself.

"What do you see, Mister Sarren?" Inspector Welling asked, flexing his fingers. The very act of flexing caused the *numina* to surge and spill and then be sucked back in.

It was like the inspector's hand was made of both napranium and dalmatium at the same time.

"I'm really not sure," Delmin said, absently eating the pastry while continuing to stare.

"Minox," Inspector Rainey said softly. "This is not the moment."

"Of course," he said, drawing his hand away. And just

that—the distance of table—made all the difference. Delmin could barely sense anything now.

"One of the reasons why we were interested in talking to you, Mister Sarren, was your decision to intervene. We spoke to many witnesses who said you engaged the Thorn—"

"I didn't say the Thorn," Delmin said, perhaps too quickly.

"No, you did not," Inspector Welling said pointedly.

"Engaged the assailant," Rainey said. "You're a magic student?"

"Code of conduct excuses students engaging in non-sanctioned magical activity in situations of dire threat. Bring in Professor Alimen right now and he'll confirm that."

"We aren't going to arrest you for that," Rainey said gently. "Or report you to the Universities or Circles or anything like that."

"Certainly not," Welling muttered.

She glared at her partner, then turned back to Delmin. "You mentioned dire threat?"

"He was going to kill the lieutenant. I didn't do more than throw up a light show, try to scare him off. I really couldn't do more than that. Again, ask Professor Alimen."

"So you acted on the lieutenant's behalf?"

"To try to save him, yes!" Delmin said. Were they being dense or just playing with him? "I'm sorry I wasn't strong enough to help the patrolman as well. I tried . . ."

He had been crying. He wasn't even sure when he had started. The thought of those arrows burying themselves in the patrolman's chest wouldn't leave his psyche.

"It's all right, son," Inspector Rainey said, moving over to him. She put one arm around his shoulder. "We know that's what you did. Lieutenant Benvin is still alive thanks to you."

"This has been very helpful, Mister Sarren," Inspector Welling said, getting to his feet. "We have your information, and may call on you on campus if we have further need of you."

He got up and left the room.

Inspector Rainey stepped back and looked at Delmin. "You need anything?"

"I'd just like to go home now," Delmin said. He was exhausted, in every way he could imagine.

"I'll get a carriage for you," she said. She walked to the door, and turned back, "Thank you, Mister Sarren, for everything you've done."

Veranix didn't go to Orchard Street to find Colin. Colin didn't trust his current crew in the slightest, and there was no place there or along Rose they could trust not to have prying ears. Colin's emergency signal meant only one thing, the only safe place they had.

Veranix left a magical mark on the alley outside the window of Colin's Orchard Street flop—a signal in case they missed each other—and fully shrouded with the cloak's *numina*-drawing powers, he bounded from rooftop to rooftop toward Saint Julian's Church.

He had never done this in broad daylight before. Shrouding didn't render him invisible, but like a shimmer in the air. Anyone not looking straight up would probably think a flock of birds flew by.

He knew it was foolish to travel this way. It probably would make far more sense to simply make himself look like an ordinary student and walk there, even with his weapons and Thorn regalia hidden by magical illusion. But he needed the air. He needed to be above the crowd. Right now, more than anything, he wanted to find someone he could blame, someone he could hit to make everything right again.

But there was no such person.

So all he had was the jump, pushing the muscles in his legs, and that indescribable feeling when in the air before gravity claimed him again.

It was the closest thing he had to home.

Saint Julian's had a clock tower, but the clock had

stopped working long before, and no one made any effort to maintain it. This made it an excellent location for Veranix to make his entrance into the church unnoticed.

Especially since Reverend Pemmick had long since agreed to leave the clock face trapdoor unlatched for him. And no one ever looked up at the clock, because it only read a few minutes past ten bells.

"I expected you earlier." Reverend Pemmick was dusting the defunct machinery.

"Were you?" Veranix unshrouded. "I take it Colin is already here."

"He is here, and he is not alone." The Reverend sighed. "Many matters have the appearance of pertaining to you, my friend."

" 'Have the appearance' is the key part of that phrase, Reverend."

"You are not responsible for the assault on the constables." It was not a question.

"You don't have any doubts?"

"I've seen your spirit, and the saints pointed me to you. I have faith in their guidance."

Veranix was never quite sure how to react to Reverend Pemmick when he talked like this. He wanted to discourage the reverend from treating him like he was some sort of saintly icon, but at the same time, he didn't want to chase away any allies. Especially at a time like this.

"I need to find out who is responsible, though," Veranix said.

"And why is that?"

"Besides the fact that he's killing Constabulary?"

"You feel that you are responsible for him."

"Can we go talk to Colin? I don't want to keep him waiting."

"Thorn," the reverend started. He still didn't know Veranix's true name, and he didn't want to know it. But his use of "Thorn" like it was a proper name was often disconcerting to Veranix. "You shouldn't avoid discussions like this."

"Fine, but we should move while we're at it."

The reverend put his hand on Veranix's shoulder. "A moment of patience. Colin is waiting, and he is not alone."

The reverend had said that before, but this time Veranix actually heard it. "Who is he here with? Someone else who wants a word with me?"

"They actually, quite pointedly, do not. But I think a word would be valuable. I need your assurances that you will curb your more aggressive instincts in this instance."

"Is . . . is it one of Fenmere's men?" He knew the reverend tried to be open to all, and wanted to broker peace between all the Aventil gangs. Would he arrange a meeting with one of Fenmere's people?

"No." The reverend chuckled. "I will admit, I have considered reaching out, but I have done proper diligence. I do not believe any of them would treat my station with the same respect that the local factions do."

"Glad to hear it." Veranix realized how that might have sounded. "Rather, I mean—"

"Worry not," the reverend said. "Still, your assurance. Which would mean more if you left your weapons here."

Veranix unhitched the bandolier that held the bow, quiver, and staff and left it on the floor.

"Appreciated," Reverend Pemmick said with a bow of his head.

He led Veranix down the tight winding staircase from the bell tower, down past the main floor to the basement quarters. There were a few others who lived at the church, the Brothers who maintained things under Pemmick's guidance, but Veranix had barely seen them and never heard a word from them. He wondered if a vow of silence was attached to serving Saint Julian.

It certainly wasn't something the Knights imposed on themselves out in the streets.

They reached a chamber door. "Your assurances," the reverend said once more.

"You're not filling me with confidence here, Rev."

He held his hand on the door. "There is someone in here who is under my protection."

"With Colin?"

"Yes."

"Then I'm sure we won't have a problem."

The reverend opened the door, revealing Colin pacing back and forth behind a chair. It was the person in the chair who held Veranix's attention. Sotch, of the Red Rabbits.

She looked up when the door opened and leaped to her feet. "Ow, rutting blazes, you tossers," she snarled. "You set me up."

"What is she doing here?" Veranix asked.

"Calm down, young lady," the reverend said. "He has promised me he would not harm you."

"Like blazes he wouldn't," she said.

"What's going on here, Prince?" Veranix asked Colin. He didn't want to show they were too close in front of Sotch. He even added a little magic twinge to his voice, made it sound deeper and echo through the room.

"Just got to clear some things up, thought the reverend could help," Colin said.

Sotch picked up the chair and held it in front of herself. "Don't you try a damn thing, bastard."

"Language, miss."

Veranix moved into the room, hands up. "Didn't know you and yours were still around."

"Yeah, you ran us out good, didn't you?" she said. "Wasn't enough for you, was it?"

"What is she talking about?" Veranix asked.

Colin answered, "She says she and Keckin were hunted down out in Benson Court. Hunted by you."

"I don't go out to Benson Court."

"Then who killed Keckin?" she snarled, tears forming at the corners of her eyes. "You tell me that, Thorn!"

"Not me," Veranix said.

"There you have it," the reverend said.

"You believe him?" Sotch wailed. "After what he did?"

"What I did, Sotch?" Veranix asked. "You helped a man nearly destroy the campus, worked with Fenmere and tried to create something worse than *effitte*. So what did I do?"

"The point is, Thorn," Colin said. "Someone did come after her and kill Keckin. Someone dressed as the Thorn."

"Dressed as the Thorn?" she wailed. "You believe that?"

"You should," Veranix said. "Because you're still breathing now. If I really wanted to hunt you down—"

"That's enough," Pemmick said with quiet authority.

"Sorry, Rev," Veranix said. "All right, Rabbit. Tell me what happened."

Sotch told her story, about a very Thorn-like character coming after her and capturing Keckin, and then Keckin ending up dead. Veranix had to admit, it sounded believable. If he didn't already know he didn't do it, he would have believed her.

"So now what?" Colin asked.

"Keep your ear out," Veranix said. "You too, Rev. There's someone out there pretending to be me, so I've got to put a stop to that."

"And the girl?" the reverend asked.

"Sorry about your friend," Veranix said to her. "You and the rest of your Rabbits clearly have trouble on your stoop, but if you're not in the drug business, it won't come from me."

"Cold comfort," Sotch said.

"Keep her safe, let her do what she will," Veranix said.

"But her tormentor?" the reverend asked.

"Yet another problem on my stoop," Veranix said. "You have a bite of something for her, Rev? She's skin and bones."

The reverend took the cue and led Sotch out of the room.

"Sorry about that," Colin said. "That was how the rev wanted to play it."

"I could have done without the drama of it all," Veranix said. "But it's fine."

"You all right?"

"Just feeling stupid," Veranix said. He had to tell someone what he did. Colin, of anyone, would understand. "You ever, you know, end up sharing a cot with an Orphan or something like that?"

A sly smile crept over Colin's face. "What did you do?"

"Remember those Deadly Birds who tried to kill me a few months back?"

"You—was it the one with the hoops?"

"No, it was— that doesn't matter."

"Because I could understand if it was the one with the hoops."

"Anyway, that's where my attention was last night, as opposed to out here. But we've got a real imposter problem."

"I thought you needed to know," Colin said.

"I already knew. The imposter also attacked the constables, from what I hear."

That was news to Colin. "Saints, I am off the circuit over on Orchid. I hear nothing, and my crew is rutting useless."

"Sorry," Veranix said. Colin never said it, but Veranix felt responsible for Colin's loss of standing in the Princes.

"Ain't nothing," he said.

Veranix remembered one of the other things from last night. "Where are you usually cooling your throat now? The Old Canal?"

"That's right," Colin said. "How did you—"

"Damn it," Veranix said. "I was in there with the tetch squad last night—"

"They win?"

"Routed, fourteen-aught. But the bartender treated us real good, and wanted me to make sure I let my brother know he did."

"Rutting saints," Colin said. "Let me see your proper face."

Veranix dropped his facade.

"I see it," Colin said. "You've been letting your hair grow out over the summer."

"That's how I like it."

"Trim it back and shave, and we won't have the problem," Colin said. He gave a bit of a smile. "Don't worry. We'll find this clod who's messing with your name."

"And you're going to protect Sotch?"

Colin shrugged. "I don't like her, but I still believe in the Pact. And the whole point of that was, no matter what's happening inside Aventil, nobody gets to come from outside and mess with it. So against this imposter, I've got Sotch's back."

Veranix didn't quite know how to respond to that. Quite a few of the Aventil gangs—even many of the Princes— would see him as someone from "outside."

"All right," he said. "Signal me if you hear anything. I've got sales creeping onto campus, so I've got my own trouble."

"Keep sharp," Colin said, taking Veranix into an embrace. "Stay away from Deadly Birds."

"Not advice I'd have thought I'd need," Veranix said.

"All right, get out of here," Colin said, breaking away. "Get out there."

Veranix put his facade back up. "Keep sharp, yourself."

"Always," Colin said.

Veranix left the room and climbed up to the clock tower, collecting his weapons. He probably would need them, especially if the Constabulary spotted him.

Minox Welling, Inspector Third Class of the Maradaine Constabulary, found his way to Lieutenant Benvin's special task force squad room. The able-bodied members of the squad sat in quiet contemplation. While Minox had never received a proper introduction, thanks to Jace he was already well versed on who they were.

Sergeant Trinnit Tripper was the ranking member of the task force with Lieutenant Benvin out of commission. Ten years of footpatrol, most of that in Dentonhill. From a southern Druth family, still with a strong Linjari accent. Smart and dedicated—they all were smart and dedicated, of course, that was why they were on this task force—but with a file jacket full of reprimands. Most of those, from what Minox had determined, were due to a failure to hold his tongue when a superior did something foolish. He had also tried to expose graft and bribery in the Dentonhill house, which resulted in his transfer and subsequent ostracism in this stationhouse. Sergeant Tripper had few friends outside of this room.

Patrolman Kendall Pollit was another unique case, and from Minox's understanding, one which required some delicacy. Had Minox not been informed by his brother, he would have presumed that Pollit was a woman dressed in disguise as a man. "That ain't rightly it," Jace had said. "Far as any of us are concerned, Pollit is a bloke. It ain't some pretend or disguise for Pollit. Rest of the house gives us sewage, gives Pollit sewage, but the Left said everybody has the right to be who they want to be. Makes a strange kind of sense to me." Minox had found himself agreeing with that principle—an Uncircled Mage who stayed in the Constabulary could hardly think anything different.

Patrolman Gummen Wheth was relatively fresh out of his cadethood, from a family that emigrated from Ch'omik-Taa. Ch'omiki immigrants had much in common with Racquin, having fled their home country in fear of war and oppression. Unlike the Racquin, who had some cultural connection with the Druth and could sometimes pass in appearance—such as Minox's mother—the Ch'omik stood out strongly. With umber brown skin and thick black hair, Wheth was probably the singular member of the Constabulary in the entire city with his heritage.

Minox sometimes wondered how Jace ended up with this group. Lieutenant Benvin had collected outcasts, and they rewarded him with loyalty. In what way was his brother one of them?

How much is Jace like me? Minox wondered. The Inemar Constabulary House might not have had a Benvin, but fortunately Captain Cinellan recognized talent and capability in whatever form it took. Which was why Minox, outsider even before he discovered he was a mage, was where he was, same as Inspector Rainey. Her impressive skill for investigation combined with her unbreakable tenacity made her the best partner he could hope for. She came into the room at his side.

"So what's the word, specs?" Tripper asked. "You finished with the questioning?"

"For the time being, I'm satisfied that I've gotten what is worthwhile from the witnesses."

"I imagine so," Tripper said. "Seemed pretty straightforward."

"It would probably seem that way," Minox said. "Many of them gave practically the same testimony."

"Right?" Tripper said. "And you talked to Saitle, right?"

"Welling," Rainey said lightly. "It's technically against protocol to discuss this with them."

"Protocol, but not regulation," Minox said. "But what is regulation, is that as part of our investigation we are empowered to utilize facilities and personnel at the stationhouse our investigation is centered at. I believe that this squad room and these officers would serve well for those ends."

Rainey gave him one of her looks, which he knew meant she was skeptical of his plan, but was not going to gainsay it.

"We did talk to Cadet Saitle," she said. "His testimony was scattered, but fundamentally in line with a majority of the ones we heard."

"Right, then, that pretty much settles it, don't it?" Tripper said. "We've got cause for full searches for the Thorn. We've already got a fair amount of legwork—"

"It isn't settled," Minox said.

"But you just said—"

"That Cadet Saitle's testimony was in line with most of the rest. And the testimony of many of the witnesses was remarkably similar. They all reported the 'Thorn' filling the street with magical smoke, then coming out and attacking Lieutenant Benvin and the others."

Tripper looked at him incredulously. "Then what, sir, is the blasted problem?"

"There's the testimony of Delmin Sarren."

"Who the blazes is he?"

Jace spoke up. "He's the one who protected the lieutenant. The magic student."

"So?"

"He explicitly noted that the smoke was not magical in nature. He knew it."

"He's a magic student, so?" This was Wheth. "I mean, he'd know, no one else in the crowd would. Makes sense."

"True," Minox said. "But Mister Sarren also did not identify the assailant as the Thorn."

"He's a Uni kid," Pollit said. "He might not know about the Thorn like the locals."

"Perhaps," Minox said. He decided not to mention that Delmin Sarren himself was quick to point out that he did not identify the assailant as the Thorn. That was crucial. It was clear to Minox that Mister Sarren knew—not suspected or didn't want to confirm, but *knew* with complete certainty—that the assailant was *not* the Thorn.

That certainty made Mister Sarren a very interesting witness.

Jace spoke up. "So what do you need from us, Mi— Inspector?"

Inspector Rainey answered. "We're going to want to go over all the lieutenant's work, and get up to speed with the details here in Aventil."

"No, look," Tripper said. "We appreciate you all coming out here to help us, but you asked your questions, you told us your opinion. We'll handle it from here."

"We're not done, Sergeant," Minox said. "And it isn't yours to say."

"And it ain't yours to dig through the Left's files!"

"Trip—" Pollit said. "I don't think it's like that."

"The blazes it ain't," Tripper said. "We shouldn't need these folks going through our business when we should be dragging the Princes in here."

Minox glanced at his notes to refresh his memories of the various gangs in the neighborhood. "Why the Rose Street Princes?"

Wheth provided the answer. "Left was pretty sure they were protecting the Thorn, or he was one of them."

"Is that just some sort of 'roses have thorns' thing?" Inspector Rainey asked. "Or is that based on something hard?"

"Kid we ironed and sent to Quarry few months back," Pollit said. "Prince who helped the Thorn, and refused to talk about him. We offered him a deal to finger the Thorn, wouldn't take it."

"Not surprised," Jace muttered.

Minox knew Jace was keeping something to himself—it would be obvious, even if Minox wasn't already privy to the information. Jace had absolutely no suspicion of the Thorn in this case, or as someone the Constabulary ought to be pursuing. The Thorn had saved Jace's life during a stampede of mad horses, and due to that, Jace couldn't believe the Thorn would do anything like attack Lieutenant Benvin.

Minox couldn't believe it either. But it was clear Sergeant Tripper was already set in his opinion, and he was willing to make the facts fit his theory.

"This is what I believe, Sergeant," Minox said. "That we are not dealing with the Thorn, but a deliberate imposter, someone who already held a grudge against the lieutenant and used the guise of the Thorn to be able to attack him in plain sight."

"That's just absurd," Tripper said.

"Why?" Inspector Rainey asked. "Anyone with a cloak and bow and a few tricks from a chemist's shop could do what the killer did."

"But the Thorn—"

"The question is simple, Sergeant," Rainey said bluntly. "Do you want to get the man responsible for Benvin, Mal, and Saitle, or do you want to whine about the Thorn?"

Tripper looked like he was going to shout at Rainey for a moment, but then pulled back. He glanced about the room, finally locking eyes with Jace. Jace gave him a little nod.

"Pol," he said quietly. "Show the inspectors what they need. I'm going to get some tea."

He stalked out of the room.

"Well," Rainey said, taking a seat at one of the desks. "Let's get to work."

Things required Kaiana's attention.

That had been the theme all day, which she had been expecting. The Tournament was giving her and the grounds staff more than enough work repairing the damage done by the previous day's events and the night's revels. The south lawn was a mess, flower beds trampled on, and at some point in the middle of the night a group had managed to uproot one of the trees.

The tree had been her priority, and with a few workers and a lot of rope, they got it back upright. She hoped that with some care it could be saved. Most of the roots were still intact, and getting it back in the soil might just keep it alive.

"Something you need to see, Miss Nell."

Kaiana sighed, having almost gotten the tree to stand up on its own. The young worker—she had forgotten his name—stood earnestly over her.

"What is it?" she asked, brushing the dirt off her knees as she stood.

"Over at the bathhouses."

"In the bathhouses, or outside near the bathhouses?" she asked. She better not be expected to deal with inside the bathhouses. For one, it wasn't the grounds, it was a building, and that should fall to housing or maintenance or some other department of the staff. For another, since the various athletes from all over Druthal had arrived, the bathhouses had more or less turned into a brothel. The usual division of baths between genders—what had always been polite custom rather than rule—had devolved into meaninglessness. When Kaiana had gone over the other day, she immediately observed coupling—and tripling and more—of flesh in every possible combination, and walked right out.

So no bath for her until this was all over, and even then

not until copious amounts of soap and vinegar had been applied to every surface.

"I wasn't told, Miss Nell. I just was told to fetch you, because you wanted to know about this sort of thing."

That got her attention. "Lead the way."

She was led behind the bathhouses, where Rennie and Lash were standing over three students—not U of M boys, but Kaiana couldn't tell where they were from. This was in no small part due to the fact that they were only wearing their linens, and their bodies were still damp. They must have been in the bathhouses recently. Now they were sitting on the grass looking terrified. Rennie and Lash hovered over the three boys like a couple of thugs, holding their pruning tools like they were ready to beat the boys.

"Here she comes," Rennie said. "Now you boys are going to get the crunch."

So now they were her thugs. Kaiana wasn't sure how she felt about that.

"What's the news?" Kaiana asked, doing her best to sound authoritative. Rennie and Lash had clearly built her up as an authority to these boys.

"We found these young men throwing some vials on the ground, can you imagine?" Lash said. "Miss Nell here has opinions about boys who do *effitte* on campus."

One of the boys burst into tears right away. All three of them were about Veranix's age and build—tetchball players, likely—but this one had a younger face than the other two. He launched into a hysterical rant. "We didn't mean . . . we just thought . . . please don't make us go to our chaperones, we won't do it again."

"Saints, boy, have some spine," Rennie said.

"Calm down," Kaiana said, squatting down in front of the boys. He was still a mess of tears, and the other two looked like they might burst out at any moment. "So you all thought you'd get yourself buzzed on *effitte*, hit the bathhouses, and get yourselves polished up while flying?"

"Something like that," one of the calmer boys said.

"You flying now?" she asked them, grabbing that one by the chin to look into his eyes. The pupils were huge and wide. He was fully in. Probably they all were.

"How'd you catch them?" she asked Rennie.

"Lash and I saw that one throwing the vials out the window of the bathhouse," Rennie said, pointing at the crying one. "So we grabbed his arms and pulled him out, and yelled to the other two that they better come out."

"Should have ran," one of the boys said. "Stupid."

"Couldn't leave Tensy."

"He was caught already. Now we all are."

"Roll your rutting hand, Gorm!" Tensy shouted over his tears. "This was your rutting plan!"

"Was it?" Kaiana asked. "Well, we have to decide what to do with you boys."

"Who even is this napa?" Gorm snarled. "She ain't a prefect or cadet or nothing."

Kaiana gave him the back of her hand, which made even Rennie and Lash gasp. "I don't care for that term, Gorm."

"Say you're sorry!" Tensy cried.

"Sorry," Gorm mumbled.

"Now, we could just bring you all to your chaperones, and you'd be scrubbed from the games, for sure."

"Please, no," Tensy said.

Kaiana glanced over at Rennie and Lash, who seemed to be enjoying this game, perhaps too much. She didn't trust either of them farther than the length of her arm, but she figured they would play along if they thought it was fun. "So, which one of you bought the stuff?"

"It was Gorm!" Tensy said.

"You rutting bastard."

"Well, you did!"

"This is the last time I ever—"

"Boys!" Kaiana barked, surprising even herself at how harsh she sounded. "I'm going to give you an opportunity here. First off, do you still have any of it?"

"Yeah," the third boy said. "It's with our clothes inside."

"Lash, go with him to fetch it. And bring their clothes as well."

"Why do I have to—"

"Lash!" Kaiana snapped.

"Saints, fine," he said, giving a glance over to Rennie. A glance that Kaiana interpreted as meaning that they had underestimated how she would handle being forced to be responsible for things. Maybe they wouldn't be bothering her anymore. More likely, they would find a new way. He pulled the third boy up to his feet and trotted him over to the bathhouse entrance.

"Rennie, take Tensy here and bring him to the tool shed."

Rennie paled. "What are we going to do to him in the tool shed?" There was a strange tone to his voice, like he was both afraid and excited at the same time.

Kaiana rolled her eyes. Perhaps she was playing the part a little too strongly. "He's going to wait there, calmly. And so are you."

Rennie looked mostly relieved, but also slightly disappointed. He took Tensy by the arm and dragged him off.

After a moment, Gorm jumped to his feet and tried to run. Kaiana grabbed him by the front of his linens and pushed him right back down to the grass. He struggled, but he couldn't push back up strong enough to get on his feet again. He looked like he was contemplating the value of actually punching her, but then thought better of it.

"So now what?" Gorm asked when he settled.

"Now you tell me where you got it."

Gorm stewed for a moment. "I heard you had to go into Dentonhill. So I went over there, and looked around, found a lady who was selling. Gave her crowns and bought it. Pretty simple."

"Pretty simple," she repeated. Too damn simple, that's what it was. Dentonhill Constabulary probably didn't even bother to crack down on it.

"So what are you going to do, lady?"

"I'll tell you what you're going to do, Gorm," she said, plan forming in her head. "You're going to be the bait."

For the first time, he really looked scared. "What does that mean?"

"I mean, while your friends are cooling their boots in the tool shed, you're going to run an errand for me."

Chapter 7

VERANIX RETURNED TO the carriage house to find everyone there waiting. Delmin sat on a crate, looking spooked and exhausted. Kaiana paced around, while Phadre watched Jiarna draw something on Kai's worktable.

"I take it there's news," Veranix said.

"Vee," Delmin said, coming over to Veranix and grabbing him in a strong embrace. "Good to see you."

"I'm fine, Del," he said. "Blazes, it sounds like you saw more . . . excitement last night than I did."

"I have," Delmin said, eyes to the floor. "I wanted to wait until you got back to tell them all."

"You're all right?" Veranix asked.

"He's not," Kaiana said.

"I just . . . I never. . . ." Delmin shook his head.

"Start at the top, chap," Phadre said.

"Right." Delmin sat back down. "So, I was with the other prefects at the end of the Endurance. Constabulary were keeping the peace when someone throws smoke powder. They obviously wanted people to think it was magic, but I knew otherwise. It had to be some kind of smoke powder."

"Easy enough to make," Jiarna said. "Any corner apothecary or chemist could do that."

Delmin nodded. "Then he came riding through the

smoke, dressed like you. A few arrows, and a few swings of his staff, and he had knocked down two of them and . . . killed a third."

Kaiana put a hand on his shoulder, and Delmin looked like he was doing his best to hold back sobs.

"Sorry you had to see that," Veranix said. "Did you get a good look at him?"

Delmin shrugged pathetically. "Sort of your height, sort of your build, face covered. I mean, I knew it wasn't you because he wasn't a mage, but if I couldn't tell that . . ."

Veranix nodded. "And how about how he moved? Was it like me? How he handled the staff? How he shot?"

"Vee!" Kaiana snapped. "Ease off."

"Sorry." She was right. It was clear that Delmin was not equipped to handle what he went through.

"I don't even know how to answer that, Vee," Delmin said. "I'm sorry, I . . . I saw him but I'm not much help."

"No, it helps. So what happened then?"

"He was going for the last constable—the lieutenant— but I did my best to protect him."

"You did? That was real good, Del."

"And the guy threw down some more smoke and slipped off. Next thing I know, I'm brought to the stationhouse as a witness, and I wait for a while. Then these two inspectors question me . . . one of them was a mage. Does that make sense?"

"Not at all," Phadre said. "I mean, Red Wolf works with Druth Intelligence, but there's no Circle that would allow their members to be a constable or marshal or something. Not even hired out, as far as I've heard."

Veranix shrugged. "I don't know."

"So what did you find out?" Kaiana asked him.

"Nothing much we didn't already know. Colin confirmed there's someone impersonating me. And whoever it was, they were hunting the Red Rabbits as well. I got a vivid depiction from one of the survivors." Veranix looked back at Delmin, still shuddering on the crate. "Damn it, I should have been there."

"Where were you, anyway?" Kaiana asked.

"Being distracted," he said. Now it made sense. Blackbird kept his attention all night, kept him in cups, while her partner went after the lieutenant. "Won't happen again."

"Good," Kaiana said. "Because I've got something."

"Bless you, Kai," Veranix said. "What is it?"

She quickly detailed her morning, where the three boys were caught, and her intention to have one of them lead the Thorn to their seller.

"Excellent, Kai," Veranix said. "That could close the box all around, at least as far as campus is concerned."

Jiarna spoke up. "So you're not going to latch on to the boys on the tetch squad tonight?"

"No need," Veranix said. "They don't have a match today, anyway."

"Who's playing today?" Phadre asked.

"Pirrell against Erien—" Veranix said.

Jiarna made a face. "Ugh, the Pirrell boys."

"All the prefects have been put out with them," Delmin offered.

"And Astonic against High Academy of Korifina. Tomorrow we play whoever wins that one."

Jiarna nodded. "We'll watch both matches, though, just in case."

"We will?" Phadre said.

"Yes, of course," Jiarna said. "It's the least we can do. And keep an eye on the social house parties. There are three tonight, and we should see what's happening in each of them."

"You're all so very diligent," Delmin said. "I just would prefer not to spend any more time in the stationhouse."

"It's fine," Veranix said. "If we've got the bait leading us to the seller, that might be all we need."

"Might not be the only seller," Kaiana said.

"Of course not," Veranix said. "That's why tonight won't be about getting just her."

"What are you going to do, exactly?" Phadre asked.

"I'll find the seller and convince her to tell me her sources."

"Convince her?" Phadre asked nervously. "How?"

"These are things I prefer not knowing about," Delmin said.

"I'll ask very nicely," Veranix said. He didn't need to inflict the things he had to do on the streets on Delmin or Phadre.

"All right, enough." Kaiana closed the trapdoor to the Spinner Run. "Lovely secret meeting. I have work to do, and you all should go to lunch or watch matches or do something other than be here." She opened the door to the carriage house and shooed them all out.

"So, lunch?" Veranix said to the other three.

Phadre looked like he was about to answer affirmatively when Jiarna pulled on his arm. "We'll get you another time," she said, dragging him toward the tetch field.

"You and I, then," Delmin said. "Campus or off?"

"Both are going to be a pain," Veranix said. "Though there are quite a bit more cookstand carts in Aventil than usual."

"Which means?"

"We'll find a culinary adventure at one of them."

The cookstand carts were taking advantage of the wide variety of clientele, offering cuisines from all over Druthal. Veranix spotted one selling Scallic-style slow-pork wraps. He had vaguely fond recollections of the food in Scaloi, though the circus hardly ever went that far south.

"What does it even mean?" Delmin asked as they approached. "What makes it 'Scallic style'?"

"The meat—specifically the belly of the pig—is marinated in lime, salt, coriander, and garlic," someone next to them by the cart said. "It's wrapped in plant leaves and cooked slowly, then served in thinly rolled flatbreads." Veranix noticed the speaker was wearing a Constabulary uniform.

Specifically, an inspector's vest.

"Mister Sarren," the inspector said coolly. "Are you feeling better?"

Colin brought Sotch back to Orchid, sent her up with Ment and Kiggy to the flop. That was as good a place for her as any. Three more Rabbits had turned up looking for her, and Ment had wasted no time slapping them about and dragging them up to the flop. He assured Colin that they had it under control up there, no need to worry.

Colin was glad of that. He needed to get a bite and come up with a proper plan for the day. No need to waste the opportunity for coin. Enough time had been spent on Red Rabbits for his taste.

He spotted a young Prince standing outside the Old Canal, not one he had ever seen before. Real new kid, the ink on his arm still raw and red. The kid looked around nervously, like he wasn't sure he was even in the right place.

"What's the word, Prince?" Colin asked, coming over.

"You Tyson?" the kid asked.

"That's me. You get sent over here to find me?"

"Yeah, yeah," the kid said.

"All right," Colin said. "So what's the word?"

"Like I said, Tyson. They sent me over to find you."

"I got that, kid—what's your name?"

"Cober."

"So, Cober. Why did they send you? You delivering a message, or are you supposed to flop out here with my crew?"

"Yeah. That. Both of those."

"You've got a message and you're flopping out here."

"Yeah. That's it."

"So?"

"I told you, that's it."

This kid was either utterly stupid, or he was on *phat* or *doph* or something. Possibly both.

Colin grabbed him by the shoulders. "Cober. What's the message?"

"Oh, yeah," Cober said. "They said to put me on your crew, show me the tricks."

"Great," Colin said. "That's it?"

"Yeah, yeah," Cober said, looking around. "So where are your boys and stuff?"

"The sew-up's place," Colin said, pointing it out. "Head up the back stairs to the that blue door, they're in there."

The kid nodded. "Good. Good. They said you taught your boys well. Right? Except when they get pinched."

Colin cuffed the kid across the head. "Get up there, say your hellos. Tell them you're our new pigeon. We'll figure out what you can do later."

The kid made off for the back stairs, and then came back over.

"What?" Colin asked.

"I remembered, there was something else. They said you needed to come out to the Turnabout right away, cuz somebody wanted to talk to you. Old Kelly or something."

"Old Casey?"

"Yeah, that's it."

"Rutting blazes, Cober," Colin said. This kid was going to be the death of him. "Next time something involves Old Casey, that comes first, hear?"

"Oh, I guess."

Colin gave him another smack. "When I say 'hear,' you say you heard it, hear?"

"Heard," Cober grumbled.

"Get up there. I'll sort you later." Colin strode off to the Turnabout, not bothering to see if the kid got inside or not. He had already wasted enough time, he wasn't going to make Casey wait any longer.

Veranix knew Delmin was still deeply troubled by what had happened last night, and the appearance of this inspector seemed to send him into a state of panic. "No, I mean . . . yes . . . that is . . ." Delmin stammered, sweat beading on his brow. "Are you following me, Inspector?"

"No such thing, Mister Sarren," the inspector said. "I just happen to be intrigued by these particular food items. 'Skizzies,' I think they are called in Scaloi."

"Skellies," Veranix corrected.

"Whatever they are, they smell disgusting." This came from the redheaded woman on the other side of the inspector, also wearing an inspector's vest.

"Who is your companion, Mister Sarren?" the inspector asked.

Delmin was frozen.

"Veranix Calbert," Veranix offered, looking to both of the inspectors for their name badges. "Inspectors Welling and Rainey, I presume."

"They're the ones," Delmin said nervously. "They're investigating that attack I saw."

"Ah," Veranix said, understanding immediately. "Good luck in that, Inspectors. Hope you get your man."

Inspector Welling stared at Veranix, his head cocked slightly to one side, his oddly large eyes looking up and down. "Uncommon name. Racquin, if I'm not mistaken."

"As is 'Minox,'" Veranix said, pulling it off the man's nameplate.

"Is this boy your classmate, Mister Sarren?"

"Yes!" Delmin almost barked. "He and I are both magic students at the University. Studying magic."

"You were very helpful, Mister Sarren," Inspector Rainey said. "We may have further questions for you. You're on campus for the summer?"

"Yes. Yes."

"Almers House," Veranix offered. Delmin was acting so strange, the inspectors were probably getting suspicious. "We're both in Almers House, though with the Tournament on, it's all rather chaotic up there."

"Indeed," Inspector Welling said. He took two of the skellies from the vendor and passed them to Veranix and Delmin, and then another one for himself. He passed a coin over to the vendor. "My compliments, gentlemen."

"Really?" Veranix asked. The fact that the inspector was buying them lunch was more disturbing than anything else.

"You're not . . . not trying it, Inspector Rainey?" Delmin asked.

"Saints, no," she said. "You boys are welcome to it. I know you need it."

Veranix wasn't sure what that meant, but it probably had something to do with magic.

One of them was a mage, Delmin had said. That was Welling. Now Veranix could feel it off the inspector, in ways he never could with other mages. *Numina* wafting and roiling around the Inspector Welling like a tidal pool. Especially from his hand—was this how it was for Delmin?

"You're missing out, Inspector," Veranix said, taking a bite. It really was everything he remembered.

"I'll learn to live with that," Inspector Rainey said, glancing around. "Mister Sarren, are we far from the place where the incident occurred?"

"No," Delmin said, his own skellie hovering a few inches from his mouth. "Not far at all."

"Good," she said. "We want to get a feel with our own eyes. You think you'd be able to walk us through it?"

"Walk you through it?" Delmin repeated.

Inspector Welling had polished off his skellie in moments, and signaled the cart cook for two more. "As best you can, Mister Sarren, show us where you were, where the attacker came from, and so forth."

Delmin stammered, looking unsure how to answer. Veranix stepped in front, putting himself between Del and the inspectors.

"He's been through quite a bit today, as I'm sure you're aware," Veranix said. "This isn't the best time."

"When would be?" Inspector Welling asked.

"Give him a few days," Veranix said. "So his nerves settle."

"Settled nerves lead to missed details," Inspector Welling said. "Fresh thoughts—"

"What is going on here?" The patrician tones of Professor Alimen intruded as he came striding across the street to them. Veranix hadn't seen the professor much during the summer, and he seemed to not be doing well. His face was a little more drawn, his beard a bit more unkempt. Despite that, he still exuded power and authority, putting himself in between Veranix and Inspector Welling. "I ask you, Inspector, what do you think you're doing?"

"Buying the boys a skellie," he said. "These young men are hungry, and—"

"Do not insult my intelligence, Inspector, you—" He paused, eyes narrowing. "How are you—"

"I'm afraid we have not been properly introduced," Inspector Rainey said, stepping up to the professor. "Inspectors Rainey and Welling. You may have heard there was an assault on some Constabulary officers last night."

"I have," Alimen said cautiously, eyes still focused on Welling.

"Mister Sarren was a key witness, Professor—" She let it hang there.

"Alimen. Gollic Alimen, Chair and Professor of Magic."

"These boys are your students?" Welling asked.

"They are indeed," Alimen said. "And as they are students under my charge, I would insist that any questions you have for them are done in my presence."

"That's not necessary, sir—" Delmin started.

"I'm quite certain it is, Mister Sarren." He gave another look at Inspector Welling. "Who are you with?"

"With the Maradaine Constabulary, Professor," Welling said. "The Grand Inspectors' Unit."

"Do not trifle with me, son. What Circle?"

"Maybe you and your students should return to campus," Inspector Rainey said.

"Not until he tells me—" Alimen started.

"Do not presume to—" Welling shot back.

"Professor!" Inspector Rainey shouted, putting her palm on his chest. "We will be in contact with you if we have further questions for Mister Sarren."

He looked like he wanted to say more, but Inspector Rainey was standing firm, staring him down. Veranix had seen that kind of stare before, and he fully believed that Rainey had the goods to back it up. Despite being old enough to be his mother, she held herself like a ring fighter. Inspector Welling, on the other hand, seemed to almost shrink back at Alimen's gaze.

That was it. Inspector Rainey was being protective of her partner. Protecting him from Alimen.

"Boys," Professor Alimen said, grabbing both Veranix and Delmin by their arms. "Let us be away from here."

"Right," Delmin said.

"Thank you for lunch, Inspectors," Veranix said.

"Mister Calbert," Inspector Welling said with a slight nod, though his eyes were on the ground.

Professor Alimen all but dragged the two of them back toward the south gate.

"Is this really necessary, Professor?" Veranix asked once they were around the street corner.

Alimen stopped, and let go of both of their arms. "My apologies, boys," he said quietly. "I saw those inspectors talking to you, and I immediately—"

"It's all right," Delmin said. "I appreciated your intersession."

"Is it true, Mister Sarren?" Alimen asked. "Were you a witness to those horrors?"

"I was, yes," Delmin said, his voice quavering a little. "I don't know what else I could tell them."

"Well, if they have need, we'll both sit down with Inspector Rainey," Alimen said. He glanced back down the street where they came from. "How dare he?"

"Is 'he' Inspector Welling, sir?" Veranix asked.

"'Inspector,' indeed," Alimen scoffed. More gently, he led them through the gate.

"He's a mage, isn't he?" Veranix said. "I mean, I could feel it, so you two must have."

"He is, but that makes no sense," Delmin said. "I mean, do any of the Circles cooperate with Constabulary?"

"None," Alimen said acidly. "Red Wolf Circle works with Druth Intelligence, and that's a . . . but, no. No Circle would allow their members to be a constable, and I cannot imagine that the Constabulary would allow their officers to also have loyalty to a Circle."

Now Veranix understood, especially Alimen's reaction. "But that would mean Inspector Welling is . . ."

Alimen finished the sentence like the word itself was damned.

"Uncircled."

Chapter 8

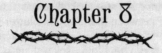

PROFESSOR ALIMEN'S MOOD soured as they continued. Once they crossed into campus, he was muttering half to himself, not giving any regard to the strange looks they were receiving from passersby. Veranix had never seen the professor so distracted, so unconcerned about how he was perceived. The professor was usually so circumspect in his demeanor.

"Very inappropriate. This has to be looked into. Someone must be made aware. I had heard a rumor—well, Olivant rambling on. I should have taken it more seriously."

"Sir?" Veranix said calmly. "Why don't we all get to the tower?"

Alimen paused and looked hard at Veranix, and then to Delmin. "Yes. Yes, I think I need a cup of tea. And then, Mister Sarren, I would like a somewhat detailed account of your encounters with Inspector Welling, and the reasons behind them."

"Of course, sir," Delmin said.

They headed toward Bolingwood Tower, where Alimen's office and residence was. "I apologize for my behavior, boys," Alimen said. "This summer has been particularly oppressive, on many levels, and to walk in the very streets outside here and . . ." He took a deep breath. "It will be cooler up in the tower."

He led them up the staircase to the top of the tower, and brought them through his office to his sitting room. This was the first time Veranix had ever been invited into the professor's more personal space, and from the look on Delmin's face, it was his as well.

The room had two worn couches, which were clearly older than Veranix, but still looked comfortable. There was a small table in between them, with a clutter of books and papers. "A clutter of books and papers" described much of the rest of the room, including several spots on the floor. The spots that weren't covered in papers were occupied by cats—at least four. Veranix wandered over to the window, where several plants were hanging.

"Sit, sit," Alimen said absently. He went over to his kitchen, pumping water into his teakettle. He put the kettle on the table next to the couches and then went back into the kitchen.

"Delmin," Veranix said, calling him over.

"What?" Delmin was sweating, and Veranix wasn't sure if it was the heat or nerves, but his friend was definitely out of sorts.

"Look out there," Veranix said, pointing out the window. It was a clear view of the south lawn, including the carriage house. "Alimen must see me coming and going."

"Us, you mean," Delmin said. "Gracious, I have become fully entrenched in your world."

"Boys, come over," Alimen said. "Though I admit the view is spectacular. One of the best in Maradaine, I imagine."

"We're high up enough," Veranix said.

As they approached the couch, Delmin said, "Sir, the kettle isn't going to get hot on the table, you know."

"I'm not quite in my dotage yet, Mister Sarren," Alimen said. He picked up an orange tabby cat to clear the couch for them, depositing it on the floor. "Though with my rambling earlier, you would be reasonable in presuming it. I am out of sorts, my boys, for more than just Inspector Welling."

"I can put it on the stove," Veranix said, reaching for it.

"Nothing doing, Mister Calbert," Alimen said. "I haven't lit the stove all summer. Far too hot already. I couldn't bear it." He snapped his fingers, and with a rush of *numina* that even Veranix could sense, the kettle started whistling with steam. "Fortunately we have other means." He picked up the kettle and poured the water into his teapot.

"So what is going on, sir?"

"Going on?" Alimen looked confused. "That's what you're supposed to be telling me. This business with constable inspectors." He stepped over to the kitchen one more time, emerging with a tray of bread, soft cheese, and cured lamb, putting that on one of the piles of papers on the table.

"Right, yes," Delmin said.

"Sorry, sir," Veranix said. "Just you said the summer has been oppressive, and you're out of sorts. I know that isn't just us."

"No, no, it isn't. It's nothing for you boys to be concerned with, truly. But I am very concerned."

Veranix was going to be concerned for the professor's mental state, especially since he brought out glass tumblers instead of teacups, but then the professor picked up the teapot, and as he poured he let another push of *numina* at it. The tea was ice cold when it reached the glass. He passed glasses to Veranix and Delmin, and then sat back on the couch with his own, sipping loudly. "Just the thing in this heat."

"Couldn't agree more, sir," Delmin said.

"Now, Mister Sarren, begin with your story."

Delmin rattled off the whole story, omitting certain elements such as why he had decided to be at the end of the Endurance, or anything relating Benvin's attacker to the Thorn. As far as Delmin's story to Professor Alimen was concerned, the constables were just attacked by some random interloper. Delmin did not omit, however, his own intervention to help Lieutenant Benvin. He played it humbly, but he made sure to mention it.

"This is quite troubling, Mister Sarren, but I applaud your acts of good citizenship. Yes, just because Circled mages would not work for or with the Constabulary, that doesn't mean we can't be helpful. You saved a life, Mister Sarren. And as you are a witness, you have a duty to assist in the investigation. That said, I will be present with you in further inquiries, and we will only interact with Inspector Rainey. I may also call in Quentin to join us."

"Who is Quentin?" Veranix asked.

"The lawyer for Lord Preston's Circle. He's a mage in the Circle as well—though honestly, he's better off practicing law."

"I'm a bit confused, sir," Delmin said. "I mean, Inspector Welling may be an Uncircled mage, but he's also clearly a Constabulary inspector. Are you saying we shouldn't respect his office?"

"Here is something you boys need to understand," Alimen said. "Circle law gives us protection and accountability. Protection, especially, from overzealous law enforcement."

"Provided the Circles actually account for themselves," Veranix said. The Blue Hand Circle certainly thought they were above everyone else.

"Any system has abuse, surely," Alimen said. "I would prefer that over being subject to Constabulary whims. But Circling also is an indication of training, discipline. Mister Sarren, you could feel the level of power radiating off Inspector Welling."

"I suppose, but that does—"

"Power like that, unchecked, untrained? It's incredibly dangerous. Inspector Welling is a menace, to himself and others, and he is part of an organization more likely to use him as an excuse to damage our credibility. No, nothing good can come from interacting with this Welling character."

"If you say so, sir," Delmin said, though he looked genuinely confused. "It's just—"

"Is there something you don't understand, Mister Sarren?" Alimen sighed, looking as if the idea of going over this with them just exhausted him. "Do I have to review this history with you? You have read about the fate of mages up through the tenth century? Hangings, burnings, torture?

And even with Circles across Druthal, that kind of behavior—especially from local Constabulary—still occurs to this day."

"Really, sir?" Veranix found the words had come out of his mouth before he could properly consider them. Alimen gave him a hard glare. "I mean, sure, in backwater towns, especially in Monim or Scaloi, I suppose. But nothing like that has happened in the city."

"Mister Calbert, do you remember my associate, Mister Harleydale from Light and Stone?"

"I think so," Veranix said. Harleydale was a decent enough fellow, though that meeting had been dominated by the presence of Kalas from the Blue Hand Circle.

"He was found dead, with his hands cut off and his eyes gouged out. Two members of the Firewings had their hearts cut out in broad daylight, and Constabulary's main concern was keeping the Circles from fighting each other. No, Mister Calbert. Always be polite to constables, respect their office, but never for a moment trust them. When it comes to the law, the only thing a mage should trust is this." He pointed to the Lord Preston's Circle tattoo on his arm.

Veranix had never imagined that Professor Alimen and Colin could sound so much alike.

"I am sorry, boys," he said after a moment. "I am . . . I am put out, and it is not your fault. You did well, Mister Sarren, and we'll leave it at that."

The professor dropped the subject completely and spent the rest of the afternoon talking with them about the Tournament, Veranix's involvement with the tetchball squad, and some plans for the next semester.

"What is the time?" he said eventually.

"About four bells," Veranix said.

"Gracious, I've kept you boys cooped up with me far too long. Be off, go to some of the events or the parties. You boys deserve it. Especially with your display in the opening ceremonies. I feel I haven't commended you for that."

"Quite all right, sir," Veranix said. "You've had a lot on your mind."

They said their good-byes and left the tower.

"I'm a bit worried for him," Delmin said. "It's not just me, he was a bit dotty, right?"

"I think Inspector Welling put him in a state," Veranix said.

"I can understand that. He confused the blazes out of me." Delmin shook his head. "Something really strange about his magic, though. It's not just an Uncircled thing. At least, I don't think so. Something connected to his hand."

"Hopefully I don't have to worry about that," Veranix said. "I would prefer not to deal with constables or inspectors at all."

"You know the best way to do that?"

"Yes, I do," Veranix said. "I'm going to meet up with Kaiana to figure out the details of following this kid out to Dentonhill to find the sellers."

"That really was not where I was going with that question."

"That may be," Veranix said. "But it's what I'm going to do. Regardless of what this imposter is doing, I'm going to keep Fenmere's paws off this campus."

Veranix didn't want to admit to Delmin how much he was looking forward to finding a few *effitte* pushers and giving them what for. The past few days had built up some righteous fury that needed a target.

Colin came into the Turnabout for the first time in weeks. Which was silly. Thinking about it, no one ever told him he was banned from the Turnabout or from Rose Street. But there had been a sense that it would be best if his face weren't seen for a while.

But now he was summoned.

Several Princes looked up and took notice of him. He gave a few nods to them, and went over to Kint behind the bar.

"You need something, Colin?" he asked.

"I need, Kint," Colin said. "Beer and two strikers."

"Two?" Kint asked.

"It's been that kind of day," Colin said.

"Usually it's a two-beer day," a woman said at his side. Deena, now with her captain stars and running his crew. Of course, all that was left of his old crew was Tooser, who sat over at a table with Theanne and a few young faces Colin didn't recognize. Tooser had his head down, not even looking at Colin.

Blazes, Colin hadn't seen him since the day Jutie got ironed and sent to Quarry.

"Let him be for now," Deena said, seeing where Colin's eyes were. "Ain't nothing good going to come from that."

"What would you know?"

"I know from having him at my right hand all this while."

"Should have been you at his."

"That ain't how it worked out, Tyson," she said. She raised up her hands. "I didn't come here to pitch a quarrel at you."

"Sporting of you," Colin said, taking the beer that Kint offered. "I came here because the bosses called for me. Wasn't even thinking about you."

"Blazes, Colin." She grabbed his arm and moved in closer. "Look, I ain't exactly proud of what I did to you, or how I got my stars." Telling the bosses about Veranix's friend, letting them know he had ties to the Thorn, it wasn't something Colin was going to forget anytime soon.

"You did what you had to. Bosses asked and you told, right? I did the same, sworn on Rose Street." Colin made the motion of shrugging it off and sipped his beer. "It's how it goes, Deena. Just keep your eye on your crew, hmm?"

She smiled nervously. "I saw that pigeon they sent over to be on your crew. Seems like you got some teaching to do."

"We'll have to see," Colin said. "So, if you saw that, you know what this is about? Why they called me in after a couple quiet months?"

"I don't know anything," she said. She lowered her voice. "Look, do you really have something tight with the Thorn?"

"I wouldn't say tight."

"Well, if you see him, ask him why the blazes he killed a stick and beat the skulls of two more, including that Left you're so fond of."

"I heard about that," Colin said. "I can tell you, wasn't the Thorn."

"Don't sell me that, Tyson. I saw it. The Thorn did it."

This was going to be trouble.

"Sewage like that ain't going to make anyone's life in Aventil any easier," Deena said. "Surely you can see that."

"No argument here," Colin said.

Kint dropped the two strikers in front of Colin. "Eat up."

Just as Colin picked up the first, Hotchins came out from the back. "Oy, Tyson. Let's have a word."

Colin took a bite and put it back down. "Keep those for me, Kint," he said. "I'm going to want them later."

Tripper's day had been a damned waste of time, with those two inspectors getting underfoot, the captain being more concerned with the folks from the Tournament, and no word from the hospital ward about the Left. They wouldn't even let him sit in there with him.

Finally Holcomb had gotten sick of Tripper and the rest of the Loyals, and put them out on footpatrol. "Lots happening out there. Need the show of color. If you're on your feet, you can walk a patrol."

Tripper sent Pollit and Wheth out together, and kept Jace on the inspectors. Blazes, Jace could probably watch over them better than anyone else. The strange one was his brother, after all. He might actually listen to Jace.

Tripper had to admit those two inspectors weren't all bad, considering how things could have gone. They were annoying, but they were at least interested in doing an investigation, even if it was damn obvious that the Thorn had done it. He had no clue why they were bothering looking beyond that. Jace had done the right thing, bringing in his strange brother, though. Anyone else would have been lazy or corrupt.

Like the rest of the stationhouse.

That was why Benvin brought the squad together. Because they were better than that. So Tripper was going to do something. Something even the Left had balked at.

He walked up the steps to Saint Julian's, taking a moment to drop a couple prayer tokens at the statue's feet. A prayer for the Left, and another for Mal. Mal had been a good stick and a good friend.

A sick feeling coursed through Tripper's stomach. Mal had a sister who lived over in Colton. Tripper had met her a couple of times. Odds were, with the Left still in long sleep, nobody went to tell her that her brother was dead. Unless Jace had handled it. He doubted Captain Holcomb did. At best, he had sent a page with a dry, lifeless letter.

Tripper would go see her later this evening, no matter what.

"My condolences, Sergeant." The priest had come up right by him. "I've heard about the events, but I don't know the details." He peered at the tokens Tripper had tossed. "One dead, one gravely injured."

"That's how it is," Tripper said, looking at the preacher. He had no idea how Pemmick could always look so damn serene. Even when his "peace meeting" with the Rabbits blew up in his face, Pemmick took it in stride. It was easy for him, though. Benvin had been the one poisoned. "The Left is laid up, Mal killed."

"I will add my prayers to yours, Sergeant. Especially for Lieutenant Benvin's recovery."

"You know who did this, don't you, Rev?"

"As a matter of fact, I don't," Pemmick said. "I've heard rumor and speculation, which I'm sure you have as well."

"It was the Thorn."

"That was the speculation."

"So, listen, Rev. You've got the ear of some of the street caps, right? Set up that disaster a few months ago."

"They see the church as a neutral territory, yes. I try to get them to listen to me. I believe that through them, God is testing my faith yet again."

"One of them knows who the Thorn is, where he holes up, or something."

The reverend nodded sagely. "I'd imagine that would be true." Though his eyes hinted he wasn't saying everything.

"You may even know who."

"What I may or may not know is my own business. Business which is a sacred pact between the souls of this community and the saints."

He definitely knew something.

"I'm talking about a killer of sticks, Rev," Tripper urged.

"And I'm talking about my ability to minister to the people who live in Aventil. Including the gangs. That requires trust in me. Trust of the people and the trust of the saints."

"But you got to—"

"Sergeant, we may possess the same underlying goal—peace in this neighborhood. But do not think for a moment that means I would betray my faith for your betterment."

"The betterment of everyone—"

"As defined by you. Not by my faith."

"Do I need to take you down to the station?"

"Would you try that? Is your soul in such a parlous state you would take an ordained reverend out of his own church without just charge? You would violate sanctity?"

Tripper shook his head. "You ever hear the name Reverend Ollicar?" He would bet that the priest had no sense of the history of these streets.

"I can't say that I have."

"Look into it. Ask your friends in the Knights." Tripper stalked off to the door. "There's sides to these streets, preacher, and you've picked yours."

"I've chosen the path of the saints, Sergeant. And I know that's never an easy path." Tripper turned back to him, seeing the priest's frustratingly calm face. "Besides, you have your own ear on the street. Why don't you go ask her what she knows? She doesn't carry the burdens of oath that I do."

The damned preacher knew about Yessa. And if he knew, Tripper wondered who else knew. Were there any damn secrets in Aventil? Or was Tripper the one on the outside of all of them? He knew damn well the whispers the rest of the stationhouse made.

"You made your call," Tripper said. "When we bring in the Thorn, you might find yourself in irons right there with him. And no church doors are going to protect you from that."

"Go with God, then," Pemmick said. "May he show more mercy than you."

Kaiana waited outside the tetchball pitch while the match raged on. She only paid cursory attention to the game itself, though it was clear that Pirrell was beating the stuffing out of whoever they were playing. Probably the most interesting thing to watch was Jiarna in the stands, whose emotional investment in every play was a sight to behold. She shouted, screamed, and cheered like she had bet money on the game. Kaiana didn't understand it, but she had to admire the pure enthusiasm of it. Phadre, for his part, was engaged in the match, but couldn't come close to the same level of energy.

Gorm spotted her and came down from the stands.

"Took you long enough," she said.

"I came when I saw you," he said. "We're level, ain't we?"

"Level?" she asked. Must be the slang in his city. "If this all works out, we'll see."

"What do you mean 'we'll see'?" He shook his head and started to walk away, then came back. "That ain't fair, lady. You got to let me know—"

"Not up to me, Gorm," she said.

"Well, who the stones is it up to?"

"Come with me."

She led him over by the east gates to one of the blossom trees hidden away behind some hedges.

"If you turn me over to the prefects or the boards, I'm ruined, you hear me?"

"You should have thought about that before."

"It was a stupid thing, and we shouldn't—"

"You've got that right. You're lucky I'm feeling nice to you."

"How are you—" He paused. "You haven't turned me over to them, have you?"

"To the prefect or the school boards? Not yet." She hardened her eyes at him. "But Misters Lash and Rennie will be reporting to them if I don't check in with them later."

"Are we just going to stand under this tree?"

"Wait."

An arc of lightning danced around them, and then Veranix dropped down from the tree in a flash of smoke and fire. Or, the Thorn did, since he was in full aspect, with his hood covering his face.

Gorm jumped, and Veranix shot the rope out like a viper, coiling loosely around his neck. "So this is the idiot who wanted to try *effitte*," he said. He was making his voice deeper, probably with magic, and adding a bit of an echo to it. It was an absurd bit of theater, and Kaiana did her best not to laugh.

"He's the one," she said.

Gorm clutched at the rope around his neck, pulling uselessly at it. "You turned me over to the Thorn? Isn't that worse?"

"What do you know about it, Gorm?" Veranix asked.

"I heard you—don't kill me, all right? I won't do anything with *effitte* ever again."

Veranix's face twitched a little. The fact that this kid thought of the Thorn as a killer didn't sit well with him. Kaiana knew he had been troubled with the imposter out there, but in that instant his face betrayed just how much.

"I wouldn't need to, Gorm. *Effitte* would probably do the job just fine."

"I didn't know! We don't have that stuff at Glennford! We just thought—"

"Enough gibbering, Gorm," Veranix said. "Nice and simple. You're going to go out that gate and go to your seller. You buy some *effitte* and you walk away. You bring it back to Miss Nell here and then you pray to every saint you've heard of that this will be the last time you ever do something so foolish."

"Just . . . just buy it and walk away?"

"That's all. I can trust you to keep your eye on him afterward, Miss Nell, and then destroy his purchases?"

Kaiana nodded, doing her part for the showmanship. "If that helps you."

"Then let's not waste any more time," Veranix said. As the rope uncoiled from Gorm's neck, Veranix leaned in close. "I'm giving you a chance, Gorm. Try not to disappoint me." With another flash of light and smoke, he leaped out of sight. The theatrics really were a bit much.

"You heard him," Kaiana said, dragging Gorm out of the sequestered hedges. She pointed to the east gate. "Let's go buy some *effitte*."

Chapter 9

THE LATE SUMMER SUN hung low, creating a harsh glare through the western window of the squad office. This was never a problem at the Inemar stationhouse, where the buildings were far too tall and densely packed to allow the setting sun to be seen through the window. Minox found it unpleasant to work at the desk he had claimed for himself—one that had belonged to a fellow named Arch, killed in the line of duty some months back. The rest of Benvin's squad, including Jace, were out of the office on patrol duty. Minox understood the necessity—the streets of Aventil were packed with visitors, and the environment fostered by the University's massive athletic competition was volatile. Minox was shocked that Captain Holcomb had not requested aid from other neighborhoods.

Shocked, but not surprised. In his brief assessment of Captain Holcomb, he noted a strange combination of pride and lethargy in the man. He was quite content to run his stationhouse in a haphazard and disorganized way, and clearly resented any outside interference.

"You two are still here?" Holcomb asked when Minox and Rainey had come to his office shortly after noon bells. "I thought you'd have cleared out by now."

"We've not identified or arrested Lieutenant Benvin's attacker."

"Didn't you have a room full of folks saying it was the Thorn?" He picked idly at his teeth. "We've already got an All-Eyes out for the man, so what's there more for you all? Head on home."

Rainey had fielded the response, as she was better at dealing with obstinate people than Minox was. "We're not satisfied with that as a proper identification."

"Yeah, well, we all want to know who the Thorn is. We'll get him, and I'll shake his hand for getting rid of the Rabbits, and then lock him down a hole."

"Captain, I don't think—"

"Just go home, and tell Brace we're all set, thanks."

Captain Holcomb acted like he was friendly with Captain Cinellan, which Minox found unlikely. Minox could not hold his tongue further. "The termination of this investigation, like any out-of-house investigation, is determined by our satisfaction in its completion, not yours." This wasn't entirely true, but it was honest enough for Captain Holcomb's purposes.

Holcomb waved them out of his office. "Then be about your business, and don't bother me anymore. I don't want to hear it."

So they had left him and continued to work out of Benvin's squad room, for all the good it had done.

"You're out of sorts," Inspector Rainey said as she came back in from an errand to the file room.

"We have not had as productive a day as I would have liked," Minox said. "I feel like we've barely gotten started assessing the situation, and the day is done."

She held up a note. "Captain Cinellan sent a page. He's giving us two more days of investigatory latitude here."

"You wrote to him requesting it." They originally had only a single day assigned to Aventil, despite the bluster Minox had made to Captain Holcomb.

"I knew you would want it." She sat on the corner of his desk and smirked. "Don't think I haven't noticed 'the Thorn' occasionally making an appearance on your board at the stationhouse."

"It's a subject which I've taken some interest in, certainly. I doubt you could use that as a justification to Captain Cinellan."

"No, of course not. I told him the truth, though. The situation in Aventil is complex and we need the time to find our footing. There's clearly a lot more to this than a standard out-of-house constable-death investigation. Most of this house—" She lowered her voice. "This house is downright unhealthy, but they've built a blazing strong Green Wall around it. From what I've seen, I'm not surprised Benvin got attacked. The only thing that surprises me is that we're not seeing an obvious stick in this house as the culprit."

"Laziness is this house's primary trait," Minox said. "Which is something I've known about for a long time, even before Jace was assigned here for his cadet year."

"How did that happen?" Rainey asked.

"I'm given to understand that this past year's cadet test had an unusual number of high-scoring candidates, so while Jace did well, he was not ranked high enough to claim his first choices. But I believe his presence here is Aventil's gain."

"Familial pride looks good on you."

"I'm not one for idle praise of relations, Inspector Rainey." He held up one of Benvin's files. "Lieutenant Benvin has nothing but commendations for Jace."

Rainey took it from him. "Including working extra shifts, not signing out or going home until late. That sounds familiar."

"It was a value instilled in us," Minox said. Though Jace had been so young when Father died, it was more likely he drew that habit off of Minox himself.

"Speaking of," Rainey said, standing up, "it is, technically, time to sign out. But I'm guessing you are not ready to leave just yet."

He nodded. "I wish to continue to sift through Benvin's files. We know that the killer is not the proper Thorn—"

"We're certain?"

"Quite," Minox said. "So the question is, who is enemy enough of Benvin to engineer this?"

"Or the Thorn," Rainey said. "Benvin and his squad are a convenient target, but the real goal is to bring the entire Aventil Constabulary on the Thorn's head."

"Which would have happened were it not for our investigation." It may still, Minox thought. "Sign out, Inspector. You've got a longer walk home than usual, after all."

"Don't stay here too late."

"I will stay only as late as Jace does, and return home with him."

"Fair enough. Tomorrow morning we should go to campus and talk some more with Mister Sarren."

"I think you should do that alone, perhaps," Minox said. "His magic professor does not approve of me."

"Tosh," Rainey said. "That isn't his business." She tapped on the desk. "Not too late."

"I already agreed to that."

"I heard what you agreed to. Make sure that Jace doesn't stay too late either. Give me a time."

He nodded. They had been partnered long enough for her to learn he could be very specific about obeying the letter of his promises. "Barring crisis, I will make sure we are both gone by nine bells."

Her eyes narrowed at him. She was likely considering what sort of loophole he was giving himself by allowing for a crisis. "Fine," she finally said with a slight smile. "I'll see you in the morning."

"My best to your husband and your family."

"And to yours," she said. With that, she was out the door.

The sun was now out of Minox's eyes. He took out his pipe and tobacco from his coat pocket, and with a bit of magic, sparked a flame to light his pipe, and then lit the oil lamp on his desk. Situated for the moment, he dug into Benvin's files on the Aventil gang known as the Rose Street Princes. Specifically a street captain named Colin Tyson.

Hotchins didn't talk as he led Colin back through the alley to the basements of the Turnabout, where the bosses kept themselves apart from the captains and the rest of the Princes. This was where Old Casey kept his office, such as it was, as the proxy boss of the Princes.

Of course, Casey still answered to Vessrin, the supposed King of Rose Street—a man who had been a total recluse for years. Most Princes thought he was dead, or some sort of myth. The Thorn—just the idea of the Thorn—had pulled Vessrin back into the world, and he was taking an active hand again. He was afraid the Thorn was making a play for Aventil, and he wasn't going to be caught unaware.

In his paranoia, Vessrin had guessed exactly who the Thorn really was—Colin's cousin, the long-lost son of Cal Tyson, based entirely on the bow Veranix had been using out on the streets. Colin avoided confirming this point as best he could. But the only thing keeping Vessrin from sending a dozen Princes to wring Veranix's neck was that he had no idea who he was. "The son of Cal Tyson" was even more of a myth, an idea of a man, than the Thorn was. And no one would expect him to be a scrawny magic student in the University.

Unless one of the old guard got a real good look at him. According to Veranix, Gabe Jensett had known who he was right away. Fortunately Jensett ended up with a wrung neck before he could tell anyone.

If Vessrin ever saw Veranix . . . Colin didn't want to know what would happen. Vessrin would see the face of the man he betrayed in him, surely. Colin sometimes wondered if half of why Vessrin had sequestered himself was so he didn't have to look at Colin.

But all that, plus the fact that all the Princes knew Colin had ties to the Thorn, meant Vessrin didn't trust Colin one jot, and that was the real cause behind his Orchid Street exile.

The usual gang of underbosses gathered around the card table outside the office: Nints, Frenty, Bottin, and Giles. Colin wondered what the blazes these old boys did to earn the right to be bosses, living off the sweat and blood of the young Princes on the street.

"How's things on Orchid?" Frenty asked.

"Can't complain," Colin said.

"Good answer," Giles said. "We hear you've been hiding something."

"I'm an empty room, gentlemen," Colin said. "I don't know what you've heard. But why don't you ask me?"

The office door opened, and Vessrin came out with Old Casey.

"Jolly idea, Tyson," Vessrin said. He came up close to Colin, grabbing him by the nape of the neck. "So I'm going to ask you. Red Rabbits?"

"You're talking about Sotch," Colin said. "Yeah, I got her squirreled away, and she's brought in some more of her Rabbits—the last few that are still around, apparently."

"And you didn't share this with us, why?"

"I just hadn't yet."

"We heard from your boys, Tyson," Casey said. "They told us you took her to the preacher."

Colin's own crew. Of course he knew this crew wasn't really his, they didn't give a blaze about him. But even then, he didn't think they'd go talk to the bosses behind his back. There was going to have to be a reckoning over that.

"Yeah, I did," Colin said, keeping his best card face on. "She had a story about the Thorn killing Keckin and some of the others, and I wanted her to bring in the few boys she had left. I thought getting her to talk to the preacher, that would get more of the story out of her than twisting her myself. And I was right."

"So the Thorn went Rabbit hunting?"

"Preacher didn't think so." Colin wasn't lying in saying that. Leaving out details, but not lying. "He thinks there's some steve pretending to be the Thorn. Same story for who hit the Left and his squad."

"Preacher thinks that wasn't the Thorn?" Hotchins asked. "Half the 'hood saw it, including Deena. They all said it was the Thorn."

"I'm just telling you what the preacher thought," Colin said. "You want to know why he thinks that, you go ask him. But I got the impression Sotch's story didn't quite line up."

"So now," Vessrin said, "you're going to bring her and her Rabbits to us."

"Here?"

"Blazes, no, Tyson, not here," Vessrin said. "How stupid would it be, even with the Rabbits *wrecked*, for us to bring any one of them here."

"Yeah, I don't see Sotch or any of hers putting roses on their arms anytime soon."

"And why the blazes would we want that?" Vessrin asked. "Last thing we want is a bunch of new Princes of questionable loyalty. Right, Tyson?"

That felt like it was being spat in Colin's face.

"No, sir," Colin said.

"Yeah," Vessrin said, giving an ugly grin. "But we do want Sotch and whoever else she has. Rabbits cost us in that whole debacle a couple months back. Ain't that right, Frenty?"

"Not all the squabbles turned out so nice as your claiming Orchid, Tyson," Frenty said. "Lost a couple captains and lot more Princes."

"Arrick, I remember," Colin said. "So that's what you're looking for, hmm? Draw some blood on Sotch and whoever?"

"You got a problem with that?" Vessrin said. "It seems the only one making examples of the Rabbits is the Thorn. How's that look on us, eh?" Vessrin's claw of a finger poked Colin in the chest. "Blood was taken, blood's owed. Prince blood."

Colin looked down at that finger, still touching him in the sternum. He felt like he should be scared, Vessrin giving him so much guff, the other bosses staring knives at him.

But there wasn't an ounce of fear. Fear meant he respected these men, and he wasn't feeling much of that right now. He'd obey them, like a loyal Prince, but if this was how they were going to talk to him, after all these years, he didn't owe them an ounce more of himself than that.

"Whatever you need, Vessrin," Colin said. "Just tell me what you want."

"What crew is going to help Colin, Nints?" Vessrin asked.

"Cabie's," Nints said. Cabie was a decent bird, well-earned stars on her arm, though she and her crew worked out by Branch, holding the line again Hallaran's Boys. Like Colin, she stayed out there and never came around to the Turnabout no more. Now Colin wondered if she had soured someone's beer like he had.

"Well, send somebody to fetch Cabie," Vessrin said. "Then she and her crew can join you and yours, and you'll drag the last of those Rabbits to a special place we've got for them."

"Where's that?" Colin asked.

"Cabie'll know."

This plan was sounding increasingly stupid. One thing to just kill Sotch and her boys. Colin didn't have a beef with that. Blazes, even Sotch might agree it was fair. But to bring them to some other place, so Vessrin or whoever could mess with them? And bring them through the streets, while it was crowded with Uni folks for the games?

That was all kinds of idiocy.

But Colin was a loyal Prince.

"All right, then," he said. "Let's get to it."

Vessrin patted Colin on the cheek. "I knew—I told all these boys—that we could count on you, Colin. Glad I was right."

Two spirited tetchball matches made for a cracking afternoon. Jiarna almost felt guilty, that she was supposed to be "working," in terms of this drug-busting business of Veranix's. She didn't really understand why Kaiana and him were so devoted to this fight, but some things didn't necessarily need a point. She understood it was important to them, that it was a calling, and that was enough. She had spent the last four years in academic devotion, and done that entirely for its own sake. Now the fruits of that labor were ripening. In a month she and Phadre would be engaged in deeper study of scientific and mystical connections with Professor Salarmin at Trenn College in Yin Mara—possibly the second greatest mind in Druthal on the subject.

She had to admit, as much as she loved pure academia and science, there was something visceral and exciting about being a part of Veranix's team.

Veranix might be academically dim—few men were her peer the way Phadre was—but she wouldn't deny the sight of him charging after Jensett like a sinner from the blazes had stirred something in her. Nothing she would ever act on, not having also met Phadre. But the prospect of having another moment like when she and Phadre saved the campus made her heart hammer in her chest.

In the meantime, the tetchball had been a solid thrill. Pirrell had roundly trounced Erien; it wasn't even fair. Two triple jacks, almost a dozen doubles, and the poor Erien players were at a loss to even pull down a runner. Shame the Pirrell boys were a bunch of uncouth rowdies. They may be great players, but they were a long way off from being the Gracious Gentlemen of Study and Sport that, in her mind, college boys ought to be.

Astonic had given a good match to the High Academy of Korifina, and that one had been tight and thrilling. Both teams had outstanding fieldwork, barely letting a point on the board in every interval. Korifina squeaked it out at the end, and Jiarna had cheered her throat raw the whole time. Frankly, she hadn't cared who won, it was a fantastic match to watch.

"Where are we to, now?" Phadre asked, hooking his arm into her elbow.

"That is an excellent question," Jiarna said. "There are several social houses throwing parties tonight. Grand Sable, again. Silverlight. Twin Moons. I think the Twin Moons is most promising."

"And why is that?" Phadre gave her a wry smile. "Is it because they have a cask of Fuergan whiskey?"

"No, it's because they're specifically hosting today's

event winners. So that part will draw the most diverse crowd, making it more likely to find information about the drug sales."

"And the whiskey?"

"Well, we'll have to blend in, darling," Jiarna said. "This is a burden I accept."

Twin Moons was a Gentlemen's Social House, and one where Jiarna had found their parties rather enjoyable in her time, and not just because the Twin Moons boys tended to have impeccable taste in imported whiskey and tobacco. Twin Moons, as opposed to more raucous houses like Whisper Fox, imposed a level of academic excellence. Their boys had to maintain top marks, even though a majority of them studied law or literature or some other useless thing. They were engaging boys, for the times when she had craved distraction, but little more. Still, heads above most of the other social house boys.

"Is that Jiarna Kay?" one Twin Moons boy called out as they approached the front stoop of the social house. "Why the blazes are you still here? I heard you received your letters."

"Of course I have," she said. She recognized him, but his name completely escaped her memory. "But it's the Grand, I wasn't going to miss that."

"Who's this lucky one on your arm?"

"Phadre Golmin," Phadre said, offering his hand to the boy.

"Caspar Caldermane." Caspar, that was it.

"Caldermane?" Phadre asked. "We're booked on a Caldermane carriage to go to Yin Mara."

"My uncle is *that* Caldermane," Caspar said. "Not that I probably won't be headed to work under him once I letter up. Yin Mara? You're leaving Maradaine, Miss Kay?"

"Trenn College made us a glorious offer for teaching and research," Jiarna said.

"You're going to be bored to tears, dear," Caspar said. "Have you been to Yin Mara before?"

"Never," Phadre said.

"It's a village compared to Maradaine. An absolute village." He shrugged. "But pass me your travel plans. I can get you the luxury package for regular cost."

"I wouldn't refuse that," Jiarna said.

Caspar smiled and waved them inside. "Let's get you both set up, shall we?"

In moments she and Phadre both found whiskeys in one hand and cigarros in the other. "See?" she said to Phadre. "Blending in." Plenty of others—students from every corner of Druthal—were clustered in the Twin Moons sitting rooms, while musicians in the corner played a jaunty number on viol and clarinet. Caspar went off to get a taper to light their smokes.

"If we must," Phadre said lightly. "Is he all right?"

"Caspar?" she asked. "He's fine, for a boy who will never be burdened with worry in his life. But he's got a solid head."

"Not the type who'd get mixed up in *effitte*, though."

"No, true," she said. "But he is the type that would mop up for his mates if they did."

"Every social house needs one of those."

Caspar came back with the taper.

"So who were today's winners, Caspar?" she asked their host as he lit her smoke up. It was good tobacco, not Little East corner den stuff.

"U of M won the oars in the river, of course." He pointed to one clutch of boys in one corner, also Twin Moons men.

"Well done," she said, taking a draw on the cigarro.

"I can't claim anything there. Pirrell and Korifina took their matches in the tetch," Caspar said.

"Knew that, we were there."

"You went to tetch instead of oars?"

"Tetch is my game."

"Fine. What else? That girl from RCM is the front placer in Floor and Beam so far." He pointed to the honey-skinned young woman talking to one of his brethren. "Hey, Royal!"

She turned to them. "Is that what you call me?"

"You're our guest," Caspar said. "People want to say hello."

"Oh, I'm being shown off," she said. She extended a hand to Jiarna. "Emilia Quope."

"Charmed," Jiarna said. "Jiarna Kay, and my friend—"

"Phadre, Phadre Golmin." He put out his hand with a bit too much enthusiasm for Jiarna's taste, though she could hardly blame him. Miss Quope definitely had an allure.

"Phadre and Jiarna?" Her eyebrow went up sharply. "We have a mutual acquaintance."

"Do we?" Jiarna asked. "Who is that?"

"Veran Calbert? No, Veranix. I met him last night, and . . . you wouldn't happen to know where I could find him?"

"He's very busy tonight," Phadre said. Jiarna sent a sharp elbow into his side.

"Busy with?" Emilia asked. She stared pointedly at Phadre.

"Didn't ask," Jiarna said quickly. "Who can keep track of that boy, you know?"

"Who, indeed?" Emilia said absently. "If you'll excuse me." She made her way to the front door.

"Eh, is she leaving?" one of the other partiers—part of a loutish-looking group—shouted at Caspar.

"Ain't yours or mine to bother," Caspar snapped back. He turned back to Phadre and Jiarna, indicating the loutish group with a nod of his head. "Blokes from Pirrell won the Quint and Archery today. Blighters."

"Good day for Pirrell, though," Phadre said.

"Doesn't mean they aren't a bunch of blighters," Caspar said. "We'll give them theirs soon enough."

"Right," Jiarna said. "If we beat Korifina and they beat whoever they play tomorrow."

"You're talking tetchball again, girl."

"What do you mean, then?"

He nearly gasped. "Oh, blazes, I shouldn't have said anything."

"What are you talking about, Caspar?" she said.

"Nothing, nothing. Look, you're going to be teaching at Trenn, so I understand—"

"We're not faculty yet, man," Phadre said. "You planning a prank on the Pirrell boys or something?"

"Oh, saints, no," Caspar said, though the look on his face made it seem like now he was considering it. "All right, lock your jawboxes on this, hear?"

"Locked," Jiarna said.

"There's a plan—the Twin Moons and Grand Sables from the various schools are putting this together. Night after tomorrow at midnight—"

Suddenly a pair of arms wrapped around Caspar and lifted him off the ground. "U of M!" the owner of the arms shouted.

Caspar just hooted in return. The arms' owner—a beefy sort who probably was one of the rowers—leaned in on Jiarna and Phadre. "I've got to steal this one away for a bit."

"Steal away," Jiarna said, sipping at her whiskey. It was, indeed, quite fine.

"What do you think that was?" Phadre asked.

"Not sure, but it might be worth finding out."

"As part of our investigation," Phadre said with a wry smile.

"Absolutely," she said, though she hardly convinced herself of the sincerity. "Let's mix it up, see if we shake anything." She pulled a draw off her smoke. "But we should make sure we dance before the evening is done."

"Yes, ma'am," Phadre said enthusiastically.

She kissed Phadre on the cheek, and moved into the crowd. One eye, still, she kept on Caspar. She couldn't shake the feeling that what he was about to tell them would be quite interesting.

Erno Don held the last note of his song a bit longer than he ought to have, but the ladies in the crowd at this Dentonhill shanty bar loved it. None of them really noticed that his throat cracked a little at the end, but that was the kind of rot-beer place this was. They were all deep in their cups or half-tranced on *effitte*.

"Thank you kindly," he said. "I'm going to yield the stage now. A wandering minstrel never outstays his welcome. But if you, well, would like to seek me later . . . you know where to find me."

He sauntered off, nodding and waving to the crowd, over to the manager at the bar.

"Not bad," the barman said. "You could do a bit more, another half-crown."

"One set a night, brother," Erno said. "I've got to keep my throat filled with silver. That means I use it sparingly."

"Your call, if you'd rather have silver in your throat than your pocket. Beer?"

"I told you, brother. I need to protect my throat. I'm heading up."

"Sleeping already? It's pretty early."

"I said nothing about sleep. I'm heading up. I won't be sleeping for hours yet."

The barman nodded. "Of course. Have a good night."

Erno went out and around to the iron stairs that led to the rented rooms above the bar, whatever it was called. The bars in Dentonhill were much the same, regardless. So were the rented rooms.

His room was at the end of the hallway, right over the alley. He noticed the door was open a little as he approached. That was hardly a surprise. He was expecting there to be company waiting for him.

Three of them, in fact. Standing around like a bunch of meaty goons, which is just what they were.

"You're a bit impatient, Bell. I was going to come over to your place."

"Sorry, Erno," Bell said. "We've got a tip about the last of the Rabbits, including that slan Sotch, hiding out in Aventil. Time to move."

"Oh, if we're hunting Rabbits, then I can see why you're so excited." Erno went over to the trunk by his bed and opened it up, taking out all the gear for his costume. "Don't forget, you're paying for the show, not the kill." Bell had already tried to run around on him over paying the full fee, just because the stick Left hadn't been killed. Didn't matter, Bell still got the results he really wanted.

"Whatever you need, Erno," Bell said. "What you're doing is worth the price."

Erno got on the cloak, hood, and bow. "Then what are we waiting for? The Thorn is ready for his performance."

Veranix watched from the top of a tenement building as the Glennford kid went down the alley. True to his word, there was the seller—a young woman in a work skirt, leather apron, and shirtsleeves. She looked respectable enough, could easily walk on campus looking like she worked the staff, or even blend in as a student, especially this week. She certainly didn't look like she used. That made a big difference.

The buy went quick and clean, and the kid skittered off. Veranix kept an eye on him just long enough to make sure he got back to the main street, and that Kaiana grabbed him by the elbow and escorted him back to campus.

So the tip was solid, and the idea that this woman was a seller who brought stuff on campus was credible. His first thought was just to dive in and take her down. She didn't look like a fighter—she wasn't obviously armed—and Veranix could take her out of commission and divest her of stash in moments.

That would be easy, but wouldn't change anything.

He needed to learn more of what she knew. That meant getting her to talk.

Fortunately, his reputation on the streets lately was that of a heartless killer.

He leaped down to the alley, willing the rope to wrap around a chimney pipe as he dropped. He dove down to her, unshrouding just as he closed the distance, and grabbed her by the front of her shirt and apron. In the same moment, he willed the rope to pull him back up to the edge of the tenement roof.

She startled, but before she could even properly scream,

he had her dangling four stories above the cobblestones. With the rope anchoring him to the roof, he held her out at arm's length, her legs thrashing uselessly in the open air.

"Thought we could have a word," he said.

Terror in her eyes transformed to anger, and she produced a knife from underneath her apron.

"By all means, stab me in the arm," he said coldly. "See how well you fare after that."

She hesitated, knife still poised.

"Drop it."

She scowled, but obeyed.

"So you've been selling to students," he said. "Didn't word get around that I don't like it when you cross Waterpath?"

"Hey, they came to me," she said. "I didn't cross anything."

"And how did they know to come to you, hmm?"

"Word gets around, and these kids want to tan their skulls, who am I to say no?"

"Well, now I want something," Veranix said. "Where does your supply come from?"

"Like I'm gonna spill to you."

"Spill?" Veranix let the rope go slack just for a moment, so they dropped almost a foot. "You want to talk about—"

"All right!" she cried out. The shirt he was holding her by was starting to tear. "There's a basement den, alley next to the barber shop on Allison! The dealer boss hangs out there!"

"Thank you kindly," Veranix said, and let her go. She screamed as she plummeted to the ground. Just before she landed, he reached out magically and grabbed hold of her. She hovered mere inches above the ground for a moment, and then he let her go again.

"Ah!" she cried out as she landed face first on the stone. "You boke by doze, you bastad!"

"All part of the service," he called back, and giving her a jaunty salute, he shrouded and leaped off to Allison Street.

Finding the alley was easy enough, same with the

basement door. There seemed to be just the one door, down a few steps, and the only windows were small, dark, and ground level. If there was another way in or out, Veranix couldn't see it.

So the main door it was. The main door, clearly guarded by a shaggy-bearded, muscle-bound heavy.

Stealth was not an option.

Veranix dropped down to the alley, about twenty feet from the guard.

"Hey."

The guard lurched forward at him, and Veranix shot the rope out, wrapping it around the guard's neck. With a magic-assisted yank, he threw the guard against the opposite wall.

That was a bit harder than he had expected it to be, took more out of him. The rope wasn't as powerful as it used to be, he needed to remember that.

The guard made no sign that he was going to be engaging anyone else for the rest of the night. He was still breathing, though.

Veranix tried the door. Latched, from the inside. Maybe even a double bar. There were no subtle options. No amount of kicking would knock that down.

He didn't need to kick it in, though.

This didn't require finesse, but it needed power. He took a moment, letting the *numina* flow into his body, through the cloak and the rope, through the air around him, and built it up like drawing and holding breath. Slow and steady. He built it up, letting it fill him until he was ready to overflow.

Then he turned that power into raw force, and channeled it out through his hands.

The door flew in, off its hinges, and through the back of the room. It was like a crack of thunder, shattering half the windows. Delmin, wherever he was, surely felt the *numina* shock wave.

Veranix dove through the door, drawing his bow as he hit the ground. Whoever was in here would be dumbfounded for a moment, and he needed to use that while he could. Two heavies were in the hallway, staring at the hole in the wall. Veranix took two quick shots, hitting them each in the leg. He charged down the hallway, nocking the next arrow. Another guy came up around the corner with a crossbow, but Veranix had the drop on him. He screamed as the arrow hit him in the chest, and Veranix knocked him in the teeth as he went past.

The hallway opened up to a large chamber, where there were several crates stacked in the center of the room. Shelves with hundreds of glass vials lined one wall—some with *effitte*, some empty. A desk sat in the corner of the room, with journals and piles of goldsmith notes. He raced over to the crates, opening one up. It was filled with jars of *effitte*. Gallons and gallons of it.

"Sweet saints," Veranix whispered. This was the biggest den he had ever found.

"It's like I always say, boys," a rough voice growled. "Big fish requires the right bait."

Veranix looked up, and saw a grizzled old soldier—scars and leathery muscle—coming through the door with a score of similar-looking gentlemen. A dozen more came in from the other entranceway. All of them had knives, crossbows, knucklestuffers, and cudgels, and they were blocking the only ways out.

"The bounty is for his head," the leader said, "so try not to bruise it too badly."

"Right," Veranix said. "Can we all agree, gentlemen, not in the face? Some decorum."

"The only thing we agree on is this is your last night plaguing us, Thorn."

"Well, I never agreed to that," Veranix said. With some hard and sloppy magic, he sent the crates flying across the room to the main entrance, crashing them into that set of heavies. Despite them being pummeled with wood, broken glass, and *effitte*, that probably would only slow them down for a short time. And that took more out of him than he was ready for.

Turning to the smaller group, Veranix quickly drew three arrows and fired them in rapid succession, aiming for the ones with crossbows. Most immediate threat. He took one out, and injured the second before that group got too close to keep firing.

Veranix flipped back to avoid the front man, a fast little rat with two knives, and put up his bow while taking out his staff. He whipped it around before his feet hit the ground, cracking the kid across the skull. No time for games or banter, he jabbed the dazed kid in the chest to bowl over the one behind him.

Veranix spun the staff in wide arcs, as fast as his hands could move. Still at least nine of this group, and the only advantage he had right now was reach. Hard, fast hits, power over precision.

"Surround him!" one shouted.

"No, thank you," Veranix said. Another quick and dirty magic blast—knocking them all to the floor, but nothing stronger than that. He followed that up with magicking up a sticky tar, coating them and the floor with the stuff. Those boys weren't going anywhere.

That left him nearly drained, as far as magic was concerned. Even with the cloak, it would take him a few minutes to recover. And the other twenty were getting up for their portion of the bout.

"So," Veranix said, holding up the staff, "anyone want to run?"

Chapter 10

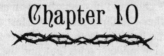

THERE WERE TOO MANY OF THEM.

For a brief time, Veranix used that against them. Twenty toughs, more muscle than brains or finesse, he got them to knock each other instead of him. He was faster, he was smarter, and with his staff, he had longer reach.

But there were too many of them, and they wouldn't stay down.

He thrust backward with his staff, knocking one of them in the chest, and then swept it to one side while dropping into a lunge. One more was knocked off his feet while a punch went over his head.

Someone else hit him in the side. He reeled back, taking a wild swing at whoever hit him. He didn't connect with anything, throwing him off balance. He corrected, using his staff to keep himself on his feet. Then the staff was wrenched out of his hands. A pair of hands grabbed his head and brought it down upon a knee.

Crying out, he charged forward, tackling the knee's owner and bringing them down to the ground. Despite his head swirling, he pulled himself up enough to pummel that person in the chest, and then face, and face again.

Two bruisers grabbed his arms and pulled him up in the air. He couldn't pull free of either of them; they had him tight. Another one moved in front and delivered a series of blows to his chest and stomach.

He couldn't breathe.

They were all laughing.

He brought up his legs in the air, first to block the punches, and then to kick as hard as he could. He connected with someone's chin, and pushed off—with as much magic as he could gather—to flip himself over, fast and hard. The two bruisers who had him by the arms didn't let go, so they went with him. He landed on his feet, and they dropped on their heads. He stomped on one of them while dodging his own staff being swung at him.

He risked the last bit of magic power he had to throw sparks and light in the face of the guy who had his staff. That guy cried out and clutched at his face. Veranix snatched his staff away and then smashed the guy with it.

Veranix's back was to the wall now. And there were still at least ten of them, including the leader, still standing in the doorframe.

"That all you got?" Veranix shouted.

The leader was about to say something, when he was yanked out of view. His screams were followed with a horrific bone-crunching noise.

All the other bruisers turned to the doorframe, giving Veranix a chance to slam another one of them with the staff. A fist connected with Veranix's face, hot blood coming out of his nose. Veranix lashed out at the closest bruiser, grabbing him by the hair and introducing his face to the brick wall.

"I thought we agreed not in the face!" he shouted.

Seven or eight left. Veranix wasn't counting or seeing all that well anymore. Blood in his eyes, brain a blur.

Another bruiser was suddenly yanked out of sight, but this time Veranix saw a rope pull him away. He instinctively grabbed at his own rope, just to make sure it was still there. He didn't have any magical strength left to use it, of course. Napranium only did so much.

"So there's a bounty," Veranix snarled at the remaining men. "If you want it you're going to have to earn it."

A rope sang out from the doorway, wrapping around the neck of one of the farthest bruisers. He was pulled off his feet, bowling over a couple of his compatriots.

Suddenly a gray figure leaped out from the hallway, and in a flurry of feet and fists, four of those bruisers were rendered insensate.

"Who in the—" one of the remaining ones started, but he was interrupted by a high kick to his chin, and then another to his chest.

One more guy decided this was his moment, and dove at Veranix with two knives out. Veranix brought up his staff to block him, but before the guy closed the distance, a rope was around one arm and he was pulled down to the ground. He struggled to stand, and got a brutal boot to the skull.

Figure in gray. Rope. This meant something familiar, but Veranix couldn't piece the fuzzy thoughts together.

He could barely stay on his feet. He let the staff fall to the ground.

The gray figure was busy with the last two bruisers, but they were swinging at empty air while she was landing wrenching blows.

She. Definitely a she. Veranix's instincts screamed danger, even though he didn't know why.

Veranix fumbled to pull up his bow, nock an arrow. He had it up, even if he couldn't focus on anything but a blur of gray.

The last of the bruisers were on the ground, out cold or dead.

"Stay back," he said, drawing back the arrow.

"Don't be absurd," the figure said, coming closer.

Veranix fired, but she dodged the arrow without even breaking stride. The bow was taken out of his hands before he could get another arrow out.

"Come to claim your prize?" he wheezed out.

Her face came into focus. Emilia—no, Blackbird.

"Saints, Thorn, you're in a state."

"I won't go easy," he said. Despite that, his knees gave out.

"I'm sure you won't," she said, catching him as he collapsed.

He tried to struggle as she pulled him out, but he could barely move his arms, and by the time she had him out the door, he couldn't even keep his eyes open.

Cabie was a scrapper, having made her bones in the Princes by fighting in knuckledusters in basements all over town. Her nose was twisted three ways, but she could take a hit and give three more back any given day. Her crew never did hustling or paper jobs, they were around for cracking skulls and holding the line against Hallaran's Boys. She was a captain Colin respected, and the bosses knew that. That was probably why they put her on this job with him. He waited outside the Turnabout—with a couple of the boss's bigger heavies keeping an eye on him—as she approached with her crew of brawlers.

"Heya, Tyson," she said with a several-gapped grin. "How's the word?"

"It is what it is," he said.

She pulled him in a quick embrace, thumping him on the back. "Hear that." In a low whisper she added, "This Orchid Street business they did to you is pure sewage."

"Appreciate that," Colin said.

"It's what it is, though." She whistled to her boys. "Let's walk."

The crowd, despite being a collection of Uni revelers deep into their cups, made a path for them rather easily. Clearly none of them wanted a piece of Cabie and her boys.

"So, last of the Rabbits, I hear?"

"That is what we've got. They're holed up in our flop, with their last captain, Sotch."

"Blazes," Cabie said. "You didn't swear on safe haven or something?"

"Nah, nothing like that."

"Good. That's just bad hoodoo, I'll tell you. Already bad enough, scrapping someone under your roof."

"I'm glad you get it," Colin said.

"I do. Still, we got orders. I just wanted you to know . . . blazes, there's a lot of not right in this." She sighed, glancing at her boys. "Still, job'll get done. Your boys are there with them."

"Such as they are."

"Problem with your boys?"

"They ain't really mine. They're just the ones I've got."

She nodded. "And this is a haul job. This is some ugly."

"We got a wagon or something to drop them into?"

"I ain't a fool, course we do."

"And you know where we're taking them."

"I know. But . . . you ain't supposed to know. That's what I've been told."

"This ain't what Princes are supposed to be, you know? Certainly not between each other."

"I know, Tyson," she said. "But it is what it is."

They were now at the sew-up's office where Colin's crew made their flop, and Cabie turned to her crew.

"All right, let's do this clean. Give them a choice to come without bruises. On my lead if it goes elsewhere. Ockie, stay here and eye out for the wagon. Give a call when she's in line."

Ockie, presumably, gave a nod, while the rest went into the sew-up's.

"You good, Tyson?" she asked him.

"I ain't ever a stranger to a brawl, Cabie. Wish it didn't have to happen."

"Maybe it won't. They could come quiet. Rabbits are already broken."

"Sotch won't, and the rest'll follow suit."

"Their choice."

They came up the stairs to the flop, where Ment and Vandy were standing watch over Sotch and the Rabbits— three of them—who were sitting around a plate of sausages and bread from the Old Canal.

"Where's Kiggy and Sella, and the new kid?" Colin asked. Might as well have as many hands available as possible.

"Went down for a sip," Vandy said.

"Blazes is this?" Sotch asked as soon as Cabie and her boys were in view.

"Time for you and your boys to come, Sotch," Colin said.

"Come where?"

"Well, you can't be staying here any longer," Colin said. "This here is a Prince flop, and you ain't Princes. So you're going to go somewhere else."

"Where is that?" Sotch asked, her hand drifting to the knife on the table.

"Where our bosses said," Cabie said. "So come along."

"Like blazes."

"You got two choices, skirt. You can come quiet, or you can come with a few things broken. Either way, you're going where we're taking you."

"Best do what she says, Sotch," Colin said.

"Damn it, Prince, I trusted you."

"Why the blazes did you do that?"

Sotch grabbed the knife and flung it right at Colin's chest. Before he got a chance to move, Cabie's hand moved like a bolt of lightning, snatching the knife in the air and hurling it right back, landing it in the thigh of one of the other Rabbits.

"Now, look," Cabie said while the Rabbit dropped to the ground wailing. "The bosses want you to come, and come still breathing. But if we lose one or two along the way, that's the price of business."

"I'm gonna make one thing clear to you, slan," Sotch said, yanking the knife out of her compatriot's leg. "I'm a goddamned Red Rabbit, and I will not go quietly."

"She's right, she ran away screaming last time I saw her."

There was a sudden buzz through the air, and three of the Rabbits dropped to the ground, arrows in their chests. Colin looked up to the sky-top window, where a cloaked figure dropped down into the room.

"The Thorn!" Cabie shouted.

But it wasn't. Colin could see why people might be fooled, if they had only heard of him, seen a fleeting glance. But this was a fraud.

"At your service," he said with a flourish. With that, he threw something on the ground, and there was a flash of light and smoke.

"He's mine," Cabie snarled.

"He ain't—" Colin said, but before he said much else, he was slashed in the arm, Sotch rushing past him.

Cabie's boys jumped in on Sotch. Colin could barely see them; the smoke filled the room. He could hear smacks and grunts. Someone was getting beaten hard, but Colin couldn't tell who.

"Everyone get him!" Colin shouted. "He's a rutting fraud!"

"How dare you!" the fake Thorn said. A hand grabbed Colin through the smoke, and another punched him in the face. Colin grappled his attacker, pulled them in close.

It was Cabie.

"We're all turned around," he hissed.

"Grab Rabbits, get them out of here."

"Rabbits are probably dead, save Sotch," Colin said. The smoke was thinner where Sotch was, and Colin could see she was holding her own against Cabie's boys.

"Then get her out of here," Cabie said. "I've got this rutter."

She dove back into the smoke. Something else came flying out of there, landing in the stairs. Another flash, but this one came with flames instead of smoke.

"Rutting sewage," Colin said. He ran over to Sotch, grabbed her wrist and wrenched the knife out of it. Then he lifted her up and threw her over his shoulder.

"The blazes you doing?" she shouted, beating on his back.

"Saving your stupid life."

He ran at the far window and jumped through it. He and Sotch fell down, crashing through the awning onto a vegetable cart, Sotch taking the worst of the landing.

"Holy saints!" Ockie shouted. "What's going on?"

Colin forced himself to get on his feet, despite his back being nothing but pain. He pushed Sotch's dazed form over to Ockie. "Where's the wagon?"

"It's over there, but it can't get through the crowd," Ockie said. "But what—"

There was a crowd, all gawking at the spectacle. Colin couldn't blame them. He could feel blood oozing down his head, and there was smoke pouring out the windows of the upper floor of the sew-up. These Uni kids were getting quite a show.

Colin spotted Kiggy and Sella amongst the slack-jawed. "Hey, flat the street! We need that wagon!"

"Clear it!" Sella shouted immediately, pushing folks out of her way. "All of you, get out of the blazing way!"

Ockie threw Sotch over his shoulder. "I can run her."

"Do it, because—"

Another crash came behind them. Cabie, battered and bloodied, lay on the remains of the cart. Colin couldn't tell if she was still breathing.

He looked up to the window, where the fake Thorn was framed in the fire and smoke, bow drawn. He released the arrow.

It flew fast and true, sinking so deep into Sotch that it took Ockie down with her. They both tumbled to the ground.

"Well, that's the last of the Rabbits," he said, drawing another arrow. "But there's still Princes to play with."

Hands were on Veranix's person. Something was being poured into his mouth. Tastes both repulsive and familiar. Scents as well.

Someone was tending to him. The memory of being pummeled came back to him.

"Kai?" he called out hoarsely. "Where am I?"

"Kai?" The voice was definitely not Kaiana. "If I jealoused up, we'd have a problem."

"Jealoused up?" Veranix knew that voice. Emilia Quope. Blackbird. He grabbed the hand that was tending to his stomach and yanked it away, bolting up to his feet as he did.

His legs were not happy with this plan. Nor his arms or stomach. Everything reacted with pain.

Emilia Quope sat there in front of him, peeling his fingers off her hand and pushing him back down on the cot.

"Let's not do that, you're in no condition for it," she said.

"So is the bounty worth more if I'm alive, Blackbird?" he asked.

She sighed. "There is a bounty on your head, yes. Two thousand crowns, I understand. It doesn't really care about the condition you're in."

Veranix noticed she had resumed rubbing in some familiar-smelling oil on his stomach. He also noticed he had been completely stripped. "Then what are you . . . why . . . where?"

"These are excellent questions."

"Damn it, Blackbird—"

"Emilia." She stared hard at him. "My name is Emilia."

"And you're a killer and assassin who's taken me and . . . is that khenas oil?"

"It is."

Veranix had run out of khenas oil long ago, in his first year at the University. The stuff was almost magic, a Racquin circus remedy for bruises and injuries.

"Why are you rubbing me with khenas oil?"

"Because you took a beating like I've never seen, by Jox. You're lucky to be alive."

"Let me rephrase," Veranix said. "Why do you care? I mean, you tried to kill me yourself not that long ago."

"That was a job, Veranix," she said, pointedly using his name. "I don't kill people for the joy of it."

"But now the job is the bounty on my head, so—" He looked around the room they were in. A rather plain sleeping chamber. It could be a cell. "Does Fenmere want me on my feet when I'm brought to him?"

"What?"

"Don't think I won't—" He tried to sit up again, despite the screaming in his bones.

"You won't what, Veranix? You going to hie and hag with every bit of you shivvy?"

"I've fought my way out shivvier," he said. "And I wouldn't have to hie and hag if you hadn't have kecked me."

"Jox and Javer," she said, "You reckon I kecked you?" She smacked him across the head. "Lie your shivvy ass on the bed so I can get this in your bones."

"Saints," Veranix said. "I don't reckon anything no jot." He suddenly felt like he had relaxed a muscle he didn't know he had been holding tense for years. Emilia, despite being an assassin who had tried to kill him, talked just like his mother and the rest of the circus Racquin.

"Then sit down so I can rub this in."

"And after?"

"And after we'll get you more *oxaym*."

That was the familiar but unpleasant taste. His mother made him drink it whenever he hurt himself.

"Wait, wait," Veranix said, his brain still catching up to the world around him. "You really for truth pulled me from the pan?"

"For real truth," she said. She sighed again.

"Why?" he asked. "So you can get the bounty for yourself?"

"Sweet stones, no," she said. "You don't see it, do you?"

"See what?"

She rolled her eyes, grabbed the sides of his head and kissed him. Slow, long, deep. Veranix reeled for a moment, responding to the kiss out of instinct. For a moment, he forgot all about who Blackbird was or why he was upset with her. He even forgot the pain.

"That's what," she whispered when she pulled back.

"I'm even more confused."

"Damn it, Veranix," she said. "You're cute, charming, and stupid."

"That I know."

Pouring more oil in her hand, she started to rub on his

chest. "Swear to the road, I didn't know you were the Thorn until this morning." He didn't realize how badly bruised he was there. He didn't think anything was broken, which was a miracle all on its own. The oil helped a lot.

The rubbing from Emilia was rather nice as well.

Then he remembered about Lieutenant Benvin.

"Wait a damn minute," he said. "Is this another ploy to keep me in place while your partner causes trouble?"

"Who the stones is my partner?" she asked. "Are you talking about Bluejay?"

"Is Bluejay killing sticks while pretending to be me?"

"What?" Emilia looked genuinely confused. "I don't know what you are talking about."

"Last night, while you and I were drinking and—"

"Rolling."

"Someone dressed like the Thorn attacked a bunch of sticks. One dead, one still out cold."

"Oh." She went over to a table and picked up a cup. "I didn't know."

Veranix took the offered cup and smelled it. *Oxaym*, all right. Smelled like a skunk ate itself and threw itself back up again. "Seriously?"

"Tell me it doesn't work," she said. "The average ottie would be on crutches for life with how my ankle was. But I'm already in prime." She was right about that. He always felt better after his mother forced it down his throat, but drinking it was a challenge.

"So straight stones on the road," he said. "You, what, just saw me last night—"

"I saw a cute quin who was passing as an ottie in the University, just like me. So I wanted to get to know you. And that guy from Pirrell really was creeping me out."

"You could have taken him, I think."

"My second option, if attaching myself to you didn't scare him off."

"And this morning you realized who I was."

"Same time you figured me out, sweets," she said. "Though I took it a lot better than you did."

"Then tell me how we ended up here."

"Kept my eye on you, saw you stalk after that one boy, then shake down the lady in the alley. Then you went into that den, and I stuck close. Soon as I realized you were in a trap, I went in for you."

"Just like that?"

"Not just like that, but they weren't expecting anyone to yank your fat clear. You were in a bad way, so I brought you here to treat you."

"And where is here?"

"Apartment I have in southern Aventil, on Clover."

"Whose patch is this? Toothless Dogs?"

"I don't know. You pay close mind to that stuff?"

"Shouldn't you if you have this apartment here?"

She looked sheepish. "To be straight, it ain't strictly mine. It's a safehouse for the Deadly Birds."

Veranix pulled himself up off the bed like a spring. "The blazes you bring me here for?"

"Because I had my oils and such here, fool," she said. "I had to treat you if you were going to be able to move again."

"I'll be fine," he said, though looking down at his body, he was a bruised and battered mess. "But I can't stay here."

"The Birds don't care about you. That contract was open and closed."

"I know there's a price on my head, they said so in there. You telling me one of your sisters wouldn't run for it?"

"We don't . . . Owl wouldn't like it."

"Owl?"

"She's the boss."

"Of course she is," Veranix said. "So you still work for them?"

"I don't not work with them," she said. "I mean, I—that's not the issue. I haven't taken a job since you."

"Because you suddenly got morals, or your ankle?"

"You're going to lecture me on morals, are you? With what you do?"

"What I do?" Veranix shot back at her. "I find people

who sell sewage that kills people or worse, and I make them stop. I do what the sticks can't, or won't."

"And you've left bodies in your wake," she said.

"When I've had to."

"Yeah, I heard about that gang kid you hunted. The Rabbit?"

"That—that wasn't me!"

"What, was that the imposter who attacked the sticks?"

"Yes!"

She laughed for a moment. "Sounds like you have a real problem, Thorn."

"Where are my things, Emilia?" he asked. "I . . . I'm sorry, it's just . . . I appreciate your help. I probably would have gotten myself killed without you."

She arched an eyebrow. "Probably? You could barely stand."

"That part hasn't changed," he said. He stumbled back over to the bed and sat down. "But if you give me my stuff, I can just get out of your hair."

"You haven't figured out, Veranix Calbert?" she said as she straddled his lap. "I rather like you in my hair."

"Oh, this is all kinds of stupid," he muttered as she came in closer to kiss him.

"Isn't that your theme for the evening?"

Her lips met his, and in the moment his whole world shook. Followed by screams outside the window and thunderous booms that made the room rattle.

Chapter 11

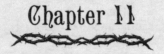

VERANIX DASHED OVER to the window. They were at least five floors up, which told Veranix exactly which building he was in—the Tenement Tower at the corner of Clover and Magnolia, probably the tallest building in Aventil, and the worst. The place was falling apart, and the people living there were the poorest families in the neighborhood. The Toothless Dogs and Kemper Street Kickers kept fighting over the corner, so brawls about the building—as well as in the building—were common. No wonder Emilia could drag him up the stairs in his condition without any trouble—no one there would lift their head to notice it.

He couldn't make out too many details on the street below, but something was on fire. A carriage that had smashed into the tenement. The building was starting to burn, and the people gathering around it were not working to put it out.

"What's going on?" Emilia asked.

"Clothes, gear," Veranix said. "We need to move."

"That didn't answer my question."

"A carriage crashed into this building, it's on fire," Veranix said.

"That's an answer," she said, pulling out a crate from under the table, where most of Veranix's gear was. She started putting on a pair of boots. The building shuddered again. "Do I want to know?"

"The carriage must have damaged one of the supports," Veranix offered. "We need to get out of here." He suited up as quick as he could, despite the pain in every part of his body, shrouding his face as soon as he had the cloak on.

"Why are you doing that?" she asked.

"Habit," he said. "Plus I'd rather not be seen in this get-up with a clear face."

"If that's the case," she said, putting on her own Blackbird mask, "might as well match my company."

"Door or window?" Veranix asked. Almost in response, the building shook, the floor lurched beneath them.

"Window," she said. "Let's go."

Veranix pushed open the window and got out on the ledge. On the street below everything was in full chaos. It was hard to make out in the darkness, but a large brawl was going on, and he imagined it was Dogs against Kickers. The only thing to wonder was, did one of them crash the carriage to start a fight, or did the carriage crash trigger a fight?

Someone was blowing a whistlebox, but no sticks or fire brigade were on their way.

"If you do a Katik Throw, you can get me to that roof," Emilia said, pointing across Magnolia to the shorter apartment building. "Best way down from this height."

"Either way, it's down into that," Veranix said. He looked up to the floor above them. "How many people in this building?"

She raised an eyebrow at him. "We need to get out of here. You can't be thinking—"

"Most folks can't get out the way we could."

"Saints, you're going to be a bad influence on me." She stepped away from the window. "Looks like it's door for both of us."

She pressed her hand on the door for a moment, and then opened it up. Smoke poured in, and several voices could be heard shouting in fear and terror.

Veranix joined her by the door. "Plan?"

"Find people, get them out," she said. "Especially the ones who can't manage themselves."

"Like the family on the carriage?" he asked. He flashed her a grin as she gave him a withering look. "And you thought I was the bad influence on you."

"That was the right thing to do, but don't make me regret it."

"Help!" someone shouted.

"Sounds like our cue," Veranix said.

The screams were coming from one of the other apartments. Veranix's first impulse was to kick the door open, but his whole body wanted nothing more than to curl up on the floor. That was with khenas oil and *oxaym*. He didn't want to think about how he would have felt without Emilia's ministrations. He could magic it, but he knew he had to conserve his strength, even with the cloak feeding him *numina*.

Emilia pounded on the door. "Are you all right?"

"Help us!"

The floor buckled, and more screams came from inside. Emilia knocked it open with a sharp kick.

"You're barely on your feet," she said to him as they went in.

"I'll manage."

This apartment was in worse shape than Emilia's. The room had cracked apart, with a section of floor hanging precariously into the open air. The wall had already collapsed to the street below. Two women—mother and daughter, likely—were stuck on the hanging section, clutching to whatever they could get a hold of.

Emilia went right up to the cracked edge in the floor, stretching out to the closer one. "Get my hand!"

"I can't!" the woman cried. She looked too terrified to even loosen her grip on the plaster, let alone pull herself up to grab Emilia.

"Two steps," Emilia said. "You can do it." She glanced over at Veranix. "Do something."

Veranix pulled out his rope. In his weakened state, it was hard to manipulate it, but he could still toss one end out to the woman. "Grab that."

The woman started to move her hand, but as soon as she did, she slipped, and desperately grabbed on to the floor again. "Get my daughter!"

Veranix whipped the rope over to the other woman—closer to the edge—and willed it to wrap around her waist. A cold sweat broke out over his brow. This was already more effort than he was ready for.

"You need a Hesker Saddle—"

"Can't really do that," he said. "I'm going to pull you up," he called out to the young woman.

The young woman nodded, and he pulled the rope tight. She didn't move much, but she was able to let go of the section of floor she was holding on to.

Emilia took her own rope and tossed an end to the young woman, who grabbed on to it eagerly. With Emilia pulling as well, the girl slid up the tilted floor to the broken edge.

"I've got her," Veranix said through strained teeth. "Pull her up."

Emilia took the woman's hand and hauled her up to safety. She scrambled to the door, clutching on to the frame like an anchor. "Mama! Come on!"

"Same play," Veranix said to Blackbird, getting ready to will the rope to the mother.

Then with a horrible crack, the floor gave way, dropping to the street below with the mother still on it.

Veranix dove after it, pushing himself down with a hint of magic. As he swooped in toward the mother, he flung one end of the rope back up, praying to the saints that he had enough strength to make this work.

He grabbed the mother and looked back up—only a few moments before they would hit the cobblestone—to see that Emilia had flung one end of her rope down. He willed his rope to wrap itself around hers, making a fast and tight knot. She braced her strong legs as the two ropes snapped tight. Veranix, still clutching on to the mother, bounced away from the falling chunk of floor, and they soared back up for a moment, and dropped down again until they hung some fifteen feet above the ground. Shattered chunks of plaster covered the street below, and the crowds were in a full panic of screams and madness.

"You got it?" Veranix called up to Emilia.

"Not for long," she called back. "Do something quick."

"But you've got me?"

She looked down at him and winked. "I've got you."

Then an arrow went into her chest. Then another. And another.

∞∞∞∞∞∞

Colin found himself shouting something he never thought he'd say in his whole life.

"Call the Constabulary!"

Another arrow sang down at him from the window, and he dove behind the fallen bodies of Sotch and Ockie.

"Rutting blazes!" Ockie coughed out. "What—"

"Stay down," Colin said. "Let's get the carriage over here."

"But she—"

Colin didn't give him a chance to finish. He leaped up, shouting to Kiggy, "Flat the rutting street!" The crowd was still far too thick for the carriage to get through.

Kiggy was still standing like a rabbit in a lamp, but Sella was on point. She drew out a knife. "Clear it out, gawkers! Burn your shoes!"

The sight of a blade made most of the crowd scream and run. Fascinating that arrows and dead bodies hadn't done the same. They screamed bloody for the sticks to come, but none had showed yet. Colin wanted them here, he wanted them to iron up that fake Thorn. This blighter going to the Quarry would put an end to plenty of Veranix's troubles, and with that, his own.

"Hey, fraud!" he shouted, throwing his arms open wide. "I thought you wanted to play with a Prince!"

The response was another arrow. Colin jumped out of the way, but not as quick as he ought to have. The fletching grazed his arm, slicing a gash right on his rose.

Colin drew a knife and threw it, but the fake Thorn was too far, too high. It hit the window frame and stuck there.

"This is hardly fair, Prince," the fake shouted, drawing out another arrow. Colin could see only four left in his quiver. Maybe he could draw all the shots, keep any other Prince from getting hit. Sella had made a path for the carriage, which was rolling up to Ockie and Cabie. She ran over to Ockie, but the fraud took aim at her. The arrow went right in her leg, but she didn't drop. Instead, she yanked it out with a shout, and then pulled Sotch's body up off of Ockie.

Damn girl must have half the sew-up's *doph* in her right now.

"That the best you got, fraud?" Colin shouted again. He held up his arm. "You don't want to go for the stars?"

"The Thorn would be happy to kill you, Prince," the fraud called back. Before he got his next arrow in place, arms wrapped around him. Ment, his head blood-soaked, was about to crush him like a grape.

A dead fake Thorn would suit Colin just fine.

"Move, Kiggy, move," he snapped. Kiggy helped load Ockie and Sotch's body into the carriage, and then pushed Sella into it as well. Colin scooped up Cabie—still wasn't sure if she was alive—and put her in it as well.

"Go, go," he shouted to the driver as he shut Kiggy in with the rest. "Get them safe."

The driver didn't question it, spurring his horses.

Colin looked back up to the window, but it hadn't gone well for Ment. The fake Thorn jabbed his arrow into Ment, and he had lost his grip. The fraud pulled the arrow out and then put it in Ment's eye. Ment fell back, but managed to grab the fake's bow as he went down, wrenching it out of his hands.

Colin sailed another knife up to the window, and this time got a piece of the fake.

"You, still?" the fraud said, turning his attention.

"We're not done, fake."

Whistles pierced the air, and a couple sticks were

running over. Colin kept his last knife in its sheath, hands away from his body, as the two of them closed. Both trained their crossbows at the fake Thorn in the window.

"Stand and be held!" they both shouted.

"Can't oblige," the fraud said, and with a flick of his wrist a plume of colored smoke poured out of his vest. The sticks both fired, but if they hit anything, Colin couldn't tell. In a moment, the smoke cleared, and the fake Thorn was gone.

One of the sticks turned on Colin. "What the blazes is going on, Prince?"

"I was attacked!" Colin said, keeping his hands high.

"Yeah, but why?"

"Thorn's going after everyone, it seems," the other stick said.

"Give me a good reason not to iron you and drag you to the stationhouse," the first stick said, grabbing Colin by the front of his shirt.

More whistles pierced the air. Fire Call. Yellowshield call. Panic Call. Several blocks away, but a lot of them.

"Because you've got better things to do, stick," Colin said.

The stick frowned, but with a glance at his partner he let Colin loose and ran off.

The sew-up came out of his office, coughing and wheezing. "What are you sinners doing up there?"

"Never you mind, doc," Colin said, grabbing the man by the scruff of the neck. "Come with me. You're earning your keep tonight."

At half past eight bells, Minox went searching through the stationhouse for Jace. He had already observed how lax the Aventil Stationhouse had been on regulations, and the engagement of cadets was no exception. Strictly speaking, cadets were students in schooling at the stationhouse, and they were supposed to spend no more than eight hours each day on duty, and half that time was to be dedicated to study and training. The other half was to fulfill duties of squad support.

Captain Holcomb seemed to treat all the cadets as underpaid footpatrol, clerks, and whatever other use he could find. Minox had long since suspected this, given Jace's typical accounts of his days, though he also presumed that Jace had chosen to push his duties out of his enthusiasm and loyalty to Lieutenant Benvin.

But the proof was in the Cadet Room itself. Other than the daily sign-in book, there was little sign of regular use. Some parts of the room had a rather thick layer of dust.

"Something you need, specs?" an old clerk asked him as he looked around the Cadet Room.

Raising any sort of fuss over this stationhouse's habits was counterproductive, and could actively hurt Jace's career before it got properly started. That was the last thing Minox wanted, despite finding the conditions of this house appalling.

"Looking for a cadet."

"Most of them went home hours ago, or they might have been roped into street patrol. You need some sort of errand?"

"I should have been more clear. I'm looking for a specific cadet, Jace Welling."

"Oh, Jace. Good kid, even if he's got his head puffed up with that Left's 'special squad.'" The clerk shook his head and went over to the sign-in book. "He ain't checked out today."

"I had already determined that. You have an issue with Lieutenant Benvin's squad?"

"Most folk do. What's it to you?"

Minox raised an eyebrow. "I'm here to investigate the attack on Lieutenant Benvin. That 'most folk' have an issue with the man is quite relevant."

"*Pff,*" the clerk said, and wandered off as if this were a sufficient explanation.

Minox was about to call him back when a bell rang out through the stationhouse. It wasn't a signal or protocol he was familiar with back in Inemar. He went out to the main work floor.

"What's the situation?"

He was given a strange regard by the floor sergeant—not surprising given he was an unfamiliar inspector—but the man answered. "Word hit that there's a row on Clover. So we're rolling out the lockwagons and making a sweep."

"Clover?" A few blocks away. He didn't remember the details of which gangs congregated there. "A 'row' is a specific term you use for gangs fighting each other, yes?"

"What are you, simple?" the sergeant asked. "Get out of the way."

Minox didn't respond before the sergeant brushed past him. He was about to rebuke the sergeant—most of the people in this house needed a lesson in respecting rank—when he recognized a different person going out the main door. He made pursuit.

"Officer Pollit!" he shouted as he went out into the street. Pollit turned on his heel, walking backward to not stop moving while looking at Minox.

"Something I can do for you, specs?"

"I would hope," Minox said, jogging forward to match pace with Pollit. "I was hoping to find Jace. He hasn't signed out, and I had no luck in the places I expected him."

Pollit shook his head. "That kid is a whip, I'll tell you. Should do you proud."

"He is quite diligent in his duty, but I would think he should go home. Cadets should not—"

"My cadet year, I was always in before the captain and the cadet commissar, and didn't leave until they did."

Minox nodded. "I'll confess similar behavior. Something our father instilled in us. Even so, I should be the responsible authority and make sure he comes home with me."

Pollit chuckled. "Right. All of you live under one big roof. Must be something."

"I should—"

"Specs, we got a brawl over on Clover. Run with me or walk away, but it's business time."

Pollit turned back front and went into a sprint. Minox sighed and followed suit. He had promised to be home, barring crisis. A brawl between two gangs on the open street while civilian crowds filled the neighborhood certainly qualified as one.

"Is there any chance that Jace is in the thick of this brawl?"

"Knowing him, absolutely."

That did not give Minox any sense of relief.

Pollit stopped to catch his breath a block away from Clover and Vine. "What are we heading into?" Minox asked.

"This is a we, specs?"

"I haven't signed out," Minox said.

"Sorry. Just most of our specs, they wouldn't bother with—"

"I am not them. What can we expect?"

"It's bad enough they're bringing in the wagon. We're about to hit where the Kickers and the Toothless Dogs butt heads. Corner of Clover and Vine has been a contention with them, and the Knights claim it's theirs as well."

"At some point I'm going to have to make a study into gangs making claims of territories," Minox said. He drew out his crossbow and checked that it was loaded.

"You don't got that in Inemar?"

"Not with the same formality. What's our strategy?"

Pollit started moving again—brisk pace without running. "Honestly, keeping the civs safe is probably more important than ironing a few gang boys. Some good whistle blasts should make some of them scatter. Push in, look for injured, make a hole for the Yellowshields. Crack the skulls of anyone who keeps making trouble."

They reached the corner, where a dozen or so young men were brawling in the intersection. More of note was the flaming carriage that had crashed through the tallest building on the corner. The building was already afire and beginning to collapse.

Minox's instinct was to blow a whistle blast he rarely had used or heard—one that he doubted most people knew how to respond to—the Evacuation Call. The building was going to fall, and people needed to get out of the way before they were crushed.

"Sticks!" one of the brawlers yelled. His fight partner took advantage of his distraction and knocked him down. Minox took aim and fired his crossbow at that boy. The blunt-tip struck him in the chest, sending him down.

Pollit blew his whistle and charged into the brawl. Minox was about to follow when there was a hand on his shoulder.

"What are you doing?" It was Jace.

"I was searching for you."

"I saw you leave the station with Pol. You shouldn't—"

"Neither should—"

The air was pierced with a harrowing scream, and Minox looked up, seeing something—someone—fall from one of the upper floors of the burning building. A whole crowd was already formed around that part of Clover Street, gawking at the spectacle. When the building came down, it would fall on them.

"Get the area cleared," Minox said. "We're about to have a worse situation."

Jace nodded, and pushed ahead, Minox right on his heels.

"Clear out, clear—" Minox shouted. "You must get safely away—"

Through the crowd he could see a figure in a burgundy cloak, cradling a woman in his arms. Someone in the crowd screamed and pointed at him.

"THORN! MURDERER!"

Chapter 12

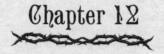

INSTINCT AND MAGIC took over as Veranix started to fall, one hand still holding the mother, while Emilia's arrow-ridden body dropped down. The world around slowed to a halt, his own descent now a crawl. He pushed a blast of wind beneath him, and twisted his body to get his feet underneath him. Cradling the old woman in his arms, his feet touched the ground as light as a feather.

Then the world jumped back into place, screams and rushing and chaos.

Emilia's body smashed onto the stones, a horrifying sight of blood and flesh. Veranix shielded the old woman's eyes, but that didn't dull the screams of horror that came from the rest of the crowd.

Veranix looked up to the roof of the building across the street. There in the moonlight, he saw the archer. A man with a bow and a crimson cloak.

"The Thorn!" someone shouted. "Murderer!" More shouted the same things. Half the people were pointing at Veranix, and the other half at the man on the roof.

Veranix let the terrified woman down onto her feet just before something hit him in the head. Just hard enough to hurt.

He had to ignore it. Up there on the roof, the imposter moved away. He drew away the rope and shot it up that building, sending enough magic into his legs to leap up. He knew he wasn't strong enough right now to reach the top, but the rope could. It coiled around a gutter outcropping, and he used it to pull himself the rest of the way.

Shouts from down below. Angry, horrified. Constabulary whistles. There was probably more happening down there, but Veranix couldn't pay it a lick of mind. There was only one thing—the imposter running across the roof. The fraud had killed Black—Emilia. Whoever this was, he had brought enough havoc to this neighborhood, especially to Veranix, and he was going to pay.

Veranix nocked and fired an arrow in a flash, which soared past the imposter.

The imposter stopped for a moment, glancing back at Veranix, and then went right back to his run, leaping to the next building. Veranix took three more steps in pursuit when a horrible cracking noise came from behind him. He turned back to see the whole building collapsing.

Tons of plaster, wood, and concrete were about to drop onto the crowd below.

He didn't think. He just pulled every drop of *numina* he could summon through the cloak.

The Thorn was already in the air and up on the roof before Minox could push his way through the crowd. The woman he had been carrying stood in a stupor, while another one lay dead on the ground, her body mangled from the fall and three redundant arrows in her chest.

"Madam, we have to get you out of—"

He was interrupted by the sound of cracking stone above him. The building was about to fall. The crowd still stood, slackjawed and gawking at the danger above them.

"Move! Run!" Minox shouted. Jace was physically pulling people away, as was Pollit and a few other officers. Yellowshields and Fire Brigade were also here, but no one was going to be able to get everyone away in time.

Minox grabbed the woman by the shoulders and pulled

her away. The crowd was panicking, and he couldn't get back through them, let alone guide her to safety. He looked back up to see a large chunk of the building coming from directly above him.

Then he felt a surge in his left hand—a burst of energy, the likes of which he had not experienced since it changed into its current inhuman form.

Instinctively, he raised his arm up to the sky, and a bolt of green light poured out of his hand. It spread out into a wide circle, covering the crowd. The chunk of the building struck the circle of light, and Minox dropped to one knee. The weight was more than he was prepared to hold.

"Go, go!" Jace was beating his way through the crowd, pushing them out of the way to get to Minox. Minox felt his body was drenched in cold sweat. "Minox, what are you—"

"Get clear," Minox grunted out through his teeth.

The energy in his arm faltered. Legs buckling, he struggled to force another surge of magic out of himself.

Another light, this one red, joined the green circle, wrapping around it.

Minox knew the red energy hadn't come from him. It was coming from above the mass of masonry that Minox was trying to hold above the crowd. The red light pressed into the green, crushing the pieces of the fallen building between them.

Minox was on both knees now. The only reason why he hadn't fallen down completely was his brother propping him up, even holding his left arm high.

"I can't . . ." Minox said. This was too much, more than he had ever borne.

He let it go, and the green light fell apart. But all that remained of the chunks of the building was a blanket of dust and powder, which fell on the remaining crowd.

Minox looked up again, and on the roof on the opposite corner, he saw the cloaked figure again. The man up there was half slumped over the eave, as spent as Minox was.

"Is that—" Minox managed to wheeze out.

"I think so," Jace said.

The figure—the Thorn—looked at Minox for several seconds before pushing himself away from the edge of the roof, out of sight.

"We need—we should—" Minox tried to say.

"Get you out of here," Jace said, pulling Minox to his feet. "You're as weak as a kitten, and this crowd could turn on you."

"But we—we need—"

"I've got you, Minox," Jace said. "Let me get you someplace safe."

As much as he wanted to, Minox was in no position to argue.

※※※※

Bells rang over campus. Emergency lockdown.

Kaiana left her carriage house, not sure what her role was in this situation. Before she had been told to stay in her damn room by Master Jolen, but in her new position, she might have a specific duty.

Sets of cadets were running in every direction, many with megaphones in hand. "Please return to dormitories immediately. This is for your safety. Campus gates are closing."

Kaiana ran up to one of the cadets. "What's going on?"

"I don't rightly know, ma'am," he said. "There's apparently all sorts of unrest in the streets. We're pulling our people inside the walls and locking it down."

Kaiana wanted to ask what kind of unrest but this cadet clearly knew nothing. "Where's your officer?"

"South gate," he said.

Kaiana ran toward the gate. Eight cadets were blocking the gateway while two more were checking the throng of people trying to get in. They were letting in only one person at a time, and the crowd looked as if it might riot and charge the gate.

"Officer," Kaiana called, approaching the man shouting orders at the other cadets. "What's happening?"

"You shouldn't be here, Miss Nell."

"I'll decide that based on what's happening," she said firmly. She had no idea what authority she had, if any, but she bet the officer didn't know either. "I have storage sheds with tools, chemicals. I need to have those secured if there's a risk on campus. I have people I need to—"

"There's no risk on campus, but we need to keep it that way," the officer said. "Real bad gang fighting on the streets. So we're locking down."

"Should I—"

"You should go back to your quarters and wait for the clearing bells. And tell anyone you see to do the same."

He put his attention back to the gate, clearing people to pass through. Kaiana ran back to the carriage house, wondering what Veranix was doing. Where he was. She hadn't heard a word from him for hours. For all she knew, he had been killed by Fenmere's men.

The carriage house door was slightly open when she returned. She didn't remember if she had closed it when she had run out earlier. Cautiously, she pushed it open and went in.

Veranix's bow and staff were on the ground, just dropped carelessly. The cloak, the rope, the quiver of arrows—all made a trail over to the stable.

"Veranix?" she called out. "Are you all right?"

He was in the stable of the Spinner Run, stripped to the waist. His body was covered in bruises, but he had a bandage on his arm, and another wrapped around his chest. Someone had tended to him already.

His face was twisted in anger, tears streaming down.

"Vee?" She reached out to touch his shoulder.

He pulled away, and with a primal scream, kicked at the slats of the stable wall. Then he did it again and again.

"Vee, Vee, stop it!" she cried. "What happened?"

"I saw him," Veranix whispered hoarsely. "I saw the rutting bastard."

"Who? Fenmere?"

He looked at her, confused. "No, why—the imposter. He's out there, dressed like me, killing—killing inno—good people. And he got away." Veranix kicked the wall again. "Where are my regular clothes? I need . . . I need to sleep."

"But what happened, where did you—"

"Kai!" he snapped. "I just need my clothes. The rest can wait."

She pointed to the Spinner Run trapdoor. "Down there."

"I'm sorry," he said. "I didn't mean to—it's just . . . I'm so tired . . ."

"It's fine," she said. "We'll figure it out tomorrow."

He went to the Run and opened it up. He looked back to her, tears streaming down his face, his hands trembling. "I didn't . . . I wish I had . . . I don't know how . . ."

His voice broke, and before Kaiana could respond, he went down the Spinner Run, closing the trapdoor behind him.

Kaiana picked up his gear and put it away. She didn't expect him to come back, and didn't wait any further to go back to sleep.

Chapter 13

COLIN BARELY SLEPT, beyond a few minutes of dozing on the floor of the safehouse. This place—a basement flop and abandoned shop in an alley off of Branch—was to be where Sotch and her remaining Rabbits would be tortured and killed. Instead it became a sew-up hut for the handful of survivors from the debacle on Orchid.

The sew-up did fine, given the situation. He didn't have any supplies, but what Cabie's crew had on hand to work over the Rabbits proved useful to him. He spent the night trying to keep everyone alive, possibly because he was afraid of what would happen to him if any Princes died.

Sotch was dead. She had been dead since Orchid Street.

Ockie wasn't doing much better. He had quite a hole in his gut, and while the sew-up got it patched up, Ockie went feverish somewhere in the middle of the night. He was still alive when the dawn came, but Colin wasn't expecting him to make it to sunset.

Cabie was asleep. The sew-up didn't think she'd wake up, and if she did, she wouldn't walk. He made a show of stabbing a needle in her foot to make that point to Colin. Colin didn't even pretend he understood, but he trusted the sew-up knew his business.

Sella started howling in pain around midnight, and

threatened to stab Colin and everyone else if they didn't get her some *doph*. She settled for a bottle of half-turned wine, which she rode to oblivion for the rest of the night.

Kiggy was unhurt, but shaken. From what Colin understood, he had been tight with Ment and Vandy since they all first got their ink. He went out in the middle of the night, despite Colin's warning. He came back a few hours later, Cober in tow. Damn kid had been hiding in the basement of the cheese shop the whole time. He confirmed that Ment and Vandy were dead, as well as the rest of the Rabbits and Cabie's crew.

So Colin only had two of his crew on their feet, plus there was Cabie's wagon man Relly. There was also Bassa, who was there to be Sotch's torturer. She seemed disappointed to have nothing to do for the night, and made no comment beyond that. Colin wasn't sure if she was part of Cabie's crew, or came directly from Vessrin. He was shocked that he had never met her before in his life, but the Rose Street tattoo on her meaty arm was old and faded.

Since Bassa hadn't seen fit to say more than two words to Colin, he sent Relly to the bosses. He made it clear to Relly not to make a full report, just to let them know how far to the left the night had turned, and that Colin would come in the morning to tell them everything.

Shortly after sunrise, Giles and Old Casey showed up with Relly. They had the decency to bring bread and a few jars of preserve with them.

"You look like sewage, Tyson," Giles said when they came in.

"And I'm the lucky one here," Colin said. "All told it could have gone worse."

Casey sat down at the rickety table and laid out the food. "Eat something before you fall over, Colin."

"What about my crew, and Relly?"

Giles tossed a coin over to Relly. "Take Tyson's boys around the corner for a bite of something. Bring the sew-up with you, too. Keep an eye on them."

Relly nodded and went off with the rest. Colin was

acutely aware that Bassa was still in the other room, and surely Giles and Casey knew that as well. The fact that they didn't send her away was a bit alarming.

"So, Relly told us what he saw," Casey said, spreading some preserves on a hunk of bread before handing it to Colin. "But he was on the street the whole time, half a block away."

"Right," Colin said. "I get to the flop with Cabie and her crew. Ockie stays on the street to wait for the carriage, the rest of us go up. My boys Ment and Vandy are up there with Sotch and the other Rabbits. Sella, Kiggy, and the kid are off somewhere else. Sotch gives us some guff, but before it gets very far, this guy comes in through the skywindow. He's got arrows and smoke-powder bombs, and in a tick he's put down the rest of the Rabbits, and filled the place with smoke."

"The Thorn," Casey said.

"Nah," Colin said. "Wearing the same colors, but not the same guy."

"You know this, huh?"

"Look, I know my credit isn't clean with you all, especially as far as the Thorn is concerned, but can we agree that I've seen and spoken to the real thing? I would know a fake."

"A fake, according to you," Giles said. "But like you said, your credit ain't that clean."

"Fair enough," Colin said. "Cabie jumps in to scrap with him, and at this point it's smoke and fire in the place. I grab Sotch and pull her out the window, fall down to the street with her. Ockie helps me hold on to her while the carriage tries to get to us, but the street ain't clear for it. Suddenly Cabie drops down to the street, beat all to blazes, and this guy up in the window puts an arrow in Sotch, which gets Ockie as well. I spot Kiggy and Sella, and yell to them to flat the street while I try and draw the fight out of this fraud. They get the carriage over, Sella takes an arrow, I help Kiggy load everyone in, and send Relly on his way. Up in the window, Ment tries to give the fake a fight, but he gets it.

Sticks show up and the fraud slips off. I grab the sew-up, since his place is burning down, and track after the carriage to bring him here."

Casey nodded. "And here you are."

"Here we all are."

"You say this Thorn who attacked you ain't the real one. Same look, same weapons, different bloke."

"Truth on Rose Street."

Giles gave him a look, like he didn't believe an oath to the street from Colin.

Casey didn't look quite as skeptical, but he stayed guarded. "So, if you came across this fake again, what would you do?"

"Try to beat him senseless, and maybe drag him back here for Bassa to have some words with him."

Casey gave what might be an approving look. "And why is that?"

"Here's what I figure. This fake Thorn, he's got an agenda."

"Does he?" Giles asked coldly.

"What have we seen him do? Go after the Rabbits, go after Aventil sticks. Who does that suit?"

"Besides the Thorn?" Giles threw at him.

Casey took the thread. "If it is a fake, he's making the Thorn look bad, and dealing with the folk who crossed Fenmere. So that's two crows in a shot for Fenmere. You think the fake is one of his?"

"Or some merc working for him. I mean, what does it take? Right colored cloak, decent shot with a bow, and a bit of showmanship. Who would know it wasn't the Thorn?"

"Only you and Jutie, it would seem," Giles said. "Sad we can't talk to him."

"Hey, you want to break Jutes out of Quarrygate to get his mind on this, I'm game." Colin had done wrong by Jutie, and that ate at him. He had heard stories of breakouts. Other gangs had done it. He'd take that shot for Jutie, if he knew how.

"Don't change the subject, Tyson," Giles said.

"What is the blazing subject? We got hit. Lots of ours are hurt or killed. Did Relly tell you different?"

They both were silent for a bit. "No, that matches his story," Casey said. "In as much as he saw. He saw someone killing our people, and you fighting like blazes to save them."

"Then why in the name of any saint are you giving me any grief about this sewage?" Colin snapped. "Eh, Giles? What's your issue?"

"I don't know what you're loyal to, Tyson."

Colin pushed Giles out of his chair onto the floor, and leaped to his feet. He held up his arm, showing his tattoo. "I've bled for Rose Street. I bled for it *tonight*. When was the last time you could say the same?"

"I ought to knock your teeth—"

"Just rutting try it, old man. Or call Bassa out here to do your dirty work, don't think I won't make her earn every drop."

"Enough," Casey said, waving Giles back. "Ain't nothing like that going to happen here." Giving another glance at Giles, he added, "Though I can see why you'd think that."

"You haven't exactly been lauding me with trust, Casey," Colin said.

"And you haven't done much to earn it."

"Ten years and my stars—"

"Which I've kept on your arm, boy. Don't you forget that."

"No, sir," Colin said.

"So here's what I've got for you. Your crash over on Orchid is gone."

"There's a basement in the secretary's shop we could use," Colin said.

"Fine. But we'll send Kiggy and Relly over there to hold our claim. Else the Orphans might run in."

"Sounds like you don't want me back there."

"We took a hard hit last night. Plus the south side of the

neighborhood had a huge dustup between the Dogs and Kickers. They managed to bring the Tower Tenements down in it."

"Bring it down?"

"Building is half gone, from what I hear," Giles said quietly. He had turned into a dog that had been whacked across the nose.

"So the sticks are probably putting on quite a show," Colin said.

"That's the word. What that means is we need to be quiet right now."

"Quiet?" Colin didn't like the sound of that.

Casey must have picked up on that. "Quiet, not silent. Fact is, whoever this guy is, Thorn or no, he came into one of our flops and killed or maimed over half a dozen Princes. We can't let that sit."

"That's the most sense you've made all morning, Casey," Colin said.

Casey frowned. "Glad you approve. So we've got to do something, but at the same time, we've got to be saints-be-damned mice about it. You hear?"

"I hear you." Colin heard, but wasn't sure where Casey was going with this.

"So you have an ear in this, know about the Thorn, and his Napa girl, right?"

"Right." Colin's stomach started to turn on him.

"So you make contact. Have a word. Find out what that girl knows, find out where this guy who hit on us is."

That was a little better. "You want me to run him down. I can do that." Colin would gladly do that, even without Casey ordering it.

Casey reached out and smacked Colin across the head. "Listen, Tyson. I want you to find him. Find where the blazes he is. If it's the real Thorn, fake Thorn, whatever. Find the bastard who did this to us, and then you let us know."

"Just let you know? But I can—"

"Use your brain, Tyson. Forget that he fed the street to

Cabie and a bunch more Princes at once. Even if you could take him out, where does that leave us?"

"Score settled."

"For you. I have to look at the bigger scene."

"Tell me what that is."

Casey frowned, but nodded. "This guy didn't just hit us. Hit the sticks too, and that beehive is going to open out on the whole damn neighborhood. Won't rest until they have someone. Princes gives the sticks a 'Thorn' they can iron up, they're going to ease back."

Colin nodded. That made sense.

"Knew you'd get that," Giles said. "We've heard how you saved the Left that one time."

Colin hadn't stopped getting sewage for that. "Made sense, right? Dead stick opens the beehive."

"Good," Casey said. "So go find that Napa girl, put your ear to the street. Come to the Turnabout tonight to tell us what the what is."

"I hear you," Colin said. He picked up the last piece of bread and took a bite. "Then I guess I better be off."

He didn't stick around to hear any further comment. He knew Casey was done, and he didn't need to hear anything else from Giles.

As he left the safehouse, the early morning was already sweltering hot. Sun was barely even up. It was bound to be an insufferable day.

No time to waste, he was going to have to break one of his rules and get on the Uni campus. He needed to talk to the Napa girl—Kaiana, was it?—and talk to Veranix. At least on the Uni grounds, no other Princes would see him.

First had to find some Uni brat who had flopped out in the neighborhood overnight and steal his clothes.

Minox wasn't sure where he was when he woke up. Most of the events after Clover Street were a bit of a blur. It was a cheap, ramshackle apartment, the kind found over just about any reputable or disreputable business in Aventil for a minimal fee. There would normally be little more than a bed, basin, and table, but this one had boxes. Several boxes filled with papers, and then more papers on the walls, on the tables. If it wasn't so organized, it would remind Minox of the barn behind the house, where his cousin Evoy charted the massive amounts of information he was chasing. But this wasn't madness, this was meticulous organization.

Minox got out of the bed to look closer, but put his foot on something soft.

"Oof, watch it!"

"What are you doing on the floor, Jace?"

"Well, you were in the bed, so that's where I slept."

"Why did you—what time is it?"

"I've got no more way of knowing that than you."

"Right," Minox said, glancing out the dirty window. Sun just barely up. Maybe six bells. "Where are we and how did we arrive here?"

"We're—we're in a flop that the lieutenant kept," Jace said, rubbing his face as he stood up. "This is sort of our back-up squad room."

"With copies of Constabulary files," Minox said, glancing at the boxes. "I take no joy in pointing out this is a serious infraction of procedure."

"Yeah, I know," Jace said. "But it—look, us in the squad, we're the only ones in that house playing a narrow game, right?"

"I've observed a fair degree of lax methodology at the Aventil stationhouse, and I have my suspicions regarding corruption—"

"It's more than that," Jace said. "We've had things go missing—files, evidence, the like. And we didn't take anything from the files. We wrote out new copies and brought it here."

"Hmm," Minox said. He wasn't quite sure what to think of this. Not that he didn't want his own version of the file archives that he could peruse at his leisure, but that was mostly so he could keep working after going home. "I have been focusing on the wrong elements here. We stayed the entire night in Aventil instead of going home. This is quite improper."

"We didn't sign out, that's true," Jace said. "But you were in no condition to do anything but sleep."

"The tower collapsing . . . I made quite a spectacle of myself, didn't I?"

"You could call it that," Jace said, pumping water in to the teakettle. "I call it saving people."

"Yes," Minox said. He flexed his hand. Jace must have taken the glove he usually wore off of him in his sleep, so he looked at it in all its black, glassy strangeness. Somehow his hand, the way he controlled it magically, was able to connect to the Thorn—the true, proper Thorn—and his magic. In some way, he could still feel a curious tendril of that connection to the Thorn. He had no idea how or why such a thing had occurred. Perhaps the Thorn was just as rough and instinctual with his magic as Minox was. He had—

"Of course!" Minox shouted.

"What is it?" Jace asked.

"Mister Sarren—the witness who saw the attack on the lieutenant—is a magic student. And the Thorn is absolutely a mage, as we saw."

"We knew that already, Minox."

"No, my point is, we—Inspector Rainey and myself—we thought Mister Sarren had known the man who attacked the lieutenant was not the Thorn because he recognized the lack of magic." Mentioning her reminded him that he had certainly broken the spirit of his promise, if not strictly the letter. "Inspector Rainey is going to be cross with me for not signing out and going home."

"My fault."

"I am the ranking officer and the adult here, Jace. But—"

"You were in no shape, Minox," Jace said forcefully. "Back to what Sarren recognized."

"Yes," Minox said, recognizing the same tone he used with Evoy, and with their grandfather before. It was a little troubling that Jace had felt the need to do that, but Jace was right. His thoughts were unfocused. "Mister Sarren knew the fake was a fake because he knew he wasn't a mage, but how does Mister Sarren know the *actual* Thorn is a mage? Is that public knowledge?"

Jace thought on this for a moment. "I don't think it's in the papers, but it's hardly a secret. Any gang kid would likely know."

"But a University student? Would they know?"

"Depends on how much attention they're paying to the world out here, you know?"

"I might be operating from the unfounded presumption regarding how sheltered the life of a University student would be, but I would think the dealings of the street gangs, Constabulary, and vigilantes wouldn't be in their field of knowledge. Unless they had cause."

"All right," Jace said. "What's the cause?"

"That the Thorn is a magic student. Therefore, it's quite likely Mister Sarren's certainty comes from *knowing who the Thorn is*."

Jace nodded. "Makes sense. The Thorn, he's about my age." Jace was having difficulty balancing his duty and his faith in the Thorn's decency, it was clear on his face. Minox wondered what Jace would do if given the opportunity to capture the Thorn.

In truth, Minox wondered that about himself.

Jace must have sensed he was lost in thought. "So what do we do?"

Minox grabbed his glove and put it on. "We hurry home—Mother and the aunts must be in a state—and then head back out here for today's sign-in."

"No need for the first part," Jace said. "I've had night pages send word to the house. We're square."

Minox shook his head. "That is beyond your station, you are aware of that."

"While you were sleeping, Ed and Ferah came in so she could check you out." Their cousins. Edard was footpatrol in Dentonhill, and Ferah was a Yellowshield in the same neighborhood. The members of the family who worked closest to here. "She said you seemed fine, but you should probably eat something once you woke up."

Minox nodded. That was imperative. "Well then, you know this neighborhood best."

"Get your boots on," Jace said, pointing them out by the door. "There's a great cresh roll shop down the street."

"Inspector Rainey will be quite cross with me still."

"Well," Jace said calmly. "I can't be expected to solve everything. I'm just a cadet."

Kaiana was awoken by someone pounding on the carriage-house doors. "Miss Nell! Miss Nell! Are you in decency?"

She got out of her bed and grabbed a shawl to wrap around herself—mostly for propriety, since it was already incredibly hot this morning—and went out to the main doors. "Who's there?"

"It's Master Bretten, Miss Nell."

Her actual boss, which was shocking. She hadn't seen him for more than five minutes since her promotion. So far he had had all his instructions delivered in writing, which Kaiana always suspected was some sort of test to see if she could actually read. She opened up the door. "Morning, sir. Is there an emergency?"

"There's madness is what there is," he said, pushing his way into the carriage house. He stopped and sniffed the air in the carriage house. "You really sleep in here?"

"My designated apartments aren't ready," she said. "I was told they wouldn't be until the end of Soran. That is, after they weren't ready at the end of Letram."

"That's appalling," Bretten said. He shook his balding head. "I don't know what that's about, but I don't approve."

"Is that why you're here?"

"No, no," he said. He reached into his satchel and pulled out a sheaf of leaflets. "The campus cadets and the Vice Dean of Safety had these printed up overnight, and want them posted all over the grounds. Someone got the idea that job falls on our shoulders." He handed them over.

WARNING! STUDENTS AND VISITING ATHLETES!
AVOID ENTERING THE AVENTIL NEIGHBORHOOD UNLESS
STRICTLY NECESSARY
ESPECIALLY IN NIGHTTIME HOURS
If you must travel in the Aventil neighborhood for any reason, be vigilant!
Always know how to find whistleboxes and Constabulary!
DO NOT ACCEPT 'SAFE WALKS' FROM STREET PEOPLE,
ESPECIALLY IN GANGS.
Aventil gangs can be recognized by their chosen markings. AVOID people
with tattoos (especially roses or collars), scars, green caps, or
handkerchiefs around their ankles.
**DO NOT TRUST ANY STREET PEOPLE!!
ONLY CITY OFFICIALS ARE SAFE!!**

"This is . . . strong," Kaiana said. "This is what they want to put out there?"

"You did hear there was a gang war on the street last night? The mutts and the booters or whatever were fighting, and tore down a whole building. Tore it down. A building. We don't know how many people died."

"I heard something about it," she said. She was still waiting to hear Veranix's side of things. He was angrier last night than she'd ever seen him.

"They want these mostly along the south lawn, especially by the gate. Put your people on it."

Kaiana nodded. "I'll get on that, in addition to our basic upkeep."

"Which reminds me, have the hedges by the tetchball pitch roped off. Those poor things have been wrecked the past couple days."

"Yes, sir."

He went to the door. "And, I'll . . . I'll lean on the housing about your apartment. That needs to be squared."

"I appreciate it, sir."

He grumbled something and went back out into the morning.

Kaiana got dressed in her work gear and finished off the last of her bread and dried lamb for breakfast. The bread smelled like it was on the verge of going moldy, but it looked fine enough. She was going to have to go to the campus stores to replenish, especially if Aventil wasn't safe. She hated that. The women in the campus stores always looked at her with such naked aggression. The Aventil grocers had the decency to merely be brusque with her.

She went off across the grounds to find her work crew, pamphlets tucked under her arm. She wondered how the students were going to take this "warning." Likely, most of them would ignore it. They wanted drinks and revels, and if they couldn't find them in the social houses like Jiarna, they would find them elsewhere.

Or worse, they'd decide Aventil wasn't safe, so they'd go into Dentonhill.

She was so lost in thought she didn't even notice the man coming up close to her.

"It's Kai, isn't it?"

She startled, and almost struck out at the man. He was wearing an ill-fitting Pirrell jacket, unshaven and unkempt, and Kaiana's instinct was to scream until she recognized his face. Veranix's Rose Street Prince cousin.

"What are you doing here? You can't be on campus." She handed him one of the pamphlets. "Especially now."

He took the pamphlet and glanced at it. "I don't care about this sewage. I need to . . . I need to talk to him, but I don't know where he would be."

She glanced around to see if anyone was noticing them. At best, Colin looked like a Pirrell boy who woke up in a very wrong place this morning. Even that wouldn't stand up to scrutiny—college boys didn't have teeth or fingernails like Colin. "Don't you send him signals?"

"Too big to wait, or to risk him coming out."

"It's that bad?"

He nodded. He looked far more spooked than she imagined any street kid ever would.

"Damn and blazes," she muttered. "All right, see that building in there?" She pointed out the carriage house. "Yeah, that your flop?"

"Go in there. Second stable, find the trapdoor. Go down that and wait at the bottom. I'll send him to find you there. Hear?"

"Heard," he said.

"And don't be seen."

"Last thing I want," he said. "I cannot wait long, though. Got?"

"Got. Go."

He slipped off toward the carriage house. Kaiana doubled her pace to find her work crew. As far as she could tell, none of the few people out on the walkways this morning paid her or Colin much mind, even though the two of them stood out far more than anyone else.

"Miss Nell?" someone called out across the lawn. Ebbily, running over to her. "Good morning to you. We've, uh, got something that—"

"Requires my attention?" Kaiana sighed. "Doesn't everything today?"

Chapter 14

VERANIX WASN'T IN any mood to eat breakfast, save for the pure necessity of it. Last night had taxed him in every way he could imagine, and sleep hadn't helped. Every bit of his body hurt, and he couldn't imagine how he'd feel if it wasn't for the khenas oil and *oxaym*. Of course, if it hadn't been for Blackbird.

Emilia. He told himself as he ate. *Her name was Emilia.*

"Vee," Delmin whispered from across the table. "Your concentration is slipping."

Veranix nodded and returned his focus to maintaining the illusion of his face not having several bruises and a gash across the eyebrow. He hadn't even noticed the last one until Delmin mentioned it in the morning. It was going to leave a scar. He was going to have to manufacture some semipublic accident to "cause" the injury, so no one would question its origins.

"What's in store for you today?" Delmin asked lightly.

"Tetch team has to play Korifina," Veranix said. "But I'm not—"

"You should be on hand," Delmin said.

"Why? For the appearance of normalcy?"

"I was thinking actual normalcy," Delmin said. "Look, you—" He lowered his voice. "You went through some real grind last night, and—"

"You don't even know," Veranix said. Which was true. Veranix had glossed over everything involving Emilia. Fortunately Delmin hadn't bothered pressing for details.

"And you need something that isn't about any of this."

"I don't think you fathom what's going on out there," Veranix said.

"I know they locked down the gates, put out those flyers," Delmin said. "It's scared the University far more than even Jensett did."

"I'm not talking about the gang fights. I'm talking about the—"

"Mister Calbert?"

They were interrupted by a young kid in a work smock. Veranix imagined he was someone on the grounds crew by the look of him.

"That's me," Veranix said.

"Beg your indulgence, sir," the boy said. "I was asked to look for you in here by Miss Nell. She said to tell you you're needed in a meeting."

"A meeting?" Veranix asked.

"She said you would know where." The boy glanced around nervously. Grounds crew never came into the dining halls, and while most of the boys eating were athletes from other universities, there were enough U of M regulars who were giving him an odd regard.

"I appreciate it," Veranix said. "We'll be there in short order."

The boy nodded and raced out.

"That was odd," Delmin said. "What could be such an emergency that Kaiana would send him in here to get us?"

Veranix took another bite of potatoes. "You think it's an emergency?"

"She thought it merited interrupting your breakfast," Delmin said.

That got through his skull. Veranix grabbed two more rolls off the tray and got to his feet. "Let's go."

Delmin caught up to him at the storage closet. "You're going this way?"

"We've already created enough spectacle in the dining hall. No need to have gawkers notice us walking over to the carriage house." He had grown far too incautious in this business. Emilia had been able to track him, and Fenmere's man had been ready for him, and the imposter . . .

Veranix magicked the door open and latched it behind them as they went down into the Spinner Run.

"Whatever this is about," Delmin said as they walked down the passage, "you can't run off like a wild chicken."

"When do I run off like a wild chicken?" Veranix snapped back.

"Regularly," Delmin said in unison with another voice at the end of the Spinner Run. Veranix drew *numina* in hard and fast, his hand glowing with power. Before he released it, the light revealed who the second speaker was. Colin.

"What the rutting blazes are you doing here?" Veranix snapped.

"Morning to you, too," Colin said.

"Vee, who is this?" Delmin asked nervously. "He's a—"

"He's Colin," Veranix said. "My cousin."

"Your—right. I had—of course."

"Things must be bad for you to actually come here," Veranix said.

"Yeah, well, I wanted to see the plush Uni life," Colin said. "Didn't know it would be a spider-filled tunnel."

"Nothing but the best here," Veranix said. "Kaiana sent you down here?"

"Guess she needed me out of sight."

"Come on," Veranix said, climbing up the ladder. "I imagine we're going to have to figure out how to get you off campus."

"Off is easy," Colin said. "I just show my arm, and a bunch of the Uni boys will come drag me away."

"Unless they drag you to the Constabulary," Delmin said.

"Good point, Uni," Colin said. "I take it this jake knows what you do?"

"Delmin, Delmin Sarren," Delmin stammered out, offering his hand to Colin. "It's a real pleasure, sir."

Colin took the hand cautiously. "Wasn't expecting that."

Delmin shrugged. "Twice now I've ended up in the thick of things as part of his—"

"Vendetta?"

"Vocation," Delmin offered. "Both times I ended up standing shoulder to shoulder with a Rose Street Prince. Both times they did the name proud."

Colin looked up to Veranix, still on the ladder. "Hetzer," Veranix said. "And Jutie."

"Good Princes both," Colin said, a hint of a crack in his voice. "Thank you for saying that, Mister Sarren."

"Let's get on with this," Veranix said, pushing open the trapdoor. "You're obviously here because things are horrible."

"What's horrible?"

Veranix jumped, again nearly drawing on magic to blast whoever was speaking. Jiarna and Phadre both were waiting in the carriage house.

"Don't do that," Veranix said, dissipating the *numina* he had built up. "Saints, it's a wonder I have any wits to me at all this morning."

"Aren't you a snarly cat," Jiarna said.

"What are you doing here?" Veranix asked.

"We came in this morning for the Tournament," Jiarna said. "Kaiana spotted us and said we should come here, and—oh, mercy my."

Colin had come out of the Spinner Run. "This is more of your crew?" he asked.

"You're acquainted with this ruffian?" Phadre asked.

"None of that," Veranix shot back. "He's family and he's part of this, and if you have a problem—"

"No one does," Jiarna said, giving a pointed stare at Phadre. "Pleased to make your acquaintance, Mister—"

"Colin," Veranix offered.

"Charmed," Colin said.

"And that's Phadre and Jiarna. They helped stop Jensett's plan."

"Oh, they're the ones?" Colin asked. "I thought it was your other girl."

"I stopped him." Kaiana had come in through the main door, latching it behind her. "They stopped his creation."

"So, we're all met," Colin said. "I didn't know you had this much of a crew in here. Thought it was just you and the . . . girl."

"Things evolved," Veranix said.

"Something drove you to come out here," Kaiana said. "You said you didn't have time to waste."

"Right," Colin said. "So, last night this imposter showed up again."

"I know," Veranix said.

"You heard about it?"

"I saw him."

"You did?" Just about everyone asked this at once.

"Yes," Veranix said cautiously. "A lot of things happened last night."

"Evident on your face," Delmin said.

"His face is fine," Colin said.

Veranix sighed. "This isn't really my face right now." He relaxed the magic. Kaiana and Phadre both visibly recoiled.

"Saints, old boy, that's quite a rollicking," Phadre said. "Is this all really worth it?"

"If it were just about the *effitte* right now, I'd gladly take a few days off to rest up," Veranix said. "But as it stands—"

"Who the blazes did that to you?" Colin asked.

"Fenmere's men."

"How many?"

"About twenty or so. I didn't exactly count."

"Twenty?" Phadre sputtered. "And you're still standing?"

"How did you manage that?" Jiarna asked.

"I . . . I got away, and holed up somewhere to rest. But

then that place was the middle of a thing between the Dogs and the Kickers, so—"

Colin nodded. "You're talking about the Tower Tenement. I heard it fell down."

"It did. I was barely able to keep the rubble from crushing folks on the street. So I couldn't chase the imposter."

"I feel like this narrative is missing key elements," Jiarna said. "You were out on the east side of campus, in Dentonhill, and then you end up holing up somewhere in the southern part of Aventil. How'd you get there, and why didn't you just come back to campus?"

"I—" Veranix wasn't sure how to explain this, not without bringing up Emilia. He glanced nervously at Kaiana, then back to Jiarna. "Someone saved me from the *effitte* dealers. And then she—"

"She?" Delmin asked, eyes going wide.

"She brought me to her safe place, which was in the Tower. But the imposter—"

"Wait," Colin said. "Was this that bird you mentioned?"

"Bird you mentioned?" Kaiana repeated, her eyebrow raised.

"I didn't call her that," Veranix said defensively. "Except, she is, because—"

"She's a Deadly Bird!" Colin half shouted, half laughed. "Wait, wait, the Deadly Bird who tried to *kill* you a month ago is the one who saved you?"

"It's a bit more complicated than that."

"Is her name Emilia?" Jiarna asked.

"What, how did you—" was all Veranix got out.

"Am I the only one completely confused?" Delmin asked.

"Oh, cousin," Colin said, putting his arm around Veranix. "You must have really done well with her."

"She was very interested in finding you," Jiarna said. "I had no idea . . ."

"What are you all talking about?" Kaiana asked.

Veranix sighed. "I met a girl named Emilia the other night, out with the tetch squad. Turns out she was the Deadly Bird named Blackbird."

"An assassin," Kaiana said coldly.

"She's the one who helped save the family on the carriage. Not one of the ones in the brewery."

"So a *nice* assassin."

"She saved me, dressed my wounds, and got killed for the trouble!" Veranix shouted. "The imposter. He . . . he killed her right in front of me."

No one spoke for a moment, until Colin patted his shoulder. "He had a busy night. Around nine bells he attacked my flop, killed half my crew."

"Nine bells?" Veranix asked. That didn't sound right. "That was about when he killed Emilia."

"Are you sure?"

"Relatively. I'm sure there were several dozen witnesses on Clover when the building came down. They certainly were shouting 'Thorn! Murderer!'"

"I know when my business went down," Colin said.

"Here's a crazy idea," Phadre said. "Perhaps there are two imposters."

"Two different imposters?" Delmin said. "That seems unlikely."

"Yes, but consider. What do we know about the imposter?"

"He killed a gang member the other night," Kaiana said.

"Keckin, of the Red Rabbits. And last night he came for Sotch. My people were just in the way, though he enjoyed taking us out."

"So, logically, one of the imposters is settling a vendetta against these Red Rabbits," Phadre said. "What else do we know?"

"He killed a constable, injured two others," Delmin said.

"And he killed Emilia," Veranix said.

"Three events, and three witnesses," Jiarna said, pointing at Veranix, Colin, and Delmin. "This is good observational data."

"This sounds like Uni stuff," Colin said.

"No, no, this is good principle," Phadre said. "By comparing the accounts the three of you have about the imposter—or imposters—"

"If your theory holds water—" Jiarna injected.

"It is just a theory, but I'm trusting that they are being accurate about the time—"

"Both incidents had other witnesses; the timing of the events is verifiable."

"Phadre, Jiarna, you're doing it again," Kaiana said.

"Sorry," they said in unison.

Jiarna picked up. "Let's get every detail we can about each of your incidents. Compare and contrast."

"Sorry, Delmin, old chap," Phadre said. "I know you don't want to hash it out again—"

"No, it's fine," Delmin said. "If it'll help."

"I can't really stick around the Uni," Colin said.

"It's fine, sit," Jiarna said, taking out a leather journal from her bags.

"I need to get back to work," Kaiana said. "But I'm sure you'll be able to handle things."

"Kai—" Veranix started.

"Go on," she said. "I really don't need to hear *all* the details about what you did last night."

She went out, and Phadre latched the door behind her. Jiarna set up her journal, pen, and ink out on the table.

"Now, Delmin," she said coolly. "Start from the beginning."

Minox was on his fourth cresh roll when they reached the Aventil Stationhouse. Inspector Rainey was waiting on the steps with a sergeant from the Grand Inspectors' Unit at her side. The sergeant was, of course, Minox's sister, Corrie. Neither of them looked pleased.

Inspector Rainey started speaking as soon as Minox noted her. "I went home last night thinking, what are the odds that Welling will actually sign out and go home? Or will he concoct some excuse to stay in Aventil all night?"

"I did not—" Minox managed to say before his sister launched onto Jace.

"And you, you little rutter," Corrie snarled. "You blazing well know better. Mother was in a state."

"I sent a page," Jace said while keeping his attention down at his feet.

"You sent a page," Corrie said. "You hear this sewage? The boy sent a rutting page. You're supposed to head home. And you!" This was at Minox.

"As I attempted to say—"

"The part that shocks me," Rainey said, "is how you employed your brother to be your blametaker."

"He did nothing of the sort," Jace said. "I swear on my coat, Inspector. Last night we legitimately had a crisis here."

"Almost always a crisis in Aventil," Corrie said.

"Damn right there is," Jace said.

Corrie cuffed him across the head. "Watch your rutting language."

"Truth, Corr. A full-on brannigan between the Toothless Dogs and the Kemper Street Kickers, which actually brought down a building."

"A building?" Rainey asked.

"The Tower Tenement. Burned and collapsed," Jace said. "The whole thing came down like Uncle Timm on his sixth beer."

"Decorum, Jace," Minox said.

"Were you hurt?" Rainey asked. She looked pointedly at Minox. "Something like that would have covered the street in brick, wood—"

"Would have," Jace said, pointing at Minox. "Except this one right here stopped it all. Just put his hand up and *whoosh*. Everyone safe."

"I was quite incapacitated from the events," Minox said pointedly. "Admonish me if you must, Inspector Rainey, but Jace made the best choices possible given my condition."

Both Corrie and Rainey raised their eyebrows at him.

"Condition how?" Corrie asked. "You having another rutting change like before?"

"No, nothing of the sort. I merely exerted myself beyond my endurance."

"Well, that was rutting stupid, Mine."

"Circumstances were dire."

"Building fall on us dire," Jace added.

"It doesn't matter," Inspector Rainey said. "Since you've spent extra time here, what have you learned?"

"I don't know if I've learned anything new. But we encountered the Thorn—the real one—however tangentially."

"The real one?" Rainey asked. "You're certain."

"Pretty sure," Jace said.

Minox lowered his voice, leaning into Rainey. "The magic to protect the people on the street. I didn't do it alone."

"The Thorn helped?" Rainey's face was full of incredulity.

"But there was the imposter as well," Jace added.

"There was?" Minox asked. "I didn't see that."

Jace nodded. "The girl fell out of the building, and the Thorn was on the ground. And people were screaming 'murderer.' Half of them were pointing at him, and the other half were pointing to the opposite roof. When I looked up, I only caught a glimpse of a cloak, but—I definitely saw it."

"And the Thorn then went up there." Minox finished the last bite of his cresh roll. "We should determine what official reports there are of the incidents last night. Namely, identify the dead girl. Corrie, I presume you aren't here simply for escort?"

"Captain wanted to ensure you were facilitating communication between the stationhouses, or some rutting sewage like that," Corrie said. "He knows the two of you can be garbage about sending pages and reports, so I get to make sure that word gets back to the house, and his messages get back to you."

"Did we get messages yesterday?"

Rainey shrugged. "We might have. Who knows in that house?"

"I'll rutting find out. Shouldn't you be signing in?" Corrie asked Jace.

"Blazes," he said, and then blocked another swat from Corrie. "Don't you be making trouble for me, Cor. I've got to stick to this house."

"You tell Minox that?"

"He didn't embarrass me."

"Let's go," Minox said.

The stationhouse was filled with activity when they entered. Officers and patrolmen were shouting across the work floor, some of them concerned with statements or reports or getting the people in the lockup properly charged and filed. Several dusty, dirty people were sitting around the place, huddled under blankets. Most likely residents of the Tower and surrounding buildings who were displaced in the events of last night.

"Jace!" Sergeant Tripper shouted. He was talking to a couple patrolmen in one corner of the work floor. "Go sign in and get to the squad room. Specs, come hear this."

Jace nodded and ran off. Minox and Rainey approached Sergeant Tripper, Corrie at their side.

"What's going on, Sergeant?" Rainey asked.

"Boys, tell him what you saw," Tripper said.

One of the patrolmen cleared his throat—the two of them both looked red-eyed and exhausted. "Last night, the brawl over on Orchid."

"There was a brawl on Orchid?" Minox asked. "I wasn't aware of that."

"Why would you be?" Tripper said. "Go on, boys."

"Yeah, this brawl, it was a bunch of Rose Street Princes, all crazy in the street, and they were fighting the Thorn. Right there, and the Thorn shot at us."

"Were you injured?" Minox asked. "And when was this?"

"No, we were all right," the second patrolman said. "But there was a lot of smoke."

"Smoke?"

"Yeah, his magic smoke, you know?"

"Smoke," Tripper said pointedly. "Like when the Left was attacked."

"Let him continue, Sergeant," Minox said. "Officer, when was this?"

"About nine bells."

"Nine bells?" Minox asked. "You are certain of this?"

"Yeah, pretty certain," the first patrolman said. "We had both come on at eight bells, and right when it happened, we wanted to grab the one Prince that was still around, but there were more whistles calling everyone to Clover and the Tower."

Tripper nodded enthusiastically. "So what do you think of that?"

"This is excellent, Sergeant," Minox said. "Gentlemen, I presume you're off shift at this point?"

They both nodded.

"Then go and rest. I appreciate your assistance."

They left, and Tripper looked triumphant. "The Thorn, attacking Princes on Orchid. Same way he attacked Benvin. I told you." Minox glanced at Rainey. She had the look in her eyes that told him she had reached the same conclusion as he had.

"You did indeed, Sergeant. If these gentlemen are giving accurate testimony—"

"Hey, now—"

"Which we think they are," Rainey supplied.

"Indeed," Minox said. "Then it proves it was a pretender, not the real Thorn, who attacked Lieutenant Benvin."

"What?" Tripper shouted so loud much of the work floor turned to them. He looked like he was about to throw a punch at Minox.

Rainey held up a hand and stepped in front of him. "You have to understand, Sergeant, that the Thorn was also seen at the Tower right when it was collapsing."

"Two of them," Corrie added.

"Who the blazes are you?" Tripper asked.

"Sergeant Corrie bloody Welling, tosser," she said. "Name's on my blasted badge."

"So how do you know that one was the real one?"

Minox decided delving into the details of the magic of

it—especially his own—would be counterproductive. "That isn't relevant at this juncture. Right now we need to move forward with our assigned investigation. Finding Lieutenant Benvin's attacker."

Tripper calmed a bit at that. "All right, so. What're you going to do for that?"

"I'll need all the reports of both incidents last night," Minox said. "Including the examinarium's reports on all the dead. Have all of that sent to the squad room immediately."

"Reports? Really?"

"In addition," Rainey said, pointedly, "we're going to need to interview witnesses. I presume you know where we can find Rose Street Princes?"

"Oh, I know, specs," Tripper said. "That I can take you to straightaway."

This Uni girl was all business, but Colin had to admit, she handled the damn business well. Annoying as all blazes. It was a right proper interrogation, but she never sounded like a constable once.

She sounded like how Colin imagined a Uni professor would.

But she would have done well with a Constabulary interrogation, he could tell that. Each time he, Veranix, or the other kid told her something, she asked a probing question that opened up new details. Colin didn't even realize how much he had really seen in the fight with the imposter.

"Well," Jiarna said as she closed her journal. "This is quite illuminating. I do think we're on point with the idea of two different imposters." She pointed to Colin and Delmin. "You two saw the same one, I'm nearly certain, but Veranix saw a different person."

"What do you base that on?" Veranix asked.

"The man Colin and Delmin saw made a point of showmanship. He wanted to be noticed, he wanted to be recognized. He wanted to engage."

"Damn right he did," Colin said.

"But yours?" Jiarna continued. "He was focused on a purpose. He killed Miss Quope—"

"Wait, was that the girl we—" Phadre started.

"Yes, the same. I'm glad you've caught up," Jiarna said.

"Well, that's a blasted shame."

Jiarna gave him a look, the kind that Colin knew meant the guy was in trouble.

"I mean that she was front placed in her category. And, you know, waste of human life."

"Certainly, darling," Jiarna said. "But if I may continue. He killed her with intent, based on your account. Three arrows for her, no one else engaged. He didn't bother coming back for you."

"Right, so?"

"So whoever he was, his mission was to kill Emilia. Nothing else."

"Why would—" Veranix started, but then he shut his trap. He was probably about to ask a stupid question, when the answer was pretty blazing clear. There were surely dozens of folks with scores to settle with a Deadly Bird.

"So you have two problems. I'm designating them the Jester and the Hunter."

"You're really going with those?" Delmin asked.

"What did you call Jensett before you knew his name?"

"The . . . Prankster."

"My names will suffice."

Colin stood up. "This is fascinating. But it's the Jester that the bosses are concerned about, and I still have to convince them that he isn't you. Or that you aren't him. Or, frankly, that I still don't really know who you are."

"How are you going to do that?" Veranix asked.

"Beats the blazes out of me," Colin said. "But I'll make the Jester my problem. Can you handle the Hunter?"

"I'm going to, have no doubt."

Colin didn't doubt it. Veranix had that same blasted intensity in his face when he talked about clearing the streets of *effitte*, or taking out Fenmere. The Hunter had stoked Veranix's fires by killing that Bird.

"All right, good. Now I need to clear off of campus in a trice."

Phadre stood up and extended his hand. "Thank you for your help."

Colin took it, still bewildered by this politeness these Uni friends of Veranix were showing him. "It's what I got to do. I took an oath to keep him safe, hear?"

"Yes," Jiarna said. "If you need assistance in some way . . ."

Colin snickered. "Yeah, thanks, skirt. But I've got enough trouble to explain to the Prince bosses, without adding you swells to it."

Veranix took him in an embrace. "We both need to be careful. Just notes with the preacher for the next few days, all right?"

"Smart," Colin said. He went to the door. "You all, keep his head on the rest of him, hmm?"

"I'll try," Delmin said.

"And he needs to get better marks."

"That's what I've been saying."

"Hey, enough," Veranix said.

"I promised your pop—"

"Get out of here," Veranix said. Colin chuckled. For once, he got to leave Veranix's space and leave him annoyed. He could get used to that.

The grounds crew were all standing around outside the tetchball field, like they didn't know they were supposed to be working.

"Gentlemen!" Kaiana shouted as she approached. "Is there some sort of problem?"

They all looked up at her. "Miss Nell," one of them called back. This was one of the new boys; she couldn't remember his name. "We need to show you something."

That was at least a new phrasing.

"What's going on?" she asked. "There are two matches here today, the first one in a couple of hours. Please tell me this field is going to be ready."

"No, we've got it nearly ready," Lash said. He looked close to nauseous. So did Rennie. The other boys, the new ones—they looked distraught, but nothing like "It's just . . . all right, we need to show this to you."

"But we got to ask you, Miss Nell," Rennie went on. "Are you having a lark of some sort on us?"

"A lark?" Kaiana asked. "Have I given you the impression that I'm having a lark of any kind?"

"It's just—" Rennie stepped away from the rest, pulling her aside with him. She yanked her arm out of his grip, but stayed with him. "Look, we may have had a laugh and gone too far with those boys—"

"I wasn't having a laugh," Kaiana said. "We let them off easy, frankly."

"And this isn't some trick that you're pulling on me and Lash, is it? I know we've been giving you the run and everything, but if this is a joke—"

"If what's a joke?"

"It needs to be over. Fair's on both sides."

"I really don't know what you're talking about, and I don't appreciate you wasting time. We need to—"

"You swear you didn't do this to prank us?"

She raised an eyebrow at him. "If nothing else, Mister Rennie, you should know how I feel about pranks."

"Ren, let's show her," Lash said. "I thought it was his joke at first, and he thought it was mine, but then it was clear it was neither of us, and these boys kept finding them . . ."

"Finding what?" Kaiana feared she already knew the answer.

Lash whistled to the other boys. One came over with a cloth sack.

"They're all over the place. By the field, under the stands, in the stands, the grass surrounding."

Kaiana looked in the sack. It was full of empty vials, all of them with residue inside.

"How many?" she asked.

"We found at least twenty," Lash said.

"And this isn't your trick?" Kaiana was surprised how angry and hard her voice sounded. Lash jumped back.

"No, ma'am, swear to the saints."

"And ain't nothing like that before yesterday's matches," Rennie added. "These are new."

Kaiana swore. Despite everything they had done, they weren't even close to stopping the flow of *effitte* on campus. It was worse than ever.

Chapter 15

SATRINE RAINEY HAD had quite enough of Sergeant Tripper this morning. He had been dismissive and annoying, though he had stopped short of actually disrespecting her rank. But she was stuck with him for the moment, since Welling had decided it was worth staying at the stationhouse to sort through the reports from last night, and Corrie went to campus to arrange the interview with Delmin Sarren and his blasted professor.

"Now, look here, specs," Tripper said as they approached the Turnabout. "This has got to be done in a delicate way, hear? We can't just charge in there."

"No?" Satrine asked. "Is it a private club? Do we need a Writ of Entry?"

"Nothing like that, no," Tripper said.

"Is this the part where you tell me that I just don't *know* Aventil or how it all works?"

Tripper made some strangling noises. "It just ain't like that, specs."

"Then tell me what it's like. This bar is the usual hangout of the—who? Orchid Street Princes?"

"Rose Street," he said.

"Yeah, that's a better name," she returned. "So I imagine the bar is where the underlings sit around at the tables in their individual crews—when they aren't out doing whatever mischiefs the gangs get into. Am I gathering?"

Tripper just huffed.

"Probably the basements under the bar, those are claimed by the bosses. That about right?"

"But you don't know—"

"What don't I know, Sergeant?"

He sighed. "Last time we went in here, one of ours got killed. His name was Arch."

"Killed by a Prince?" She saw something in his eyes. Anger? Fear? "I won't let that stop me from doing my job, Sergeant. I hope you can say the same."

"I'm just saying it's a dangerous place, and these colors won't protect you, ma'am."

"I never count on the colors to protect me." They were at the Turnabout now. Two boys with rose tattoos on their arms gave Rainey and Tripper some hard glares, but didn't say anything. "But do you have my back in there? Or do I have to call in help?"

"No, specs. I'm just saying, have care."

"I'll have care, all right." She went right past the two boys through the doors of the Turnabout, sticking her whistle in her mouth as she entered. She gave a strong, sharp blast.

"Do I have your attention?" she asked, letting the whistle drop back into her hand. Many eyes were on her, most of them belonging to people with that rose tattoo on their arms. None of them looked pleased to see her.

"What the blazes you want, stick?" A young woman with stars on her rose tattoo.

"The *inspector* has some questions," Tripper said. "She's looking into the attack on Lieutenant Benvin."

"We didn't have nothing to do with that, stick," she said.

"Maybe you didn't," Satrine said. "But it seems whoever did it also knocked you and yours over on Orchid last night. At least that's what we hear."

"That's what you hear? Who'd you hear that from?" The

Prince girl got up close, almost pressing her nose into Satrine's.

Satrine bit her cheek to not laugh at this girl's bravado. Another life, another path, she'd have been the same way. "There was a blasted open brawl in the street, girl. You think we wouldn't hear a thing or two about it?"

"So what's it to us?"

"You're delightful," Satrine said, this time with a laugh. "I don't care what it is to you. What it is to me is one of you is a witness, and I want to hear from them."

"Anybody see anything?" the girl called out to the room. No one spoke up. "Looks like you're out of luck, Waishen." The girl even dared to reach out and twirl a strand of Satrine's hair around her finger.

"Oh, look," Satrine said, grabbing the girl's wrist, "you put hands on an officer of the Constabulary." She spun the girl around, pinning her arm behind her back. The girl went for a knife on her hip, but Satrine had her other hand on it before the girl could reach it. "Let's not be doing that."

Princes got on their feet, and Tripper had his handstick half drawn before Satrine spoke out to the room. "Let's no one get too damn hasty. We'd hate to come in here just for questions and things get messy."

"So sit it down!" Tripper snapped. "We ain't looking to iron any of you. At least not today."

"You wanna let me go, Waishen?"

Satrine took the knife from her and pushed her away. "Cool down a bit, girl."

"I'm a winter's day," the girl said.

"What's the situation here, officers?" An old man, all white hair and beard, came from the back, ambling easily over to them. "Can I help you with something?" He gave them a large, toothy smile, which put Satrine in the mind of a Waish snow fox.

"As I was telling your friend here, we're looking into the attack on your people on Orchid last night."

"Attack? Oh, Inspector—Rainey, is it?" He peered at

her badge. "That's an exaggeration of events. I hear a few boys had a few too many at the Old Canal and started an argument over a pretty lady. You know how these stories get out of control."

"Don't sell us your nonsense, Casey," Tripper said.

"Do I know you, Sergeant?" Casey asked, regarding Tripper like an old fish. "Oh, you're one of the lieutenant's people, aren't you? His little merry band? Well, you tell him all of us at the Turnabout are wishing him a speedy recovery." Before Tripper spoke, Casey waved him off. "Never mind. I have a few friends at the stationhouse who can do that for me."

Tripper lunged at Casey, but Satrine quickly grabbed him by the collar and pulled him back. "We'll leave it at that, Sergeant."

"I'm going to bring a city of pain on your head," Tripper snarled at Casey. "Mark me, old man."

Satrine yanked him back, almost throwing him at the door. "Mister Casey, if you think of anything that might be of note to our investigation, please don't hesitate to leave word for me at the stationhouse."

"This isn't your house or neighborhood, is it, Inspector?"

"Attacks on constables are always handled out-of-house," Satrine said, shooting a glare at Tripper. "It keeps biases from entering into the investigation." Tripper stewed, but stepped back by the door.

"I see you've got a good head, Inspector. So I'll tell you, something like this, you shouldn't worry about."

"Why is that?"

"Because Aventil takes care of its own, Inspector. Right now, the Dogs and the Kickers are working out some issues, but that will sort itself in due course. A few new players are trying to get noticed, but they'll be taught their place. Everything will settle shortly. Not a matter for the sticks."

"See, Mister Casey," Satrine said, moving in a bit closer to him, "this is where we don't quite see the same street. You think everything will settle of its own accord. I think

I'm going to have to keep coming to Aventil until the man who attacked Lieutenant Benvin is on his way to Quarrygate. Now, I live in High River."

"Oo, la, High River," Casey said, snorting with derision.

"So I don't like coming into Aventil. It takes me twice as long to get out here, twice as long to get home. Each day I have to come out here, the more annoyed I am with everyone here. With this one right here"—she pointed to Tripper—"and all of you in here. The more annoyed I am, the more I'm going to come into this place and express my annoyance."

"What kind of—"

"That one there"—she pointed to the girl—"I could have popped irons on her and dragged her to the station and no one would have given a damn. But I'll give you this one for free. Tomorrow I won't be so inclined."

"You think you can come in here—"

"Yes, I do, Mister Casey. I really think I can. Because this isn't my neighborhood." She went over to the door, adding, "I don't give a damn about how the Dogs or the Campers or Princes or whatever feel things will sort themselves. I just want to solve my case and go home. And you will want me to solve my case and go home. Hear?"

She didn't wait for an answer, marching out of the Turnabout with Sergeant Tripper at her heels.

"Saints, Inspector," he said. "The blazes you think you're doing?"

"What I do best, Sergeant," she said. "Piss people off and get stuff done. Let's head to campus. Corrie should have arranged our next interview by now."

The tetch match would be a nail-biter if Veranix had cared about it. The game was on its third interval, and U of M was two points down with only three batters remaining. If they didn't make up the difference, they wouldn't even play the back half of the interval. Korifina was fielding like an oiled clock, and the boys of the Mary squad had managed the ten points only with one-point Jack Line crossings. The Korifina boys had managed a particularly brutal Double Jack cross in the second interval that had put them in the lead. This interval, U of M hadn't managed to put a single point on the board.

Veranix's head wasn't in the game. His thoughts swirled with Emilia, with the imposter—two imposters—and Inspector Welling. Emilia, he hadn't trusted her, despite saving him from that *effitte* den. He felt such a fool, said such horrible things to her, and yet she stayed there with him. She stayed and died for it. Killed by one of the imposters— the Hunter, as Jiarna had dubbed him. Then there was the Jester, who made Veranix even more nervous. A complete mystery, and willing and able to murder constables, go after the Princes and Orphans. And from Colin's description, a capable fighter. What did he want? Just to make the Thorn look bad?

And then Inspector Welling. Professor Alimen had gone into a state just upon being near him, and Veranix could understand why now. The man seemed downright ordinary, except for the strange flavor of *numina* flowing out of him. Specifically coming from his hand. A flavor that somehow Veranix was able to instinctively harmonize with—that was the only word that he could think of that applied. Or perhaps Inspector Welling had harmonized with him.

Their magical abilities linked to each other, in a way Veranix had never done in a practical lesson or anywhere else. In that moment, they worked together to save the people on the street from the fallen building. But that had been a fluke, a sudden convergence of their power that Veranix felt he didn't even properly control. Had Inspector Welling managed to control him and his magical ability? Was that even possible?

Was this because Inspector Welling was Uncircled? Or in spite of it? Did his lack of training lead him to using magic in ways no proper mage had ever worked out?

Veranix's mind reeled with the possibilities and implications, but it scared him far more than facing Fenmere. He understood why Professor Alimen had been so disturbed by the man.

He would have to ask Delmin about it.

No, not Delmin. He'd panic. Jiarna, perhaps. She'd look at it rationally, scientifically.

He glanced up to the stands. Jiarna was next to Phadre, both dressed in blue and white, screaming in excitement. Veranix glanced back at the pitch, to see that Needle—Needle, of all people—had just hit a Double Jack. Good for him. Veranix didn't think he had it in him. Needle sprinted past the Jack Line and the Double Jack as the Korifina Triple Warder dove for the tetchball, which had landed just a few feet shy of the Triple Jack. The Triple Warder had the ball in hand the moment Needle crossed the Double Jack, and threw it to their Deep Double as he charged at Needle. The Triple Warder had a good five inches and thirty pounds on Needle. This wasn't going to end pretty for him.

"Dive knock!" Veranix shouted.

Needle remembered the play. Instead of trying to outrun the Triple Warder, Needle barreled toward him, and dropped to the ground in a roll right before the Warder got his hands on him.

Needle crashed into the Warder's legs at full stride, while the Warder had nothing to grab on to. He went face first into the dirt, while Needle rolled back up onto his feet and crossed the Triple Jack.

Needle was already turned back around and running toward the Tetch Rail before the Triple Warder could pull himself up, blood gushing from his nose. As soon as Needle was back over the Double Jack, the Right and Left Feet were on him, pulling him hard to the ground.

"Restore!" the Watcher called. "Four points to University of Maradaine!"

Veranix turned back toward the stands to see Jiarna—as well as the rest of the U of M fans—go wild for that play, but he saw something else past the stands, outside the pitch.

Kaiana, and three largish boys grouped around her.

Veranix didn't waste any time moving over there.

"You all can be about your business," Kaiana was saying, staring hard at the middle boy looming over her. Veranix recognized these three bruisers once he closed the distance. Pirrell boys, the same ones who had been giving him a hard time in Almers. What the blazes was their problem?

"Come on, skirt," he was saying. "We saw you watching us, we know what you—"

"Let's not finish that thought," Veranix said, stepping in next to Kaiana. "She told you to be about your business."

The middle one scoffed. "Get the depths out of our way before we make you our business."

"You tried once, let's not bother again."

"Oh, the rabbit," the one on the left said. "You gonna jump around on us again?"

"I'm no rabbit," Veranix said sharply. He wasn't going to accept that particular epithet, not ever.

"That jumping might save your skin, but not the skirt's," the middle one said. "You want to play hero, you might have to actually fight us."

"If that's what it's got to be," Veranix said.

"Still, three of us, and you're mighty short. Do the math."

Veranix didn't have any urge to play around with these boys. With a rush of *numina*, he surrounded his head and fists in bright blue flame. "Mage. Do the math."

They all stumbled back, and while the middle one looked like he still wanted to give a fight, the other two pulled him away. As they retreated, Veranix turned off the flame and turned to Kaiana.

"You all right?"

"I'm fine," she said hotly. "I didn't need you coming to make a spectacle."

"I wasn't making a spectacle," Veranix said.

She just glared at him. A glare that said he had screwed up.

"I thought you were in trouble," he said meekly.

"I can handle it. Why don't you worry about Emilia or whatever her name was?"

Veranix almost choked, Kaiana's venom shocking words out of his throat for a moment.

"She's dead, that's why," he said.

Kaiana looked abashed for a moment. "Right. Sorry."

"How could you—"

"Sorry!"

"I was just coming to help you—"

"Well, you finally were paying attention for once—"

"What the blazes is that supposed to mean?"

She shoved a bag that she was carrying—he hadn't even noticed before—into his hands, opening it up. It was filled with empty *effitte* vials. "That's what it means. We didn't stop a blasted thing."

"Where did you find these?"

"All over campus, Vee. Especially here at the tetchball pitch. I was finding more now, and saw those boys from Pirrell acting suspicious—"

"Were they using?"

"Do you even care?"

That hit him in the heart like ice. He handed the bag back to her. "I don't know how you could even ask that. I nearly died last night facing Fenmere's goons."

"I'm sorry," she said coldly. "It just seems like this on campus hasn't been your priority."

"You'll forgive me that I've had a few things pulling at my attention."

"I can bet," she muttered.

Veranix let that drop. With everything swirling in his skull, the last thing he needed was to fight more with Kai. "I've got to deal with these imposters," he said. "And the *effitte*."

"How?" It was almost a threat the way she spat it at him.

"The vials have mostly been around the pitch?"

She nodded.

"Then I'll stick to the tetch squad again tonight." He sighed hard.

"Is it that bad?" she asked, and he couldn't tell if she was being sympathetic or not.

"I'm going to stay out of the cups, no matter what they're doing."

"Finally, some wisdom," she said.

She turned to walk off, and Veranix almost reached out to her. She pulled her arm away, as if she sensed he was going to do that.

The crowd cheered. The top of the interval was over, and the U of M boys were about to take the field. If they held the lead, sticking with them through the night meant a victory crawl.

Veranix almost wished for another fight with Fenmere's men.

He glanced back in Kai's direction, where something else grabbed his attention. Walking along the south lawn, toward Bolingwood Tower, were two women in Constabulary uniforms. One of them, with her red hair and inspector's vest, he immediately recognized as Welling's partner, Inspector Rainey.

She was going to talk to Professor Alimen.

Veranix couldn't imagine anything good would come from that.

"You were a Uni gal, right, Tricky?" Corrie asked as she led Satrine toward the professor's office, which appeared to be in an actual tower isolated away from the rest of the buildings. A magic professor in a tower. Satrine thought it was like something out of the old storybooks. Sergeant Tripper walked a few paces behind them, keeping whatever thoughts he had to himself.

"Most definitely not," Satrine said.

"Yet you're all refined and educated," Corrie said. "How'd you rutting manage that?"

"Painfully," Satrine said. That was the easiest honest answer she could give.

"So tell me this, Trick," Corrie said. "I ain't never known Minox to take a pass on questioning someone. So why the blazes are you and I here without him?"

"You did note that the Professor Alimen was a mage, yes?"

"Yeah, and?"

"You haven't noticed that mages don't like your brother?"

"Yeah, but he doesn't give a toss about that sewage."

"This mage professor nearly threw a fit in the street just looking at Minox."

"And rutting Circle law kept you from just ironing him there."

"That and not having a real charge," Satrine said.

They heard someone huffing and puffing as footsteps came crashing up to them. Jace, running at full tilt across the campus lawn.

"Slow the blazes down, Jace," Corrie admonished him.

"You didn't notice when I blew a call, or shouted," he said. "I had to catch up."

"Didn't hear you," Satrine said. "What's the call?"

"Minox, er—Inspector Welling—" Satrine noticed Sergeant Tripper giving Jace a glare. "He said that the girl who was killed at the Tower was a student participating in the games here named Emilia Quope. And get this—she was dressed all in leather, with a mask."

"More of these crazies," Tripper said. "Just what we need."

"We only were able to get a name because someone recognized her from the charcoal sketch. She's competing in the games. She was winning whatever competition she was in."

Satrine nodded. "So we should start looking into her."

"Why we need to do that?" Tripper asked.

"Because that girl was killed by either the Thorn or someone pretending to be the Thorn," Satrine said. "You couldn't figure that out?"

"So whoever it was might tie to the Left's attack. Fine." He sighed. "I ain't got no questions for this professor or nothing, so why don't I head over to student administration and start getting us a couple steps ahead for this girl, and see what's what?"

"Excellent plan," Satrine said. "Keep Jace with you."

"Right," he said. "Come on, kid."

"You were anxious to get rid of him, weren't you?" Corrie asked as soon as they were out of earshot.

Satrine started walking toward the tower. "I get it, this special squad of Benvin's—the one Jace is on. They're clearly the only ones in Aventil who give a blaze about enforcing the law in this neighborhood."

"But something still sits in your rutting teeth, hmm?"

Corrie wasn't half as dumb as she pretended to be. "They've got the drive, but not the vision. Tripper there wants someone in Quarry for Benvin, and I really don't think he cares who. If he could use it to drag in all the gang kids, he would. Jace ever talk about Benvin at home?"

"Only like a rutting schoolgirl. 'The lieutenant said this.' 'The lieutenant told me that.'"

"I just wonder if Tripper's the same way. I think the squad is foundering without the lieutenant to hold the reins."

They reached the tower, and the door opened before they had a chance to, though Satrine was surprised to see a familiar figure emerge.

"Major," she said to her old friend from Druth Intelligence. "What are you doing here?"

Altom Dresser, retired major in Druth Intelligence and mage in the Red Wolf Circle, looked a bit put out, as if he had been caught in the midst of something embarrassing. Strangest of all, he was actually wearing the gray Druth Intelligence uniform, something that was almost never worn. He still greeted her back with warm regard.

"I could ask you the same," he said as he took her in a quick embrace. "You aren't trying to investigate the professor or something?"

"No, one of his students was a witness to an attack. Professor Alimen didn't want us asking any questions without his supervision."

"Hmmm," Major Dresser said, nodding absently.

"Were you pulled out of retirement?"

"Hmm, what?" he asked. He looked down at his uniform.

"Oh, yes. Well, there's never really retirement for us, hmm? Needed to look official just now, is all."

This raised several questions in Satrine's mind that she was certain Major Dresser would not answer. Especially with Corrie Welling—or anyone else—a few feet away. And she was curious about the answers to those questions, but she also knew they bore minimal connection to the case, or anything else in her life. There was no need to prolong things with Major Dresser out of her idle curiosity.

"It all worked out well, then?" she asked.

"Fine, yes. I really must be—"

"Of course, yes, I wouldn't want to keep you."

They gave perfunctory good-byes, while Dresser gave her a small signal with a scratch of his nose and ear. Much to her annoyance, Satrine couldn't remember exactly what that signal meant. She knew it, generally, was a warning to be cautious, but there was a nuance to it that she had forgotten.

Be cautious with Professor Alimen? She had already presumed that.

"What the rutting blazes was all that?" Corrie asked once the major had walked away.

"I'm not entirely sure."

"That ain't an army uniform, Tricky."

"I know what kind of uniform it is. Let's go on."

They had just gotten inside the tower when Professor Alimen confronted them on the staircase, his face hard. Delmin Sarren stood a few feet behind him.

"What in the name of the saints was that, Inspector?" he asked coldly, every syllable punctuated.

"What was what?"

"I saw you out there with Major Dresser." That was an accusation.

"Just saying hello, Professor. Nothing—"

"So you do know him!" he said. "Who are you? What is all this?"

"Professor—" Sarren started, but the professor cut him off. The poor kid looked like he had no idea what was happening.

"Tell me, Inspector Rainey. You know Dresser. You have an Uncircled mage working in the Constabulary, your partner, and he—"

"Best watch your tongue—" Corrie started. Satrine grabbed her wrist before she went too far.

"What are you trying to do?" Alimen asked. "Are you part of the Altarn Initiative? Is that what his hand is about?"

Satrine was definitely confused by that. "I'm only here about the attack on Lieutenant Benvin—"

"No, no, I'll none of it," Alimen said. "I'll not be bullied or tricked by you."

Satrine held up her hands, trying to show a sign of calm. "Professor, I think there is a misunderstanding here—"

"Yes, I know it now," Alimen said. "We are done, Inspector. You have no further questions for my student. Or business on this campus without the proper writs."

He marched back up the stairs, and as he did, the door behind Satrine flew open.

"That's our rutting cue to walk out," Corrie said.

"Most definitely," Satrine said, and did exactly that.

"Just so we're clear," Corrie said, "I've no blasted clue what the blazes just happened."

"You're not the only one," Satrine said. Unfortunately, whatever was going on between Major Dresser and Professor Alimen would have to go into her own Unresolved file. Dealing with that wouldn't get her any closer to solving this case and getting out of Aventil.

Chapter 16

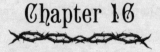

A THICK, meaty hand was on the back of Veranix's neck. "What are you just standing there for, Calbert? Let's get inside."

Hoovie and Chippit, the Right and Left Foots of the tetchball squad, flanked Veranix outside the Turnabout. Much of the rest of the squad were already heading inside, charged off their fourteen-to-twelve win over the High Academy of Korifina. They were now one of the four teams in the final rounds. The day after tomorrow, they would play whoever won in Pirrell versus Cape Institute.

So tonight they were on another victory crawl, and Veranix followed along. Not because he cared about celebrating—at this point he didn't give a blazes what happened on the tetchball field—but because going back to Jiarna's social strategy was the only way he could think of to keep a finger on the *effitte* problem on campus.

That one finger was all he could spare. Between the *effitte*, the two imposters, and an Uncircled mage inspector, he couldn't juggle anything else. He certainly couldn't just go hunting as the Thorn right now. He didn't have any idea how to handle any of it, other than being out with the squad, ready to take action if something sprang up. So with the tetch squad he went.

He didn't know they'd be heading into the Turnabout, though.

"I've heard some things about this place—" he started.

"Yeah, it's a gang hangout," Hoovie said. "But they'll let us in."

"You read those blasted pamphlets?" Chippit asked.

"Crazy," Hoovie said. "It ain't nothing. These gang kids wouldn't hurt us."

"Not all of us." Catfish, the Far Bumper, said coming up from behind them. "What the blazes are you prattles waiting for?"

"Vee has stuck feet," Chippit said.

"Well, unstick them." Catfish tried to give Veranix a playful shove, but Veranix jumped ahead before Catfish properly put hands on him. If he had touched him, he would have felt Veranix hiding his bow and quiver under the napranium cloak. Except for his staff, Veranix was ready to be the Thorn in a moment, all masked under an illusion held up by the cloak.

"All right, all right, I'm going," he said. "If this is where you all want." He went in, keeping himself behind the squad members who had already gone in.

This wasn't the first time Veranix had been in the Turnabout, but it was the first time while wearing his own face. Of course, he was masking the bruises, and even with the cloak and rope on, it was a challenge to hold that on top of the rest of his masking.

He had considered and rejected the idea of changing his face to look slightly less like himself. It would probably confuse the tetch squad, but he definitely wouldn't be able to keep it consistent. He'd make a mistake, and he couldn't afford that.

There had been too many already.

"You boys in the right place?" someone asked.

Tosler was at the front of the group. "We've got coin for beers and strikers, so I think so!"

Veranix noted the bartender giving a look to an old man in the corner, who gave a nod of approval.

"What'll it be?" the bartender asked.

Tosler threw some coins down on the counter and started rattling an order off, while other boys on the squad went to claim a table. At a gesture from the old man, a handful of Princes cleared away from one of them. It seemed the Princes wanted to avoid trouble, and that suited Veranix just fine.

Veranix moved over to the table with the other boys, making sure to keep someone between him and the old man in the corner. Whoever that was, he was the most likely to have known Veranix's father, and make a connection.

"Oy." Before he realized it, a woman was right in his face. Prince with captain stars tattooed on her arm. "Let's make something clear."

"All right," Veranix said, keeping his head down a bit. No eye contact. "We're just here to celebrate the win is all."

"Celebration is good. Just don't get too many ideas about making this a place you come on the usual."

"Fine," Veranix said. He glanced up, noting that she was still staring hard at him. "Why are you telling me this?"

"Because you look like the one who has half a lick of sense in this crew. Keep your boys in line."

"I'll do what I can."

The squad had all sat down and Tosler had brought over beers for all. "Gentlemen, gentlemen," he said. "This one was hard won, they gave us what for . . ."

"Hey, let Vee do it," Ottie said.

"Me do what?"

"Give the salute!" Needle said.

"He does it best!" Ottie said.

"They're right on that score," Tosler said. "Beers up, gents!"

"No, I don't think I should—"

"Vee! Vee! Vee!" they all chanted. Far too many Prince eyes were looking his way.

"All right, all right, hush," he said, raising his beer. "Today you all—you . . . Today you had a fight out there. Those Korifina boys played good and hard and you did not let them earn a single point easily. At one point one of them crawled over the Double Jack with three of you hanging on him."

"You praising them or us, Vee?" Blute asked.

"Give me a moment, Blute," Veranix said. "I am saying these boys were *worthy* adversaries, and we should treat them with honor as we raise up our glasses. They played hard and strong, and it was only due to the power and team-work each and every one of you brought to this match that you came out on top. You put blood and sweat and heart on that field."

"Aye!" they all shouted.

"I left a fair amount of blood out there," Catfish said. He still had some caked on his face from the hit to the nose he took during the match.

"That's because you're a bleeder," Veranix said. "If I can give you all any advice, it's this—don't get hit in the face, less you want to be as ugly as Catfish here."

"Aye!" they all shouted again.

"So drink up," Veranix said, "You've all earned it."

They raced to finish their beers, while Veranix just took a meager sip from his own. No need to get lost in his cups tonight, for any reason.

"Another set!" Blute shouted.

"Another set!" Tosler echoed, and he went back to the bar.

The Prince captain was at the table, standing far too close to Veranix for his own comfort. He recognized her now. She had been the one who fought Blackbird with Jutie the first time he encountered her.

Emilia, he reminded himself, *not Blackbird*. Treat her with the honor of her own blazing name.

"Boys," she said sternly. "I gather you are celebrating a victory."

"We are!" Catfish said, moving a little too close to her for his safety.

"Bring it down, steve," she said, pushing him back into his chair. "We ain't really a raucous, yelling sort of establishment. Most of ours are just ... tolerant of you Uni boys, you hear?"

"We hear," Veranix said before anyone else could respond. "We're doing a victory crawl, so we'll just have one more here and move on to the next place, right?"

"Right," she said. She gave him another look, eyebrow up. "You got good sense for a Uni."

"Vee!" Tosler yelled from the bar. "Help me carry!"

Far too much attention was being placed on Veranix for his comfort. He moved over to the bar to help Tosler.

"You managed on your own last time," he muttered to Tosler.

"Last time there wasn't that dark-eyed nimble asking for you to come talk to her," he said back with a grin. "Vee, you've got the magic, in every way."

Veranix noted the young woman he was indicating. She was stunning, no doubt, and almost every eye not on him and the tetch squad was looking at her.

Veranix's attention was completely on her, because he knew perfectly well who it was, even without her bladed hoops spinning around her body. She slinked closer to him as Tosler carried some of the beers over to the table.

"Hello, Thorn," Bluejay whispered.

"You must be confused, miss," he said.

"I'm not. I saw you last night, and I know damn well who you are." Her voice was almost silky with her eastern Druth accent, but Veranix wasn't enticed at all. "You're going to play nice and follow me to the alley."

"And why would I—"

"Because if you don't, 'Vee,'" she said with a purring smile, "I'm going to kill every last one of those boys over there. So it's your choice."

She strolled over to the back doors, casting an eye over her shoulder as she went.

Tosler was back over. "What did she want?"

Veranix answered honestly. "She wants me to follow her."

"Then you better get out there, my friend, or you're an idiot."

"Tosler," Veranix said, taking a gulp of one of the beers. "You're more right than you know." He went to the back door after Bluejay, and as he left, he could tell that the old man had definitely noticed him.

Satrine had embraced the fact that there was no going home on time this evening. Everything about this case had sent Welling into his mode, where things like rest or signing out or spending time with family went completely out the window. Of course, none of those things were ever particularly high priorities for Welling in the first place.

Though, if anything, working with Jace had brought out an interesting new spark. In the past few months of partnership, she had seen Minox Welling be excited, intrigued, and invested in solving a case, but usually for the sake of the answers, for the sake of justice. But she had never seen him so animated, and it seemed entirely about working with his brother for the first time.

Jace was fascinating to observe—he had all his brother's better qualities, wrapped up in youthful enthusiasm.

"Are you going to tell me where Minox is right now?" she asked Jace as he led them down the street. Welling had gone off somewhere to further investigate his ideas, and Satrine once again had to carry the water of sending official messages back to the captain at the Grand Inspectors' Unit on their behalf. This time Captain Cinellan wrote back that she should not sign out or leave the neighborhood without Minox. She knew damn well that what the captain meant was that she should drag him out and bring him back home, but in practice it meant she was stuck with him until he was satisfied that he had done everything he could.

Welling was never satisfied.

So Satrine had sent word home to her daughters and Missus Abernand not to expect her anytime soon. Corrie, amazingly, had agreed to do that for her, though she shuddered to think what a few minutes of exposure to Corrie Welling would do to her daughters' vocabulary.

"I'm showing you," Jace said, half jogging down the street. Saints, that boy had energy.

"Did your mother never teach you boys about giving straight answers?"

"That all went to Corrie," Jace said, flashing a grin.

"She also signed out and went home."

"Yeah, maybe she got all the common sense."

Jace led her to a pub in the heart of the part of the neighborhood controlled by the Waterpath Orphans. "Don't tell me he's in there."

"They serve food," Jace said.

"You go in there?"

"Not in this coat," he said. "I don't know what you've got in Inemar, but here, we don't go into any of *these* pubs unless it's business. Blazes, Lieutenant Benvin got straight up poisoned by the Red Rabbits."

"Really?" That was information Satrine would have thought was relevant. "The same Red Rabbits that the Thorn embarrassed?"

"Yeah," Jace said plainly. Then realization crossed his face. "Oh, you think—but there are none around no more."

"Except the ones who were killed by the other Thorn on Orchid, according to the report."

"I don't know, specs," Jace said.

"Well, that's why you're the cadet. So, if not the pub, what? You all have a flop up top there?"

"Yeah, come on."

The flop in question was crowded. Welling was in there with Tripper and Pollit, the latter of whom was dozing on the bed. Tripper had left campus while they were questioning associates of Emilia Quope. Welling was going through papers and documents—the same sort of files that ought to be at the stationhouse.

"Looks like quite the party," Satrine said. "Should I have brought cider or wine?"

"Tea would be better," Welling said dryly. "The lieutenant's squad have been doing good work here, Rainey. They've compiled quite a bit of information. Not—"

"Let me guess," Satrine said. "Nothing actionable for arrests, right?"

"Is this a familiar song?" Tripper asked.

"Quite," Satrine said. "We've got a thing we call 'unresolved.'"

"Oh, we've got that in cords," Tripper said. "That's the order of the day in Aventil."

"All right," Satrine said, taking a seat at the table. "Do you want to hear what I have?"

"Eagerly," Welling said, though he didn't look up from the files he was reading.

This was nothing new.

Satrine took a seat. "So, a bulk of my day, when not trying to rattle gang members or getting screamed at by magic professors—"

"Screamed?"

"You don't even want to know. Needless to say, Professor Alimen was not cooperative with my investigation."

"So, no further questioning of Delmin Sarren?"

"Not a chance, unless we get a Writ of Compulsion."

"You ain't going to get that, not from our Protector's Office," Tripper said. "He ain't about to piss off anyone above him to Compel someone on campus, especially not a professor."

"Especially not a magic professor," Pollit added, not rising from the bed.

"Anyhow," Satrine said. She was eager to get through this. Maybe with her information, Welling would be willing to go home, sleep, and let his brain work on things. "So I looked into Emilia Quope."

"That's a waste of your time," Tripper said. He had been dismissive of that investigation the entire time.

"Student at the Royal College of Maradaine, in her fourth year. Was competing in Floor and Beam, and had been the ranking contender after the first day of events. But none of the RCM chaperones or athletes had much of a strong opinion of her personally. Seemed she was distant with them."

Welling looked up. "She should have been housed on campus for the games. All the athletes are."

"She had a room. I was shown it. Nothing of note to be found there."

"Yes, but my point is more, she had a room. So what was she doing at the Tower Tenement last night?"

"Carousing? Celebrating?" Tripper offered. "She was in the lead."

"Well, I have something on that," Satrine said. "She was at a social house party last night until about seven bells, and she left abruptly."

"We don't know why," Welling said.

"We don't," Satrine said.

"We also don't know why she was wearing that outfit and mask, near the Thorn. I must do some further research."

"Here's what we do know. The night before she had been seen out on the town, and several boys on the U of M tetchball squad remembered her. She had wandered off with their batting coach."

"While her personal dalliances might be relevant as to why she was at the Tower, I don't think it is appropriate—"

"I'm hardly gossip mongering," Satrine said. "Because this is where we have an interesting coincidence."

Welling raised his eyebrow at her. "Coincidence" was always a word to get his attention. "As you know—"

"Yes, coincidence rarely occurs naturally. I've been listening." She went on. "The coach is one Veranix Calbert. Who you might recall is—"

"The magic student, friends with Delmin Sarren," Welling said. "That is certainly curious." He took a moment in thought, and then dug back into his box of papers.

He was going to keep this up unless Satrine actively stopped him. "I know you love a box full of papers to sort through, especially if there are newsprints involved—"

"Saitle's out collecting those," Pollit muttered from the bed.

"Shouldn't that boy be home in bed or something?" Satrine asked. "Saints, shouldn't all of you?"

"Pollit is in bed," Tripper said.

"I'm just resting my eyes."

Satrine sighed. "I'm saying, I admire this devotion, gentlemen, but—"

Welling looked up from his papers. "You can feel free to sign out and go home, Inspector. I do know your family needs your devotion as well."

"Yeah, except the captain sent word not to let you spend the night here in Aventil without me."

"That is an unreasonable order. If it helps you, Rainey, I can go in to sign out with you, and then you can go home."

"And then you come back here," she said. "No, nothing doing. You're going to kill yourself slogging through work. I'm not about to—"

Suddenly Welling's left hand—his gloved, altered hand—shot up and pointed to the window.

"What the blazes is that?" Tripper asked.

"I am not certain," Welling said, straining to bring his arm back down. "A curious sensation has just intensified."

"Like last night?" Jace asked.

Welling raised an eyebrow. "Not dissimilar."

"What, what last night?" Satrine asked.

"When we encountered the Thorn," Welling said. "Our use of magic . . . synchronized. I've been feeling some of that throughout the day, but it has taken on a different flavor. It is difficult to explain."

"What is he talking about?" Tripper asked.

"It don't matter," Jace snapped. "Point is, maybe the Thorn is nearby?"

Welling was on his feet. "Yes, I believe so. Actively."

"Wait, what?" Tripper was hard-eyed. "How the blazes is he—what's with his—"

"That's of no moment, Sergeant," Satrine said harshly.

"Point is we've got a lead, and we should move. On your feet, Pollit."

Pollit was up with crossbow in hand. "Let's get this bastard."

"In irons," Satrine said firmly. "We do this clean and right, hear?"

"Heard," Tripper said. "Let's move."

They filed out of the room, Satrine taking up the rear with Welling. "You now a compass with that thing?"

"I do not profess full understanding of the altered nature of my hand," Welling said. "As you well know."

"You'll forgive me if I don't put complete faith in it."

"Nor do I," he said. "You do know that I don't believe the Thorn is responsible for Lieutenant Benvin."

"I don't either," Satrine said. "But that's hardly the only wrong the Thorn has to answer for."

Welling gave a noncommittal nod, as if he did not fully believe that either.

Satrine gave it no mind. It wasn't their call if the Thorn was guilty. They just needed to deliver him into the hands of law and justice. Hopefully those hands would do the right thing.

Once on the street, Welling looked around, and then pointed north. "This way," he said. "Something is definitely happening."

"What is it?"

Welling didn't answer. Suddenly he broke into a run, as if his feet had taken hold of him.

"Where's he—" Tripper started. Welling was already half a block ahead, he had run so fast.

"Don't just stand there," Satrine said, sprinting after her partner. "Run!"

By the time Veranix was in the back alley, he had shed any illusion, putting on his appearance as the Thorn, rope in hand. He willed it to coil up around his arm and move like a snake. Maybe that would put a bit of fear into Bluejay.

Of course, she was the one who damaged the rope in the first place.

She was there, her circular blades in her hands. She didn't have the bladed hoops spinning around her waist—perhaps too impractical to take into the Turnabout.

"So you had the guts to come out, bastard," she said.

"You're the one who threatened to murder people," Thorn said. "You didn't give me much choice."

"Good. I only want to kill you." Her eyes showed none of the madcap joy she had when they had fought before. She was pure anger.

This wasn't a hired hit. This was her, looking to settle something.

"Why?" he asked.

"You have the audacity to even ask that?"

"Humor me."

She launched herself at him, her whole body a whirlwind of strength and grace while the blades came spinning at his head.

He ducked and rolled, willing the rope to lash out and wrap around her ankle. With a sharp yank, he threw her at the brick wall by the backhouse. She spun in the air to hit the wall feet first, and jump off to land on the ground.

"Not going for the kill with me, Thorn?" she snarled.

"You're the one trying to kill me." There was no space here in the back alley to move, get out his bow. He needed to change that if he was to have any chance here.

"You've earned it," she said, her blades coming in toward his neck. Easy to dodge. Her anger was making her sloppy. That was something in his favor.

"Tell me why!" A blast of quick magic, covering one of her blades in sticky resin.

"What the blazes is going on out there?" A door in the alley opened up, a huge man with a Prince tattoo coming out.

"None of yours!" Bluejay shouted, throwing her other blade at the Prince. It hit him in the gut, and he shouted in pain.

"Help! Murderers!" he cried.

Too little space, too much attention. "Follow along if you want to kill me," he shouted at Bluejay, and magicked a jump up onto the roof.

He only had a moment to breathe once he was up there, drawing out the bow. He had an arrow nocked when she came over the ledge, one blade still stuck to her hand.

"Hold it right there, Bluejay," he said.

"So this is how you kill me?"

"You came after me!"

"Because you killed her!"

That startled him, and he lowered his bow. "You mean Emilia?"

"You don't get to use her name!" She launched into a furious attack, pulling out a new blade. Veranix pulled up and fired, which she blocked easily. He had another arrow nocked and fired before she was on him, but the shot went wild when he jumped out of her way.

"I didn't kill her!" He swung his bow around and cracked her over the skull. It probably would ruin the bow, but that didn't matter right now.

She was already turned back toward him, blade whirling in one hand. "She helped you and that was how you repaid her?"

She pressed on him, and he was forced to use the bow to hold her back, keep her blades away from him. "How did you—"

"You think she carried you from Dentonhill and up four flights alone? I was there, you fool—"

"Then you would know—"

"I don't know why she trusted you—"

Veranix dropped and rolled backward, bringing his foot up into her gut as he went. She was flung off to the far side of the roof, landing like a cat.

"It wasn't me!"

"Who else could it have been? And who killed Cormorant and Sparrow?"

An arrow came from the distance, striking Bluejay in the shoulder.

"I did, you filthy bird."

A cloaked figure came closer, bow raised. "I gave all of them what they deserved." The Hunter. It was too dark to get a good look at him, his face covered with the hood. He fired two more arrows at her. Bluejay was ready, blocking both with her blades, then breaking off the arrow in her shoulder.

Veranix had his own bow up, arrow at the ready. "Back away, fraud."

"Stay out of this," the Hunter said. "This isn't your fight."

"You play at being me, you make it my fight."

"This isn't about you. I just want the Bird."

"I'll kill you," Bluejay said. "Both of you!" She leaped at the Hunter while throwing one blade at Veranix. He dodged, barely, as it shaved past his head. Bluejay sliced with the stuck blade, catching the Hunter's hood as he fired another arrow. Blood flew from his face and her chest. Despite the arrow through her body, she swung two more times at him before he grabbed her wrist.

Veranix aimed and fired, but the arrow missed, short and far to the right. His bow was too damaged.

The Hunter dropped his own bow and took Bluejay by the throat. Despite her face turning beet red, blood pouring out of her chest, she swung her legs up and wrapped them around his neck. But then she went limp, and the Hunter dropped her to the ground.

"Don't you move!" Veranix shouted, putting up his useless bow and grabbing the rope.

"The world is better without her, like her friends," the Hunter said. He picked up his bow.

Veranix drew up the rope and shot it out to entangle the Hunter, but only snatched his bow. The Hunter let go of it, allowing it to fly at Veranix while he ran.

Veranix pulled the rope into a coil and caught the Hunter's bow, ready to use it to take the Hunter down. But when he looked up to take aim, the Hunter was already gone.

"I told them . . . it was you," Bluejay gurgled through her bloody mouth, her eyes filled with hatred. "The Birds . . . they'll come for you . . ."

She wheezed a final breath when he heard someone else approach.

"Constabulary! Stand and be held by law!"

Veranix spun, bow raised, to see Inspector Minox Welling up on the roof, his crossbow aimed right for Veranix's heart.

Chapter 17

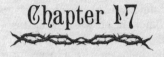

"I'M NOT THE one you want here, Inspector," Veranix said, keeping his aim trained on the man.

"Perhaps not," Inspector Welling said. "But there's a dead woman at your feet."

"I didn't kill her."

"Or Emilia Quope?" Welling kept the crossbow up. Veranix felt his stomach churn.

"The killer slipped away just now, dressed like me. He did them both."

"How many Thorns are there?" Veranix expected a mocking tone from the question, but it actually seemed genuine.

"Only one," Veranix said. "But there's two fakes out there."

Inspector Welling's face almost lit up. "I knew it!"

"Then let's just step away, so you can bring them in," Veranix said.

"My duty compels me," Welling said. "Lower your bow and this can go peacefully."

Sounds came of others coming up to the roof, from two sides, as well as shouts from constables and Princes in the street. Soon Welling wouldn't be the only one up here. Veranix was going to have to get out of here, and quickly.

"Peacefully is exactly how I'll go," he said. He built up

a rush of *numina* and channeled it to his legs. He had already leaped up high in the air when Welling fired the crossbow.

"No!" Welling shouted, and he reached out with his gloved hand.

The rope uncoiled, flying right to Welling's hand. Veranix snatched at it instinctively, having already launched into the air. Before he knew it, he was towing Inspector Welling along with him.

"Minox!" The shout came from Inspector Rainey, having reached the roof in time to see the two of them fly off half a block.

Veranix landed ugly on the next rooftop, his whole jump thrown off by the extra weight of Inspector Welling. It was just shy of a crash, rolling when he hit the roof to avoid breaking anything. He spun and sprang to his feet just in time to see Welling hurling through the air at him, head first.

The man would be killed if he landed like that.

A quick and dirty rush of *numina*, he slowed the world and made the air around them thick and liquid. Welling sloshed through, slowing down enough for Veranix to catch him before he broke his neck. They both collapsed in a heap together.

Inspector Welling immediately grabbed Veranix's wrist and twisted it behind his back, flipping Veranix over face down in the process. Welling put a knee on Veranix's back, pinning him down to the floor. Veranix was initially too dazed by the fast magic and crash to do anything about it.

"You are bound by law. You will be ironed and taken under arrest. Do you want your charges named?"

Welling grabbed Veranix's wrist with his gloved hand, and suddenly there was a surge of *numina* running through him. Veranix's mind snapped into place, and he willed the rope around Welling's body, pulling him off.

Veranix rolled back up, attempting to keep Welling bound in the rope.

Again Welling exerted sway over the rope. Their mutual

attempt to control it caused *numina* to spark and storm around them.

"You don't know what you're doing," Veranix said.

"I think I have an inkling," Welling said. Suddenly Veranix's end of the rope swirled around his arm and started to work its way behind his back. "More familiar than you could imagine."

His hand. Veranix had no idea what Welling's hand was or why it felt like napranium and dalmatium at the same time, but he could feel it still, even with Welling ten feet away.

He could feel it the same way he could feel the rope and the cloak.

"I'm very sorry about this, Inspector," he said, pulling in as much *numina* as he could manage to channel into himself.

Welling gave a confused look, as if he was trying to hear something just out of earshot.

Veranix shoved all the *numina* he had into that hand. He willed it into a fist, with so much power that the hand itself burst into blue flame.

"How—" was all Inspector Welling managed to say before his own left hand smashed into his face.

Welling went down like a sack, and the rope released. Veranix quickly willed it back into a coil at his belt.

"Terribly sorry," he said, and took another magical leap off the roof before the man could regain his senses.

"I'm very sorry about this, Inspector."

Minox considered himself gifted in determining when he was being lied to. Even with the Thorn's face obscured, every instinct in his gut told him the vigilante—and this was the true one, of that he was certain—was being honest. The Thorn did not wish to fight or injure him.

It was accompanied with a rush of magical power that was unlike any Minox had ever felt before. Even with his untrained abilities, he recognized the sheer power that had suddenly manifested. Minox was surprised enough by this that he didn't even realize that his left hand had balled into a fist and burst into flame.

The Thorn had taken control of his own hand.

"How—" was all he managed to ask.

And then his own hand knocked him in the face.

"Terribly sorry."

Minox lost track of the moments between hearing that and hearing the rush of boot-clad footsteps coming toward him.

"Minox! Minox!"

Inspector Rainey must be truly concerned if she was using his given name.

She was kneeling next to him, hands on his face, checking him for injuries.

Still dazed, he spoke up before she pawed at him further. "I am largely unharmed, save my pride."

"What the blazes happened?" she asked, looking around. "The Thorn got away?"

"A singular experience," Minox said, sitting up. He flexed his left hand, the glove covering its black, glassy appearance now destroyed. He seemed to have full control over it again. At least for the moment. "What did you see?"

"He jumped off, tangling you in that rope of his," she said. She glanced off, muttering, "I should ask the major about that . . ."

"He did not entangle me. Quite the opposite. I was able to exert control over it, and pull myself along with him."

She turned back, face astonished. "How did you do that?"

"I'm not entirely certain," he said. "It was not unlike how I'm able to control my hand. Which might explain how he was able to take control of it."

"He controlled your hand?" She reached out to touch it, her own fingers hovering a few inches away. Inspector Rainey rarely showed trepidation, but his transformed hand still made her nervous. He could hardly fault her for that. It had been nearly two months since his hand had been transformed, and he still barely understood what it was or how it functioned. Nights like tonight only confirmed that.

"He used it to knock me out," Minox said.

"Let's get you off this roof," Rainey said, taking his normal hand and pulling him to his feet. "We'll have Tripper and his folks whistle up a group of footpatrol, sweep south. That's where he seems to be going . . ."

"No," Minox said. "There is a dead body left over there, and that should be attended to. But more importantly, this encounter has given me much to consider, and has taxed me far more than I can easily bear."

"So what should we do?" she asked.

"Exactly what you counseled an hour ago, Inspector," he said. "Let us allow the local Constabulary to handle the body and other elements here. It is their job, after all. We should sign out and go home. The proper sleep will do me good."

When Colin came to the Turnabout, a bunch of sticks were milling about outside, even nosing around the alley to the basement. For a half a click he thought that they had raided the Turnabout, but that would mean a passel of lockwagons, friends in irons. That wasn't happening at all. The sticks were too calm, too weary.

Something had happened, but given that he could see the Turnabout was still full of Princes, it couldn't have been too bad for the gang.

Plus he walked past the sticks to the door, and none of them made a move to stop him. If there had been a scene in the Turnabout, if someone had been arrested from there, that wouldn't have happened.

All the Princes inside were quiet, heads down. Tooser looked up when Colin came in, but he quickly looked down at his beer. No one was looking at him. Or one another.

"What's the word?" he asked Kint as he approached the bar.

"Ain't mine to know," Kint said. "I just serve, friend."

"All right, then I need a beer," Colin said.

"No, you don't." This came from behind. Colin turned. Two of the heavies from downstairs loomed over him.

"I don't?" Colin asked. "How's that?"

"You need to come downstairs. Now."

"That's what I came here for," Colin said pointedly.

"Then let's go." They moved closer to him like they were going to force him. Colin was getting tired of this sewage.

"First hand that touches me is forfeit," Colin said.

One of them—Iggs, Colin thought his name was— snickered and grabbed Colin's arm. He pulled him out the back and to the basement. Colin noticed a trail of blood from the back alley door down to the bosses' card room.

Old Casey was sitting at the front table, with Giles, Frenty, and Bottin. Their glasses of beer were all near empty, a tapped keg sitting in the corner. Colin recognized it as part of the special stash that had been stored away in his old flop with the double-bolt lock. If the bosses were drinking that, they'd have to be celebrating something huge, or really upset about something. Since they all looked ready to eat glass, it couldn't be the first one.

"Colin, glad you could join us," Casey said coldly. He was not offered a chair. In fact, Iggs was still holding on to his arm.

"I was here, and coming down. There was no need for this insult," Colin said. He pulled out of Iggs's grip.

"We weren't that sure about that," Frenty said.

"Oh, really?" Colin asked. "Why the blazes is that? Did I hide or make a run?"

Frenty didn't say anything. None of them did, but Giles stared so hard and hateful, they could have burned the stars off Colin's arm.

"I take that as a no," Colin said.

"Not yet," Giles said.

"Fine," Colin said. He quickly pulled out one knife, grabbed Iggs by the wrist and plunged the knife into his hand. Iggs screamed, blood everywhere. Colin kicked him in the knee and sent him crumpling down, while twisting his knife as he pulled it out of the mangled hand. The other goons moved in, but Colin pointed the blade at them.

"I told him—a rutting Prince captain told him—not to lay a hand on me or he'd lose it. If you tossers want to lose something, try me."

Casey waved to the goons to take Iggs out. With ugly looks at Colin, they picked Iggs up off the floor and pulled him out of the room.

"I'm getting really tired of this sort of treatment, Casey," Colin said. "I thought we were square this morning."

"This morning I told you to come to the Turnabout tonight to tell us what you found."

"And I'm rutting well here."

"Later than I'd like."

"And so you have the muscle grab me? That's a lack of respect, Casey."

"And, what, you won't have it?" Frenty asked.

Frenty was a skinny bag of nothing. Colin had no idea how he ever made captain, let alone becoming a Basement Boss. Giles and Bottin had plenty of scrap back in their day, but not Frenty.

"I won't have it, no. And neither would any of you if you were in my place. Next time you send boys like that for me, be ready for a lot more blood than that."

"Tough talk from a captain without a crew," Bottin said.

"I don't have a crew anymore? You're taking the ones I kept alive away from me?"

"No, we ain't," Casey said, glaring at the other three. "We just want some goddamned answers from you."

"What the blazes did you think I came here to do, Casey? You said go find things out, and I did that. Don't act like I'm holding out on you all."

"Aren't you?" Giles asked.

Casey waved Giles down.

"So, what did you learn?" Frenty asked. "Did you go and talk to the Thorn's girl?"

"Yeah, I did," Colin said. "Talked with the Thorn's whole crew."

"Thorn has a crew now?"

Colin regretted saying that. Might as well dive into the creek.

"Yeah, you think he does everything alone? Of course he has people."

"I told you," Giles said. "He's gearing up to make a play!"

"Enough." Casey pounded a fist on the table. "So what happened?"

"Well, there's not one fake Thorn out there, there's two."

"Two?"

"At the same time one of them was killing Sotch and our folks, the real one and the other fake were tussling in that dustup at the Tower. From what I hear whispered from the sticks, and the Dogs and Kickers, that all tracks." Not that he had actually gone and talked to anyone else about that. But he knew the bosses needed further confirmation. "Here's what I figure—"

"You're figuring now?" This was Giles.

"Yeah, I am. You ask me to find things out, be boots on the street, then I'm gonna figure a few things. You wanna hear?"

"Enlighten me," Giles said, leaning back in his chair.

"The thing we got to worry about is the fake who hit us. The real one, the other fake, that ain't our problem. At best, they're each other's problem, or the sticks'. But we got to shut down the fake who cost us in blood."

"That's great, Tyson," Frenty said. "Glad you figured that out. Anything else you want to tell us about how we should do things?"

"Hey, if you—"

"Here's what you don't blazing know, you sewage-spilling prat," Giles snarled. "While you were figuring with your boots on the street, the *Thorn*, the blasted, actually real *Thorn*, killed some bird right here on our blazing roof!"

"What?" Colin was honestly shocked by that. "When did this happen?"

"Less than an hour ago," Frenty said. "Why do you think all those sticks are milling about up there? Because they tried to grab the Thorn, they're investigating the girl, and they're still parked on top of us!"

"I didn't know anything about that," Colin said. Had Veranix killed some girl? Or had the Hunter, but these fools thought it was really the Thorn? And who was the girl?

"At least he admits that," Giles said, mostly to Casey. "He doesn't know anything!"

"I know what's going on out there—"

"You didn't know the Thorn would hit the Turnabout!"

"Did he hit it?" Colin asked. "Hmm? Did he kill one of ours? Rob the till? Make off with Vessrin's shoes or something?"

"He was on our roof!"

"I heard you the first time, Giles. If the Thorn wanted to hit the Turnabout, then it would look like the Trusted Friend does. You can be sure about that."

"So," Casey said quietly, "since you're such a loyal Prince, Colin, I want to know what you're going to do for us."

Colin's thoughts raced. The best thing for him right now, the best thing for the Princes, would be to nail this Jester fraud. Find him, hit him hard and good, and once the Princes had gotten their cup of blood from him, drop his body off on the Constabulary Stationhouse steps. That would get the heat off the street and off of Veranix. The only question was how to draw the Jester out.

"All right, all right, I got a blasted idea," Colin said.

"You blazing well better, because—"

That tore it. "I swear to the saints, Giles, if you want to eat your teeth—"

"Bring it down, Tyson," Old Casey said. "Giles, enough of your guff, though."

Giles went off to the tap and filled his glass, grumbling the whole time.

"He's been giving me—"

"I don't blazing care! You know how often I've stepped up to the rail for you? To these tossers, and to Vessrin? Give me something, Colin."

"Yeah, and I think I've got something. Look, whoever is making noise, fake Thorn, real Thorn, I don't know . . . but—"

"I don't care real or fake. I don't care if there's one or three. Tell me what you're going to do."

"Right, so . . . the guy who hit us, whoever he really is, he wanted the Rabbits, right?"

"Rabbits are all dead now," Bottin said.

"Yeah, but who knows that Sotch didn't make it? Just a few of our people. We spread out the word that she's all right, where she's hiding, we dress up someone to play the part . . ."

Old Casey's face brightened. "Then you flush this bastard out."

"It's not terrible," Giles said.

"How are you gonna do it, though?" Frenty asked.

How was he going to do it? It was clear they were putting it all on him. Let him take the risk of fighting the Jester. Let him do all the work. And all the blame if it goes bad. There was only one way he could think of, though.

"I'll get word out that she's going to go to the church, hide with the preacher. Put on a gripe act, like I'm talking out of turn."

"And people would buy that from you," Giles said.

Colin didn't give that a response.

"That should spread the word enough that it could filter to this guy," Bottin said. "Then you bring a ringer over to the church, and you're ready when he comes?"

"Something like that," Colin said. "I'm guessing Cabie isn't on her feet."

"Might never be," Casey said.

"Bassa?" Frenty offered.

"She's a good foot taller than Sotch was," Colin said. "Deena is the right height."

Giles scoffed. "Risky job, you're suggesting the bird who rolled you over and took your crew?"

"I'm just saying, she's a match. Give me whoever you want. Give me a crew or don't. If you want me all on my own, I can work in the wind. You want me to play second to someone, fine. Whatever you all need."

"A loyal Prince," Giles said with a sneer.

"Let it rutting be, Giles," Casey said. He turned back to Colin. "Deena's good. And her crew as backup. Work it out with them."

"Thanks, Casey," Colin said. "We'll get this tosser."

"Damn well better," Casey said.

"Sorry about the blood," Colin said. "Just next time—"

"That was a mistake," Casey said, glaring over at Frenty. He came out from the table and led Colin to the door. He lowered his voice as they crossed over. "It ain't just these guys here. Vessrin keeps muttering about how you're just like your father. Show me, show *him*, that you've got a handle on things in the streets, for *all of us*. That's what I need to keep these boys off your back."

"I hear, boss," Colin said.

"All right," Casey said, clapping a friendly hand on Colin's neck. For once, it really did feel like some form of filial affection from Casey. Colin had almost forgotten what that was like.

"I'll get it done, you can count on that," Colin said.

"You better count on it," Casey said. "Now get out of here."

Colin didn't waste any time getting back out into the night. As he left the basement, Iggs and the other boys were lurking in the alley. They kept their distance, but Colin could see that they were glowering at him. That was going to be a problem. Between them and the bosses under Casey, he had all sorts of problems brewing right in his house.

Blazes.

Of all the things he had to worry about, the last thing he needed was to feel like he couldn't trust someone with a Rose on their arm.

But that was exactly where he was right now.

Almers Hall was quiet when he slipped in. At this hour, the doors probably should be locked, and he'd have to climb up to the second floor to jimmy his way into his room through the window. The interim prefects set up for the summer clearly had a lot to learn about keeping things secure. But that suited his needs well enough. No one was noting his comings or goings, nor did anyone give any mind when he slipped off campus. He made his way up the stairwell to the second floor, where it was only a few quick steps to his room.

"Hey, Hence."

Depths, he didn't want to deal with anyone right now.

"Hence, hey." There was insistence in the voice. No avoiding it.

Enzin turned to see Poncher, the delving thick-skulled addle who captained the Pirrell tetchball squad, ambling over to his room. He was a half-witted addle, but he had plenty of coin in his pocket, so Enzin put on a smile.

"Sorry, Ponch. Didn't hear you just then."

"Yeah, didn't want to be too loud," Poncher said. "Folks are sleeping. Or out making revels. That where you were?"

"Revels. Exactly."

"Were you invited to something fancy?" Poncher said.

"Why do you—"

"You got the cape of your dress uniform," Poncher said, grabbing the crimson cloak with his meaty fingers.

"Yes, that's right," Enzin said, pulling it free. "Special dinner."

"Guess that's what happens when you win your event," Poncher said with a dull laugh. Enzin had received plenty of praise and attention for claiming the top prize in Archery for Pirrell. Winning that had been utter simplicity compared to his own agenda. "I guess we'll see what that's like ourselves, huh?"

"You seem to be on your way," Enzin said. "You're playing Central Academy tomorrow, yes?"

"Yeah, which is why I wanted to catch you before you racked down. Those Academy boys, they're, like, military cadets. Well trained, organized."

"Your squad should be fine."

"Yeah, but . . ." He glanced around the hallway, despite no one else being around. "We already finished all the Fist you sold us on that last game. We're gonna need more."

Enzin hid his disgust. Selling Soldier's Fist to these boys just so they could cheat their way to a tetchball victory was necessary to pay his way from Kyst to Maradaine. As much as he hated it—he only had so much Fist, and he needed it—he also was going to need to pay his tuition to finish his schooling, and pay for further travels if he didn't finish his task in Maradaine.

"It's gonna cost," Enzin said. "And I mean significantly."

"Yeah, sure, sure," Poncher said. "We got it, whatever you need."

"Give me a second," Enzin said. Waving Poncher off, he went into his room and shut the door behind him. He noticed his hand was starting to tremor as he latched it. His own dose of Fist was running out. The slice he had gotten on his cheek, the bruises on his neck—he was starting to feel them. He'd need a bit more Fist tonight. Just a few drops, he still needed to be able to sleep. But a few drops.

He stripped off the cloak and the rest of his gear, putting the quiver under the bed. He lost the bow, which was fine. He had two more, thanks to Pirrell University, but that bow had been special. That had been his father's bow, and now this Thorn had it.

Delving, meddling Thorn. What were the odds that Maradaine would have someone else with a bow, a crimson cloak, and a grudge with the Birds? Or something with the Birds. The Thorn had been far too chummy with Blackbird.

Didn't matter. Blackbird was dead. Bluejay was dead as well, now. He'd sleep well knowing that. Of all the Deadly Birds on his list, she was the one he had wanted most. She was the one who had killed his sister Anzi.

But all the Deadly Birds were going to pay. They had

taken Pop and Mama, Perri, Fermo, and most of all Anzi. They only didn't get Enzin because of their strange rules about only hunting their targets for a set number of days. But they had left him with nothing.

Nothing but his bow and a few casks of Fist. He had already sold some of it, used some to give him the edge he needed to fight those delving Birds. Now there were just two jugs left. He pulled that out from under the bed, and grabbed a handful of the glass vials he had bought from Pop's old friend Benny. Those were a handy way to pass out doses of the stuff to the addles on the tetchball squad.

Despite the tremor in his hand, he measured out a few dozen vials, nearly finishing the jug in the process. Those few remaining drops, he emptied into his own mouth.

As soon as the drops hit his tongue, he felt that exquisite rush mixed with a numbing bliss. The pain in his face and neck, the rest of his body, all washed away.

Just one jug left.

That last jug was going to have to be enough for him. He was going to need it to finish his fight with the Birds.

And if the Thorn got in his way again, saints and sinners help that poor soul.

Veranix didn't dare head to campus. Something about Inspector Welling's hand could connect to him. Or to the napranium tools. It was strange, and beyond Veranix's capability to understand. Delmin would have to figure it out. More likely Phadre and Jiarna. This was something on their level.

But it meant that Welling might be able to track him, find him. How the blazes else was he able to be up on that roof?

He jumped from roof to roof, pushing south all the way to Kemper and Low Bridge. Welling might be able to track him, but he couldn't match his speed. Maybe with enough distance, changing directions, he'd leave a tangle of *numina* that Welling couldn't possibly follow.

He needed to get rid of the rope and cloak, somewhere

safe. The flop over the laundry wasn't an option, and not just because Phadre and Jiarna were staying there. He couldn't risk leading the Constabulary there. He might as well turn himself in.

He was on the roof of a cheap tenement, one covered in paint jobs marking it as Kemper Street Kickers territory. This whole block was like that—run-down and marked. Even the shops had a blue K painted on the door, and those that didn't had broken windows.

He could hear a few Kickers on the street below, mostly just laughing and carousing. This part of the neighborhood wasn't crowded at all. Veranix wondered if anyone who came to town for the games even bothered renting rooms down here. He couldn't imagine it would be worth it.

There was no telling if Welling still was after him. Though if a cadre of Constabulary came rushing down in this part of town, the Kickers would give them trouble.

Veranix didn't care for that thought, even though it would help him.

He needed to rest, hide his gear. He needed a safe sanctuary.

As soon as he thought that, he almost wanted to kick himself for the obviousness of what he needed to do.

He went west, across the Toothless Dogs' territory, where he saw several groups of Dogs huddled around corners, also carousing and griping. Even up on the roofs, racing his way along, he could hear them snarl and shout about the Kickers. These two gangs were more trouble than the other four combined. He wasn't sure if the carriage crash at the Tower Tenements was caused by their fight, or if their row came up due to the crash. Either way, they made the situation worse.

Or had he done it?

Did his war with Fenmere lead to the end of the Rabbits, which cracked the balance in Aventil? Was whatever was happening between the Dogs and Kickers his job to clean up?

Kaiana would probably say it was. And she'd probably be right.

One more thing for the list.

Into the Hallaran's Boys part of the neighborhood, by Drum and Bear, he turned back up north. Making his way to Saint Julian's.

There was no sign of a Constabulary action by the time he reached the church. At least, no more than could be expected. Each block closer to campus, he saw more constables on the street, but they seemed to be concerned with safety and patrol. None of them looked like they were on an active search. He definitely didn't see—or sense—Inspector Welling.

He went into the clock tower and stripped off his gear, forming a bundle of the cloak, rope, and weapons. As soon as he removed the cloak, exhaustion set in. He hadn't paid attention to how hard he had been pushing himself.

He must have been making noise as he stumbled out of the tower and down the stairs, and Reverend Pemmick was coming up, lamp in hand.

"I wasn't expecting you," he said with a slight grin. "Well, when I heard someone clomping around, I expected it was you. I didn't think you'd being coming here tonight, though."

"I wasn't planning on it either, but trouble found its way to me."

"That seems to be your habit. You look a fright."

"I just need to sit down for a bit," Veranix said. His legs buckled for a moment as he stepped down. "Maybe something to eat if you can spare it."

"We always spare what we can," Pemmick said. "Come along."

They went down to the cells beneath the church, where Pemmick found some bread, cheese, and mustard in the larder. "It isn't much . . ."

"It's fine, Reverend," Veranix said. "I'm very grateful."

"Why did you come here tonight?"

Veranix had to answer honestly. With the support and openness that Reverend Pemmick had given him, anything less would an insult.

"There's a constable inspector—he's here investigating the attack on Benvin."

"And you're suspected."

"Not exactly," Veranix said. "I don't know, I think this inspector, he—"

He knew about the two imposters. Inspector Welling *already* knew.

"Thorn?" Pemmick asked.

Veranix realized he must have gone silent mid-sentence.

"Sorry, Reverend," Veranix said. "I just realized something. Anyhow, this inspector is also a mage—"

"That's allowed?"

"My professor doesn't seem to think so, but the inspector has a vest, so who is he to say? But he's a mage who can also connect to my rope and cloak. And perhaps sense me as well. I'm not sure, exactly, but I need some place safe to recover."

Pemmick furrowed his brow. "I confess the areas of magic have been a shortfall in my studies, so I don't fully understand the things you're telling me, Thorn."

"It's Vera—"

"Do not tell me unless we are performing Absolution, son." He sighed. "I do not understand about the magic involved, but I do understand your need for refuge. You should rest here for the night."

Veranix considered what the reverend just said. There was so much on his shoulders, so much on his soul. He wasn't sure how much longer he could carry it. "Maybe that is what I should do."

"I'll prepare one of the sleeping cells for you—"

"No, Reverend," Veranix said. "Absolution."

Reverend Pemmick gave the barest of smiles. He went over to one of the cupboards and produced a bottle of wine and two cups. He quietly poured for them both and sat down. He took Veranix's hand and closed his eyes.

"May our voices be heard by only God and the saints, for our words are for no one else."

He opened his eyes and picked up his wine.

"I'm going to tell you everything, Reverend," Veranix said. "Absolutely everything."

"That was why I got the wine out," Pemmick said. "I have a feeling we'll be at this for a while. Go ahead. I am bound to silence."

Veranix took a sip of his own wine, and then a deep breath.

"My name is Veranix Calbert. I'm a magic student at the University of Maradaine, and I am the son of Cal Tyson."

Chapter 18

THE SCENT OF TEA and honeyed oats woke Veranix. He opened his eyes to Reverend Pemmick watching over him.

"Is it morning?" he asked.

"Only just," the reverend said. "You do not sleep with a peaceful face."

"I never noticed," Veranix said, sitting up from the cot in the basement cell. "Were you watching me long?"

The reverend picked up a mug from the tray sitting next to him. "There's a passage in the 'Tale of Saint Irina'—"

Veranix nodded, taking the offered tea. "'Look upon my face while I rest, and you shall see if I hold any guile there.' I know it."

"You've studied your *Tales of the Saints*. I'm pleasantly surprised."

"Well, you aren't helping a complete heathen," Veranix said. "I don't have much to be peaceful about. I'm lucky to have made it through the past few nights. Saints, I'm lucky to be alive at all."

Pemmick scowled, sitting on the cot. "I am not a fan of luck. It feels like belief in a fickle faith." He thought deeply for a moment, looking like what he wanted to say was almost painful for him. Finally he said quietly, "Blessed might be a better word for you."

"Blessed, Reverend?" Veranix asked. He could tell the reverend wasn't using the word lightly—he was using it in its saintly context. "I wouldn't make that claim."

"What else would you say? Random fortune being responsible for your continued survival strikes me as short-sighted. For example—how was that unpleasantness on campus stopped?"

"You're going to have to be more specific, Rev."

"A few months ago, at the Ceremony of Letters. It was stopped while you were holding off the two assassins. When we met."

The reverend had told Veranix he'd seen him as an image of Saint Benton during that fight with Bluejay and Magpie two months ago. That was what had made him decide to help Veranix. Veranix tried not to think too much on that revelation. Being compared to a saint in any context was disquieting.

"Right," Veranix said. "I didn't have anything to do with that, really. My friends did it, disrupting the alchemical magic."

"And how did they do it?"

Veranix realized the reverend was using the Method of Questions, like all his least favorite professors used. He wanted Veranix to reach a conclusion he had already made. Veranix sipped at the tea and played along.

"They used the napranium rope," he said, pointing to it, draped across the chair in the corner of the cell. "Channeling the *numina* powering the alchemy away from the campus—"

"And to?"

"To the cloak, and me, in Cantarell Square."

"Which did what?"

"Saved me from being killed by Bluejay and Magpie. Yes, I know, Rev, but that doesn't mean—"

"I'm not done, son," Pemmick said. "This part is important. Why did your friends have that rope and not you?"

"Kai brought it with her hoping Del could use it to track me—"

"Yes, but why was it available to her? Why didn't you have it?"

"It wasn't working right. Bluejay cut it in our first fight."

"Rather peculiar, hmm?" Pemmick asked. "A small event—inconsequential—cascaded to other events that proved crucial for saving your life, as well as everyone on campus."

"And you're trying to convince me I'm not lucky?"

"Luck? And not the design of a higher power?"

"No," Veranix said, his emotions suddenly rising up in his chest. He got up from the cot and picked up his shirt. He was so stricken, he could barely get words out. "My life—you would have me—by design?" was all he managed at first.

"You're upset, obviously—"

His real feelings found voice, "You want me to believe that I'm living a *plan* set for me by God or the saints? Did they kill my father, destroy my mother, just to set me on it?"

"That's not quite what I—"

"That they would make me suffer to be their instrument?"

"Most of the saints suffered. But they still chose what was right. I see that in you."

"I'm sorry, Rev, I have a hard time swallowing that. I'd far prefer the terrible things in my life have been just part of normal tragedy. Don't tell me it's a path to beatification."

The reverend was silent for a bit. "I'm sorry."

"I need to get moving. Folks on campus will be worried." He started to get dressed.

"Before you leave, I may have a solution for your other problem."

"You're going to have to be more specific."

Reverend Pemmick laughed. "You told me about these . . . Deadly Birds. You fear they'll be hunting you."

"Right," Veranix said. "If you've got a solution to that, I'm listening."

"You know that the various gang captains meet in the church as a neutral ground. They respect it as a place of peace."

Veranix didn't explicitly know that, but he nodded. "Sure."

"Perhaps we can arrange a similar parley between you and these Birds."

"I'm for it," Veranix said. If they thought he killed Emilia, Bluejay, and those others Bluejay named, then he'd need a chance to explain himself. One less problem on his shoulders right now. "How would we even do that? Colin?"

Pemmick shook his head. "This morning a different Rose Street Prince captain visited in the early hours, and when I inquired about your cousin, she implied that he is being kept quite busy right now by his bosses. I fear he is out of favor."

"He's got plenty of problems, and I shouldn't add to them."

"The Prince captain has already left, but she met with one of the Waterpath Orphan captains. I think she might be someone we can use to contact the Birds."

Veranix wasn't sure how he felt about the Orphans. They didn't seem to care for Fenmere—holding the line between Aventil and Dentonhill mattered to them. Maybe that was enough. Maybe he should be friendlier with the other Aventil gangs. Or at least cordial.

"And it might be best if you take a few actions so those on the streets do not think you favor the Princes," Pemmick said, as if he had heard his thoughts.

"She's still here?"

"I instructed her to wait, taking her back to my study. Though we should probably not leave her alone any longer."

"All right," Veranix said, grabbing the last of his gear and putting it on. He pulled the hood over his head and magicked the mask of darkness over his face. "Let's go talk to her."

They went up to Pemmick's study, where the Orphan captain was waiting restlessly, twirling one of her knives around absently. She looked like a Waterpath Orphan— dingy, shabby clothes, scars on her cheeks.

"Yessa?" the reverend said as they entered. "Apologies for making you wait."

"I ain't got much better place to be, Rev, so—saints on fire!"

That was when she saw Veranix.

"Morning to you, too," Veranix said, augmenting his voice to echo when he spoke.

"That—" she said, pointing with her knife, as if she didn't realize how threatening that appeared, "that is the rutting *Thorn*, Reverend."

"I'm aware of that," Pemmick said.

"Me too," Veranix said.

"I didn't know you wanted me to wait to church meet with the Thorn. Blazes, I thought—" She chuckled, shaking her head. "Don't matter. So, Thorn. Pleasure to meet you."

"Yessa, was it?"

"Yessa, indeed. No one's daughter and no one's mother. What does the Thorn want from me?"

"I've got a bit of a problem—"

She burst out laughing. "I'd say. The sticks want you locked up, the Princes want you knocked around, and Fenmere's folk put two thousand crowns on your head."

"I've heard that figure as well," Veranix said.

"I'm surprised the sticks aren't after you to cash in on that," Yessa said. She sat down in one of the chairs, flipping the knife absently. "I can tell you, Orphans won't go for that. Not for two thousand. Mostly because they wouldn't want to do Fenmere the favor."

"I appreciate that."

"So we have some common ground," Pemmick said. "I had hoped you would."

"You got something for my throat, Reverend? Wine or cider?"

"It's nine bells in the morning."

"And I've got to parley with the Thorn, so I need a bit of a kick."

Pemmick sighed and went to a cabinet.

"So Orphans wouldn't want to hurt me—"

"I didn't say that. But you fight Fenmere, broke up the

Rabbits, and are pissing off the Princes and the sticks, so I like your style."

She was giving him credit for things the imposters had done, but he wasn't going to bother to disabuse her of that notion.

"The Deadly Birds might be coming after me," Veranix said. "They think I've been hunting them."

"Haven't you? I heard about that tussle in Cantarell Square." She took the wine offered from the reverend. A sip, and she added, "You watered it."

"Allow me that," he said.

Veranix waved off the cup he was offered. The Thorn needed to have some mystique, and what little he had left with Yessa would bleed out on the floor if he was drinking wine. "I'm not interested in the Birds, but I also can't have them coming after me. I have enough concerns."

"Fine, but what the blazes do you think I can do about it?"

"I want to talk to them. Here. Tonight. At midnight."

"And you think I can set that up?"

"Can you?" Pemmick asked.

She thought about it for a moment. "All right, I may know someone who can contact the Birds. I'll see if I can get them here."

"Good. Let the reverend know if you do." Veranix went to leave.

"Hey, Thorn!" she shouted. "Let's make one thing clear. You're gonna owe the Orphans a favor. That's a marker I am going to get my crowns for."

"Fair enough," Veranix said. Time to add in a bit of that mystique. "But you better earn what you ask for." That sounded enough like a vague threat to exit on, magicking up black curls of smoke and darkness to surround himself with before slipping out the door.

Of course, had anyone been in the hallway, that bit of theater would have looked ridiculous. He shrouded himself and went up to the bell tower. Time to get back home to the campus before Kaiana and the others burned the city down looking for him.

Colin had been through more than his share of sewage, especially from the bosses, and he'd take whatever came his way. But nothing felt stranger and wronger to him than what he had to do this morning.

He knocked on the door of his old flop, where his old crew were still crashed in, so he could ask their captain for help.

He could hear the double-latch flip inside, and the door opened up. Tooser, that great big lug, opened it up just enough to look through.

"Hey there, Toos," Colin said. "How you doing?"

"What are you doing here, Colin?"

"I'm a Prince, this is a Prince flop, ain't it?"

"You shouldn't be here."

"When did we turn Princes away when I was the cap here, Toos?"

"That ain't it—"

"And I need to talk to your captain," Colin said. "So open the blazing door."

Tooser paused. "She ain't here right now."

"Where the blazes is she?"

"Does she answer to you or something?"

"Sweet saints, Tooser, why are you making this so blasted hard?"

"Because I know what you did," Tooser said, nearly spitting in Colin's face as he said it. Colin wasn't about to take that.

"What do you think I did?"

"You left Jutie in the wind."

That hit Colin right in the gut, because it was true. Colin had to choose between fighting sticks to save Jutie, or saving Veranix. "I didn't have a choice . . ."

"You choose to be loyal to your crew, the bodies under you. That's what being a captain is supposed to mean."

"It wasn't like that, Toos . . ."

Before he could continue, Deena strolled up the alley to

the door, smile brighter than two full moons. "Colin Tyson, what can we do for you?"

"We've got a job to do, you and me," Colin said.

"You're taking my crew, Tyson?" she asked.

"No, Deena, I'm taking *you*. Bosses said. Whether you want to bring the rest of your crew in or not is up to you." He wasn't going to give her a hint of anything resembling disrespect about her being the captain of this crew now.

"You and me, on some gig together?" she asked. "Am I being punished?"

"Pardon?"

"She means your partners tend to end out bad," Tooser said. "Like your current crew."

"Or Cabie," Deena added.

"Not funny," Colin said. "My crew got hit hard, same with Cabie's, and we've got to do something about the tosser who did it."

"And what are we going to do?"

"We're going to go inside so we can talk in private, Deena," Colin said. "So open the blazes up."

"What do you think, Tooser?"

"I think I don't like it."

"Tooser doesn't like it."

"Oh, I see," Colin said. "I'll go let Old Casey know that Tooser doesn't like the plan, so it's not happening. I'm sure he'll be thrilled." He stepped away from the door.

"Hey, hey," Deena said. "No need to be that way, Tyson. Come on in, tell us what we're doing."

So naming Casey got her attention. Either she already knew what was happening, or she knew Colin wouldn't drop Casey's name lightly. Tooser opened the door and let them in.

The flop was brighter and better smelling than Colin remembered it. Tooser went in the back while Deena took a jug of cider out of the cupboard—Colin could see it was far better stocked than it had ever been when this was his flop—and poured cups for the two of them.

"So what are we doing?" she asked.

"This guy who hit us, he's pretending to be the Thorn—"

"Because you know the difference between a pretender and the real thing."

"Yeah, I do," Colin said. "Don't be causing a problem about that."

"It's your problem, not mine. So, this pretender."

"His whole thing was taking out the Red Rabbits. That's why he hit us, because we had Sotch."

"All right," Deena said. "And now you want to hit him back."

"Right, but we don't know where this guy is. We got to draw him out."

"And how do you—oh." She got to it quick. "Yeah, I'm the right height and build, ain't I?"

"Pretty much. We put out some whispers that Sotch is going to go to the church for sanctuary."

"Which she ain't, because she's dead, yes?"

"Yes."

"But we're hoping this guy doesn't realize that he won already."

"And when he comes, we'll be ready for him."

"We better, cuz I'm the one who'll be wearing the fur."

"All right, good," Colin said. "Do we bring your crew along as backup?" He really wanted to let this be her call. He didn't want anyone to claim he tried to push it one direction or the other.

She thought about it for a bit, sipping at her cider. "Nah," she said finally. "It's got to look like we're doing this as mouse quiet as we can manage. More bodies in the street, even if they're discreet, it'll look like a trap."

"We've got to presume this tosser is smart," Colin said. "He did track down my crew's flop, take out my folks and Cabie's."

"I got something here, something Theanne put together." She went into the back room and came back out in a moment carrying a vest. "Crazy idea the kid had, sewing some metal plates into this vest." She put it on. "Bit bulky, but if I'm wearing a Rabbit coat over it, then an arrow is going to have a harder time finding my heart."

Colin nodded. "Clever. Normally it'd be obvious you were wearing it, but you're right. With the coat, it'll work."

"So how do we go with it?"

"Meet me at this safehouse—it's on Branch, just in the second alley south of Rose. Number nineteen. Come around nine bells tonight."

"Nine bells. Branch number nineteen. Got it. And I should bring a lot of knives?"

"Blazes, yes. As many as you can manage." Colin got to his feet. No reason to stick around here, especially since Tooser clearly didn't want to talk to him. "See you then."

"Right," she said, getting the door for him. "We'll get this guy. For Cabie."

"For Cabie," Colin said, heading out. The door shut behind him, and the double was loudly latched as soon as it was.

Colin didn't have a place to be right now, so he went to the Rose & Bush. He could be sure no other Princes would bother going in there. He could have a few ciders in peace.

Minox met Inspector Rainey in the morning at their Constabulary House in Inemar, as they had agreed upon the night before. He had agreed to go home and sleep a full six hours, meet her at Inemar at eight bells and quickly brief their captain on their progress before going to Aventil.

It had been a necessary step after the events of the past two nights. He had been neglectful of his health and other responsibilities. He had received a literal knock to the skull, reminding him to refresh himself to regain perspective. He had to examine the facts impartially, not filtered through the magical connection between his hand and the Thorn.

After sending a page ahead with a note for Sergeant Tripper, he and Inspector Rainey made their way into Aventil.

"You told the captain what's happened in Aventil, but you weren't forthcoming about what you think," Rainey said.

"I'm still processing what I think," Minox said.

"Is that why we're walking to Aventil instead of taking the carriage?" she asked. "I don't mind the walk—"

"It helps me think it through," Minox said. "Though once we know the identity of the woman killed on the roof last night, I think I will have significantly more information to work with."

"Here's my concern, Welling. I'm not sure what your end goal in Aventil is. I have a suspicion of how things are going to end—"

"Enlighten me."

"We will find and arrest someone who will satisfy the Aventil constables for the attack against Benvin and the others. This someone will likely be guilty of *something*, not necessarily that attack. You will be dissatisfied and have a large amount of fodder for the unresolved pile."

"That prediction is not unlikely," Minox said. "I fear that—"

"I fear that you're trying to 'solve' Aventil, and that's not going to happen."

"Understand, not solve," Minox said. "I had wondered if Aventil was plagued with the same deep corruption that the Dentonhill house has. Its afflictions—as far as the Constabulary are concerned—are quite different."

"They slam back and forth between apathy and overreaction?"

Minox nodded. "Though most of the house leans toward the apathy, with Benvin's squad, including my brother, on the overreaction side."

"But you like the squad."

"I like that they care about what they are doing. But I wonder if that translates to doing good work."

She gave him a puzzled look.

"I'm thinking specifically with regard to the Thorn."

"Your encounter with him last night has enlightened you?"

"I want to know more about the woman last night, and Emilia Quope—"

"There's a connection between them?"

"My instinct says yes. Two women, killed near the Thorn by a Thorn imposter in similar ways? And the one last night was armed with atypical weapons—"

"A *dektha*. It's Kellirac."

Minox felt like he should have known that. "I must verse myself better in foreign arms. The point is she was armed. And Miss Quope was hardly dressed like a collegiate student when she died. I have a theory—"

"Please do not keep it to yourself."

"It's ill-formed."

"Yes, but when you share your ill-formed theories, I know where your thoughts are going. This prevents me from feeling foolish later."

"There is a group of notorious assassins referred to as the Deadly Birds. One of them was arrested a few months ago, here in Aventil, after an encounter with the Thorn."

"So Quope and the other victim might have been part of these Birds, and were after the Thorn now? But someone else killed them?"

"Evidence and instinct points to two Thorn pretenders active right now. One flamboyant—who I think attacked the Rose Street Princes and Benvin—and the other purposeful—who attacked our presumed Deadly Birds."

"This is pure supposition, Welling," she said. "I mean, we know the Thorn is a mage, yes?"

"Of that we're certain."

"And a powerful one, you've experienced."

"Granted."

"So how sure are we that this series of pretenders isn't some elaborate ruse on his part? Magical illusions? Compatriots?"

"I spoke to him, though, and I felt he was being honest—"

"You have been fooled before," she said. She stopped in the road, looking hard at him. "You are excellent at detecting dishonesty, like no one I've ever met. But you are not infallible. And he seems to be a trickster."

Thoughts fired all across Minox's skull.

Minox's mother, being Racquin—of Kellirac descent—sometimes preferred to go outside the city limits to a specific church. Minox would occasionally accompany her. It was a Church of Druthal church, named after a saint, but it appealed to Minox's mother because it catered to Racquin sensibilities. Which made sense, because Saint Veran was appropriated from old Kellirac myths of a trickster figure.

Named *Veranix*.

That was all largely circumstantial, as were many other elements surrounding the Thorn. But the points clicked. A magical young man with a Racquin name. Many Racquin were in traveling circuses, and the Thorn had acrobatic skills. He was friends with Delmin Sarren, the witness who knew for certain that the man who attacked Lieutenant Benvin was not the Thorn.

"Now what are you thinking?"

"Nothing actionable," he said. The ideas in his head made perfect sense, but it was also a construction as solid as his pipe smoke.

They arrived at the apartment over the Broken Spindle. "You're certain you want to conduct ourselves out of here instead of the stationhouse?" Rainey asked.

"I have little trust for the infrastructure there," Minox said.

"Granted. But this is—unusually off regulation for you."

He glanced at her. "I wouldn't think you would mind."

She chuckled. "I don't at all. I'm just surprised that you don't."

They entered the flop, to find Sergeant Tripper already there, with a young woman who was certainly not Constabulary.

"Oh, hey, what the blazes is this?" the girl snarled as soon as she saw Minox and Rainey. She was in threadbare clothes, and notably had sizable scars on her cheeks. Minox's research into the neighborhood specifics told him this marked her as a Waterpath Orphan.

"It's fine, it's fine," Tripper said, grabbing her wrist as she went for a knife. "These are special inspectors."

"How the blazes is that fine?"

"They aren't from our house, Yessa," he said. "They're here because of what happened to the Left."

"Oh," Yessa said. She smiled. "So you all are some special sticks brought in to hunt the Thorn."

"Something like that," Rainey said, switching to her childhood accent from growing up on the Inemar streets. Minox knew exactly why—she was trying to form a quick connection with this young woman. It was the sort of ruse Rainey did effortlessly. "So who the blazes are you?"

"Oh, Red, I'm your Terrentin present come early."

"What's that mean?" Rainey asked.

"Apparently the Thorn came to Yessa this morning," Tripper said. "He wanted her help with something."

"So if you want to catch him, sticks," Yessa said. "I know exactly where he's going to be at midnight tonight."

Minox was curiously surprised at how conflicted he felt about this development.

Chapter 19

VERANIX RETURNED TO campus with little issue. The night before, despite his encounters, had not caused additional alarm on campus. There was plenty of activity, as the games remained in full swing. As Veranix made his way back to Almers, he overheard plenty of discussion of the results of yesterday's events, the anticipation of today's, and which colleges were ahead in the total rankings. There was a lot of chatter about the tetchball match scheduled today—Pirrell against Cape Institute. People definitely talked about that as the event to see.

Veranix wished he was interested in that.

He got to Almers, stashed his gear in the closet, and headed to the water closet to clean off. He was tempted to go to the bathhouses, but given how many fresh bruises and scars he had right now, it would bring up too many questions. A handcloth washing would have to do.

He returned to the room to find Delmin there.

"You're back," Delmin said quietly.

"Sorry, last night—went wrong." That was the easiest way to explain it.

"I gathered that when you didn't come back. Look, you can't take advantage of the fact that I'm the prefect on this floor—"

That had never occurred to Veranix, and he said so. "Besides, we don't have strict curfew right now."

"I'm talking about precedent. I don't want you getting into the habit of staying out at all hours once the proper semester starts up again."

"I won't," Veranix said. "And I'm sure Professor Alimen will put enough on my plate that I won't be able to."

"Good."

"But as for right now—"

"No, don't even," Delmin said. "Kaiana said to drag your skinny butt to the carriage house when I found you. So let's go."

"Don't you want to—"

"Save the full story for when we get there." He sighed. "Did you eat anything?"

"Yeah, I'm all right," Veranix said. He gathered up his gear and put it in a pack. "I'm not going to have the carriage house as a place to hide my gear much longer."

"I'm not keen on regularly sharing a room with that cloak and rope," Delmin said.

"We'll work something out," Veranix said. He *could* keep the gear in the apartment above the laundry shop, but he didn't feel like that was particularly secure. He couldn't dismiss the idea that a group like the Blue Hand Circle was out there, people who could track and find them, with the only protection being a door that even Delmin could kick open. The heightened magical activity on campus at least masked the items from casual notice. "There is something that happened last night—"

"Again, just wait."

The carriage house was a surprising sight. Phadre and Jiarna had set up a full workshop and laboratory. On one table they had unpacked equipment, as well as maps of the campus, Dentonhill, and Aventil. Jiarna had lined up the empty vials that Kaiana had collected throughout campus, each one tagged. She was examining them with her eyepiece. The scattered teacups and crumb-filled plates made him wonder how long they had been working here. Kaiana, for her part, was pacing around the room restlessly.

"You found him," she said to Delmin when they came in.

"He was in the dorm," Delmin said.

She looked over at Veranix, her face hard to read. "You didn't spend the night there." It was stated as simple fact, making it sound colder and harsher than any of the times when she had been angry.

"Things happened last night. I thought it wise not to come back to campus where I could have been tracked. So I went to the church."

"Fine," Kaiana said, taking his pack from him. She started to empty it. "Tell us what happened."

He quickly went into the story—sticking with the tetchball squad to see if that led anywhere, Bluejay coming at him, the imposter and the fight with Inspector Welling.

Kaiana focused on the fact that Veranix had broken his bow. "You've gone through three bows in as many months," she said. "It's very irresponsible, given what they cost."

"But he's got the Hunter's bow, instead," Delmin said. "So that's something."

"It's not a great bow for me, actually," Veranix said. The pull was stronger, and it felt wrong. The Hunter must have incredible arm strength.

"This is excellent, actually," Phadre said, taking the bow from Kaiana. "I mean, I don't know anything about bows, but surely we can determine something useful from it. Style, composition."

"Leave it on the table," Jiarna said, still focused on examining the vials.

"What are you doing, exactly?" Veranix asked her.

"I'm trying to determine what magiochemical properties this substance has. Perhaps by knowing that, there's a way to *numinic*ally excite them in a way that Phadre's device can track."

"Or Delmin himself," Phadre added.

"Yes, but I'm more comfortable with the device," Jiarna said. "No offense, Delmin."

"None taken," Delmin said. "I'm more comfortable with nothing being my responsibility here."

"Unfortunately I don't have a significant sample size to work with." Jiarna sighed, looking up from her work at Veranix. "Tell me more about this Inspector Welling and his hand."

"Yes," Phadre said. "I'm quite curious about it."

"How does this help us with the *effitte*?" Kaiana asked. "I'm sorry, but the amount of discarded vials on campus has reached absurd levels." She looked pointedly at Veranix. "We *need* to do something about that."

"And I want to—" Veranix said.

"Sorry," Phadre said, talking over Veranix. "But this is fascinating. It's his hand, an actual part of him, but it's not flesh."

"And you can control it in the same way you control the rope."

"And he could control the rope," Veranix said. "I think he actually uses his hand the same way."

"He's dangerous," Delmin said. "That hand is probably the result of uncontrolled, untaught magic."

This brightened Phadre up. "Maybe he came into contact with napranium—"

"Or some other substance," Jiarna said excitedly. "And he absorbed it into his body. Phadre, have you ever worked with quicksilver?"

"I've read a bit, but I don't recall it being magiochemically—"

"Of course it is, anything might be, that's not the point. Perhaps there is—"

"Jiarna!" Kaiana snapped. "I'm sure what happened to Veranix and the inspector's hand might be fascinating, but we need to do something about the *effitte* on campus. We need to find out where it is, where it's coming from, and stop it. That's what you need to be doing."

That last part was quite pointedly aimed at Veranix.

"I am. I've been trying, but—"

"But it's getting worse! Every night there's more!"

His head was swirling. "Look, all of you, there are so many problems right now, and I need to focus. Between this imposter—"

"Imposters," Delmin said.

"Right," Veranix said. He had yet to even see the Jester. He couldn't get himself to worry about what that one was doing. Not with everything else happening. "Regardless, between them and the Deadly Birds, I've got a lot of fire to cool. Until I settle those things, I can't be thinking—"

"Of *effitte* on campus?" Kaiana asked. "You can't be serious."

"Ease off, Kai!" Veranix said. "Don't you dare question my resolve in this! I was almost killed the other night by Fenmere's men. Me, fighting against the *effitte*. I'm in this, all of this. But everyone is after me out there. Tell me what I can do, because I am out of ideas."

"We might have heard something," Jiarna broke in. "It's a strange thing, but it might lead somewhere."

"Lead where?" Veranix asked, eager to hear anything that would change the conversation. "How could it help?"

"All right," she said cautiously, looking back and forth between him and Kai. "We hit the social parties again last night, and we heard there's a secret midnight match of crownball being put together tonight."

"Crownball is banned!" Delmin said.

"Yes, I know," Jiarna said. "Thus the secret midnight match."

"And secret gatherings bring other illicit things out in the open," Veranix said. "I'll admit, that's not terrible."

"Folks putting it together want it kept hush. So if we want to get in, we need a player."

"Tonight at midnight?" Veranix asked. "I mean, I can't. Like I said, the church meeting with the Birds."

Jiarna shook her head. "We can't get in there to check it out without a player. You're the obvious choice."

"No, he needs to deal with the assassins," Kaiana said.

Her voice was quiet, conciliatory. "That's going to get worse unless you fix it."

"Del?" Veranix asked.

"Me? Play crownball?" He asked. "I can't swim."

"You can't?" Kaiana asked.

"I could give it a go," Phadre said. "I mean, I won't do well or anything in the match, but we don't need to win, do we? We just need to get in."

"You know people have died playing crownball, right?" Delmin asked.

"Yes, we know," Jiarna said. "Thus it was banned. But you know how folks are."

"All right," Veranix said. "Can all four of you go? More eyes out there, the better."

"We'll do that, and you do what you need to," Kaiana said. "But get that other business squared away. We need to stop what's happening here, before some student ends up in trance or worse."

"In the meantime," Jiarna said, putting down her eye-piece, "we should all go out and behave as normal as possible. Be seen enjoying matches, eating meals—"

"Doing our jobs," Kaiana added.

"Exactly. Put up the appearances."

Phadre smirked at her. "You're just saying that because you want to see the matches today."

"Yes, of course I am. Pirrell versus Central Academy? That's going to be cracking."

Colin had put a good show on at the Rose & Bush, followed by one at the Old Canal, and another at the Walking Eye— a run-down hole of a pub on the Dentonhill side of Water-path. Each place, he put up the pretense of having quite a few ciders, talking a bit too loudly to his neighbor, complaining about how he was going to have to keep eye on Sotch to sneak her over to the church tonight. He griped about the bosses, and the way they were treating him, putting this on his shoulders. He felt he did a pretty good job of it. He'd never be a player in Cantarell Square, but he thought he played it well enough.

Of course that wasn't all performance. But he didn't drink anywhere near as much cider as he pretended to.

Hopefully, all that would trickle over to the Jester and he'd come running for them.

Colin made his way over to the safehouse, and once there availed himself of Bassa's selection of blades. The woman had quite a lot of knives, and they were damn fine ones as well. Better than anything Colin was carrying. She groused—or more grunted—but didn't stop him from taking what he wanted.

He was in the process of putting the blades in his belt and boots when Deena arrived. Late. Not that he had expected anything different. She didn't say much, but took the pile of Sotch's clothes—someone had laundered them, Colin had no idea who—and went into the water closet.

About a half hour later she came out dressed in Sotch's stuff, hair wet, but now that same purple-black that Sotch had dyed hers. Colin had to admit, with the hair and the clothes, she was a pretty damn good likeness for Sotch. In the dark of night, no one would be able to tell the difference.

"All right," Colin said. "We ready to do this?"

"What happens if he doesn't show?" Deena asked.

"Then you'll have ruined your hair for nothing," Colin said.

"Ugh," Deena said. "Smells like I shoved my head in a flowerpot."

"Worse fates," Colin said.

"Let's hope we don't find one." She opened up the fur-lined Red Rabbit coat to show she had filled its inner pockets with knives. "The Rabbits had a blasted good idea with these coats, I can tell you that."

"See where it got them," Colin said. "I've wasted enough time. Let's go to the church."

><><><><

Minox had found the events of the day troubling, but he could not explain to Inspector Rainey exactly why. They had a solid lead on the future location of the man who, as far as anyone could prove, was responsible for the attack on Lieutenant Benvin. They were putting together a plan of action to capture this man, one that was strategically sound. Everything was proceeding in what should be considered an ideal manner.

Except Minox knew it wasn't right.

He couldn't *prove* it, though.

The theory that there were multiple Thorns was solid, but lacked evidence. The theory that one of them was the true Thorn, and the others were acting in ways opposed to his goals had no basis in anything other than Minox's intuition.

And Jace's. He could see it in his brother's eyes as the plan was discussed. Jace had had his own experience with the Thorn. His attempts to bring that up had been shot down quite strongly by Sergeant Tripper.

"Look, the point isn't *just* what he did to the Left—"

"Allegedly," Jace said.

"Yeah, sure. We've got a good pile of additional charges we can put onto the Thorn. And it's our job to catch these guys and iron them. The Thorn will get his trial, and the City Protector and the People's Advocate can hash it out."

As much as Minox was uncomfortable with the plan, he couldn't argue with that point. There were elements he did try to argue. They were technically going to break the sanctity of the church. Tripper argued that the priest had asked Yessa to bring in the Birds, and, through Yessa, they were invited. It was sophistry, but sophistry that had enough legal teeth to suit their needs.

"All right, tell us how this looks," Inspector Rainey called from behind the makeshift curtain they had hung in the middle of the apartment. She emerged, now dressed in disguise as a Deadly Bird—leather corset over her white blouse, a belt with several knives on it, her hair up in elaborate braids, and an absurd amount of makeup on her eyes. It was an effective costume.

"Acceptable," Minox said. He would have preferred that they all could wear Constabulary riot gear, but there was no way the disguises would have worked that way. The Deadly Birds were known for flamboyance, especially in dress. Rainey and Corrie were taking a risk, but they were well aware of it.

"Bloody well better be rutting acceptable," Corrie said, coming out behind her. Her costume was far more outrageous, with Linjari-style short pants and stockings, and a blouse that left her arms and collar quite exposed. She also wore excessive face paint, with green and red streaks around her eyes and temples. There was something fitting about the fact that his sister, even in this absurd costume, would make a point of sporting the Constabulary colors. She had armed herself with a pair of handsticks.

"It's fine," Jace said, looking down at the floor.

"And if you laugh, I take your teeth." This was Pollit, having volunteered to back up Rainey and Corrie in disguise. If he had any reservations in dressing as a woman, he didn't express them. In fact, he argued hotly that someone from the Aventil house had to be in the church with Rainey and Corrie, and that he was the best one to do it. Pollit's outfit was far more conservative than either Rainey's or Corrie's, but still accentuated the feminine features that Pollit normally took distinct pains in hiding. A pair of crossbows hung at his hips. Pollit also wore a short coat, despite the heat, to hide the mage shackles he was carrying.

"No, looks good," Tripper said. The man glared at Jace, Wheth, and Saitle, as if to make it clear that none of them were to give Pollit any trouble. Though Minox also noticed a flush that came to the sergeant's cheeks when Pollit first came out.

None of Minox's business, not relevant to the case.

"All right," Tripper said. "Specs, you take point going into the church, with Corrie and . . . Pollit."

"Where's your snitch going to meet us?" Rainey asked.

"A block from here, Tulip and Tree. For her sake, stay in character the whole time over. You'll be going through territory that's contested between the Orphans, Knights, and Princes."

Wheth added, "Knights and Princes should give her and you a pass if you're going to the church. But if they think you're sticks . . ."

"Then it's fair game," Rainey said.

"I'm walking into a rutting church wearing this," Corrie muttered.

Minox didn't want his sister to feel uncomfortable in this venture. He was already feeling enough of that. "If you want to wear something else—"

"Nah, Mine, it's fine. I got to look the part. But not a word to Ma, either of you."

"Sworn to the saints," Jace said.

Tripper continued. "Once they're in, the rest of us take our spots. Jace and Saitle, whistles at the ready at the two intersections. You all just bring in the patrol if things turn left, nothing else. Hear, Jace?"

"Heard."

"Wheth, you take the roof of the shop across from the church, crossbow at the ready. I'm in the alley below you."

"And I'll be trailing the ladies from a discreet distance," Minox said. Originally Minox wanted to be at the alley, but Tripper argued that whoever was there also needed to be carrying the other pair of mage shackles. Minox couldn't do that and also use his left hand, a fact he discovered when he brought the shackles over from the Grand Inspectors' Unit offices.

"You sure you can do that?" Tripper said.

"It's where I want his eyes," Rainey said. "Watching my back."

"Fine," Tripper said. "This is your show. Let's get on it."

All the Aventil constables took a brief moment, their heads down. Minox presumed it was a prayer or benediction, possibly a ritual with Lieutenant Benvin. He respected these officers and their need to acknowledge their bond, and said nothing.

He knew these were good officers at heart. That made this all so disappointing.

They all headed out, Inspector Rainey hanging behind.

"You're not happy about this," she said.

"Nor are you," Minox said. "Though mostly because we are to remain on duty past midnight."

"My caretaker at home isn't happy about that. I'm mostly worried that this seems too neat."

"A solution dropped into our laps? Indeed."

"You're more concerned if this is the right thing to do."

"I've mentioned that we are technically violating church sanctity, for one," Minox said.

"That isn't what's eating at you. You think we're catching the wrong man here," she said. She glanced over at Corrie and Pollit, already waiting for her to catch up. "Though I did tell you this morning how this case was going to end."

She jogged off ahead to join the others in their ruse. Minox stayed back for a moment, checking his crossbow. It was loaded with blunt-tip quarrels. If the Thorn was to be arrested today, he would make sure that the man was taken alive.

Per Jiarna's instructions, Veranix went about the day as normally as he could manage. He went to the tetchball match—which Pirrell won in a rout, twenty-three to six—and visited the tetchball squad over at Whisper Fox House around suppertime to give them his insights on facing Pirrell tomorrow. His insights boiled down to Pirrell being strong and brutal in their style. Two of the Central Academy players were carried off the field. Veranix told them to be ready to get hit, and to hit hard and hit first, because the Pirrell boys weren't going to be afraid to do the same. After that, he went back to his room to rest for a few hours. He needed to be at his best strength possible, in case anything went wrong.

It was already late into the hot evening when he casually strolled over to the carriage house. The campus was still active, but in a far more subdued way than the previous nights. Perhaps the revelers had cooled their ardor after heavy parties for several days, perhaps the dangers of the Aventil neighborhood had scared them into a calm. Veranix didn't care, but he appreciated that he didn't have to fight his way through the walkway.

The other four were already in the carriage house when he arrived. Delmin, Phadre, and Jiarna were all dressed oddly fashionable for the night, including Jiarna wearing a pageboy cap that somehow didn't make her look ridiculous. Kaiana was wearing a simple blouse and skirt—hardly that fashionable, but she didn't look too out of place compared to the rest.

Jiarna was sitting at the worktable, sorting the empty vials into groups, while Phadre and Delmin were tuning one of his devices. Kaiana was laying out Veranix's Thorn clothes and equipment.

"Is your idea going to work?" he asked Jiarna. "You'll have some way to track the *effitte* on campus?"

"It's not impossible," she said. "There are magiochemical properties in the residue of some of these vials. With a large enough sample, I should be able to determine what they are and how to best activate them." She sighed. "I did spend much of the evening researching this."

"No socials tonight," Phadre said wistfully. "Though I think this secret match will make up for it."

"It's frightfully exciting," Jiarna said. "There is a secret password and everything."

"But you've learned how we get in?" Kaiana asked, taking the Hunter's bow off the table.

"Oh, yes. We'll be able to. We had to have a secret team name, though. We are the Defenders of Rationality."

"So, you picked the name," Delmin said.

"I most certainly did," she said.

"Vee," Kaiana said, handing him the bow. "Twenty practice shots, far wall. Right now."

"Why do you want—"

"Because this is the bow you have to use tonight. That's just how it is, so get accustomed to it."

"All right," he said, giving her a bit of a smile. She didn't give anything back to him. He accepted that, no need to belabor things right now. Last thing he wanted was another argument over his priorities. He took the bow and started the practice shots. It was a heavier pull, hard on his arm, but after a few arrows he adapted, putting the arrows where he wanted them.

"Now that's what we needed in Archery," Phadre said behind him. "U of M was one of the lowest-ranked in this one."

"You know the rules about mages competing," Veranix said, taking another shot.

"How did you ever learn this?" Phadre asked.

"My father," Veranix said. "He was a trick-shot performer in the circus, and before that . . ." Veranix faltered, not sure how much of his father's history in the Aventil streets he needed to share right now. Blazes, it wasn't like he knew it all, either. "Before that he was a soldier in the island war."

"Whose father wasn't?" Phadre asked genially. "Blazes, I'm the first Golmin in four generations not to serve."

"Good with that bow?" Kaiana asked, coming up to them.

"Good enough," Veranix said. He took one more shot to confirm, and then went to collect the arrows. "Though the Hunter definitely has more arm strength than I do."

"Be aware for him tonight," Kaiana said. "He's been right with you the past two nights—"

"No, it's the Deadly Birds he wants," Veranix said. "That much is clear, he's got an agenda that's all about them. Blazes, that's what I've got to negotiate with them."

"So why is he dressed like you?" Phadre asked. "I mean, that's the obvious question there."

"I don't know, and I don't care," Veranix said, though the thought had been itching in his brain. The Jester, from everything Del and Colin described, seemed to be trying to use or sully the Thorn's reputation in some way. The Hunter didn't care about the Thorn, he just wanted the Birds.

That didn't matter, though. Veranix just needed to solve the problems he could. First, make peace with the Birds, then the *effitte* infestation on campus. If he was very lucky,

Inspector Welling would catch one of the imposters and solve two problems at once.

Kaiana took the bow and attached it to Veranix's bandolier with his staff and quiver. "Suit up," she said. "You've got a meeting to get to."

"You all need to be off as well, yes?" Veranix said.

"I heard eleven bells a while ago," Phadre said. "We should get going."

Jiarna put her work away while Veranix finished getting dressed. "Should one of us be going with you?" she asked. "I mean, in case things go wrong, you shouldn't be alone."

"Like the other night," Kaiana said. "I should have stayed near when you went into that den. Then maybe—"

"No, not for this," Veranix said. "If things turn left, my best choice is to just get the blazes away. That's easier to do if I'm on my own."

"And that is what you'll do?" Delmin asked.

"Like blazes it is. The last thing I want is to have a fight with the Deadly Birds. I will happily run away from that."

"Good," Kaiana said. She looked him over, now that he was fully dressed and equipped. "I think you're ready. Good luck."

"And to all of you," Veranix said. "Especially you, Phadre. Crownball gets rough."

"I won't be playing to win, just to get them in the door," he said. "No worries about me. Like I said, four generations in the army. I'm tougher than I look."

"There's our team motto," Jiarna said.

"All right, no more time to waste," Veranix said, shrouding into the background.

"If you aren't back by two bells, I'm storming the church," Kaiana called out.

"Damn well better," Veranix threw back as he went off into the night.

Not that he was worried. He wasn't charging into a fight this time. If all went to plan, this would just be a simple parley, and he'd be back home in an hour with no trouble.

Chapter 20

KAIANA DIDN'T KNOW how the students who had put this illegal match together had managed to get into the bathhouses, but clearly someone had dropped enough money in someone's pockets to make it happen. Probably some of those social house kids. Saints knew they had the wealth to do it.

Jiarna led them to one of the side doors—usually only used by the bathhouse staff—and gave some special knock.

"How'd she learn all this?" Delmin asked Phadre.

"She listens to everyone," Phadre said.

"Yeah, but how did she get them to tell her?"

"No, that's not what I mean," Phadre said. "She has a knack for being able to hear several conversations at once and pick what she needs out of it. So if people are talking about it near her, she gets it all without seeming to pay attention."

"Good ears," Jiarna said, waiting by the door. "Someone's coming."

The door opened up, and a slack-jawed student peered out. "You got bait?" he asked.

"No, we've got the big fish," she returned. He nodded and let them in.

They were led over to the bathhouse's deep pool, where torches had been set up all around the perimeter of the water. Several groups of folks, from all the different schools, were clustered around the edges.

A young woman—the social-house type—came up to them. "What's your team?"

"Defenders of Rationality," Jiarna said. The social house girl rolled her eyes.

"Who's your player?"

"Me," Phadre said.

"It's ten crowns," she said. "Winner takes the pot."

"Ten crowns?" Delmin asked. He echoed Kaiana's thoughts. This whole thing was limited to the wealthy students, clearly. Maybe they put this together just because the regular matches weren't interesting enough for them. Or they needed some exclusive thing to set them off from the rest of the students.

"I got it," Jiarna told the social girl, giving her some coins. "Tell Vee he owes me, though."

"I'll make sure he's good for it," Kaiana said.

"Oh, you will?" the social girl said, sneering at Kaiana. "Aren't you a good thrall?"

Kaiana's cheeks flushed with anger at that, but she didn't let it move her, as much as she wanted to clock this girl in the teeth. The girl laughed and pointed to the pool.

"All right, boy," the girl told Phadre. "Skiv down and get in place."

They found a spot by the side of the pool, and Phadre started to strip down to his skivs. "The things we must do, hmm?" he said.

"Jiarna," Kaiana said sharply, noticing her attention was mostly on Phadre, "remember what we need to keep our eyes out for."

"Right," Jiarna said, breaking her gaze away. She glanced around the other groups. "Once the match is going, we should move about as best we can, mingle."

"Hey, hey!" the social girl yelled. "What's this sewage you've got there!" She was pointing at Phadre.

"What do you mean?" Jiarna asked.

"On his arm, what is that?" She was pointing to his tattoo—the L and P in flames together.

"Lord Preston's Circle," Phadre said, holding it up.

"A rutting mage?" she screamed. "No, no, no. No jot on him."

"What?" Jiarna asked. "Just because he's a mage—"

"Yeah, he'll make himself a fish and cheat everyone," social girl said. "Only natural folk playing in this game."

"Really?" Delmin asked. "An illegal secret game, but you've got that rule?"

"You got a problem, mage-lover?" she asked. "You and your skinny boy here can go magic whatever you want somewhere else. All of you. Especially with no player."

Kaiana wasn't about to let this girl kick them out.

"We've got a player," Kaiana said.

"I told you magic boy can't do it."

"I know," Kaiana said, unbuttoning her blouse. "I'll do it."

"You, napa slan?" the girl asked. "You're going to dive with those boys?" She pointed to the other players taking position around the pool—all of them muscle-bound young men, many of them a good foot taller and wider than her.

"Yes," Kaiana said, handing her blouse to Jiarna. "Unless any of them are afraid of me."

"Pah," the social girl said. "You want to breathe the drink, that's on you."

"Kai," Delmin said, his gaze firmly on the ground as she took off her skirt. "You know people have died doing this game. Like, a lot."

"You can swim, yes?" Jiarna asked, taking Kai's skirt. Many of the other players and their friends were hooting and hollering at Kai in her skivs, but she did her best to ignore them.

"Since I was born," Kaiana said. She might not remember much about her early years in the islands before her father brought her to Maradaine, but she did remember the ocean.

"Gentlemen," the social girl called out to the crowd. "And lady," she added, sneering at Kaiana again. "Welcome to crownball!"

She pulled a pouch off of her belt, and emptied its contents into her hands. "Three crowns," she called out, and threw them into the pool, where they splashed and sank to the bottom. Another girl came over to her holding two small leather balls—much smaller than a tetchball. The social girl took them and tossed them into the pool, where they floated. "Find, call, and claim for a point. First to five without tapping wins."

"Someone better tell me the rules quick," Kaiana whispered.

"Dive down, find one of the crowns," Jiarna said.

Kaiana nodded. That was easy. "Then?"

"Then you surface and call out 'crown.' That's crucial. If you have a crown and don't call it, you'll get tapped."

"Tapped?"

"Pulled out of the game. Same if you hold on to the side of the pool for longer than a count of five. Once you have a coin and call it, then grab a ball and claim your point."

"So I get a point for finding a crown and grabbing a ball?"

"You have to be holding the crown when you get the ball. Grabbing the ball without holding the coin—"

"Get tapped, all right," Kaiana said.

"Right, but—"

"Play!" the girl shouted. All the boys playing jumped into the pool. Kaiana did the same, making a line for one of the coins.

Under the water, it was dim, but Kai could still see a bit. One of the coins was shining on the bottom, and Kaiana swam straight for it. Other boys, she saw, were searching around, but they seemed to be having a harder time spotting the coins. As she grabbed the coin, she saw several of them going up for air. Kaiana pushed off the bottom of the pool and jetted up to the surface.

"Crown!" she called out, and looked around to spot one of the balls bobbing on the surface.

Suddenly four hands grabbed her from every direction, pushing her back under. She hadn't gotten a chance to catch a breath, and she thrashed trying to get free of the people holding her.

One of the hands holding her twisted her arm behind her. She struggled to get him off of her, and shoved hard at him with her other hand. That was the hand that she was holding the crown with, and she dropped it as she pushed at him. She wanted to dive down and grab it again, but she needed to breathe.

"Kai!" she heard when she surfaced. Delmin was yelling to her. "When you call, every other player can do whatever they want to keep you from scoring!"

She swam closer, making sure not to come all the way to the edge. She didn't want to risk tapping. "Anything?"

"Pretty much," Phadre said. "Though things like eye-gouging and choking are considered poor form."

"Crown!" someone called.

"Got it," she said, swimming back under, moving like a shark to the boy who called crown.

She swept up from underneath him, yanking on his skivs as she ascended, and then grabbed the back of his head and pushed him down. He struggled and brought a clutched hand up to push her away.

Kaiana grabbed his wrist and twisted, while working her legs around his neck to keep him under the water. His hand opened up, revealing the coin he was holding. Kaiana snatched it before it dropped.

"Crown!" she called, and took a deep breath and dove down deep to the bottom. Several boys swarmed to where she had been on the surface, but she had already slipped away from there. They were hunting in the wrong place. From the bottom of the pool, her lungs were starting to ache. She could hold it. If she had ever needed to be her mother's daughter, a fishcatcher of the Gotapa, now was the moment.

There, bobbing on the surface, was one of the balls. None of the other players were near it. She launched herself up, hand outstretched, snatching it as she surfaced.

"Point!" she yelled. She held up both the crown and the ball.

"Crownball! Point to the napa thrall! All to your places!"

The boys all swam to their places on the edge, and Kaiana did the same. The hostess claimed the crown and ball from Kaiana. Delmin was still in place for her, while Jiarna and Phadre were moving around and chatting.

"Thought it was best if they handled that," Delmin said. "Not my scene."

"Thanks," Kaiana said, treading water. "I can see why these kids wanted to have this game."

"Are you having fun?"

"I get to swim and thrash rich Uni boys," Kaiana said. "This is glorious."

Delmin laughed a bit, then his eyes caught something. "Someone just passed a vial to a swimmer."

"Who? From where?" She turned to look at the other players, but didn't see anything.

"I can't tell. I don't know any of these people, and no one is in uniform. But I've got my eye on them."

The hostess threw in the crown and the ball. "Play!"

"Get on that. Don't worry about me." Kaiana swam out and dove under. One of the crowns was near her, and she went for it. Another swimmer was charging at the same crown, but Kaiana was at it before him. She had the crown in hand and was about to spring up to the surface when she felt his fist in her chest. It wasn't a hard punch, but it surprised her and forced air from her lungs. Reeling, fighting the instinct to gasp, she pushed away from him.

He came at her, grabbing her wrist. She needed to get to the surface, needed to breathe, but couldn't pull away. He wasn't letting go, squeezing her wrist and twisting.

She rolled in the water with the twist, losing her sense of where the surface was for a moment. She lashed out with her legs, planting them on his chest. She couldn't get any leverage to push him off.

Driving one foot into his face, she let go of the crown she

was holding. Maybe that would get him off of her. He ignored that, grabbing her foot and pulling.

Her lungs were screaming, and she couldn't move away. He twisted her arm and leg behind her, keeping her trapped under the water.

Then a sound struck them both, like thunder. Then again. Suddenly the water pulled away from them both. She gulped madly at the air as she found herself hurled up, landing by the side of the pool next to her assailant. He was gasping maniacally. It was almost as if he had forgotten that he needed to breathe until this moment.

"Tapped, tapped, what the rutting blazes was that?"

The hostess came charging over, and as Kaiana's vision cleared, she saw that Delmin and Phadre were standing over her, their hands both charged with magic. They must have pulled her out.

Delmin was barely able to stand as he stared down the hostess. "He was killing her."

"And you two are rotten, filthy mages! Cheaters!"

"You're going to say that while—"

"Get the blazes out of here before—"

"Before what?" Delmin's voice echoed unnaturally throughout the hall. The girl backed away, her face paling.

"Just get out," she said quietly. "All of you get out."

Phadre handed Kaiana her clothes while everyone stared at the group of them. The faces were filled with fear and hatred. Kaiana wondered if this was the sort of thing Veranix, Delmin, and Phadre faced all the time.

"Come on," Jiarna said, approaching the rest of them. "We certainly don't need these people." She strode past like she was in charge of everything, bumping into the hostess as she passed. The girl lost her balance and went into the pool. "Terribly sorry."

Kaiana had her blouse on and pulled up her skirt enough for the sake of decency, and the four of them hurried out the door. Jeers and hisses chased them as they got outside.

"I really should put the campus cadets on this," Delmin said once they stopped. "I think that would be a good plan."

"I'm sure it wouldn't do any good," Kaiana said. "Whoever put this together must have a few in their pocket."

"Well, it wasn't a total loss," Jiarna said. "While everyone was paying attention to the three of you, I managed to get a vial from the group that Delmin saw." She held up a vial, filled will a grayish-green liquid.

"That's not *effitte*," Kaiana said.

"You're sure?" Jiarna said. "I mean, it is dark out here, we should get back to the carriage house."

"The one who attacked you," Delmin said. "He's the one they gave the vial to. And that doesn't make any sense, right? *Effitte* makes you giddy and happy. He certainly wasn't that."

Delmin was right. It didn't make any sense.

"Let's get back to the carriage house. Maybe with the full vial, Jiarna can make some sense of it."

Veranix landed in the church bell tower. From up there, he quickly surveyed the street below. It looked relatively quiet, though he could see a patch of Knights of Saint Julian chumming around some pub on Tulip. A bit to the north on Vine, there were a couple Rose Street Princes. He knew this corner was disputed between the two of them, and the Waterpath Orphans were also encroaching in the direction.

Waterpath Orphans. One of them—Yessa, from what he could tell—was coming up Tulip toward the church. Three women were with her, definitely not Orphans. Veranix couldn't get a good look at them from up in the bell tower, but they certainly looked like they could be Birds. They had the same style as the ones he had tangled with before.

Their approach got the attention of the Knights. The Knights stayed in place at their street corner, but they definitely noticed. Hopefully nothing would happen to give them further cause than that.

Veranix made his way down the tower. Reverend Pemmick was waiting for him in the hallway. "It seems we have a parley on our hands," he said. "I just heard a knock on the door."

"You're oddly pleased," Veranix said. The man was practically beaming.

"I enjoy when peaceful solutions take hold."

"Let's see if we're there yet, Reverend."

"It won't surprise you that I have faith."

There was another pounding knock. Veranix followed the reverend to the chapel.

"I'm going to stay in the shadows by the rostrum," Veranix said. "I'm all for a peaceful talk, but I'm not going to give them a target."

"There is wisdom in that, my friend. I'll get the door."

Veranix moved up on the church podium and shrouded himself into the background. He toyed with the idea of creating an illusory version of himself in another part of the room, a target to give them in case they decided to attack. He wasn't sure how to do that, and it might drain him more than he could afford.

Instead he went for a circus trick, with a little magical enhancement.

Three women approached up the aisle, with Yessa hanging in the back of the church with the reverend. They were decked out in leather and face paint, armed with knives, crossbows, and batons. The center one, with red Waishen hair, called out.

"So where's the Thorn?" Her Waish accent was like butter on a hot day.

"Here," Veranix said, making his voice echo throughout the room, so to them it sounded like it was coming from every direction. They all spun around, looking every which way.

"Clever rutting trick," the one with the batons and stockings said. "Come out and talk to us."

"Who am I talking to?" Veranix asked. "I would need to know it's worth my while."

"We came from the Deadly Birds," the Waish one said. "We thought you wanted to talk with us."

"That's true," Veranix said. "But who am I talking to? Names."

"I'm Hummingbird," the Waish one said. "They're Crow and Cormorant." Crossbows and handsticks, respectively.

"Pleasure," Veranix said. Crow and Cormorant were both scanning the room intently. Trying to spot him. His shrouding made him hard to see, but not impossible. Sharp eyes could find him.

Cormorant.

Bluejay said Cormorant had been killed. Hunter admitted to it.

Something wasn't right.

"Why don't you talk to us square?" Hummingbird asked. "This game is tedious."

"Why don't you first tell me what your grievance is with me?" Veranix asked.

Hummingbird didn't blink. "Two of ours are dead, and it's looking like the Thorn killed them."

Crow and Cormorant fanned out to the sides. Crow, in particular, was coming closer to Veranix than he would have liked, her hand fingering the trigger on her crossbow a little too eagerly.

"Just two?" Veranix asked. "I wouldn't think the Birds would start an unpaid hunt just for that."

"Yeah, well," Hummingbird said, looking around. "There's business and there's personal. Those girls were friends of ours."

Quiet as he could, Veranix took a few steps away from Crow, who was moving far too close for his personal comfort. This brought him closer to Hummingbird, who was keeping still. That didn't make him any more comfortable.

"Fair enough," he said, maintaining the echoes. "But that wasn't me who killed them."

"I don't suppose you can prove that?" Hummingbird asked. "Any friends we can talk to who'll vouch for you?"

That sounded very Constabulary.

Crow had crossbows.

Cormorant had handsticks.

And Hummingbird—he took a closer look at her. The face paint hid it, but now that he was close it was obvious. Inspector Rainey.

Trap.

"I'm very disappointed, Yessa." He let his voice not just echo, but boom, shaking the rafters. "I don't know if you were tricked, or part of the trick, but I expected better."

"I . . . I don't know what you're talking about . . ." Yessa stammered.

"Maybe you don't," Veranix said. "But I'm sure Inspector Rainey here does."

"Rutting find him!" the false Cormorant shouted.

Suddenly the door of the church kicked open, and a cloaked figure with a bow stormed in. "Look what I found," the Hunter said. "Three more Birds to send to the ground."

Chapter 21

COLIN AND DEENA had taken a convoluted path from the safehouse to the church, making it look like they were trying not to be seen or followed. The real reason was to give this rutting Jester ample opportunity to come at them.

They were now almost there, and he still hadn't shown up.

"I think this is a bust," Deena whispered. "Let's end this little game."

"I think you're right," Colin said. "Rutting mess, this all is."

Shouts and cries broke through the night air in the distance. Something was happening up by the church.

"We should get out of here," Deena said.

"Or this could be our man," Colin said. "Come on." He grabbed her arm and pulled her forward.

"Easy, Tyson," she said, pulling away. "I've had just about—"

Two arrows sang through the air and hit Deena in the chest, making a satisfying clang as they hit the metal plates. She fell down, mostly from surprise, as bursts of colored smoke filled the street in front of them.

"Didn't think you'd be running around so quickly, Sotch," a voice in the smoke said. "I thought I got you good."

Colin dove into the smoke. He knew it wasn't magic—nothing more than a chemist trick, and the Jester was in there.

"But now I'll have another play at you and the Prince, and that will be good for a shout."

"You want to shout?" Deena cried out. Colin could barely see her get on her feet in the smoke and moonlight, and he could make out a shadow of the Jester as well.

"Still some fight in you!" the Jester snarled. Colin could barely see his bow come up. Knife drawn, he jumped in and slashed at the bowstring.

The string snapped, and the Jester screamed as the ends slashed at his fingers.

Deena was on him, sending two punches to the Jester's chest. Colin slashed, getting a piece of his arm.

"Oh, an ambush!" he said. Fast as lightning, he threw a series of punches at Deena, and then an elbow at Colin, cracking him in the nose.

"Normally I'd be amused," the Jester said, sending another blow at Deena. "But you hurt my fingers, and I take that very seriously."

"You should take me seriously," Colin said. A punch came at him, but now the smoke was working against the Jester. Thin enough that Colin could see him, thick enough that it gave away his attacks. Colin saw it coming and ducked. He jabbed the Jester in the stomach, then raked his knife across the man's gut.

The Jester screamed, and then slammed his hands down on Colin's back.

Colin dropped to his knees. Not willing to give an inch, not to this tosser, not again, Colin lurched forward, grabbing him by the waist. As they went down together, Colin stabbed wildly in the Jester's leg.

The Jester cried out, clawing at the top of Colin's head, trying to get his thumbs into his eyes. Colin stabbed his leg again and left the knife there. Then he grabbed the Jester by the wrists and twisted the man's hands off his face.

"You take me seriously," Colin said, crawling on top of him. "You take Rose Street seriously." Now kneeling on the Jester's chest, Colin knocked him in the jaw. "And you take the Princes seriously."

With that, he grabbed the Jester's head and pounded it onto the cobblestone.

The Jester moaned, but didn't move.

"Is he dead?" Deena asked. She looked a bit off balance, like her head was still reeling, and she was holding her chest.

"He'll live. Theanne's trick worked, I see."

"Still hurt like blazes," Deena said.

"Come on," Colin said, pulling this fake Thorn's cloak off of him. "Let's get him back to the safehouse but quick. That had to be a spectacle." He started to tie the Jester's hands behind him with the cloak.

"Blazes, but there's a real spectacle," Deena said. Colin looked up. A huge brawl was going on right by the church. Colin couldn't make out the details, but it seemed to be Knights fighting Orphans.

"All the more reason to clear out," Colin said. "Can you walk all right?"

"I'll manage," Deena said. "But why are you messing with him? Kill him here, let the sticks find him."

"Oh, no," Colin said. "We're not done with this fellow. We've got some questions for him."

Deena sighed, grabbing one arm of the senseless Jester and hauling him to his feet. "Let's do it."

The Hunter had the bow raised and before Veranix could even blink, three arrows were nocked and released in rapid succession.

Veranix jumped off the podium, drawing on his magic to slow the world around him. He couldn't do that and hold on to his shrouding, but that didn't matter. The arrows were creeping toward Inspector Rainey and the other fake Birds.

Staff out, Veranix closed the distance to the first arrow, smashing it out of the air as it flew through the molasses of time.

He crossed the aisle to knock the second out of the way. In the slowed world, Inspector Rainey was throwing herself into the pews, but she would have been too slow. The arrow was just a couple feet from her when Veranix smashed it, shredding it into splinters.

He pushed, physically and magically, to hold the world slowed until he reached that third arrow, inching its way at Crow. The point was literally touching her chest when Veranix snatched it out of the air, slamming back into normal speed as soon as he did.

Rainey and Cormorant both dropped down to the ground, both seemingly equally surprised that they didn't have an arrow in their chest.

"What happened?" the Hunter asked.

"I did!" Veranix shouted. "And next I'm going to rip that cloak off of you."

Suddenly his left arm was grabbed, and something cold and harsh wrapped around his wrist. It didn't just hit his wrist, it jarred his whole body, an anchor on his heart.

"Stand and be held," Crow said. "You have been ironed—"

Veranix yanked his arm out of her grip, but one shackle was on his wrist. The other end of the shackle ripped from Crow's hand and clocked her in the teeth. She reeled, and he was able to pull away.

But his connection to the *numina*, even through the rope and cloak, was numb. Mage shackles, steel blended with dalmatium. He was barely able to keep his face darkened.

Crow hadn't recovered, and he took the moment to get out of her reach. The last thing he needed was to have both wrists shackled. Or to have to actively fight a constable to stop it.

"You," the Hunter said, malice in his voice. "You should be helping me kill them."

"Idiot," Veranix said, jumping over to the aisle, staff twirling. "I don't have time to explain how stupid you are."

The Hunter drew and fired an arrow at Veranix, but he was able to dodge and close the distance. No magic, just muscle, bone, and wit.

A cry ripped through the air behind them. Veranix let it

distract him, turned his head to see the arrow he dodged had found a target. Inspector Rainey was hit in the leg.

"Specs!" Cormorant called out. "Rutting bastards!"

The Hunter nocked another arrow, but before he could draw it back, the reverend was on him, grabbing his arm.

"Shed no more blood in this house!"

The Hunter swung out his fist, connecting with the reverend's face. Pemmick crumpled, blood gushing from his nose.

"This isn't a house that's helped me," the Hunter said. "Stay down, preacher."

That was enough to set Veranix off. He launched at the Hunter, twirling the staff savagely. The Hunter was ready—fast, skilled. He blocked those attacks, parrying with his arms. Veranix was astonished that anyone could do that—he was hitting hard enough to break bones, but the Hunter just took the hits. It surprised Veranix enough that he didn't have his own guard up when the Hunter punched him in the face.

That punch hit like a speeding carriage.

Then another blow hit Veranix in the back. Cormorant ran past him, clocking him with one of her handsticks while diving into it with the Hunter.

Veranix was dazed, but his vision cleared enough to see Cormorant battering the Hunter with her sticks, all the while letting lose a stream of profanity unlike anything Veranix had ever heard.

Rage welled up inside Veranix. He had to get this fight out of the church, get the Hunter down before he killed one of these constables. He channeled that anger, pushed it through the deadening cold of the mage shackle. He still couldn't pull enough *numina* through it.

Cormorant put up a hard fight, but then the Hunter caught her handstick. He ripped the weapon out of her hand, and then brought it down on her head.

Veranix could only think of one more play. He pulled off the cloak and wrapped it around the shackle and his wrist. Maybe direct contact would cancel out somehow. Holding the rope in his other hand, stretched as far away from his shackled hand as possible, he forced himself to draw *numina* through the swirling fire of the napranium and the icy deadness of the dalmatium. He charged past the Hunter while putting all the power he could channel into the rope, wrapping it around the man before he could deliver a devastating blow onto Cormorant's head.

And with every ounce he had in him, he pulled the Hunter out the door and hurled him onto the street.

The street was madness. A haze of smoke filled the night air, and all around Waterpath Orphans and Knights of Saint Julian were brawling. A few constables and pages were trying to bring order, but there was too much chaos to get control over it. It would take an army of sticks.

Veranix didn't care. The Hunter was on the ground now, and Veranix had no intention of letting him back up.

"Well, well," a soft voice cooed. "We heard the Thorn was throwing a party for us. We didn't know it would be double."

Four women stood in the street, all armed with blades, staves, and chains.

Veranix's gut told him that these were the real Deadly Birds.

Five minutes after Inspector Rainey and the others went into the church, everything turned into chaos. Minox wasn't sure what happened at first. He was keeping his distance from the church, when there was a disturbance up Vine Street. He moved to investigate, but only saw the street filling with smoke.

At the same time, a group of Waterpath Orphans came marching up Tulip. They must have been following after Yessa just as he had followed after Rainey. He should have noticed them. Failure on his part.

That had an immediate response from the group of Knights of Saint Julian hanging outside a bar, who whistled for more Knights to come to them. The Knights and

Orphans then charged at each other, pushing past him. They didn't seem to notice or care that he was a constable.

Someone was fighting in the smoke.

Smoke, like the false Thorn used. Minox drew out his crossbow, about to move in, when there was another horrible sound. Wood cracking, from the direction of the church. Like the door breaking.

Inspector Rainey might be in peril, and that was a higher priority in this moment.

Whistle calls pierced the air. Minox turned back to the square, now a full brannigan between the Orphans and Knights. Sergeant Tripper had left his post to charge in, pull them apart. Whistle in mouth, handstick high, he blasted shrills and did his best to get between them. None of them paid him any notice.

Minox drew magic into his body, with the intent of creating a blast of light or fire. Nothing that would hurt the fighting gangs, but dazzle them enough that they might disperse.

A wave of energy hit him from the church, vibrating through his hand. The Thorn. He was inside, and the door was hanging open.

Minox reeled, the magical energy from the Thorn drawing him—and then suddenly it stopped. Like a window slamming shut.

"Specs!" Wheth up on the roof across the street. He was pointing to something down the street. The haze of the smoke had drifted into the square, and Minox couldn't make out what Wheth was pointing to. Saitle was down that way.

"Saitle!" Minox called. "Report!"

"Welling!" Tripper shouted. He was barely holding his own in the brawl. Minox had to help the officer, and trust Inspector Rainey's competence. He could hear a fight going on inside the church, and strange waves of magic vibrated in his hand. As Minox went to pry an Orphan's hands off Tripper's throat, he realized that the Thorn must have been put in mage shackles. That would explain the change in energy.

Then another wave of magic rattled Minox, just as he grabbed the Orphan. The Orphan screamed in agony just at the touch of his left hand.

"What the blazes?" another Orphan said. "What did you do?"

Minox grabbed at the Orphan in answer, mostly as an experiment. The wave of energy had passed, and the effect was not repeated.

Tripper clubbed that Orphan, and grabbed Minox and pulled him out.

"We need a Riot Call!" Minox said.

"Wouldn't hurt, but I don't think it'll get much response," Tripper said. "The blazes is that?"

At the bottom of the church's front steps, one Thorn— the real one, by Minox's senses—had another wrapped in his rope. But there were four women—Deadly Birds, actual Deadly Birds, Minox was certain—standing in a half circle around the both of them.

This could not end well without intervention.

"Get the street clear, Sergeant Tripper," Minox said. "I will handle this."

"How the blazes you gonna—"

Minox was already moving away. He remembered what the Thorn had done to him before, and he knew what that felt like. Taking up his crossbow in his right hand—still loaded with the blunt tip—he grabbed his irons in the left hand.

And primed his hand with magic, so it and the chains burst into blue flame.

"All of you," he announced to the Thorns and Birds, "Stand and be held, for you are bound by law."

Veranix thought he might have convinced these Birds that he wasn't their enemy, that the Hunter was who had been killing their numbers. He didn't even get a chance to speak before Inspector Welling dove into the situation.

And it went exactly as well as could be expected.

Three of the Birds turned onto Welling. One of them, wielding something that looked like a double-headed oar — or a tetchbat — laid into the constable with a series of furious attacks. "None of yours, stick!"

"Wait, wait!" Veranix said. "You don't have —"

An arrow struck another Bird — the one who seemed to be the leader. She cried out as blood burst out from her shoulder.

"Yellowtail!" the Hunter shouted. "You're the only one on my list!" He bolted off.

"I'll get him," Yellowtail said to the other two. "Take care of the other Thorn and the stick."

"Not today," Veranix said, seeing that a pair of Orphans and Knights were about to collide into the tall blonde one. He rolled away from her first strike, knowing that she was about to be bowled down by the brawl. He popped back onto his feet, chasing behind Yellowtail, who went into an alley after the Hunter. He reached the alley to find Yellowtail on the ground, two more arrows in her chest. The Hunter was climbing up a back alley iron stairway to the roof.

Veranix leaped up. No magic, not this time. He didn't need it. Three bounds, and he was at the top of the steps, staff spinning. Three cracks — knee, back, head — he sent the Hunter reeling. The Hunter tried to turn around, bow raised but Veranix wasn't about to let him. Staff dropped, rope in hand, he willed it to wrap around the Hunter and hold him as tight as steel. The Hunter strained — stronger than Veranix imagined he could, but Veranix held him fast.

"You aren't going anywhere," Veranix said.

"What the depths is your problem?" the Hunter snarled. "I thought you —"

"I will not bear the debt of the deaths you caused," Veranix said. "How dare you assume my mantle —"

"Your mantle? I killed *killers*. Who deserved it. You've done the same, I know —"

"And I'll answer to the saints for it, but you'll answer to me. And since the constables want a Thorn —"

The Hunter grinned — an ugly grin with gray stained

teeth. "The constable? Provided he survives against that pack of killers."

"You are bound—" Veranix heard in the alley below, followed by a bone-crunching blow. "You are bound—"

"One of ours dead, stick, and you'll answer for it."

Veranix dared a glance down. Inspector Welling was in the alley—he must have pursued behind them all—and the other three Birds had him pinned. He still held up his flaming hand and shackles, but his crossbow was gone.

Another Bird hit him across the face. "Tell us again."

"You are bound by law—" he got out before another strike across the jaw.

They were toying with him, making him suffer.

"Blazes," Veranix muttered. He didn't have any choice.

Chapter 22

"**Y**OU ARE BOUND—" Minox began again. He would say the words. He would make them respect the words. He grabbed the arm of the short woman with the bladed oar-weapon—Seagull, if his research was correct. She cried out in pain—his hand was still burning bright blue—and hit him with the flat of her weapon.

Dazed, Minox let go of her. The flame around his hand burned out.

"We are the last thing you'll see, stick," she said.

"You are bound by law," he said. "Stand and be held—"

"Shut it," the tall Bardinic blonde said. Albatross. She smashed him in the jaw with a mighty fist, loosening a tooth. Under these repeated blows, he could not maintain focus, keep any magic flowing. She raised up her arm again.

And then was smashed across the skull by a fighting staff.

Suddenly the Thorn dropped down in front of him, staff in one hand, his strange rope wrapped around the other, magic and energy swirling and diving all around him. The Thorn, with his back to Minox. There to protect him.

"Back off," the Thorn said to the Birds. "Only warning."

"Warning us?" Seagull mocked. "Aren't you as sweet as a pie?"

Minox took the chance to draw his handstick. "You are

resisting a lawful arrest," he said. "That will be added to your charges."

"Let's kill them slowly." The third one spoke with a heavy accent, raising up her wicked curved weapon. Jackdaw, a Ch'omik woman with traditional bare arms, covered in tattoos and scars. "For Yellowtail."

The Thorn spun his weapon, feinting at Seagull, but hitting a true strike at Albatross. "A little help, Inspector."

"Do not think that—" Minox said, dodging a swipe from Jackdaw, "this absolves—"

"Let's live first," the Thorn said, blocking Seagull's weapon from coming down on Minox's skull. "Unless you ladies would like to stop."

"You've got some stones, Thorn," Seagull said, launching on him. "Killing ours and calling us out."

"Wasn't me," Thorn said, blocking her with his roped hand. A blast of blue glow came from it. "I don't want a fight with you."

"Strange way to show it," Albatross said, her mighty fist coming at the Thorn.

"I don't suppose you have backup coming," the Thorn said, swinging in a wide arc to force all the Birds back.

"I'm afraid their hands are full," Minox said, using the opening to slam his handstick into Albatross's gut. Her strength made her the greatest threat. Jackdaw and Seagull were effectively equal. He dodged another swipe from Jackdaw, noting that the blow did little but anger Albatross.

The Thorn sighed, sending a backhanded thrust at Jackdaw. "That was your cue to lie, Inspector."

"Apologies," Minox said. The Thorn was a formidable fighter, but all he was going to be able to do was hold off the Birds for a brief time. It was likely they would both die without additional intervention or a succinct change in strategy.

Fortunately, he had an idea for the latter.

He hurled the handstick at Jackdaw—just as a distraction—while taking the moment to fuel his hand with magic.

"Apologies for this as well."

Minox grabbed the rope wrapped around the Thorn's arm.

And the whole world changed.

Veranix didn't know how he was going to hold off the three Birds, and he wasn't going to last much longer against them. Any one of them was one solid blow away from putting him down.

Then Inspector Welling grabbed his wrist. Or more specifically, the rope—wrapped around the mage shackle to cancel out its influence as best as possible—with his strange, magical hand.

Suddenly Veranix could feel the flow of *numina* through his body and Welling's, as if they were one person. It was a rush of power that made the influence of the cloak and rope seem insignificant.

But Veranix knew it was fleeting. It was a raging fire; they couldn't hold it long.

Veranix channeled some of that energy into a hard blast out of their bodies. Like a game of Eight Fallen Pins, the Birds went tumbling down to the ground. With the rest, he slowed the world down, down to a crawl.

"Irons," Veranix said.

Welling was in the slowed world with him. He held up his shackles. "I only have the one pair."

"We can't let go," Veranix said.

Welling nodded, and grabbed the chains from the dead Bird off the ground. With a quizzical look on his face, he channeled *numina* into the shackles and the chains themselves. They snaked into each other, wrapping around the three Birds on the ground, pulling them together to bind them.

"Did you just make those grow?" Veranix asked.

"I believe I did."

"I didn't think that was possible," Veranix said. The world was still a crawl. The *numinic* flow between them was almost bled out, faltering. "What happens when you let go?"

"Do you mean magically, or our next choices?"

"The latter," Veranix said. "Though the former has me worried." He wondered if he could channel *numina* to his legs and leap magically the moment they disconnected. But he felt everything Welling had done to the chain; there was no reason to believe Welling wouldn't be aware of his actions.

"I have a duty I should not ignore," Welling said, his grip still tight on Veranix's wrist. "You have several charges to answer for."

"It was the fraud who killed Emilia and Bluejay. And attacked Inspector Rainey and the others."

"Are they injured?" A furious rise in *numina* rushed from Welling to Veranix. It was a vibration, building between them. The connection wouldn't hold much longer.

"I don't know," Veranix said. "Do whatever you have to, Inspector."

Welling looked torn, uncertain. Looking back at Veranix, he nodded. "Thank you." With the *numina* between them on the verge of becoming volatile, he let go.

The world slammed back to normal, and Veranix found himself hurtling at incredible velocity.

Welling hadn't just let go.

He'd *pushed*.

Veranix had rocketed out the other side of the alley. The world was no longer slowed down, but Veranix was still moving as if it was.

He only had a second to realize that before he was about to crash into the side of a building.

He shaped the last residual *numina* from the harmonization into a cushion of air around his body. He collided into the building like hitting a pillow, but it still hurt like blazes. He dropped to the ground, winded but unhurt.

He was a block away from Inspector Welling and the rest of the fracas. He still had the mage shackle on his wrist, and he wanted to sleep for a week, but he was away from all that.

He took a deep breath and pulled himself to his feet. He still needed to get back home.

He realized he no longer was masking his face. How long had that been the case? Had Inspector Welling seen his face? He couldn't remember. The last time he was certain it was still on was before he jumped back down into the alley.

He couldn't worry about that now. Painfully, exhaustingly, he pulled enough *numina* through the cloak and rope, over the numbing power of the shackle, and wrapped himself in the illusion of an ordinary U of M student. He'd have to push himself to hold it as he walked back to campus, but it should get him through the gates and home.

Right now, that was all he cared about.

As soon as they got to the safehouse, they dropped the Jester on the floor. Deena washed her hands and face, stripped out of her disguise, put her own clothes on, and left. She had very little to say.

That didn't matter. She wasn't the one Colin wanted to talk.

He filled a pot and put it on the stove. He pulled the Jester into the back room, tied him to one of the cots.

"Wass going on?" a sleepy voice asked. Colin looked up. Meaty-armed Bassa, in just a sleeping shift.

"You crash here?" he asked. He wasn't counting on her being here. He was hoping he'd have the place to himself.

"What'd you think?" she sent back. "Who's that?"

"The one who hit us."

"Thorn?"

"Ain't the Thorn," Colin said. "I been calling him the Jester, because he thinks he's funny."

She looked at the Jester, and then at the pot on the stove. "You seem to have something in mind."

There was no use in lying to her. "I'm gonna wake him up, and get some answers," Colin said.

She raised an eyebrow. "That's my job, you know."

"And you'll tell the answers to the bosses. But I got my own questions, want my own answers."

She gave him a look he couldn't quite figure out. He didn't know her, despite her obvious years in the Princes.

Had she been here, doing Vessrin's dirtiest work, apart from the rest of the Princes all this time? He had no idea.

"Why?"

"Because I have my own numbers to balance, and I want to know how this guy figures in it."

Bassa crossed over, looking at the Jester. "He's a fingers man."

"What?"

"Look at the nails on him. He takes care of them. He values his fingers."

That was right. He said something like that in the fight.

"Thanks."

"I'm going back to sleep. Anyone asks, I didn't wake up when you came. I never saw you."

Colin couldn't help himself. It didn't make sense. "Why?"

She glanced back at him. "Because I owed your pop from way back. He never got to call that marker." She went back into her room.

Colin went to the water on the stove. It was hot. Not scalding: he could stick a finger in there for a moment. Hot enough. He took the pot over to the Jester. Unmasked, decloaked, he was just some guy. More Colin's age than Veranix's. Nothing very remarkable about him.

Colin threw the water in his face.

The Jester woke up, sputtering invectives and curses.

"Welcome back," Colin said. "I've got a few questions for you."

"Oh, the Prince has questions. Lovely."

Colin grabbed one of Bassa's sharp tools. "I do. And if I don't get answers, you lose a finger."

"I lose what?"

"So, first off, are you acting on your own, or were you working with someone?" He slid the blades of the tool around the Jester's first finger.

"Oh, saints," the Jester said. "Leave it be. I was hired. And not paid enough for this."

"Really?" Colin asked, leaving the tool right where it was. "Who hired you, and to do what, exactly?"

"I did what I was asked. Play the Thorn. Go after the old Red Rabbits. And hit the constables so they would go after him."

"The plan was as simple as that?"

"As far as he cared to tell me."

"Who's 'he'?"

"A bloke by the name of Bell."

Bell. That was interesting. One of Fenmere's lieutenants. The one Vee liked to taunt.

"All right, Mister—"

"Don. Erno Don. Wandering troubadour and bow for hire."

"And mouthy bastard."

"Make no claims to the contrary. Blazes, that's what Bell liked about me."

"So you were the one who attacked the constables? Including the lieutenant?"

"I can tell you, Prince. It ain't gonna go to a court or nothing. That was my job. The whole neighborhood thought I was the Thorn. Quite the performance."

"You're quite pleased with yourself."

"I did what I was hired to do, and I did it well. Who wouldn't be pleased by that?"

"You think the Princes are going to let you live with what you did?"

Erno raised an eyebrow. "You talk like you're not one of them."

"Not one of the bosses. I don't think they'll be as . . . gentle as I'm being."

"Look, I need my fingers. They're my real livelihood."

"This the troubadour thing?"

"These fingers are magic on the guit-box and viol."

"Well," Colin said, sliding the cutting tool so it almost sliced the skin on Erno's first finger. "Then let's talk about where I'll find Mister Bell."

Kaiana was done waiting. It was enough after two bells to be worried. She dug out a pair of work boots, slacks, and leather apron. She dressed quickly and quietly, and went back out into the stables of the carriage house.

Delmin had dozed off in a corner, while Jiarna was hard at work at her table. Kaiana was astounded at how quickly Jiarna had taken to everything they did, how fully she embraced it. She was still working at her method of tracking the drug—which may not have been *effitte*, a point that troubled Kaiana—despite it being the middle of the night.

Phadre had gone off for supplies and food. Where he was going to procure those things in the middle of the night was a mystery to Kaiana, but he had left with such confidence she wasn't going to question it.

"Are you the Gardener?" Jiarna asked, not looking up from her notebook.

"I was going to bring the big shovel with me," Kaiana said. "It's a solid weapon."

"I think it's a mistake." Jiarna pushed the book away and rubbed at her eyes. "I mean, I understand why, don't get me wrong. But if Veranix is in trouble, all you'll accomplish is getting yourself in a similar mess."

"If I believed that, he'd have died in the brewery and the campus would have burned."

"Fair enough." She smiled ruefully. "Truth is, I wish I had something here in all my work I could give you to help. But I've been so focused—"

"You've done amazing things here, Jiarna," Kaiana said. "I'm still wondering why."

"I spent four years here, studying and fighting to be noticed. Fighting for my work. Professors ignored me, scoffed at my ideas. Veranix didn't. Of course, he thought I was the Prankster, but that was kind of flattering. He believed I was capable of that."

"Aren't you?"

"In terms of the science? Not yet. I would love to look at Cuse Jensett's notebooks. He figured out things . . . But that's not the point. You all take me seriously. And there is something positively thrilling in what he does."

Kaiana picked up the shovel. "Thrilling, but very stupid. Which is why I'm going to have to—"

The doors opened, and Phadre poked his head in. "A little assistance, if you would." He came in the rest of the way, half dragging Veranix along with him.

"What the blazes happened?" Kaiana asked, coming to help take Veranix off of him. "Is he hurt?"

"No," Veranix muttered. He looked up with effort, as if his head was too heavy for his neck. "Just exhausted."

"I found him on the grass, crawling," Phadre said. "Lucky it was me, and not campus cadets."

"Getting over the wall took it out of me," Veranix mumbled.

"Why is he—what's wrong with him?" Kaiana asked.

Delmin had roused. "What's going on?"

"Vee's back, but he's a mess."

"Just need to rest."

Delmin came over. "Saints, what all is that?" He pointed to Veranix's left arm. The cloak was wrapped around it. "Get it off him. The *numinic* swirls, they're . . . mad."

Kaiana and Jiarna unwrapped his arm, finding the rope under the cloak. Taking that off, there was a shackle bound to his wrist.

"Great saints," Delmin said. "That's—"

"A mage shackle," Veranix said. "Can someone get it off of me?"

"The rutting blazes?" Delmin shouted. "How the rutting blazes do you have a blazing *mage shackle* on your wrist? Were you arrested?"

"Things—things didn't progress that far. Some interruptions."

"Interruptions." Delmin stalked off. "This is all too much. What am I doing here? Why am I—"

"Ease down, chap," Phadre said. "This looks bad, but—"

"Looks bad? It looks like he was a hair away from being dragged off to Quarrygate! And what do you think would have happened when it went to trial? You think it wouldn't have ended with each of us being dragged out in irons?"

Phadre nodded, trying to reach out to Delmin. "It didn't, though, so let's stay calm."

"Everything is falling apart. Everything. You, the professor, the department."

Kaiana didn't have time to deal with Delmin's panic. She dug a hammer and trowel out of her tools. "Let's get that off him."

"Delmin," Veranix wheezed. "Come over here."

"You think you can get it off with that?" Jiarna asked Kaiana quietly. "Phadre and Delmin wouldn't be able to magic it off."

"I presumed," Kaiana said. "I think I can break it." She knelt down next to Veranix.

"I cannot handle this," Delmin said.

"Talk to him," Kaiana said. "Distract him while I do this." She looked at the shackle, finding the seam.

"Is it going to hurt?" Veranix asked. He looked so exhausted.

"I can't promise that it won't. Delmin."

Delmin came over. "This is getting too dangerous. I don't think you should—"

"You said something, Del. The professor. The department. What's happening?"

Kaiana wedged the tip of the trowel into the crack of the shackle. "Tell him."

"I was at the professor's office," Delmin began. "I was supposed to have another interview with Inspector Rainey, under the professor's supervision."

"Inspector Rainey," Veranix said. "She was there tonight . . ."

"She's not important, not entirely," Delmin said. "When I got there, the professor was meeting with someone from Druth Intelligence. A mage."

"What for?"

Kaiana had the trowel in place. She lined up the hammer to the handle.

"I only heard a bit," Delmin said. "But, from what I understood, the department is lacking in funds, or is being pressured financially—"

Veranix nodded weakly. "That's why he was being amicable with the Blue Hand Circle."

Kaiana gave Delmin a hard look. She was ready to hit the shackle.

"So this Intelligence officer is going to be a professor," Delmin said. "But he's going to be part of some special projects. Alimen was very upset about it."

"What kind of projects?" Veranix asked.

Kaiana brought down the hammer.

"Rolling rutting blazes!" Veranix shouted.

The shackle cracked a little, but didn't open.

"Going to have to do it again," Kaiana said.

"Do what you have to." Veranix turned back to Delmin, keeping his eyes on him. "What kind of projects?"

"I'm not sure. But—this was the really strange part."

Kaiana brought the hammer down again. Veranix screamed again. The shackle loosened a bit more.

"The officer, he was upset that Alimen had failed to hold on to Golmin and Kay." He nodded over to Phadre and Jiarna. "That their work was the sort of thing he needed for the Altarn Initiative."

"Professor Salarmin made us a very generous offer," Phadre said. "I was quite surprised that word of our work had reached Trenn College."

"I had been writing him for months," Jiarna said. "But he hadn't paid attention until after we got our letters."

"This officer really laid into Alimen over you two going to Trenn," Delmin said.

"Well, we are quite a loss to U of M," Jiarna said. "I'm glad that's appreciated." She clicked her tongue. "Did you say Altarn Initiative?"

"That mean something to you?" Delmin asked.

"It's familiar," Jiarna said, shaking her head. "I can't recall where I read it, though."

"One more blow," Kaiana said.

"Do it," Veranix said. He reached out and grabbed Delmin's hand, squeezing tight.

Kaiana brought down the hammer hard.

The shackle cracked off.

Veranix cried out, pulling Delmin in close to him.

"That's such a relief," he said after a moment, releasing Delmin.

"Did I break your wrist?"

"No," he said. "But it hurts like blazes."

"And the rest of you?"

"Sleep," Veranix said drowsily. "Can I just fall here?"

Kaiana nodded. "Of course."

"I didn't ask," Veranix said almost inaudibly. "How did it go for you?"

"I played crownball," Kaiana said.

"That's dangerous," he mumbled.

"Scored a point, got kicked out, but we got hold of the drug."

"So we know who's selling?"

"Not that simple. It's . . . it's not *effitte*. But it's still dangerous."

He nodded. "Then we'll get this as well."

She smiled. "Jiarna is working on a plan."

"Good." His eyes were closed, he was almost out. "Wake me when we're going to get the bastards."

Chapter 23

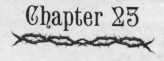

SATRINE HAD TO take command of the situation when the whistle calls were finally responded to. Lockwagons and footpatrol and Yellowshields rolled into the church square, and Satrine was the closest thing to an authority in the area. Fortunately, no one questioned her authority, despite her outrageous costume.

She had to do it with a Yellowshield nearly attached to her leg. She barely sat down long enough for the poor man to dress her wound. She made the Yellowshields focus on Corrie and Pollit. Pollit was mostly dazed from getting the shackle knocked across his head, but Corrie had an open gash on her hairline. The only reason why Satrine hadn't arrested the preacher was because he—despite his own bleeding nose—had leaped onto Corrie to stem her bleeding.

Tripper, Wheth, and the cadets had had their hands full with the Knights and Orphans, many of whom scattered once the wagons had rolled in. Satrine had let that Orphan captain Yessa slip off into the night, despite her better judgment. That had been the deal, and she recognized that the girl was an asset to Benvin's squad as long as she was on the streets. It wasn't her place to remove that. Besides, that girl was about the only one who hadn't attacked anyone.

"Has anyone seen Welling?" she asked once the Yellowshield let her walk away. "Sweep the area until we find him."

"He chased after the Thorns," Wheth said. "I saw that when I came down from my perch to help the sergeant. I didn't see what happened to him next."

"Which way?"

Wheth led toward the mouth of an alley, where she came upon an incredible sight.

Three women—actual Deadly Birds, she presumed from their dress—were wrapped in an absurdly giant chain, struggling to get free. A fourth lay dead on the ground from arrow wounds.

And Minox Welling—he lay on the ground, eyes shut, peaceful expression on his face. As if he had simply decided to take a nap once he caught these women. He was breathing, and despite the torn-up uniform and cuts and bruises on his face, there was something oddly serene in his expression. In their months together, through many bizarre circumstances, this was one of the strangest things she'd seen.

"Go get a Yellowshield," she told Wheth, and he ran off.

"Welling?" she asked, shaking his shoulder.

He opened his eyes. "Inspector Rainey?" he said calmly. "Are you injured?"

"Yes, but—" She was surprised by the serenity in his question. "I'll be all right, I think. You?"

"I've had a singular experience, which I will need to process." He sat up. "I presume we can process these arrests, so this endeavor will not be a complete loss."

"The Thorn escaped," she said. "Both of them." Though one of them—the true Thorn—had protected her and the others from the fraud, despite their attempts to apprehend him.

"Yes, he did. Both of them."

"You saw them? The real one and the fraud?"

"As I said, Inspector Rainey. A singular experience."

He was keeping his own counsel for the moment. She was used to that. "You couldn't have done . . . this on your own."

"And I do not claim that. Nor can I claim, in good conscience, that I have acted in full accord with my office."

She decided not to let him dance around it anymore. "Did you let the Thorn go, Minox?"

He thought for a moment. "Strictly speaking, to let him go, I would have had to have him under my authority. That never occurred."

"You're convinced of his innocence."

"I am convinced, beyond any shade, that he is not responsible for the attack on Lieutenant Benvin." That was an interesting specification.

She sighed. "You aren't the only one."

"Your own singular experience?"

"Arrows from the imposter, coming for my throat. And Corrie's. But the Thorn stopped them."

Welling's eyes lit up. "Did he put himself at risk for your safety?"

She thought about what happened. It had all been a bit of a blur. "Yes, I think so. Even after Pollit slapped the mage shackles on him."

"He was—" Welling thought for a moment. "Remarkable."

Wheth came running back over with a Yellowshield. "Who's hurt?"

"I should probably be checked over, as I took quite a few blows to the body and head," Welling said. That was unusual for Welling. He usually resisted any medical ministrations beyond the most obviously necessary. "Mister Wheth, make sure these three get put into a lockwagon, and call for a bodyman for the fourth."

Satrine walked out of the alley with Welling and the Yellowshield. "So, is this it? Are we done with Aventil, at least for this investigation?"

"I am loath to say yes," Welling said as he sat down on a Yellowshield cart. The 'shield started checking his eyes and ears while he spoke. "Strictly speaking, we have not achieved anything resembling closing our investigation. We may have eliminated the Thorn as a suspect, but we are not closer to apprehending or even identifying a proper one. But perhaps the arrest of wanted assassins fulfills the requirements of the hollow victory you spoke of."

"And a bunch of Orphans and Knights." Jace had approached, adding this insight.

"Hardly remarkable in this neighborhood."

"The question is, do we go back to Inemar tomorrow?" Rainey asked. "No offense, Jace, but I'm rather done with Aventil."

"It has its charms."

"I don't know about your investigation," the Yellowshield said. "But I'd like to get both of you back to the stationhouse ward, if not Lower Trenn. He's got a bruise on his temple that warrants further observation. And you, lady. How are you even standing up?"

"Painfully," Satrine admitted.

Jace added, "One of the other 'shields wanted to bring Corrie in for the same reason. Though she has a duck egg swelling on her head."

"I consent to that," Welling said. "And I think you should let yourself be brought in as well, Inspector Rainey."

"It's already one bell in the dark, so why not," Satrine said. "Jace, you're unhurt?"

"Followed the rules this time, specs," he said. "Stayed out of the fracas."

"Hope for him yet," she said to Welling.

"Go directly home," Welling said to Jace. "Make sure Mother knows Corrie and I are fine and not to worry. Then get some sleep. Don't come in until nine bells in the morning."

"So you want me to lie to Mother."

"I want you to make sure she does not worry."

"Lie."

Welling chuckled lightly. "As you see fit."

><><><><

"Veranix, wake up." Delmin, shaking him.

"Is there class?" Veranix asked, wondering why he was sleeping on the floor.

"Still summer, fool," Delmin said.

Veranix opened his eyes. Carriage house. Now he remembered.

"We been here all night?"

"Jiarna's been at it all night," he said. "We've been napping, but . . ."

"What?"

"Colin is here."

"Oh." Veranix looked around. Jiarna was still working at her table, with Phadre and Kaiana looking over her shoulders. Colin stood to the side, looking like he had spent the night in a sewer tunnel. "How is that all going?"

"Jiarna says she's just about ready, but she'll need you."

"All right," Veranix said. "Give me a minute." There was something in Colin's energy that made it seem as if he wanted to talk privately.

"I'll be right over there," Delmin said, going back to the table. Colin came over, furtive glances at the rest. As he came close, it was clear his hands and shirt were spattered with blood. He had clearly gone through something during the night.

"You look like blazes," Veranix said.

"You as well," Colin said. "Who'd your face tangle with?"

"The Hunter, some deadly Birds—"

"Then you're lucky to still have a face."

Veranix grimaced. "The Hunter still got away. Plus I had a group of constables pretending to be Birds."

Colin raised an eyebrow. "You going to have more of a stick problem?"

"I have one, period. I don't know how I could have more of one." Though Inspector Welling didn't stop him from getting away. He could have, but didn't. "Though you should know, the sticks pretending to be Birds? That was set up by Yessa."

"The Orphan captain?" Colin scowled. "The blazes you go to her for?"

"Priest's idea. A bad one."

"I'll say. Blazes, Yessa is snitching to the sticks?"

"Maybe," Veranix said, hands up. "I wouldn't swear it. She might have been tricked or something."

"Orphan problem, not mine," Colin said. "All right, I've got real news to tell you."

"I hope it's good."

"It is, but you won't like it all. The Jester isn't an issue anymore."

"What?" Veranix couldn't believe it. "When, how?"

"I tussled with him, took him down. He's still alive, but he ain't happy about it."

"I'm . . . thank you. So who the blazes was he?"

"Some wandering bow-for-hire, or minstrel. Or both."

"For hire?"

"Hired by Bell."

"You mean Fenmere."

"From what I gathered from this guy, Bell isn't in Fenmere's good graces. Maybe this was a play to get back in. But he wanted the Rabbits done, wanted you disgraced. So he found this guy."

"From what you gathered?" Veranix wasn't sure he wanted to know the details.

"Don't worry about it. Or the rest."

"What do you mean?"

"I mean Bell. Don't—I've got it. I'm going to pay him a little visit."

"You are?" That meant Colin was going to cross into Dentonhill. Walking those streets with the Rose on his arm was a huge risk for him to take.

"Don't worry about it."

Veranix glanced back over to Kaiana and the others, finalizing Jiarna's strange plan. "I've got enough to handle."

"But if you need it—if it can help you, I can give you this. The guy, and all his toys, are at a house. Number nineteen Branch. Maybe give him to the sticks, get them off your back."

"Leaving me with just the Hunter, Birds, and a campus filled with some strange drug."

"*Effitte?*"

"No. I—I don't even know. But I can't let whatever it is come in here, any more than I would *effitte*."

"All right," Colin said. He grabbed Veranix and pulled him into an embrace. "You keep yourself together, cousin."

Veranix hugged him back, and he wondered just what Colin was planning. "You too. Don't do anything too stupid."

"I know," Colin said. "That's your job."

He broke off, heading over to the worktable. He peered around, clearly making Delmin and Phadre a bit uncomfortable. Jiarna, of course, was unfazed.

"Hey, shags," Colin said to Delmin. "No matter what, ride him like a pedalcart this year. Full marks, you hear?"

Delmin smiled. "I'll tie him to the desk."

"You kids—I wish I had a crew of Princes like you all. I'd own the streets."

Before anyone could respond to that, he slipped out the door, one last salute to Veranix as he went into the dawn.

It hit Veranix like thunder. He might never see his cousin again.

"We're ready," Jiarna said. "Veranix, I need you."

Time to go to work.

Minox didn't sleep much, partly because the night doctor on duty at the Aventil stationhouse made a point of waking him at regular intervals. There was, apparently, a medical cause for this that Minox neither understood nor cared about. He was more concerned about Corrie. She had been lucid, even jovial, but the welt on her head was grossly swollen. The doctor insisted she rest, and he made arrangements for a Yellowshield cart to take her to a proper ward hospital. Minox had to spend some time arguing to send her to Ironheart in Inemar before the doctor finally relented.

Inspector Rainey had dozed off once she was given a dose of *doph* for the pain in her leg. It was the same leg she had injured months before, so the long-term effects would not slow her down any more than she already had been by that incident. He was impressed by how well she had borne the pain, kept going on with her duty despite the injury. Not surprised, but impressed. Inspector Rainey always impressed him.

Minox's lack of sleep was not just due to the doctor's ministrations or his concern for his sister and partner. There was also much to think about throughout the night, specifically about the Thorn.

There was no mystery left about the Thorn himself, at least his identity and intentions. He had seen both with his own eyes.

Veranix Calbert, magic student.

A good young man, dedicated to right, if not to law.

It was this insight he had made into Mister Calbert's character that had caused him the most consternation. By law, now that he knew the Thorn's identity he should be dedicated to gathering enough evidence to make an arrest. His own statement of witness would not be proof, but it would be enough to acquire writs and perform searches and compulsions. With those, it was likely any Constabulary inspector worthy of their vest could gather enough physical and testimonial evidence to make a proper case.

But that would not be right. Veranix Calbert did not deserve to go to Quarrygate, or worse.

Once the doctor had started ignoring Minox, he went down to Lieutenant Benvin's squad room to pore over his files once more. Everything the lieutenant had on the Thorn, which was mostly speculation. Minox had read through these files several times already, but before he was focused on what the Thorn was doing, not why.

The why took shape quickly. Willem Fenmere. The Thorn was obviously attacking the man's empire of *effitte*, smuggling, prostitution, and corruption, a festering wound in the Dentonhill neighborhood. Minox had long taken a passing interest in Fenmere, despite it being out of his usual jurisdiction. But the Dentonhill Constabulary was hopelessly in the man's pocket. Minox even suspected his cousin Edard was too deeply embroiled in such things to be fully trusted.

No one in Dentonhill Constabulary could be trusted to

enact legal justice on Fenmere. It would never happen that way.

It could only happen—

These were dangerous thoughts Minox was having. He pushed them out of his mind.

"Hey, specs." Officer Pollit knocking on the doorframe. He was back in his usual attire, no sign of his disguise or activity from the night besides the bruise on his face. "Why aren't you in the infirmary ward?"

"A bit of research," Minox said. "Though I may be wasting my time. Why are you here?"

"Looking for you. It's the lieutenant. He's awake, and he's already biting to jump out of bed and get to work."

Chapter 24

"ALL RIGHT," Veranix said. "That's definitely not *ef-fitte*." In the light of morning, the stuff was a pale grayish-green. The vials were the same kind that the *effitte* would come in, but it didn't look or smell the same way. "You really didn't need to tell me that."

"Yes, I know," Jiarna said. "I'm starting with the givens, and then we work from there. I just want to make sure you're following."

"I'm with you so far."

"Now, these three vials—" She pointed to ones she had labeled with a different code than the others. "Those three are the ones that Kaiana got directly from the boys who admitted to buying *effitte* in Dentonhill."

"Which led me to the trap."

"Incidental," Jiarna said. She took a moment, adding, "Not that it wasn't troublesome for you, but it doesn't tie directly to my point."

"This isn't a Letters Defense," Veranix said.

"We're engaging in a bit of academic rigor in this moment," Phadre said. "We'll want to document it all, at least for our own records." He tapped on one of his journals. "This sort of work—"

"The point!" Veranix said.

Jiarna took over. "Those three vials are our control. We

know they held *effitte*. And the magiochemical properties of the residue is completely different from all the other vials, which match that of our full sample."

"So the real problem on campus is this green stuff, not *effitte*." He caught a harsh look from Kaiana for a moment. "Which is still a problem, yes."

Her face softened. "I wasn't sure if that registered with you."

"Whatever this stuff is, whatever it does, we should find who's selling it and knock them down."

"What it does," Jiarna said. "I have some theories. Theories supported by data, but still just theories."

"Data?" Delmin asked.

"First, observation. We saw someone take Substance Green One—"

"That's what you're calling it?" Delmin asked.

"It's a useful moniker."

"You don't get to name anything," Veranix said. "But please continue."

She scowled. "We saw one of the athletes at the crownball game take it, and then act with significant aggression toward Kaiana."

"So it makes you angry?" Kaiana asked.

"Not just that. I did another test during the night. Darling, that bucket, please."

Phadre fetched the bucket. "Oh, there's a mouse in here!"

"Yes, I caught it and put it in the bucket, dear, that was the point. Bring it here." Phadre did as he was instructed. Jiarna put on a leather glove and grabbed the mouse. She then took a small sample of the green drug in a dropper, and put a few drops in the mouse's mouth.

"That's horrible," Delmin said. "You don't know what—"

"Which is the point of using a mouse instead of a person, Delmin," Jiarna said sharply. "The latter would be irresponsible." She dropped the mouse back into the bucket.

"Are we supposed to be—" Kaiana began.

The mouse began running against the side of the bucket.

Again and again, harder and harder, until one of the slats cracked open. It smashed again, pushing through the hole it had made, and then bolted across the table. It snarled as it went, leaping at Delmin with bared teeth.

"Ah!" Delmin screeched, before Jiarna grabbed it out of the air with her gloved hand.

"No, you don't get to bite me," she said to the mouse. She held it tight. "It is, as you can see, not merely aggressive, but demonstrating impressive strength and resistance to pain. For a mouse."

"How—" Veranix started.

"The how is outside of my expertise," Jiarna said. "But it explains why that player didn't even seem to notice he was drowning."

"He was so intent on beating me, he didn't care what happened," Kaiana said.

"Now, with a properly regulated dosage, the recipient might not be so maniacal. But I can't be sure. I would have to—"

"This isn't really what we need to know, Jiarna," Veranix said. "What about tracking it? Finding it?"

"Right, of course. I was excited for the possible—"

"Another time, perhaps," Delmin said.

She took a deep breath. "So, I may not understand the physiological properties of Substance Green One, but I have isolated one of its key magiochemical properties. It has a unique aspect that can be excited, for lack of a better word, which will cause *numinic* vibrations at a specific resonance. Which I can detect with my devices, and likely Delmin can recognize it as well."

Delmin gave a weary nod. "I imagine so."

"Now, for exciting it." She slid a small monstrosity of bronze and glass closer to Veranix.

"I presume you have a plan, and it involves this?" Veranix asked.

"Indeed," she said. "I've taken one of Phadre's calibration instruments, and made some adjustments to make it into a *numinic* emitter. I had to shave a tiny bit of napranium from the rope—it shouldn't adversely affect its effectiveness."

"If you say so," Veranix said.

"Now, all it needs is application of power. That's you."

"I presumed," Veranix said.

"What you'll need to do is apply about six barins of *numina*—that's a lot, but with the cloak on, you should be able to do it—at the crystal lens here."

"Which will create a wide blanket pulse of *numinic* resonance over the whole campus—" Phadre added.

"Won't, say, Professor Alimen and the other magic faculty notice that?" Delmin asked.

"Probably," Phadre admitted. "But there's minimal risk they'd be able to pinpoint who or where it came from. So powerful, so wide—"

"It'd be deafening," Delmin said. "And for someone as sensitive as me . . ."

"I thought of that, yes," Jiarna said. She picked up the mage shackle, dropping it into his hands. "Hold that."

His knees buckled. "All right, that . . . might work."

"And this *numinic* resonance—" Veranix started. All of this made his head spin.

"Ought to latch on to anything with these magiochemical properties—which, I believe, are unique to this drug—making all sources of it emit a vibration that this instrument here *should* be able to track." She held up one of the devices Phadre had built.

"There's a lot of ought to and should in this plan," Kaiana said.

"But it's not like we have anything better," Veranix said. "It's almost eight bells. Campus is going to get active. The tetch match between us and Pirrell will be starting in an hour."

"So," Jiarna said, picking up the cloak and putting it on Veranix's shoulders. "Six barins, at the lens."

"I really don't know what six barins feels like."

"Easily solved!" Phadre said, pulling another device out of a crate. "A barinometer!" He pointed to the glass dial on the front. "It reads in centibarins, so you'll want to get it up to . . . how many? Six hundred."

"Obviously," Veranix said, even though he wasn't sure what Phadre was talking about. "Then let's do it."

He pulled *numina* into himself, gauging what would be a very strong flow, and sent it into the crystal.

The dial on the barinometer went up to three hundred fifty.

"Not good enough," Jiarna said. "Sorry. It's going to take six hundred to trigger the reaction."

"All right, then," Veranix said. He pulled in even more, letting the cloak feed him as strongly as possible. He let it build, filling him through every fiber and vessel. It crackled in his ears and eyes.

"Saints," Phadre whispered.

He sent it out through his hands, raw and untempered, into the crystal.

The meter hit seven fifty.

"How did you—" Phadre whispered.

"Cover your eyes!" Jiarna shouted.

The device glowed bright white, and the light burst and filled the whole room.

The damned doctors wanted to keep him in bed. To blazes with that. Lieutenant Benvin got on his feet as soon as he could keep them under him. He was weak, hungry, thirsty . . . and too angry to care about any of that.

"What time is it?" he shouted as he got up. "What blasted time is it?"

"Left?" Tripper came running over from some far corner. "You got to take it easy."

"Easy, Tripper?" Benvin shook his head. Where were his clothes? "Ain't no easy to take. The blasted Thorn came at us, we got to—"

"I know, Left," Tripper said, holding Benvin's arm. "That was—it's the sixteenth, boss. You've been down for four days."

"Four days?" Benvin shook that off. "Saints, no wonder I'm hungry. Don't matter. We've got work to do. Get everyone in here. We need—"

Mal. The image of Mal, arrows in his chest, flooded his memory.

"Mal. He's—"

"Yeah, boss. He's gone."

"We need to—his sister—"

"I already took care of it, boss. We didn't—we weren't sure when you'd wake up. Or if."

Benvin held Tripper by the side of his head. It was good to have men like this, men he could count on. He had already lost too many. "Thanks. And Saitle? He was there, did he—I couldn't bear—"

Tripper nodded. "He got his skull addled pretty good, but he's all right."

Benvin chuckled wryly. "I don't how much addling that boy's skull can take. You've been holding it together, Tripper?"

"Doing what I could, especially with the specs right on top of us."

"What specs?" He looked around the wardroom. "Do I have some damn clothes in here, Tripper?"

"Sent Saitle for them when I heard you were awake, left."

"So, the specs?"

"Sent here to investigate your attack. Officially, we weren't supposed to touch it."

Benvin lowered his voice. "Sent. So none of the chairwarmers from our house?"

"No. These folk—they're pains, but in a good way."

Benvin wasn't sure what that meant. "How?"

"They don't like easy answers. Even though we knew what was going on here, they wanted to go deeper."

"Deeper than what?" Benvin shook it off. "I'm up, so we don't need to worry about them."

"Worry about what?" A Waishen-haired woman in shirtsleeves and skivs, with a bandaged leg, came limping in.

"The blazes are you?"

"I was saying . . ." Tripper whispered.

"Inspector Satrine Rainey," she said, extending her hand. "You'll have to forgive my appearance, we had a bit of a night. And, frankly, I'm still a bit fuzzy from the *doph*."

"You're the spec assigned to my case?" He'd heard stories about this woman. She was a fraud who tricked her way into an inspectorship, but the Inemar house kept her on when she was found out. They even called her "Tricky." No one he had heard about her from was clear on why she hadn't been sent to Quarrygate, but that was the story.

"My partner and I," she said. She had clearly picked up on his enmity. Her eyes narrowed, her voice tensed.

"Her partner," Tripper said. "Inspector Welling."

"Welling?" Jace's family name. His brother, he was an inspector somewhere in town.

"Pollit went to go find him," Tripper said. "Should be here in a minute."

"Now that you're up—" Rainey said, obviously about to start a line of questions.

"Now that I'm up, I've got work to do. Four days on my back is enough."

"Yes, I know you're anxious."

"I'm not anxious, Inspector. I'm ready. Ready to put an end to the sewage in the neighborhood, starting with the ones who put me on my back."

"And who are those?"

This came from a newcomer, who had walked in with Pollit. This was clearly Inspector Welling, even if Benvin hadn't been expecting him. The man looked like an older, skinnier version of Jace. Stick-bones skinny.

"Aventil streets are full of the bastards," Benvin said. "And I'm gonna start rounding them up. Now I've got cause."

"What cause is that?" Welling asked. "We've been deeply investigating the attack on you, your case work, the situation here—"

"Four days here, you've *deeply* investigated it? That's the sewage you're selling me, specs?" He shook his head in disgust. "Really, Tripper. Pollit? You've put up with this?"

"If you have some new information that could result in arrest—"

"Or closing the case," Rainey said. "Frankly, we would love to sign off this case as done and go back to Inemar."

"Then consider it done," Benvin said. "I can handle it with my people."

"That isn't how it works, Lieutenant," Rainey said. "You damn well know an attack on an officer—"

"Attack and murder," Benvin said hotly. He still couldn't believe that Mal was gone. He had probably died protecting Benvin. Loyal to the end.

"All the more reason," Rainey said.

"I'm not here to argue it with you," Benvin said. "I'll get Captain Holcomb to throw you out of this house if I have to. I don't need to deal with your nonsense. I have work to do."

"Part of that work—" Welling started to say, and then his face changed. It was like he was hearing something in the distance, something no one else noticed. Benvin had no clue what that might be; he certainly didn't hear anything. "Excuse me," Welling said suddenly, and ran off.

"Welling! Welling!" Rainey limped off after her partner.

"Well, that solves that problem," Benvin said.

"They've really been a good sort this whole time," Pollit said. "They ain't like this house's specs at all."

"I couldn't care any less about that," Benvin said. "I want a uniform, top quick. Then Quiet Call whoever you think you can bring in and will keep it dark. Gather everyone down in the stables in half an hour, ready to roll."

"Quiet Call?" Tripper asked. "Why is that?"

"Because I don't want those specs—or anyone else—giving warning. Don't even tell the folks you bring in what we're doing, just promise them the action. We're going to hit high and hard."

"Plenty who will come for that," Pollit said. "You at least telling us the plan?"

"Saints, yes," Benvin said. "We're going to clean up this neighborhood for good. Starting with the ones who've been working with the Thorn. The rutting Rose Street Princes. We'll crack through there and drag the lot of them in."

"Without a writ?" Tripper looked nervous.

"Blazes, no," Benvin said. Last thing he needed was the Justice Advocate Office crashing the whole thing over something so basic. "You get that moving. I'm going to find the City Protector, and by saints, he will write me a writ for whatever place I rutting want."

It was time to put an end to all this nonsense. No more Princes. No more Orphans, Knights, or anything else in Aventil when he was done.

Colin had made his way through Dentonhill in the early morning, weaving through the usual trudge of folks heading to the poultry slaughterhouse and the tannery and other wretched jobs they worked. He just needed to get to the right tenement without getting noticed. Head down, coat on, arms covered.

The place was just another gray brick building, no different than any other dreary tenement in Dentonhill. Perfect place for an *effitte* den or a dealer to hide out in. No one would notice or care about anything. Which is what Colin counted on. He went in with no trouble—the latch on the door had been broken so many times it couldn't even stay closed—and went up to the top floor.

He stood outside the flop door. He could hear voices on the other side—at least three, probably more. Jovial talk—eating or playing cards, most likely.

No more waiting. He dropped the coat on the floor—that thing had been so damn hot to wear. Anyone who noticed him on his way over knew he was up to no good, and they didn't give a damn. That's how corrupt Dentonhill was, of course. Plain folk, sticks, whoever—they could see trouble coming, and more often than not, they'd watch it happen.

That suited Colin just fine.

He rolled up his shirtsleeves. Prince tattoo showing. He wanted this bastard to know exactly who had come for him. He slid knucklestuffers on both hands, real nasty pieces of work with spikes at each finger. He drew out the two knives at his belt, checked his grip on them with the knuckle-stuffers on. Made sure they felt right in his hands. He didn't want to screw this up by having a knife slip out of his grip.

Ready. Committed. Taking a deep breath, he kicked in the door.

"The blazes—" was all one bruiser right by the door-frame said before earning a knife in the throat. He collapsed, choking in his own blood, while three other thugs got up from the table. They were all in skivs and linens, which was no dignified way for any of them to die.

But that was how it was going to go.

Colin leaped in at the closest one, slicing open his belly and kicking him in the knee. That one dropped like a heavy sack. The second Colin popped in the face with his left hand, then slashed with that knife. The bruiser reeled for a moment, and, before he recovered, Colin's right-hand knife was in his chest.

The knife stuck, so Colin let it go, kicking that bruiser into his friend. That one dodged out of the way, and was able to close in on Colin before he could get his left-hand blade back up. The bruiser got hold of Colin's left wrist, tried to twist the knife out of it. The other hand shot out, finding Colin's throat. This guy was a good six inches taller than Colin, all muscle, and he lifted Colin up off the ground by his neck.

"What you playing at, Prince?" he snarled, squeezing his neck.

Colin couldn't answer, but he could land a knuckle-stuffed punch at the guy's ribs. Then another, as hard as he could, and a third. That was the one that forced the bruiser to let go of his wrist.

That mistake earned the bruiser a knife in the ribs.

He let go of Colin's neck and dropped to the ground.

"Blazes is going on?" came a call from the back room. A lean, bushy-haired man came out, just the one Colin was looking for.

"You're Bell, aren't you?" Colin asked.

Bell dove for one of the knives on the table, but Colin jumped on him, pounding him in the face with the knuckle-stuffer. Bell collapsed, and Colin let himself go to the floor with him, knocking him again and again.

Colin got on Bell's arms, pinning him down.

"You know who I am, Bell?"

"You're a Prince," Bell said through bloodied teeth. "Rose Street is going to burn for this."

"I don't think so," Colin said, smashing his fist into Bell's eye. "But do you know who I am?"

"One Prince or another, all the same." Colin was impressed that Bell still could speak despite the beating.

"Oh no, Bell," Colin said. "I'm Colin Tyson. Den Tyson was my father. Cal Tyson was my uncle. Your boss killed my uncle and turned his wife into a thoughtless blank, and there will be a reckoning for that."

Colin punched three more times. Bell was in a fog now, his face so much bloody meat. Colin got on his feet, kicking Bell in the ribs for good measure.

"But that isn't why I'm here, Bell. You crossed into Aventil, you had your boy pretend to be the Thorn, and you had him kill Rabbits and sticks."

Bell just moaned.

"The Thorn would probably want to have his own words with you, but I thought you should hear it from a Prince." Colin leaned down. "You do not cross Waterpath. Not in any way. You let Fenmere know that if I even hear a whisper of his people putting a toe over that line, I will find whatever place he lays his head down and I will burn it to the ground. Do you understand?"

Bell only gurgled blood in response.

Colin went to the water pump and rinsed the blood off his hands and the knucklestuffers. He put those back in his pocket. He splashed his face as well. Clean enough to walk in the streets. He looked around the flop, notice the small stack of goldsmith notes that had fallen on the floor in the fight. He scooped that up and put it in his pocket. No reason not to hold on to that, keep it out of Bell's hands. It wasn't like he would get in less trouble for not doing it.

"The Thorn will be looking for you, Bell," Colin said. "I hear he didn't take too kindly to your ploy. I don't know if he'll be as merciful as I was."

He rolled down his sleeves and picked up his coat. Closing it over his bloody shirt, he left the flop, now quiet save for Bell's wheezing breaths.

Chapter 25

"**T**HAT FELT LIKE IT WORKED," Veranix said once the bright light had faded. "Tell me everyone on campus didn't see all that."

"That was the device," Phadre said, rubbing at his temples. "But I'm sure even the first-year mage students felt that."

"Oh, saints, yes." Delmin was lying on the ground, still clutching the mage shackles. "Even with my senses blunted, that was intense."

"I must remember goggles in the future," Jiarna muttered. She picked up the sensor device. "Well, it's definitely doing something. I'm getting readings from our samples here. This is working."

"And maybe a few clicks before we get cadets bursting in here," Veranix said. "How do we do this now?"

"That is what I'm trying to determine," Jiarna said. She turned in circles, holding the device in front of her.

Kaiana stuck her head outside, and then pulled back in. "No one is rushing over here. People seem to be vaguely confused, but otherwise going about their business."

"Wait until a professor focuses on this place," Delmin said, getting to his feet. "Or any other magic student on this campus."

"I'm less worried about that," Jiarna said. "If anything,

they'd be drawn to the drug. Are you feeling anything, Delmin?"

He crouched in front of the vials. "Yes. It's definitely putting out a unique . . . scent."

"Scent?" Veranix asked.

"Best word I have," Delmin said. "Though I don't know how many students or professors would distinguish it from usual background *numina*."

"You can?" Jiarna asked.

"Barely."

"Same here," she said, making an adjustment on her device. "Yes, I've got it tuned now."

"We should move throughout campus, try to get closer," Phadre said.

"I agree," Jiarna said. "Split up. I'll go with Veranix, you with Delmin and Kaiana."

Kaiana raised an eyebrow. "Why do that?"

"We have two ways to track—Delmin and this device. So two teams, two and three. We have to presume trouble. Veranix should be on the team of two, as he's more capable of handling trouble alone."

"But—" Phadre started. Jiarna stepped on his objections.

"I've already worked out the risk value, and . . ."

"Can we go?" Veranix asked, slinging his weapons over his shoulder.

"Yes, let's," Phadre said. "Though perhaps . . ." He looked expectantly at Veranix.

"What do you need?"

"The rope?" Phadre said. "I can use it, and it'd be good for me to have some sort of defense, in case—"

Veranix didn't want to give up the rope, but he also didn't think he could deny Phadre. The man had already done so much for them. Handing it over, he said, "Be careful. All of you."

They all stepped out to the lawn, Veranix masking himself to look like he was just in uniform.

"I'm feeling like there's a concentration of it over there, and over there," Delmin said, pointing in two directions. One was in the direction of the tetch field, the other the cluster of southern dorms, including Almers.

"Makes sense," Jiarna said, swinging her device between the two directions. "Yes, I agree."

"We'll take the dorms," Delmin said. "I am still a prefect. I can use that authority if we need it."

"Us to the field," Veranix said. "Where half of campus is."

Jiarna nodded. "It does not narrow things down."

"Be safe," Kaiana said as Delmin and Phadre started to move.

"Keep them safe," Veranix told her. She was holding a short garden tool that could work as a truncheon. "When in doubt, run and get my attention."

"I was going to tell you the same thing," she said. "Who saved you last time?"

"You. Every time."

"Vee!" Jiarna said sharply.

He went off with her as the rest peeled off. She sighed as they approached the field. "I also split us this way so our emotions won't make us sloppy. Phadre and I would make mistakes if one of us were in danger."

"I suppose," Veranix said.

"You and Kaiana are the same way. Well, not the same, but have . . . similar blind spots."

"You know that Kai and I, we aren't . . . we don't . . ."

"I'm aware," Jiarna said. "You wouldn't have had that fling with Emilia Quope if you were. It's not in your nature. But you two would both leap in front of a stampede for each other. That is clear to anyone."

"Hopefully there won't be a stampede."

The crowd around the tetch field belied that. It was a horde of people, already nearly in a frenzy of anticipation.

"You're reading it in there?" Veranix asked.

Jiarna gave him a withering look. "This is hardly that precise a device." In fact, it looked like a box with a handful of sewing needles attached to it, the needles quivering and pointing toward the field. "But the signature this is attuned to is strong, and it's right in the center."

Veranix wasn't sure how she could gauge that from a bunch of sewing needles, but he didn't question it. "The match is about to start."

"And you, in theory, are supposed to be with the squad. Wouldn't they be expecting you?"

"Yes," Veranix said. "Frankly, last thing on my mind right now."

They pushed their way through the crowd to the squad, who were in the midst of their pregame stretches.

"Just like you taught us, huh, Calbert?" Tosler said as Veranix approached. "Glad you could make it. Worried we wouldn't have our good-luck charm."

"Wouldn't miss it," Veranix said halfheartedly. "You all got a tough one today." He looked around, trying to see anything obvious in the crowd. He glanced at Jiarna.

"Not sure," she said. She had now put in her eyepiece. "You might be damaging the readings. You're . . . bristling with *numina*."

"I'm a bit on edge."

"Ain't we all?" Tosler said absently. "We got this, though. No matter how broiled those Pirrell pikers are."

He pointed over to the Pirrell team, whose own pregame seemed to involve pounding each other on the arms and shoulders and screaming at each other.

"We've got the field first," Tosler said. "Any last words?"

"Try not to give them any hits," Veranix said. "You don't want to let any of them run if you can."

Tosler gave an almost disparaging grin. "Like I don't do that every game. All right, boys, let's get out there."

The squad took the field, while the Pirrell team lined up on the Hold Line.

"Veranix, we have a real problem," Jiarna said. "The Pirrell team is the source."

"They've got the drug?" Veranix asked.

"No." Jiarna took out her eyepiece. "The *numinic* signature is coming from them. Coursing through their bodies. All of them are filled with it."

"Oh, blazes," Veranix said. If the Pirrell squad were about to play like the mouse in the bucket, the U of M boys would get clobbered.

"And I am incredibly stupid," Jiarna added. "Why didn't I think of it?"

"Think of what?" He saw her face was pale with fear.

"We've *numinic*ally excited the drug. That altered its magiochemical properties. There's no telling how that would affect its efficacy."

Tosler threw his first pitch at the Pirrell at the tetch.

"I could use an educated guess *right now*, Jiarna."

Her voice was a terrified whisper. "Amplification."

As the pitch went by, the Pirrell student swung hard, but instead of hitting the ball, he clocked Blute in the head. The ball sailed past, over the Hold Line. Normally that would break the Hold, allow the batting team to storm the field—but not if the batter struck the Wall.

"No break!" the Watcher called. "Hold isn't broken!"

The Pirrell players did not listen. They charged together at full steam, like wild dogs coming for the kill.

"Welling! Welling!" Inspector Rainey had caught up to Minox a block away from the Constabulary stationhouse. He hadn't realized how far he had gone, almost entirely on instinct. She was still in her shirtsleeves and skivs, not even boots on.

"You've been chasing me undressed, and with that leg?" Minox asked.

"Yes, you idiot," she said. She rarely employed such directed insults at him, so she must be rather angry. "You went running off and didn't give me time to find my slacks. And it hurts like blazes, but you've been too blasted deaf to notice me screaming for you."

"My . . . my apologies, Inspector Rainey," he said. He could still feel the energy humming in the distance, at the north end of the neighborhood. Possibly even on campus. "Something has happened, or is happening, and—"

"It's magical," she said. "But does that mean it's relevant to what we need to do?"

"My instinct—which is admittedly not an appropriate tool to use to judge this—says that it is. It is certainly a large event—strong enough for me to feel it from the stationhouse. And it—smells familiar."

"Smells?"

"That is the best way I can put this sensation into words. It is at the edge of all my senses, but not directly in the domain of any one of them. But it is reminiscent of a familiar scent that triggers memory."

"Do you mean you think it's the Thorn? The real one?"

"Doing something of incredible power," he said again, starting to walk. "It would be remiss of me to not investigate further."

"Then let's go," she said, walking with him. "Is it north neighborhood, or campus?"

"I'm not sure," he said. "I'll know more as we get closer."

"If it's campus, that professor—"

"I am unconcerned about that at the moment," he said. His thoughts went back to what was happening before he felt the energy. Events in the stationhouse played out in his head, the observations he had made when he first came upon the lieutenant. So obvious, and he had walked away. He had seen it clearly in the moment, only he had allowed himself to be distracted by the magic energy. Foolish, but it couldn't be helped now. "However, there is another concern. And I fear you should attend to that while I attend to this."

"Splitting up never goes well for us, Welling."

"Regardless, it may be necessary." He stopped. "I believe Lieutenant Benvin is going to organize his people, as well as the regulars of the stationhouse, to perform a police action of dubious legality. Most likely strike at one or more of the gangs in the neighborhood."

"Why . . . how . . ."

"His bearing was one of determination to action. 'Work

to do.' 'We'll handle it.' He has made a determination of the guilty party."

"He said he has cause, I remember. But why do you think he'll engage in dubious legality?"

"He was ready to drive us out, against the advice of his loyal people. He felt he lost time. Impatience is driving him. Everything I read of the man—"

"He'll do something reckless and urgent." Her expression told him she agreed with his conclusion. "I can imagine he'll hit one of the gang hangouts. Probably the Rose Street Princes one."

"Why that one?"

"One of his men was killed there a few months ago."

Sound reasoning. "Keep Benvin in check. I'll go—"

The scent changed. Still familiar, but yet . . . sour.

"Something is changing. I fear it is dangerous."

"We should both—"

"Benvin!" he said sharply. "The situation here is fraught enough without him behaving unethically." He waved her off, and then ran over to a young man with a pedalcart. "Constabulary officer. I must claim Eminent Right over your vehicle and make use of it."

"What does that mean?" the young man said.

"I must take your pedalcart for emergent Constabulary business. Report to the stationhouse, and it shall be returned to you in short order, or the city will compensate you."

"But—"

"My apologies," Minox said, getting on the pedalcart. He unhitched the tow section. Now it was a sleek, two-wheeled vehicle, unencumbered with a back wagon of goods. With a glance back, he noted Inspector Rainey pushing herself back toward the stationhouse.

He pedaled as hard as he could, racing and weaving up through the traffic toward the strange magical disturbance that called to him.

"I can't believe it's in Almers," Delmin said. Kaiana had let him take the lead, and he had stopped in front of the dorm building. "Right under my nose."

"You hardly could have known," Kaiana said.

"It's not like you could sense it earlier, right, old boy?" Phadre said. He looked like he was trying to seem calm and composed, but he was holding Veranix's rope like it was a live snake.

"I thought you could control that," Kaiana said. "Should I take it?"

"No, I've—I've got a sense of it," he said. "Just needs some adjusting to, you know?" Kaiana decided not to hurt his pride by gainsaying him. It wasn't like she could use it at all. In her hands it was just a rope.

"Let's go," Delmin said, squinting upward. "Second floor."

"You can tell that from here?" Kaiana asked.

"At this distance, it's painfully clear. And . . ." He tilted his head, like he was listening intently. "There's a lot."

"The source?" Kaiana asked.

"That would be my guess." He opened the main doors and led Kaiana and Phadre in.

"Hey, Sarren!" someone shouted as soon as they entered. "That bird can't come in here!"

"Special circumstances," Delmin said, his tone suddenly confident and commanding. "She's grounds staff, and we have a situation on the second floor to attend to."

"Oy, what?" The young man came over. "I really should have been brought in the circle on this one. Who's this guy?"

"Phadre Golmin, recent graduate." Phadre started to extend his hand to the man, and then pulled back to grab the rope.

Delmin pushed his way past. "This doesn't matter. We've got word that there's a resident with large amounts of contraband in his room on the second floor."

"Wait, wait," the other prefect said, jumping up on the stairs to keep them from ascending. "I have so many questions. What contraband? How do you know? Why not call in cadets, or at least housing authority?"

Delmin stopped. "That's a good point, Dannick. Why do you think I have Miss Nell from the grounds staff here? What do you think her job is?"

"She . . . I'm sorry, I don't know." He looked her up and down. Kaiana had to admit, in her canvas slacks and apron, short hoe menacingly in her hand, she hardly looked like the sort of person who would be brought into the dorms to deal with contraband.

"Exactly, Dannick. You don't know. She's here in an official capacity, and Mister Golmin is an expert here to handle the materials if they turn out to be volatile."

"Volatile?" Dannick went pale. "What sort of contraband are we talking about?"

Kaiana decided this was her moment to step in. What would Veranix do here? If punching someone wasn't an option, he'd bluff. Delmin had given her a good opportunity, and she just needed to take hold of it. "I'm afraid we can't discuss that. Dannick, is it?"

"Yes, that's right."

"Look." She lowered her voice. "We want, ideally, to keep this quiet. Merely the fact that this stuff got onto campus, that a student has it in his room, in Almers . . . that's an embarrassment for a lot of people on campus. You included."

"Me?"

"This was under our noses, Dannick," Delmin said. "We dropped our watch."

"I guess, but—"

"There's no time for guessing," Phadre said, loud and unnatural. Bluffing was not his skill. "We have to get on this!"

He went up the stairs, and Kaiana followed right behind him. Delmin and Dannick caught up with them at the second floor.

"Where is it?" Kaiana asked.

"Third door on the left," Delmin said. "There's little bits in other rooms, but in that one . . . it's intense."

"What are you—" Dannick started. "Oh, sweet saints, is this a magic thing?"

"Who's staying in this room?" Kaiana said sharply.

Dannick was still worked up. "Oh, it *is* some magic thing. That's why you have this guy here. Expert to handle. Is that what this is?"

"This isn't the time," Delmin said.

"Whose room is it?" Kaiana asked again.

"Most of this hall are Pirrell athletes. They took the second and third floors. Of course, most of them are out on the field. But that one is—"

"Tetch match, right," Delmin said. "Maybe no one will be here."

"I've got a master key," Dannick said, fumbling at his pockets. "Let me—"

Kaiana took the key from him. "We've got this."

"But—look, that room is Enzin Hence."

"So?" Kaiana asked. "Should that mean something to me?"

"He won Archery for Pirrell," Phadre said.

"All the more reason to do this quiet," Kaiana said. "We don't want this to be any more of an embarrassment for Pirrell than it is for U of M." She went to unlock the door when it flew open.

"You talking about me?" A shirtless young man, heavily muscled, was in the doorframe. His impressive build wasn't the most noticeable thing about him. His body and arms were covered with bruises—horrifying purple and yellow welts almost anywhere he had exposed skin.

"Mister Hence," Delmin said, stepping forward. "We're the summer prefects of this hall."

"Yeah, so what the depths is that to me?" His Kystian accent was thick and coarse.

"We are given to understand—" Delmin took a deep breath, like he was puffing up his courage. "You have some illicit material in your room."

Hence blinked, glancing back in his room. "I don't know what you mean," he said unconvincingly.

"We mean the drugs, Hence," Kaiana said. "We know you're the source."

"How do you know that?" He blinked more. "You . . . you should step away from here."

"Let's do this quiet and easy," Delmin said. "We don't need any—"

Hence's hand shot out and grabbed Delmin at the throat. "Don't you tell me what I need. I've had to—"

Kaiana didn't waste time, swinging the hoe into Hence's back, and then again on his leg. Both blows were like hitting stone.

He didn't flinch or budge, squeezing at Delmin's throat while turning to Kaiana. "Who the depths do you think you are?" With his free hand he ripped the hoe from her hand and threw it down the hall.

The rope flew out from Phadre and wrapped around Hence's arms. Hence dropped Delmin to the floor.

"You?" Hence said. "Here I thought the Birds or the sticks got you."

"I—what—" Phadre stammered out, struggling to hold on to the rope as it twisted around Hence.

"You aren't going to stop me now, either," Hence said. He twisted his arm to get a grip on the rope, and pulled, bringing Phadre to him. Phadre was drawn in close, and then knocked down with Hence's fist. The rope fell to the ground, limp.

"That was too easy," Hence said, pointing at Phadre. "You ain't him."

Kaiana dove to get to Delmin, pulling him away from Hence.

"He recognizes the rope," Delmin whispered.

"I get it," Kaiana said. "He's the Hunter."

Hence focused on her. "That's what you call me? Cute. But none of you are the Thorn, are you?"

"Hunter? Thorn? The blazes is this?" Dannick shouted.

"This is me getting rid of—" was all Hence got out before the rope, coiled into a ball around Phadre's fist, smashed into his face.

"Run, all of you," Phadre said, holding up his hands like he was in a collegiate fighting sport ring. Blood gushed from his nose onto his shirt and vest. "I will keep him at bay."

"Keep me at bay?" Hence chuckled. "Oh, you are rich, Mary. You're no Thorn."

"No," Phadre said, pulling his rope-laden fist back. "But I am a scholar."

He whipped his arm out wide, and the rope flew out down the hall. It grabbed Kaiana's hoe from the floor and hurled it back. The hoe smashed into Hence's face before it was gently deposited into Kaiana's hand.

"And a gentleman," Phadre said. "Now yield to your betters."

Despite the blood and bruises, Hence didn't look even slightly fazed. "My betters? You polished Marys really think that's what you are?"

Delmin had gotten to his feet. Dannick was nowhere to be seen. Perhaps he had taken the advice to run. His voice was hoarse when he rasped out, "Better than a salt-scrubbing, clam-eating caker who thinks he can be the Thorn."

"Oh, you're going to eat it, Mary." He swung at Delmin, who ducked out of the way, while Kaiana took her moment. She hammered the hoe into Hence's knee, hoping it would drop him.

No such luck. He wound up another punch, knocking Kaiana across the skull.

That hit like a horse.

Another punch was coming, Kaiana too dazed from the first to get out of the way. Green and purple magical energy suddenly danced in front of her, and Hence's blow smashed into it instead of her face.

"That's how you want it, Marys?" Hence said, grabbing Delmin by the front of his shirt, his hands shaking visibly. Purple energy still flowed from Delmin's hands, which sputtered and sparked. "You want a real fight, let's have it." He threw Delmin into Phadre, and then went back in his room.

The stars cleared from Kaiana's vision, and she helped

Delmin and Phadre to their feet. "Go, go get the Thorn. We need him—"

Hence emerged from his room, quiver strapped over his bare chest, bow in his hand. In his other hand, he carried a clay jug.

"That's it," Delmin said. "It's in the jug."

"You want a fight, Marys, then let's do it," Hence said. He pulled the cork out of the jug with his teeth, spitting it at Kaiana. Then he brought the jug to his lips, pouring into his mouth while green liquid oozed over his face.

"Oh, sweet saints," Phadre said. "If he's anything like the mouse—"

Hence howled, and dropped the jug. The veins in his neck and arms bulged, and the yellowing bruises turned darker. His eyes went all black, and Kaiana would swear the seams of his pants tore.

"Now, let's fight," his voice boomed.

Chapter 26

NO WHISTLES FROM the Watcher had quelled the charge of the Pirrell squad, nor had the rules of the game or boundaries of the field halted their actions. In moments, they were on the Maradaine squad, showing no interest in points or scoring, simply doling out violence.

"I need to—" Veranix started, before he realized one of the Pirrell players, having slammed Catfish into the dirt, was coming straight at him and Jiarna.

Jiarna yelped, as Veranix kicked up a tetchbat from the ground into his hand. Despite the massive presence of the player, Veranix put himself between the man and Jiarna, poised to crack him over the head if he kept coming.

The implied threat did nothing to stop the player. As he charged in, his eyes vacant, drool dripping from his mouth, Veranix leaped up and smashed the tetchbat across his skull, sweetening the blow with magic.

The bat shattered, but it barely slowed the player down.

Jiarna scrambled out of the way, and Veranix flipped over the player, adroitly dodging the massive arms that threatened to crush him.

At this point, the spectators were in a frenzy, and they charged from the stands into the field. Veranix grabbed hold of Jiarna and magically fueled a jump to the only place he could see that was remotely safe—the announcer's perch. The young woman—magic student—was still up there, away from the madness.

Veranix shed his illusions while he and Jiarna sailed through the air, fully in Thorn persona when he landed. He had to hope no one had been paying much mind in the chaos.

The magic student cried out when they landed in her box.

"Sorry," Veranix said. "We need a plan."

"A what?" the magic student shouted. "Who—what—why—"

"There's no plan," Jiarna said. "They're in a mad rage."

"You have a bow!" the magic student said frantically. "Shoot them!"

Veranix hesitated for a moment. Even in this state, none of the Pirrell players deserved to be killed. Also, while they were the most dangerous on the field, it was now a mess of players, spectators, and other folk. Simply taking out the Pirrell squad would hardly quash the full riot.

He looked to Jiarna. "You're brilliant, she's magical, come up with something. I'll do my best." He leaped up on the railing of the perch and drew out the bow. Behind him, he could hear Jiarna rattling off ideas to the terrified girl.

Amid the madness, one of the Pirrell squad had Marmot pinned to the ground, and was smashing his face into bloody meat. Veranix took aim and fired. The arrow landed square in the Pirrell player's thigh.

That got the Pirrell player's attention. He spun around and howled at Veranix.

"Come on, clam-eaters!" he boomed out, magically augmenting his voice to echo throughout the field. "Why don't you try a real fight!"

The rioting stopped for a moment, all eyes on him. Most of the brawlers went right back to the fight they were in. Some of the Pirrell squad kept their attention on him.

He took another shot, nailing a Pirrell player in the leg.

"What are you doing?" Jiarna hissed.

"I'm drawing the real danger out of here. Figure out a way to cool the rest of the crowd."

"I'm thinking," she said.

The Pirrell players were coming toward him now, just about all of them.

"You salt-scrubbers couldn't stop a real runner!" he shouted out. Firing another shot, he jumped down to the ground below. "Thorn for the Triple Jack!"

With that, he ran away from the field. Hopefully the Pirrell boys were in such a state they wouldn't realize he was running in the opposite direction of the Triple Jack line.

They came. All eleven Pirrell boys, heaving rage-filled masses of muscle and bone in crimson and white, came pounding after him as he cleared the field and went to the south lawn.

"Saint Senea, Saint Justin, anyone else who's listening," he muttered as he ran. "This may or may not be the stupidest thing I've done, but if you have any grace left for me, I could use it right now."

In the middle of the lawn, far enough from the field that they were no longer embroiled in the riot, Veranix spun on his heel and drew another arrow. He fired, then another, then another, aiming for the legs and knees.

Four of the players stumbled and fell.

Four.

He had fired three arrows.

Before he could register the meaning of that, before he could bring up his guard to defend himself from the first of the Pirrell bruisers to collide into him, a pedalcart came flying through the air, smashing into the lot of them.

Inspector Minox Welling dropped down on the ground next to Veranix, loading his crossbow as he regained his footing.

"Don't stand there gawping, Mister Thorn," he said. "Let us dispatch these madmen with due haste."

"As you wish, Inspector." Veranix put up the bow and brought out his staff. With magically assisted leaps, he flipped over the Pirrell squad, cracking one in the skull as he went.

"This is off your usual beat," Welling said, blocking a punch with his handstick in his left hand.

"And yours. But I won't complain about the assistance." Cries and screams came from every direction. "We shouldn't waste time on these fools."

"No," Welling said. A pulse of *numina* blasted from his hand, sending more of the Pirrell squad to the ground.

More screams. Veranix saw Kaiana running, half carrying Delmin, with Phadre right on their heels. They didn't stop as they passed him, which meant something worse was happening. Veranix turned to see what they were running from.

What he saw could only be described as grotesque. A young man, wearing a crimson cloak and carrying a bow—but misshapen and monstrous. The muscles on his arms, legs, and chest were bulging with terrifying yellow and purple veins. His muscles appeared to be still growing, all at different rates. He roared as he chased after Veranix's friends.

Veranix didn't blink. Arrow drawn, fired right for the monster's eye.

The arrow hit him in the face, sticking in the engorged muscle of his cheek. He turned his attention toward Veranix.

"The Thorn," he boomed. He then glanced at Inspector Welling. "And the constable. I'll enjoy tearing you apart."

Welling flashed another wave of *numina* from his hand, and suddenly the fallen Pirrell players were coated in a layer of ice. Then he looked to Veranix with hard, determined eyes.

"It appears we have a new priority."

Satrine's head was fully clear of the *doph* by the time she found the rest of her clothing, and her leg was hurting like blazes. Twice this year she had taken a hit to the same spot. She had reached the point where it had nearly healed completely, now she had to start all over again.

That seemed like a message in her life.

The stationhouse was quiet once she had dressed, certainly no sign of Benvin or his squad. Which meant

Welling's theory was probably right on target. No time to waste getting to the Turnabout.

Given her leg, she pulled rank on a horsepatrolman and took his ride.

When she made it to Rose Street, it was clear that Benvin was already about to work his not-so-quiet Quiet Call. Three lockwagons were staged a few blocks away, and clusters of Constabulary were milling about, looking like they were trying to make the pretense of just doing a regular patrol. But any fool could see that two dozen of them were about to converge on the Turnabout. Benvin, Tripper, Wheth, and Pollit were strolling up Rose Street on the opposite side from the Turnabout, making like they were about to race up to the door at any moment.

Rainey brought her horse in front of the lot of them, making a racket right in front of the Turnabout's doors.

"What's your action, Lieutenant?" she said loudly. If the Princes inside hadn't noticed her yet, they certainly would now.

"I don't answer to you," Benvin said, starting to move around the horse.

"Like blazes you don't." Satrine dismounted with a hard drop. Her leg screamed out—it was not going to forgive her for that—but she didn't let it show on her face. "I am an inspector—an inspector with the city's Grand Inspectors' Unit—and you are interfering with my case, Lieutenant."

"Don't you—"

"Do not underestimate what I am empowered to do here. The rules about investigating an attack on a constable exist for a reason. You are not allowed to take action on your own attack—or someone in your squad or your house—for a reason. So you don't pull half-cocked sewage like this."

"I have a writ—" He held up the paper, ink on the stamp barely dry.

She took it from him, reading aloud. "Any and all self-proclaimed members of the organization Rose Street Princes for collusion and coordination of the assault and murder of—" She stopped reading. "Are you an idiot, Benvin? The wettest, freshest lawyer in the Justice Advocate Office could get this thrown out, and no magistrate would accept it as just cause."

"These bastards—"

"I don't care, Lieutenant. I do not care what you think. You want to crack skulls and make arrests on this writ, you know they'll be set free in hours. You'll end up with a street full of angry Princes in a day." She tore the paper up. "It won't hold, and does nothing but soothe your pride."

"Don't you—" Benvin's hand went up, coming at her face.

"Boss!" Tripper said, but it was too late. Satrine grabbed Benvin's arm mid-strike and twisted it behind his back. She considered shoving him to the ground as well, but that seemed a step too far. His dignity was already injured.

"If you had struck me, you'd be eating your hand," she hissed in his ear. "And then be busted down to shoveling out the horsepatrol stables."

"You can't—"

"Now walk with me," she said, pulling him along toward the alley.

"I am going to file . . ." Benvin said once they got in there.

"No you aren't, Benvin," she said. She tossed him over to the wall, now that they were out of view. "Don't give me your sewage right now, hear?"

"How do you even dare—"

"Because I actually like you," she said honestly. "I read your jacket, and it's an impressive list of pissing people up and down. You don't give a blazes what anyone thinks about you, and that's bounced you through two cities and three houses."

For once he didn't sputter something for her to interrupt.

"Also you've got a squad who are damn fine constables, who'll walk through fire and damnation for you. You've earned that."

"So why are you giving me the rutting, Inspector?"

"Precisely why I told you. That writ was sewage and it

would have caused you nothing but grief. I'm shocked your Protector even wrote it up."

He looked guiltily at the ground. "Protector Ossick never really looks at what he's signing."

"Goddamn it, Benvin," she said despite herself. "In this house, in this neighborhood, you're the one who's supposed to be better than that."

"Who the blazes are you to say?"

"I'm the one who's been listening to Jace Welling. He'll go on and on about how rutting amazing you are. I'm the one who took an arrow in the leg chasing your obsession with the Thorn."

"I didn't ask you to."

"Yeah, well, you got it anyway. So cool your head."

He sighed. "Being the better man got my people killed, my skull cracked open. I got to end this before we lose anyone else."

"This isn't the right way."

He scowled at her. "I know your story, Tricky. You've got no place talking about the right way."

"You're probably right," she said. "But this could have trashed your career, and that of your squad. They deserve better. You are better."

"You can't tell me—"

"You got right now to walk away from it. Or I walk you in front of them all."

He held her gaze for a good long while before backing off. "Fine," he said. "Then what?"

"You send your folk back to the house, or on patrol, or whatever. And hopefully the Princes will think you're unhinged enough that you *just might* come in cracking skulls any damn time."

"They already do," he said with a slight smile.

"All right." She gave him the smile back. "Look, I've seen your house. It doesn't give much of a blazes about anything. Most of the sticks in there are either lazy or too anxious to crack skulls."

"I'm aware," Benvin said.

"So if you need help cleaning up Aventil—after you have a real case, built strong—then send word to me at the GIU."

"Don't they hate you there?"

"Sure they do," Satrine said. "But I'm like you. I don't give a blazes."

Arrows weren't stopping him. Veranix had put four in the Hunter, and Welling had two more crossbow bolts. It didn't even slow him down.

The only thing that was keeping either of them alive right now was the fact that the Hunter insisted on fighting with his bow, and his fingers and hands were far too engorged to properly hold it.

Finally in a rage, he threw the bow away and then swung out with a massive fist, knocking Inspector Welling several yards away. Veranix dodged another punch, while drawing in enough *numina* to coat the Hunter in magical paste, stuck to the ground. The Hunter thrashed and howled as he tried to pull himself out of the goo.

Veranix used the chance to breathe, assess the situation. He jumped over to Kaiana while lining up another shot. "What the blazes happened?"

"The drug," she said. "He took a lot of it."

"What do you mean, a lot?"

"As in he became that," she said.

"And the drug was magically augmented," he said. "Jiarna realized that might be . . . bad."

"You think?" she said.

Welling approached, looking shaken but unharmed. He glanced over at the Hunter, who was pulling his leg out of the paste. "That will not hold. A better strategy should be employed."

"Open to suggestion, Inspector."

Jiarna sprinted across the field to the lawn, stopping some distance from the monstrous Hunter. "Sweet saints, what did we do?"

Veranix took Kaiana's hoe from her, passing it to Welling. "You're a Racquin, Inspector. Ever play Knock-a-Vase?"

"I—once."

"Then let's act like his head is filled with sweets," Veranix said. He raised his staff and leaped at the Hunter, fueling his jump and his arm with *numina*, swinging at his head like he was going for the Triple Jack.

The staff shattered over his skull, but didn't seem to hurt him. Before Veranix could land, the Hunter swatted him out of the air. He didn't smash into the ground, thanks to a magical catch from Welling.

"That was ineffective."

"You have an idea?"

Jiarna had slipped over to Phadre and Delmin, and called out, grabbing the rope from Phadre. "Got one!"

"Who's she?" Welling asked.

"Someone brilliant. Keep him busy while I find out her plan."

"Busy it is."

Veranix dashed over to Jiarna.

"The drug was magically excited, causing enhanced effects," she said, her words stumbling over each other in a rush. "That *numinic* excitement is still there, coursing through his body."

"Del?"

"Clear as day," Delmin said.

"So if you can perhaps drain that excitement—" she prompted.

"I don't suppose those mage shackles are handy," Veranix said.

"No," Kaiana said. "I could—"

"You're not thinking," Jiarna said, holding up the rope. "Napranium."

"Draws *numina*," Veranix said, her point clicking in his head. He took the rope from Jiarna, looking back to Inspector Welling, who was attempting to hammer at the Hunter with raw magical force. "I've got a crazy idea."

Veranix leaped over to the other side of the Hunter, hurling the rope out so it wrapped around the man's massive torso. The other end then flew over to Welling, who caught it in his left hand.

"Follow my lead, Inspector!"

Welling nodded, and Veranix felt his own *numinic* energy harmonize with the inspector's. Through the rope, he could feel the energy drumming through the Hunter's veins. He could only hope that Welling was sensing what he did, sensed his plan, that their harmonization could work like it did at the Tower.

The Hunter howled and grabbed at the rope, pulling both Veranix and Welling in close, smashing them into each other.

No more time.

Veranix first sent a charge like lightning through the rope, which Welling matched. Hunter screamed and dropped them to the ground.

"Now, Inspector!"

Veranix imagined what the mage shackles felt like, feeling for the *numina* pulsing through every part of the Hunter's body. Then he pulled that energy away, drawing it into himself as if he was a mage shackle.

Welling did the same, his hand like dalmatium.

The Hunter screamed again, this time horrific and unearthly. His whole body began to wither and shrink as he collapsed to his knees.

Then there was nothing left to pull. The Hunter had fallen to all fours, now an emaciated body wheezing and gasping.

Welling dropped his end of the rope and grabbed one of the Hunter's hands, putting him in irons. "You are lawfully bound. You are accused of crimes and will stand a fair trial." Veranix was amazed he had the strength to do that. Despite pulling the *numina* into himself, he felt drained and empty.

The Hunter made no attempt to resist or question. The poor fool looked like just breathing was all he could manage.

Delmin came over. "His name is Enzin Hence. He's an athlete with Pirrell University. Just like that lot over there."

"Mister Sarren," Welling said. "I appreciate your good character in identifying the suspect." He looked back and forth at Veranix and Delmin. "I've also determined that this is the man who attacked the church last night, injuring Inspector Rainey and Sergeant Welling. He's also wanted for the murders of Emilia Quope and three other women."

"You're certain?" Veranix asked.

Welling gave a knowing nod of his head. "Despite the physical changes, I think it's quite clear. Establishing a case won't be challenging."

Kaiana stepped forward. "He's also been distributing drugs during the games."

"Drugs? What sort?"

Jiarna took the lead on this. "I can only give you a cursory analysis, Inspector, but it seems to be a strength and aggression enhancer. All these boys took too much—"

"Much too much in this one's case," Phadre added, shaking his head at the Hunter's prone form.

"And this is the result," Jiarna said.

"Is there evidence?" Welling asked.

"There's still some of the drug in his room, Inspector," Delmin offered. "I'm one of the prefects of that dorm, so I can authorize a search without a writ."

"Then I will need to make use of campus cadets. But this man, between the drugs, the attacks at the church and on Lieutenant Benvin—"

"This is not who attacked Lieutenant Benvin," Veranix said quickly. Campus cadets had kept their distance during the fight, but they were now approaching. "You helped me when you didn't need to, so I'll do the same. The Rose Street Princes have that imposter in a safehouse at number nineteen Branch Street."

"He was a Prince?"

"Not at all," Veranix said. He coiled the rope to his belt. In addition to campus cadets, he could see in the distance

Professor Alimen coming up the lawn. "Now if you'll excuse me, Inspector."

Veranix shrouded himself, and channeling what *numina* he still could muster, he leaped high and far away, landing on the roof of Almers. From there, he could see the aftermath on campus. Cadets and Yellowshields swarming into the disaster. Injuries, destruction.

This wasn't his fault.

This was the Hunter, this was the drug he was giving to the Pirrell players. This was them cheating, and it built to an explosion.

This wasn't his fault.

This would have happened even if he wasn't the Thorn.

This wasn't his fault.

No repetition of those words made him believe that.

He slipped down from the roof to his third-floor window. Quickly he stashed away his gear and Thorn costume and changed to regular clothes. He was exhausted, especially after taking off the cloak, but he needed to have enough strength to do a little bit more.

Shrouding himself without the cloak, just on his own magic, was much harder than he imagined it would be, but he needed to do it. Climbing up to the window, he pushed *numina* into his legs and leaped back over to the tetchball field.

There was still a crowd—a subdued crowd, but a crowd. Many were slumped down on the ground. Some were being put in irons by campus cadets, some were being tended to by Yellowshields.

Veranix saw someone lying facedown in the dirt. Dropping the shroud, dropping all illusions of the bruises on his face, he went over to them.

Marmot, the squad's Deep Double. He was out of his senses, but still breathing. Blood and dirt were caked onto the side of his head. On top of that, his left arm was broken in at least two places.

Veranix pulled Marmot up, putting him over his

shoulder in a rescue carry. He ran over to one of the Yellow-shields.

"Hey! Hey! I need some help over here!"

***

Kaiana breathed a sigh of relief that Veranix had vanished before the cadets and Professor Alimen had reached them. With everything that had happened, there was no need to also include getting caught with that.

Which puzzled her all the more about this inspector, who not only helped Veranix stop Hence, but didn't try to arrest him. He was busy making whistle calls when the cadets and the professor came over. The professor was already in a frenzied state, shouting as he approached.

"Inspector, how dare you come on this campus—"

Inspector Welling seemed unbothered, writing out several notes as he interrupted the professor. "My position in the Grand Inspectors' Unit gives me broad jurisdiction authority in the city, Professor. We sought permissions from you and the campus cadets out of courtesy, not legal necessity."

Alimen looked very put out by that, his face turning beet red. "And then you harass my students—"

"I've done nothing of the sort, Professor," Inspector Welling said. He finished his notes and handed it to a cadet, who ran off.

"It's true, sir," Delmin said quickly.

Alimen scowled at Delmin, but nodded in acceptance. Looking around at the damage, he asked, "Can someone explain to me what the blazes is happening? Not you, Inspector."

"I wouldn't bother trying, Professor," Inspector Welling said, going over to confer with the campus cadets.

"I can try, Professor," Kaiana said.

"Miss Nell," he said, his tone softening. "I trust that you've been instrumental in quelling whatever calamity has befallen our campus."

"I don't know all the details, sir, but these boys were all using some sort of drug—"

"A magiochemically altered drug, sir," Jiarna offered.

"Which caused them to do . . . all this." Kaiana waved at the chaos all around.

"And how do you know about it?" he asked with a raised eyebrow.

"I had discovered signs of it on campus, but nothing that the campus cadets would be able to take action on. It was really Delmin who figured it out, of course."

"Mister Sarren?" Alimen raised his eyebrow.

"Yes, sir? Right, sir. Well, this morning there had been that blast of *numinic* energy . . ."

"Indeed. It woke me up."

"Me as well, sir. Shot up right in my bed. My bed in Almers, of course, sir."

"Lit up my instruments as well, sir," Phadre said plainly. "Quite a powerful phenomenon."

"Indeed. Something—or someone—powerful and volatile must have caused it." Alimen was staring at Inspector Welling with loathing when he said that.

Delmin jumped back in. "But that's when I realized that there was a strange source of *numinic* energy right in Almers. In this young man's room. I confronted him on it, and he then drank the substance and turned monstrous."

"*Pamph*, I believe," Inspector Welling said. "Also called The Soldier's Fist. Not often seen in Maradaine. More common on the Sauriyan coast and Corvia."

"Thank you, Inspector, I have heard enough from you."

"And we saw Delmin in trouble, chased by him," Kaiana said. "We came to help him, and then the inspector stopped the rampaging boys."

"Hmm," Alimen said, still looking at Inspector Welling with skepticism.

Veranix then came limping over from the tetchball field, looking battered and bruised. "Are all of you all right? Was it as bad here as it was over there?"

"Mister Calbert, you look a fright," Alimen said.

"And I feel it, sir. The Pirrell boys went crazy, charging

the field, and then the spectators rioted, and, before I knew it, I was trampled by a bunch of people."

Kaiana stifled a smile. Just like that, Veranix gave himself deniability in everything that happened.

Inspector Welling gave him a curious look. "You are fortunate, Mister Calbert, that your clothing was largely unscathed by this encounter."

Professor Alimen moved in on the inspector, his eyes hard. "This is enough from you. It is clear you are an Uncircled menace, and working against the very—" He paused, shaking his head. "I suspect all this is damage caused by your careless magic. I imagine you were the source of the . . . I should have you—" Energy seemed to swirl around the professor, strong enough that Kaiana could feel the hairs on her arms stand on end. Veranix jumped in between him and Welling.

"Professor, sir. He's still an inspector. Still a constable."

The professor huffed, glowering at the inspector, who seemed to return a cold anger back. After a moment, the professor nodded. "Well reasoned, Mister Calbert. Inspector, I demand that you leave this campus at once. I will be contacting your superiors. I may even file formal complaint."

"No need, Professor," Welling said. "I have nothing else to do here at the moment." He looked to the rest of the group. "I thank you for your able assistance in apprehending Mister Hence. All of you."

That last part seemed aimed at Veranix.

He nodded and went off to the south gate.

"A disaster, a disaster," Alimen said. "Veranix, you should get to the hospital ward."

"A Yellowshield checked me over, sir," Veranix said. "There are far too many people who need more serious care for me to take up their time."

"I will trust in your judgment," Alimen said. He shook his head. "This will cost, it certainly will come down. And I am not done with that Uncircled inspector."

"Sir?" Kaiana said. "He did fight that beast of a man. He

saved us all." It wasn't right for the professor to pursue Inspector Welling when he did nothing wrong. He certainly shouldn't get punished for the magic blast they all caused to find the drug.

"That isn't the point, Miss Nell," Alimen said.

"Isn't it, sir? And now we have a campus to clean up."

"Indeed," he said, a bit calmer. "I'm sure you will have your hands full for the days to come. I will see what aid I can be. The rest of you all should probably stay clear."

"Yes, sir," Delmin said. Alimen went off, and Delmin let out a enormous breath. "I've never lied that much to him. Or to anyone. This is what you've done to me."

"We should clear off," Phadre said. "Perhaps retire to the carriage house or some other venue."

"A venue with food," Veranix said. "I am only standing on my feet out of sheer force of will."

"Let's do that then," Phadre said. "I think I know a place that's enough away to be unaffected by this." He led them toward the west side of the campus.

"Are you all right?" Kaiana asked Veranix.

"Nothing a hot meal and three days of sleep shouldn't fix," he said.

"That inspector, he—he definitely knows—" There was no way he wouldn't be coming back to arrest Veranix. Perhaps all of them.

"A problem for another time," Veranix said. He nodded solemnly. "And when it comes, it won't be your problem, I'll make sure."

"But—"

"Another time," he said again. "For now, hot meal. Sleep for three days."

Chapter 27

MINOX LEFT THE south gates of the campus to find Inspector Rainey waiting for him with Benvin's squad, minus his own brother. It was good to see her, as it meant he did not have to wait for the instructions he had sent out to be executed. He was quite exhausted from the engagement with Mister Hence and the Thorn.

Mister Calbert. Who again, bravely and selflessly, fought to protect others and stop danger. This was not a man he could, in any good conscience, arrest as criminal. This would be challenging to square with his oath as officer of the law. He would have to contemplate this for some time. Allow it to remain unresolved. Before that, though, he would need to rest and eat.

"We got your messages," Rainey said. "And Jace went running off with one of them."

"That was efficient," he said. "I must commend the campus cadets."

"We weren't far," Rainey said. "Just by the Turnabout." Her looked was pointed.

"So, specs, you say you have something for us," Benvin said. He still looked irritated, but no longer anxious. Since he saw no signs that they had been in an additional brawl, it was likely that Inspector Rainey stopped his ill-conceived raid. Which was excellent, because it made what was about to happen easier.

"Looks like some stuff went down on campus," Pollit said. "They don't need our help?"

"I believe the worst has played out," Minox said. He was quite famished. Flipping a crown over to the cadet, he said, "Mister Saitle. If you would be so kind to procure me a striker, skellie, or similar source of nourishment."

"You're eating?" Benvin said as Saitle ran off.

"Let it be," Rainey said. Looking to Minox, "You all right?"

"I am uninjured, which is more than many people on campus can say." He signaled for them to come closer so they could confer with some privacy. "In short order, there will be two arrests logged at the Aventil Stationhouse. Once those are processed, Inspector Rainey and I will have fulfilled our duties on this assignment."

"We will?" Rainey asked.

"You mean, you got the Thorn?" Tripper asked.

"I have apprehended the man who is responsible for the attack at the church. You will have to do some additional legwork, Lieutenant, to finalize collection of evidence and testimony, but this man should also face a number of charges involving the smuggling, possession, and sale of a drug called *pamph*."

"Soldier's Fist," Benvin said. "That's made it to Maradaine?"

"Hopefully this is an isolated incursion that we have cut off. However, Lieutenant, you should maintain some diligence in the coming months."

"What else was I going to do?" Benvin said. "I suppose our squad isn't going to get the credit for that one?"

Saitle came running over with something that involved hot meat and toasted bread, and Minox did not question or care further. He ate it greedily as he continued. "Given the circumstances, the first credit will have to go to the campus and the Grand Inspectors' Unit. But the process will still go through Aventil, as the campus cadets are not equipped to—"

"You said two arrests. What's the second?"

Minox spotted Jace running up the avenue toward them, waving a paper in his hand.

"Presuming my brother is carrying the necessary writ, and presuming my information is correct, we will be proceeding to an address where you will find the man you want."

"The Thorn?" Benvin asked.

Minox answered honestly, though he knew Benvin would take it differently than he intended. "The man responsible for your attack and Officer Malored's death."

Jace ran in, slapping the paper in Minox's hand. "Fresh from the Protector. Writ of Search for 19 Branch Lane."

Benvin raised an eyebrow. "We've suspected that's a Prince safehouse."

"I don't know about that," Minox said. "But let's go see."

Benvin took the writ and led the way to Branch.

Rainey sighed wistfully as they went, as if being done here had already made her melancholic.

"I thought you were sick of Aventil," he said.

"I am," she said. "But like an infection, it's grown on me."

"This is your inscrutable sense of humor."

"Rather. So is this really it? We're done. Clean arrests, right man, nothing unresolved?"

"We're done," Minox said. "Clean arrests and the right man."

But there would remain the unresolved.

It had taken a whole day before they came for Colin. He had been surprised it took that long. He wasn't hiding. After cleaning himself up and getting fresh clothes—courtesy of Bell's money—he slept in the basement of the cheese shop, and once he woke he took his usual chair in the Old Canal and ate as many sausage plates as he could handle.

It was dusk when they came in. Five of them, Iggs with his bandaged hand at the front.

Colin stood up, addressing the boys loudly. "I'm not going to make trouble, so don't cause trouble for the people who run this place." He threw a hundred-crown note on the table. "That's not what Princes do, hear?" He walked past them outside.

They had a wagon in front of the Canal. Iggs snapped his fingers and three of them grabbed Colin and threw him in the back. No pleasantries, no words.

This was how it was going to be. He had expected it.

While one drove the wagon, the other four all but sat on top of Colin, making sure he wasn't going anywhere. Colin stared at Iggs, glancing at his hand.

"Hurts, don't it?"

Iggs glowered.

"It's gonna scar like blazes, you know. Won't ever be right again."

"It'll have company," Iggs said quietly.

The wagon pulled up to the Turnabout, and the heavies took him out.

"Through the alley?" he asked, "Or are you marching me in front of the other Princes before taking me down?"

"Not taking you down," Iggs said. He grabbed Colin by the back of the neck and pushed him into the Turnabout.

Every damn Prince was in there. Every pigeon, tough, heavy, captain, and boss. Except Bassa. Colin noted she was absent.

All of them looked pissed. All but Giles, whose face was beaming with joy.

Rutting bastard, Giles.

Despite the place being completely full of Princes, there was a chair alone in an empty circle of floor, facing the collected bosses. And next to the chair, sitting in a bowl of hot coals, was a pressing iron.

They were coming for his stars, and making a whole goddamned show of it.

Iggs pushed him inside and deposited him in the chair.

"Here he is, the man of the night," Giles said. "Mister Colin Tyson, captain of the Rose Street Princes."

"This is quite the party you're throwing for me," Colin said. "I'm actually rather impressed."

"Tyson, you rutting idiot," Old Casey said. He stood up

and addressed the crowd. "I want all of you to hear, to really understand what this moron did. First of all, he does something great. He hatches a plan for all of us, and with it, he captures the Thorn."

"Wasn't the Thorn," Colin said.

"He catches the Thorn and brings him back to a safehouse. That would have been great, Tyson. You know? You would have gotten your flop back for that, you know?"

"What?" Deena said from the side.

"Not now," Casey hissed. "Because it doesn't matter. First, once you have him, you take him for yourself for a bit. Get him to answer some questions. The Thorn told you all his secrets, hmm?"

"Wasn't. The. Thorn." Colin shook his head. "Get it clear. That guy was a—"

"I don't rutting care!" Casey started pacing the floor. "Because then this guy, this loyal captain of the Rose Street Princes, he takes it upon himself to go into Dentonhill. He crosses Waterpath, and with his arm proudly showing—"

"Ain't no other way to be."

"He takes a hit on Fenmere's boys. Hits them hard, but leaves one of them around to say who he was and what he's done."

"Damn right," Colin said. Everything Casey was doing was theater, but he wasn't going to play any part other than himself. Colin Tyson, truest man in the room.

"Now of course Fenmere's people reach out to us, concerned. Why are we causing trouble in their neighborhood? How are we going to make it right?"

"You don't make it right with Fenmere's people," Colin said. He looked around at the crowd. "Really, any of you going to back that? They send that guy to hit Rabbits, hit Aventil sticks, hit us, and they ask how *we* make it right?"

"Yeah, we make it right, because we don't need a war, Tyson," Giles said. "Not one you decided to start, at least."

"You don't get to decide that," Frenty added.

Casey went on. "So we decide to give the Thorn to them. Except he's gone. Did he escape? Did Tyson set him free?"

"No," Colin said.

"No. He's gone because *THE RUTTING STICKS CAME INTO OUR SAFEHOUSE AND ARRESTED HIM!*"

"Really?" This actually surprised Colin.

That, instead of anything else, earned a punch from Iggs on Casey's nod.

"You told the sticks, the rutting sticks, where to find him. Because, why? You thought the arrest would get them off our necks?"

"I did nothing of the sort."

Another punch.

"I could understand that this was some sort of misplaced pride. Standing up to Fenmere, arm out. Giving the Thorn to the sticks so they wouldn't swat on us anymore. But even still, you told the sticks to go to our safehouse."

"I did—"

Another punch came, but Colin ducked, grabbing Iggs's wrist and twisting for all he was worth. Iggs screamed and dropped down. Colin was on his feet, knife drawn.

"I did nothing of the sort."

"Sit down, Tyson," Casey said.

Colin threw the knife down to the floor. Not that he didn't have five more.

"Making it clear, Casey. I didn't tell the sticks anything." He sat down. "I told the Thorn."

The room exploded in shouts and cries.

"Ease it down!" Casey shouted. "You told the Thorn. You told the Thorn, what, where he was tied up?"

"Again, for the slow people," Colin said. "The guy wasn't the Thorn. He was hired by Fenmere's boys to hit us dressed as the Thorn."

"Dressed as the Thorn." This came from the back doorway. The crowd opened up, and Vessrin strolled in. Some people were shocked, though most of them had no idea who this old man was or why anyone would defer to him. "What the blazes does it matter? Dressed as the Thorn? How is that not the Thorn?"

"Be—" Colin started. He bit his tongue.

"Because you know the Thorn, hmm?" Vessrin came over. "Not just that you've met him or have talked to him, but you *know* him, don't you, Tyson? You trust the Thorn, more than you trust your own. Right?"

"Of course I do, Vessrin," Colin said, making sure to say the name so even the pigeons would know what was happening. "Because I'm the son of the man who trusted you, so I've learned. The only thing you can trust is blood."

Vessrin, despite his age, roared and grabbed Colin by the throat. Colin wasn't about to have that. He brought his arm up and knocked Vessrin in the teeth. The old man let go, and Colin punched him again to send him to the floor.

The room was silent.

Iggs's boys started to move, but Colin grabbed the hot iron, holding it out at them. He put his foot on Vessrin's chest, holding the old man to the floor.

"You all wanted my stars tonight," Colin said. "But you can have it all. I'm done with the lot of you."

He pressed the iron against his arm, burning the flesh of his rose and his stars. It hurt worse than anything he had ever felt, but he didn't show it on his face. He didn't give them an inch on his face.

"I'm the king of Rose Street," Vessrin started. "You ain't gonna—"

"I'm not listening to you, traitor," Colin said. "I ain't a Prince. I'm a son of Tyson. And so is the Thorn."

He dropped the iron on Vessrin's face.

He turned away to walk out the door, hearing searing flesh and Vessrin's screams. No one moved to stop him as he went into the street.

Rose Street.

Rose Street wasn't his anymore. He didn't have his crew, he didn't have his street, he didn't have anything on his arm.

But it didn't matter. He had family.

Chapter 28

BENVIN WANTED TO be happy with the headline in the *South Maradaine Gazette* that Tripper had slapped onto his desk.

THORN ARRESTED! LIEUTENANT HENRITH BENVIN APPREHENDS THE VIGILANTE!

It felt hollow. The man they got, a cocky bit of sewage named Erno Don, had the tools, the look, everything. The moment he spoke, Benvin knew his voice, remembered it from that night. This was their man, like the inspector said.

But it was too damn easy. Getting the Thorn should have been harder, rather than trussed up in a Rose Street Prince flop. It wasn't right at all. Especially since he had a bag of tricks—mostly smoke powder—instead of being a mage. Captain Holcomb and Protector Ossick said that made sense, that a real mage would have been noticed by the University. Benvin didn't like it, and he didn't like getting credit for it.

But it was what it was, and he was going to have to accept that.

"So what's next, Left?" Tripper asked. "Still plenty to do."

"Yeah, I know," Benvin said. "Next is me going over to the church to play nice with the preacher, so he doesn't raise blazes on all of us for breaking sanctity. And the lot of you are coming with me for that."

"We gotta, Left?" Wheth asked. "I mean, I was on the roof across the street, so I never broke it."

"Technically I didn't either," Tripper said.

"You rutters are not hanging me on the line alone," Pollit said. "Not after what I did that night."

"You're all coming," Benvin said. "And you're all gonna scrape to the priest, do absolution, whatever it takes. Last thing I need is a church action placed on this squad."

"Left!" Jace had come running into the squad room, out of breath.

"Slow the blazes down, Jace. What could possibly—"

"You have to come see, sir," Jace said. "It's pretty horrible."

"Where?"

"Clover Street."

Benvin went out, Jace running ahead, while the rest of the squad was at his heels. The squad had been hurt, hurt bad, but they held together. They were the best in Aventil, and even with the priest squawking, he was proud of what they did when he was down. With them, and with Jace and Saitle once they took their patrolman tests next month, he would clean all the filth out of this neighborhood. One gang, one street at a time.

Jace hadn't exaggerated about Clover Street. It was a horror show, pure and simple. At least two dozen bodies laid out in a row, every one of them Toothless Dogs. And every one of them with a Kemper Street Kicker tag painted on their chest.

A crowd of gawkers had formed, of course. Aventil liked a show.

"This part of Clover, it's Dog territory, ain't it?" Benvin asked.

"Pretty solidly," Pollit said. "Last I knew, the line between them and the Kickers was over at Vine."

"Looks like the Kickers have drawn a new line," Wheth said.

"All right," Benvin said. "Let's get the bodywagons over here, and then we need to get to work. This isn't just a new line. It's a declaration of war."

Wheth and Pollit went to work driving the crowd away, while Jace started blowing whistle calls. Tripper came in close and lowered his voice.

"This is going to get really bad, ain't it, boss?"

"Yeah," Benvin said. "Just another day in Aventil."

Satrine was surprised how calming she found the usual business of bodies and mayhem in Inemar after the week in Aventil. She was even glad to be at her desk, covered in paperwork. Perhaps it was just comfortable. Inemar was ugly madness, but it was her madness. Her position in the Grand Inspectors' Unit was going to keep taking her outside the neighborhood, throughout the entire city. Aventil would call again.

The experience in Aventil had altered Welling slightly. Since then, he'd been withdrawn, spending more time in the archives. She couldn't quite identify what was going on with him, and he wasn't talking about it. She had long since learned it was useless to press him, especially if the subject was magic or his hand. His encounters with the Thorn seemed to qualify.

Not that she blamed him. She knew that, strictly speaking, the Thorn was a criminal and should face charges. But she also knew the Thorn had put himself between her and an arrow. He had pulled Hence off of Corrie, possibly saving her life.

And Aventil had arrested someone they could call the Thorn, so that made most of them happy.

Except Benvin. He had already written to her about a street war brewing between the Dogs and Kickers, and he was putting together a proper case for the GIU to take on.

She'd make good on that, even if it meant going back to Aventil.

"I know I got hit in the rutting head," Corrie said as she came over to Satrine's desk. After a few days in the hospital ward she'd been back to her usual profane self. "But that tosser you chatted up on campus . . ."

"I'd hardly say I chatted him up," Satrine sent back.

"Right, well, he was Intelligence, wasn't he?"

"That was his uniform," Satrine said. That was an honest answer without actually confirming it.

"Major Dresser," Corrie said. She held up two letters, one with a wax seal, the other with the seal broken. "Messenger just delivered these. Said I was bound by 'oath and blood' to give this one to you." She handed over the sealed one.

That was a familiar phrase. "The other one was to you?"

"Yeah." She leaned in close. "Saying that I'm ordered by crown and country to not blazing speak of anything of my meeting with Major Dresser under charges of sedition and treason."

Satrine made a show of opening hers and glancing at it. "Same," she lied. Shrugging, she added, "That's how Intelligence operates."

"Rutting sewage is what it is," Corrie said. "So that's delivered. I've got reports to file." She stalked off.

Satrine looked over the letter again. It did tell her to keep her mouth shut, but with an additional note in different handwriting. Major Dresser's, if her memory served. "Don't start digging. Altarn Initiative is need to know. I'll loop you in if I can."

Satrine folded up the letter and held it to the oil lamp until it caught flame, and then dropped it in the can where Minox dumped his tobacco ashes.

Nothing else to do with a letter like that. Nothing else to do but go about her day like it was any other.

⋙━━⋘

The household was in order. Every room was in pristine condition, ready for Mister Fenmere to return. The cooks were getting luncheon together—simple and tasteful, cold sandwiches and tea. Perfect for this hot weather.

Everything would be perfect, were it not for the guests waiting for Mister Fenmere in the sitting room.

Corman waited in the outer garden, not wanting to share air with the visitors. The carriage approached the household, coming to a stop while the gates closed behind it. The driver hopped down and opened up the back.

"Corman!" Mister Fenmere said jovially as he stepped out. His skin was bronzed, and he looked rested, even joyful. "You missed a lovely summer on the coast."

"I'm sure I did," Corman said. Gerrick came out behind Mister Fenmere, similarly colored but looking far more worn out.

"I thought we left the heat behind in Yinara," he said. "It's sweltering."

"It's been this way all summer," Corman said. "Quite unpleasant."

"Hmm," Fenmere said. "I've heard there's been quite a bit of unpleasant over the summer."

"I won't bore you with details now, sir, though there are several," Corman said. "I presume you are both hungry—"

"And hot," Gerrick said, fanning his shirt open.

"I've prepared for all that, however—"

Fenmere raised an eyebrow. "Something urgent?"

"I would say no, certainly not that required your immediate attention, but I've not been entirely given that option."

Fenmere nodded somberly. He knew there were few people who would be able to make Corman say that.

"He's already here?" Fenmere asked.

"Dejri Adfezh," Corman said. "And he's in an—intense state."

"Well, that's nothing new for him," Fenmere said.

"He's with . . . escort."

"Armed?"

"Quite."

Fenmere grunted. "It's his way. I'm sure it's nothing to worry about."

Corman sighed. He wished he could feel as confident as Mister Fenmere did about these matters. He went up the front steps to open the door into the house.

"We'll have to deal with this before we luncheon, I suppose," Fenmere said. "It'll keep?"

"Yes, sir," Corman said. "I planned it that way."

That was the necessity of the situation. Almost anyone else, they would have invited them to sit down to eat with them. Even the Firewings, despite the fact that Corman couldn't stand to watch mages eat.

But one couldn't do that with Poasians. They were very peculiar about eating, especially in front of other people, or having others eat in front of them. They saw that as obscene vulgarity, on par with using the water closet in mixed company.

Adfezh and the other Poasians had to be kept happy. And keeping Poasians happy was a tightwire walk like nothing else Corman knew.

"Sitting room?" Fenmere asked.

"Indeed."

"And you've—"

"Our men are in position to come in at a signal from any of us."

"Good, good." Fenmere took a handkerchief out of Corman's coat pocket and blotted the sweat on his face, and then brushed off his suit for any dust or dirt. Satisfied, he strode into the sitting room, Corman and Gerrick matching pace behind him.

The Poasians were all standing when they entered. Three of them—all sickly pale with thick black hair, dressed all in black. Corman had only had limited interaction with any of the Poasians, and he had yet to discern the minute differences in clothing style to determine rank or social standing.

That said, the two men flanking Adfezh were both sporting long convex Poasian blades at their hips, wearing heavy leather coats. Soldiers, mercenaries, some type of Poasian knight, Corman couldn't say. It didn't matter. Both men looked like the type who could remove someone's head from their neck in a moment, and not have the slightest concern about it.

Adfezh was a smaller, thinner man, his black hair having taken on some wisps of gray at the temples.

"Willem Fenmere," he said coldly as they entered. "We have been waiting overlong."

"*Khiere pul*, Adfezh," Fenmere said cordially. "I could not come any sooner. I was out of the city until today."

"I have little time to prattle," Adfezh said. "Arrangements need to be made for alterations."

"Alterations?" Fenmere said, expression turning dark. He took his customary chair, though Adfezh and the other Poasians stayed standing. "What exactly is being altered?"

"Do not presume to treat me as a fool. I am well aware of your attempts to manufacture your own version of the *effitte*."

"Now how could I do that? The *effitssa* only grows in the Napolic Islands."

"I am also aware of the *effitssa* hothouses you have built, with limited success." The man managed to say the name of the plant with not only a distinctly different pronunciation of the "f" and "s" sounds, but with a hint of genuine revulsion in how Fenmere had said it.

This was the way with the Poasians. They weren't fazed by duplicity, but pronounce a word incorrectly, and they might just walk out on the business completely.

"It has been a challenge, certainly," Fenmere said lightly. "So how does that bring us to this meeting today?"

"I'm here to tell you that you do not need to bother." He reached into his coat and pulled out a small vial, placing it on the table by Fenmere. Fenmere picked up the vial and held it up to the light. It was filled with a lavender powder.

"What am I looking at?"

"The result of our continued diligence in refining the resin of the *effitssa*. This is the *efhân*."

"*Efhân?*" Fenmere said. He clearly took care to match Adfezh's accent and pitch in pronouncing the word. "I presume it's more potent?"

"What you are holding is equivalent to—" He took a moment and consulted one of his men in their native tongue. "To nearly a gallon of *effitte*."

"A what?" Fenmere jumped out of his chair. The

bodyguards, just outside the other door, started to move. On a signal from Fenmere, Corman motioned for them stay in place.

"Needless to say, in this form it will be far easier to bring in quantities of far greater equivalence. You will be able to charge more for much less. This is beneficial to us all."

Fenmere opened up the vial and cautiously sniffed at it. "You've tested it, and you're satisfied with these claims?"

"I would never say such things if I was not."

"Very well," Fenmere said. "So you want to ship this instead of the *effitte*. It's going to take a bit of work to shift the market, for the customers to accept the new product. You understand that?"

"We are confident in your ability to make the sales to meet our needs," Adfezh said. "Which brings us to the next point."

"Our payments have been on time," Fenmere said.

"Indeed they have, and we are appreciative. However, this refinement process was the result of much effort and development . . ."

"More money? Really?"

"If you are not interested in continuing our arrangement, I'm certain there are competitors here who would find it lucrative."

"You won't find anyone matching my resources."

"Which is why we still find you useful," Adfezh said. "You have proven the most efficient in receiving the *effitte* and other goods. And regarding other goods, you'll be pleased to know—"

"I don't want the rest of the Blue Hand's . . . material," Fenmere said sharply. "Gerrick, we did make that clear. We weren't interested, yes?"

"Certainly, we had canceled those requests," Gerrick said. "Mister Adfezh, I know you received those letters, as you had acknowledged other points."

Adfezh's jaw tightened, and he held out his hand as if he were directing his men not to murder everyone. Perhaps that was to be their next action, but Corman couldn't tell.

"Your cancellations are of no moment," Adfezh said coldly. "My associates have been quite diligent in crafting what was requested, and that work will be completed, the materials will come to Maradaine, and we will receive our recompense. What you do with it once it arrives is not my concern."

"No, I want nothing to do with—"

"Your cancellations are of no moment," Adfezh said again. "I must withdraw before I am sickened further by this engagement. The shipments of the *efhân* will commence shortly, so use that vial to determine what you must in terms of market, dosage, and pricing. I will send documents with further information for you all."

He walked out of the sitting room, his men in tow, heading right for the front door.

"Well," Gerrick said, "You can't say that Poasians waste time with pleasantries."

Mister Fenmere was holding up the vial, staring at the violet powder.

"Sir?" Corman asked. "What do you think of this?"

He tossed the vial up and caught it in his fist. "I think we need to get this to Jads straight away. The wind shifts, and we set our sails to match."

He smiled, handing the vial to Corman. "Besides, if Adfezh is telling something even remotely close to the truth, then everything is going to change. We must make sure we are the ones with our boots on when it comes."

"Yes, sir."

"Corman," Fenmere said quietly. He held up the copy of the *South Maradaine Gazette* with the frustratingly inaccurate headline. "Is this our good fortune?"

"It is not, sir," Corman said. "I am given to understand that Mister Bell—operating on his own volition—contracted someone to pretend to be the Thorn to murder the Red Rabbits and confound the Constabulary."

"Bell?" He mused for a moment. "I'm pleasantly surprised. He'll need to be sanctioned, of course, but I won't deny that I'm impressed he had such a play in him."

"This play backfired. His man was the one arrested. Bell drew the attention of the Rose Street Princes. Or, at least, one of them."

"Hmmm. You've taken steps?"

"Our displeasure is known."

"Good. Though I heard you took your own initiative. Two thousand crowns for the Thorn's head?"

"I was responding to the situation on the ground, sir. Mostly to inspire men like Smiley and Benny to not be complacent. Some men need the apple instead of the whip."

"Of course, and it's fine," Fenmere said. "Though I'm glad it didn't really result in anything, other than to whet their appetite. If the *efhân* proves to be what it's claimed to be, we will have the means to put a price on the Thorn's head that would make even his own mother go after him."

Veranix had no responsibilities for the Closing Ceremonies. The whole event was subdued, far from the original plan that Madam Castilane had mapped out. Rather than a festive celebration, it was a solemn affair. Five people died in what was called The Tetchball Riot, including Pinter from the squad. Several dozen more were injured. The closing ceremony was transformed into a memorial on the south lawn, involving string quintets and candle-lighting, and a few poems recited by Vellia Sansar and the rest of the Ovation Squad.

The campus gossip had quickly spread about what had happened. The Pirrell tetchball squad had been indicted in using the drug to cheat. The Pirrell players quickly confessed and testified that Hence was the source of the drug. How and why Hence had done that had been fodder for stories and rumors, each one more wild than the next.

"The funny thing is," Delmin had said the night before, "he wasn't really pretending to be you, I don't think. He had a bow because he was an archer, and he wore a crimson cloak because he made his Hunter outfit out of a Pirrell dress uniform. Crimson and white."

None of the stories explained why he had been hunting the Deadly Birds. Of course, most of the campus had no idea about that part of it. As far as any of the stories went, Emilia Quope was an exceptional and promising student and athlete from RCM, and all mourned her as his victim. After the fact, people had remembered Hence constantly watching Emilia, staring after her. Veranix even remembered the first night, there had been a creepy Pirrell student watching her. It had probably been Hence, but he didn't trust his memory enough to say for certain.

The last days of the games had continued, though with far less enthusiasm. There was a final game in the tetchball matches, between U of M and the Acorian Conservatory. The U of M squad took the field with only seven players, and the Acorians were in their right to demand a forfeit. Instead, the Acorians had decided to play a gentleman's game, and fielded only seven as well. The Conservatory won, nineteen to seventeen, but they had to play hard to earn that win.

"It was better that way," Tosler had said. "I'd rather lose a real game than have them not play us out of pity."

Tosler didn't speak much of Pinter, or of Blute—who was alive but hadn't woken up.

Veranix watched the ceremonies from a distance, huddled with Jiarna, Phadre, Kaiana, and Delmin under one of the trees. Most of them were watching the ceremony, but Jiarna was stewing over a copy of the *South Maradaine Gazette*.

"Thorn captured! This is sewage. Not only that this is filled with lies, but after everything we did, this Lieutenant Benvin gets the credit and crows about it!"

"Let it be," Veranix said.

"I almost wish we didn't have to go next week," Jiarna said wistfully. "I am going to miss this."

"You mean the University?" Kaiana asked.

"Well, that, of course. Though Trenn will be lovely in that regard."

"She's talking about the adventure," Phadre said.

"Yes, exactly," Jiarna said.

"I could stand a little less mortal peril," Phadre said.

"A little less?" Delmin asked.

"You have to admit, it does get the blood up, darling," Jiarna said. "And Kaiana told me you took to it quite well."

"Did she?" Phadre asked, surprised. "You did?"

Kaiana teasingly put her hands up in a ring-boxing pose. "Yield to your betters."

"I am quite disappointed that I did not get to see that," Jiarna said. She looked over to Veranix. "And you, brooding over there."

"Am I brooding?" Veranix asked. "I thought I was matching the mood of the ceremony."

"Yes, which is dismal."

"People died," Veranix said.

"But not as many as might have, thanks to your actions. The numbers lean in your favor, Veranix." She placed a tender hand on his cheek. "Promise you are going to write to us at Trenn. I will need to know that you haven't gotten yourself killed without our assistance."

"Yes," Veranix said. "Though I don't think I'll have much to write about."

The string quintet started up a new strain, and it drew their attention back to the ceremony for a few minutes.

Kaiana moved close to him, curiosity in her eyes. She kept her voice low to not disturb the other three. "Are you going to be all right?"

"What do you mean?"

"I mean . . . I don't think I've ever seen you this tired before. I just wonder—"

"If I'm thinking about stopping?" Veranix asked.

She nodded. "Which I would understand. This has been—harrowing. For all of us."

"Don't worry, I'm not thinking about it," he said. She smiled, breathing out a sigh of relief. He knew she would have accepted it if he stopped, but she still believed in what he was doing, that it needed to be done.

He laughed a little. "Well, that's not true, I thought about it. But I also thought about everyone hurt by Fenmere, everyone hurt or killed so I could keep going. All of you who have trusted and helped me." He had already had another conversation like this with Reverend Pemmick. Pemmick didn't encourage him to continue, but his counsel had solidified Veranix's feelings on the matter. "There's still a job to do. I'm not going to quit until it's done."

"Good afternoon, Mister Calbert."

Veranix turned to see Inspector Welling standing next to him. He had no idea how long he had been standing there.

"Inspector," Veranix said cautiously. "Here to see the closing ceremonies?"

"No, Mister Calbert. I came to speak to you. Can we step away?"

"Why?"

"Mister Calbert," Welling said, gesturing to his clothing. "I am not wearing my inspector's vest, nor do I have arms or irons. I'm not here in any official capacity." Indeed, he was wearing a plain clasped shirt and brown slacks. His left hand was still gloved, but beyond that, he was dressed like any other man on the street. The only thing uncommon about his appearance was the heavy leather satchel hanging on his shoulder.

"This way," Veranix said. He walked away from the group, noting that his friends all looked at him with concern. Especially Kaiana. He gave them a signal not to worry.

At worst, he could get away from an unarmed inspector, even Welling.

He led Welling to a spot near the edge of the lawn, from which he could see the carriage house. If he needed to, he could run to it, get his gear.

"So, Inspector, you came to speak to me," he said.

Welling watched him intently for a moment. "I am not here as an inspector."

"Mister Welling, then."

"Yes, I think that's best." He gritted his teeth, eyes to the ground for a moment. "Mister Calbert, I am quite aware of the fact that you are the Thorn."

This was what Veranix was expecting. "That's quite absurd. There was a headline in the *Gazette*—"

"It's not absurd, Mister Calbert, and we both know the truth behind that headline. Please recall that I rely on far more than my eyes to determine things." He held up his gloved hand. "I can feel you."

"I don't even understand what you're talking about," Veranix feigned.

"Rest assured, Mister Calbert, that I cannot prove your identity as the Thorn in any way that the law would recognize. Nor am I interested in doing so."

That was a surprise. "Why not, Mister Welling?" Welling struck him as a decent and honest constable, though it was entirely possible in knowing Veranix was the Thorn, he was looking for what he could get from it. He might want a payoff to not tell Benvin. Or even Fenmere.

"Let me explain something to you, Mister Calbert. I have dedicated my life to serving the Constabulary of this city. My family has served for generations. My grandparents were inspectors. My father was killed in the line of duty. It isn't a job for me, it's a calling. I think you might understand that."

"That doesn't answer my question. If anything—"

"It confounds it, yes. I have dedicated my life to the Constabulary, because I love what it is supposed to be. However, I am under no illusion that what it is supposed to be is a very different creature than what it is."

"And what is that?"

"Troubled. Shackled. Corrupt." Those words dripped like venom from his lips. "My home stationhouse is in Inemar, and it is teeming with problems. But compared to the houses in Aventil or Dentonhill, it could be considered pristine."

Veranix couldn't withhold a laugh, but he bit his lip on an icy glance from Inspector Welling.

"Even Lieutenant Benvin—the best, most incorruptible officer in Aventil—"

"Don't tell me he's corrupt." Veranix had no love for the

lieutenant, but he believed the man was fighting for a clean, safe Aventil.

"No, but he is more interested in expedience than truth. Note that headline in the *Gazette* the other day. In this case, however, the man arrested was guilty, but not the Thorn. I believe that he'd have no qualms in locking up a good man"—Welling gave Veranix a pointed look—"if that makes his life easier."

"Is that a warning, Inspector?"

"Please, Mister Calbert, listen to what I am telling you."

"You have my attention."

"Are you familiar with the Dentonhill Constabulary?"

"Not overly."

"Rest assured that they do not have a Benvin in their number. And from what I know of their captain, they never will."

Veranix raised an eyebrow. "Are you telling me I should spend less time in Aventil?"

"If your aims are what I believe them to be, that would be obvious. But more importantly, I'm telling you something about my own frustrations. I have a great interest in the larger scope of justice. I keep a list of cases that are not resolved to my satisfaction, and continue to investigate them on my own time."

"Is that what you're doing now?"

"Indirectly, Mister Calbert. Allow me to continue."

"Go on."

"Sometimes my investigations bear fruit, and lead to something I can take action on. Now that the commissioner has formed the Grand Inspectors' Unit, with its expanded jurisdiction, I have an even wider view of what is happening in this city, and what I can do for it."

He paused, looking at the ground. He took a deep breath and continued, locking his eyes on Veranix. "But even with all my information and authority, nothing I can do will lead to the arrest of a man like Willem Fenmere."

That had Veranix's attention.

"Even if that was your priority?"

"Even if it was, I would need evidence and investigation, which would require the resources and cooperation of the Dentonhill stationhouse. My experience here in Aventil has thoroughly convinced me I would never receive that, even if that stationhouse wasn't appallingly infested with corruption from top to bottom."

Veranix wasn't sure how to take this, but he recognized in Inspector Welling the same righteous anger he felt when thinking about Fenmere and his *effitte* trade.

"So what do you want, Mister Welling?"

Welling gave him a strange regard, something that seemed not quite like amusement on his face. "I have come to a decision, Mister Calbert. As I said, I am an officer and inspector in this city's Constabulary. I am bound by rules and law, as I should be. I cannot take justice into my own hands, no matter how much I might want to."

Veranix wasn't sure how to respond to that, but took a chance. "That's because you're a good man, Mister Welling."

"Perhaps," he said ruefully. He took the bag off his shoulder and put it on the ground between them. "However, what that means is that the contents of this satchel—every file, report, and unresolved scrap of information that I've compiled on Fenmere and his organization—is useless to me."

He gestured to the satchel.

"What are you saying?"

"I am saying that you might find it more useful than I would. Because I fear that the only way Fenmere will be brought to justice is if the Thorn is the one doing it."

Veranix crouched down to pick it up. "And what's the cost?"

"I'm not going to hold this over your head, Mister Calbert. As far as I'm concerned, you're a bolt in my crossbow. Giving you this is aiming and firing. I can only hope it finds my target."

"You can do more than hope," Veranix said, looking at Welling's gloved hand. "You're not just an inspector."

"And you're not just a magic student."

Intellectually, he knew this could be a trap of some sort, a way for Benvin or the rest of the Constabulary to catch him. But every instinct told him that wasn't the case. This inspector had been at his back in the thick of a fight, and could have dragged him to the stationhouse in irons if that had been his intention.

Veranix picked up the satchel and put it over his shoulder. "Thank you, Inspector Welling. This . . . this could mean a lot to me."

"If you need something that's in my power to help you with, Mister Calbert—"

"Veranix," he said, extending his hand.

Inspector Welling took it. "Minox."

"If there's something in my power, Minox—"

Minox looked to the satchel. "I believe you will already be focused on that. And it will be quite perilous to you." This time he actually smiled slightly. "Keep your feet moving."

A Racquin farewell deserved the appropriate response. "Until our roads cross."

With that, Inspector Minox Welling nodded and walked away.

Veranix held the satchel, cautiously opening it. As Minox had promised, it was filled with files, reports, and sketches. More information than Veranix had ever had on Fenmere. It would require some study—hopefully Kaiana and Delmin would help with that—but if it panned out, it would mean everything he needed to dismantle Fenmere's empire piece by piece.

"I've got you now, old man," he whispered. "You're going to have a constant thorn in your side."

Appendix

Education and Sport in Maradaine and Druthal

There are multiple systems of early education in the city of Maradaine. Throughout the city, there are nearly fifty public preparatories—part of an initiative spearheaded by the Duke of Maradaine and Alderman Tullen of the City Council. These schools are free and available for any child in the city between the ages of eight and fourteen, and teach basic reading, writing, mathematics, and civics. While these schools are free, children's attendance is not compulsory. It is considered their own (or their parents') obligation to attend if they so desire it, and the city makes only a minimal effort to encourage children to go to school. As many of these public preparatories are on the north and east of the city, it is more challenging for children who live in the poorer neighborhoods in the southwest portion of Maradaine to attend. There are several private preparatories, which require tuition and, in some cases, only admit children of noble birth. There are similar models in other cities around Druthal, as well as less formalized systems in towns and villages.

Strictly speaking, any child who attends a preparatory of any kind (or demonstrates equivalent learning) is eligible to apply to the various institutes of higher learning throughout the country. While there are scores of such institutes around the country, there are twenty-four which have been established as belonging to the High Colleges of Druthal, which represent the most acclaimed bodies of higher education, having met a universally agreed upon standard of curriculum and instruction.

The most prestigious among the High Colleges are

referred to as "The Elevens," as they are eleven schools founded in the eleventh century by specific grants and royal decrees enacted by King Maradaine XI. These are The Royal College of Maradaine (in Maradaine), Coanware University (Vargox), Pirrell University (Kyst), Trenn College (Yin Mara), The Acorian Conservatory (Porvence), Central Academy (Fencal), The Cape Institute (Lacanja), The University of Hechard (Hechard), The Great College of Scaloi (Iscala), Riverview University (Marikar), and Glennford University (Yoleanne).

Of the other High Colleges, the largest and most diverse in courses of study is the University of Maradaine, which has schools of Literature, Moral Philosophy, Natural Philosophy, Theology, Mathematics, History, Law, Protocol, Magic, and Officer Training (whose students serve in the campus cadets.)

The various High Colleges often convene for academic conferences and athletic tournaments, as the stated ideal for students in the High Colleges are to be "Gracious Gentles of Study and Sport."

The most notable of the athletic competitions is, of course, the Grand Tournament of the High Colleges, which encompasses many different sports and disciplines. The centerpiece of every Grand Tournament, though, is the national sport of Druthal: tetchball.

The field consists of a long rectangle, with the "green" of the field marked with a trapezoid. The two out-of-bounds areas on either side are referred to as "the yellow"—and on some fields they will go so far as to paint the grass to mark it. The field is then crossed with four lines to mark the different sections of the playing zone: the Hold Line, Jack Line, Double Jack, and Triple Jack.

There are two teams of eleven players each. Each match is played in three intervals, and each interval is split into the top and bottom. In the top, one team takes the field (fielding team) while the other one (batting team) lines up behind the Hold Line, and in the bottom they switch places.

The eleven players take the field in their designated

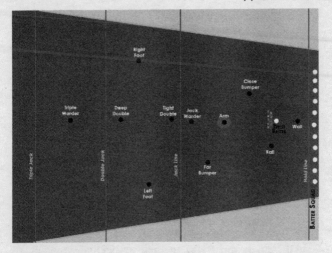

places: the Arm in the Arm's Circle, and in the zone between the Hold Line and the Jack Line (First Zone): the
Rail, Wall, Close Bumper, Far Bumper, and Jack Warder. In
between the Jack Line and the Double Jack (Second Zone)
are the Tight Double, Deep Double, Left Foot, and Right
Foot. Finally, in the Third Zone, between the Double Jack
and the Triple Jack, is the Triple Warder.

In each interval, the batting team sends one player at a
time to the Tetch Rail, a beam of wood about four feet long,
resting on two posts. The batter stands behind the rail with
a tetchbat, ready to bat. The Arm takes the tetchball (a bit
larger and softer than a softball) and pitches it over the
Tetch Rail for the batter to try to hit it. The batter gets two
pitches to try to hit the ball.

If the batter misses both pitches, they return behind the
Hold Line and the next batter comes forth.

If the batter hits the ball, then the batter will start to
run—first through the rail, knocking it to the ground, and
then toward the Jack Line. Their goal is to run past the Jack
Line, past the Double Jack, and to the Triple Jack, and then
turning around and running back to the Hold Line, all

before the Tetch Rail is restored. Restoring the rail means that the beam is back in place on its posts, and the ball is being touched to the rail. Each line crossed gains the runner one point for their team, for a maximum of six points for each batting.

What the fielding team can do to stop him depends on where the ball lands. Players in any zone are frozen if the ball lands past their zone, until the batter runs past that line. In other words, if the ball lands in the Second Zone (a "Jack Hit"), then the players in the First Zone can do nothing until the batter runs past the Jack Line. If the batter hits a Triple Jack — the ball lands past the Triple Jack line, beyond any of the playing zones, then all the fielders are frozen until the batter reaches the Triple Jack line. If the ball lands in the yellow, then the batter must return behind the Hold Line and the next batter comes up.

All fielders must stay in their respective zones at all times, save the Triple Warder, who can cross the Triple Jack line if they are not frozen.

While the batter is running, four players have the primary goal of impeding his run: the Close and Far Bumpers and the Right and Left Feet. If they are free to move, they can grapple and hold the batter to keep him from running. For the Jack Warder, the Tight and Deep Doubles, and the Triple Warder, their primary goal is to get the ball back to the Tetch Rail so the rail can be restored. Restoring the rail is the responsibility of the fielder playing Rail, though it is acceptable for the Arm and the Wall to assist in this. It should be noted, however, that any player who is free to move can both handle the ball and grapple the running batter, as long as they do not cross out of their zones.

If the ball ever crosses the Hold Line, then the Hold is broken, and all of the batting team can rush the field while the batter runs. Only the batter can score points, but every other player can impede the fielding team from stopping the batter or restoring the Rail, as long as they do not touch either the rail or the ball.

The Wall's primary job is to make sure the ball does not cross the Hold Line.

Each interval is concluded when every player on both teams have had a turn at bat. Once three intervals have been played, the match is concluded. The team with the most points is the winner.